"*God's Teeth and Other Phenomena* is electric. Forget all the rubbish you've been told about how to write, the requirements of the marketplace and the much vaunted 'readability' that is supposed to be sacrosanct. This is a book about how art gets made, its murky, obsessive, unedifying demands and the endless, sometimes hilarious, humiliations literary life inflicts on even its most successful names."
—Eimear McBride, author of *A Girl Is a Half-Formed Thing* and *The Lesser Bohemians*

"James Kelman is an extraordinary writer—smart and incisive, witty and warm, with prose so alive it practically sparks off the page. *God's Teeth and Other Phenomena* is one of the wisest, funniest, and most brutally honest books I've read in ages. I loved it."
—Molly Antopol, author of *The UnAmericans*

"Probably the most influential novelist of the post-war period."
—*The Times*

"Kelman has the knack, maybe more than anyone since Joyce, of fixing in his writing the lyricism of ordinary people's speech.... Pure aesthete, undaunted democrat—somehow Kelman manages to reconcile his two halves."
—*Esquire* (London)

"The greatest British novelist of our time."
—*Sunday Herald*

"A true original.... A real artist ... it's now very difficult to see which of his peers can seriously be ranked alongside [Kelman] without ironic eyebrows being raised."
—Irvine Welsh, *Guardian*

God's Teeth and
Other Phenomena

Books available by the same author

God's Teeth and Other Phenomena

James Kelman

God's Teeth, and Other Phenomena
© 2022 James Kelman
This edition © 2022 PM Press

ISBN: 978-1-62963-939-0
ISBN: 978-1-62963-940-6 (hardcover)
ISBN: 978-1-62963-954-3 (ebook)
Library of Congress Control Number: 2021945068

Cover by Drohan DiSanto
Interior design by briandesign
Project Editor: Cara Hoffman
Proofreaders: Michael Ryan, Gregory Nipper, Allan Kausch

10 9 8 7 6 5 4 3 2 1

PM Press
PO Box 23912
Oakland, CA 94623
www.pmpress.org

Printed in the USA.

for
Marie
but for whose enthusiasm and persistence
this novel would not have been created.
She knew it was good for a laugh and
gave me the space to batter on with it.

Chapters

Eighteen Months Later

I was at the computer trying to finish a sentence. Hannah was here and my attention would go and I was trying not to let it, to finish the damn—the sentence, the thought, before my memory snapped altogether. What the hell was it? It was just there and I would get it I would get it except Hannah standing there studying the diary chart above my right shoulder, that stupit diary chart tacked up on the wall by my desk, why was she studying that? What was she wanting me to do! Stop work to hammer in another drawing pin jesus christ. Hang on a second eh I'm just eh ... hang on a second.

But snap and gone, gone. She had not spoken a word. She never had to. Her presence just. In mid-sentence when she opened the door, and pausing so not to interrupt me, finishing the sentence, a sentence being a sentence and is one sentence from inside. It is from inside and I was finishing it. Inside. I was inside. The thing about "inside" as opposed to outside concerns perception and reality, if we are inside then our outpourings, the utterings, cries and squeals that we pour out, within the writing, becoming "outside," about eh

one toty wee sentence.

She had placed her hand on my shoulder and was peering at the thing, this diary chart and what was it, the perfume, the perfume. In former days I worked in typescript and her bending forwards, craning to read, her bosom against my cheek, one could just ... one nestled, my hand round her waist, resting on her hip. Nowadays a 21.5-inch screen, creating aloofness, aloofity; one's lady with her hand on one's shoulder, a distancing: What is that? she said and was pointing.

The diary chart. Every xmas she got me one in the expectation I examine it hourly. Every year for the whole of January she waited to see if I would stick it up myself. I never did. I had not forgotten. I just didnt get to do it, the whole time it took, drawing pins and all that stuff, even unrolling the thing. It was just time, the time it took to get it up on the bloody wall, and then once it was there, I never looked at the damn thing. Bloody drawing pins aye broke anyway, the spike part flattened or twisted or just fell out the fucking wall and ye wound up stepping on it. My heels were permanently punctured by these fuckers. So now it was another one, another drawing pin, another bloody

Fuck it.

When she knew I was beyond the heart attack stage she pointed again to a space on the diary chart, one of the paltry few I had penned an entry. What is that? she said, her finger covering the space: a nice finger, a nice hand, a strong hand; slender but strong; unlike mine, thick and grasping, a grasping hand for a grasping bastard for that was me, a grasper.

I drew hands as a boy. I drew hers when we met. I liked drawing her, the curve of her bosom and shaded nipples, so much in the shading, I could never get the shading, the valley as they say, valley; one strokes, one's fingers, one's chin nestles; nestling, burrowing. God's teeth! I was too old for sex anyway. Damn sex man one believes one is past it, has passed it. We married young. Bunny rabbits! She didnt like me using such language. Nay wonder. Sex sex and sex but that was us and why not, that was the age we were and this was the generation, our generation, pre–online porn. I was working on a story based on that. And writing about sex one aye craves it, who was that writer ... Henry Miller or somebody, writing with a hardon—I hadnt read him for forty years—the constant sensitivity and I try to capture it, something there, touch me; touch me and I am yours, a goner: me so; he, she or it am; I am, yours for ever, and ever amen: I touched her wrist and smiled but she frowned, had frowned. She was speaking and I was not hearing. I was not listening. The sentence was gone, was long gone; the thought of, the thought thereof; all of it. What does it matter,

what

does

it

Why bother anyway. Who cares apart from me, the right word or the wrong word, whether or not I finish such a question—is it a question, an exclamation, a proposition: who gives a fuck. Agents and publishers, accountants; lawyers, all these fuckers at yer shoulder, sweetsmelling breath disguising the rotten gums.

Ach it wasnt even true. I couldnt blame a soul except myself. I was skint and that was that. People dont buy yer books and ye cannay fucking force them man imagine it! waiting outside the bookshop with yer Winchester rifle: buy the bastard's book or I'll blow yer fuckin heid aff! One would be arrested for foul language.

Talking about accountants, mine was a pal. He only cared as a pal: the work petered out a while ago. When was he last paid? When was I last paid?

And Hannah was still pointing. Why does one have a diary chart if one never peruses the thing? That was her question, unstated.

The diary chart about fourteen inches from the upper right side of my cranium. All I needed to do was squint sideways to see it. And in the seeing I saw, in a lush sumptuous hand, The House of Art and Aesthetics. What in the name of god was that?

You've to be there in ten days, she said.

Pardon?

How could ye forget something like this?

I didnt forget I just eh ... Other entries were there too; actions planned, actions beholden, arrows indicating all manner of potential manoueverings in regard to bodies and other substances; dentists and tooth scrapers, the birth dates of assorted relatives; jeesoh man where do they all come frae! Fucking grandkids!

Hannah sighed. That particular sigh. Hannah had this amazing attribute: the sigh. Sigh was a set. Double click on the sigh and up came a dozen entries. This one now

Oh god ... and the word required a capital it was of such significance. Oh God!!!!! I didnt forget, I said: The House of Art and Aesthetics?

But what the fuck was it? Some kind of residence, residential. I was to be there in ten days, and it took an airoplane to get there! God's teeth!

Phone Rob.

I'm not phoning Rob.

He's your agent.

Yeah well ...

Hannah sighed. It was her fault anyway. But for her I wouldnt have considered the damn thing, that or anything else. I dont need any damn thing else. Scraps from dustbins. Who needs money. Except one has a partner, one has offspring; offspring of the offspring; appendages to one's existence. Without Hannah there would have been none of that, without Hannah ...

I would be dead.

Quality of Life: I had been trying to improve such. Put an end to this compulsive way of living. Electronic scribbling man it does yer fucking nut in. Henceforth I would accompany Hannah to the Cine Complex twice per week. Maybe I could bring the laptop.

The House of Art and Aesthetics? Was it a hotel, a bunkhouse, a barracks? Whatever man it was a job and jobs paid dough. Okay. Here I was having signed my name for some residential thing without knowing what it was. Fair enough. Not for Hannah but it was not enough for her. She was a facts and and reality kind of individual. Had she asked me directly the nature of this House I could not have told her. She did not ask, but remained hovering. "Hovering" is a silent beseech. "Hovering" is an action designed to interrupt one's thought, reminding one of the existence of the world, that one occupies a place in it. Never mind anyway. Because

may be expressed also as sequence. And that sequence, whatever it was, could not come out come out wherever you are, it had gone forever. Hannah entered the room and dynamite, splattered brains and propositions, destroyed, destroyed propositions, lost and gone forever. Statements in kind and of kind. An infinity of the fuckers. My memory had snapped. That sequence had gone. Who cares. Precision is a life-sentence. Although if one enters the racket, so-to-speak numbers-game, if one so chooses—some would say chosen, if one is so chosen, among the elect, thus one's entry into the great hereafter,

Concentrate. Slivers of thought. Form & Substance: Metaphysical Division.

A familiarity therein. But my mind was incapable, incapable. I might have made of it a sketch, or a song. Either may work. I had acquired the habit from a fellow who applied pen to paper in the construction of Truth-Tables: for sketching he used only pencil. Lead is life! (who wrote that?) It is true, sketching is a means and means is life: breathing laughing singing dancing making love; sex, sex and sex, the square and the root. People are pencils and must always be pencils, if we dont have pencils there is no red blood. Blue is blue, ink, absence. Pencils do not mark the absence.

Now dead. A good fellow. I glanced at Hannah and breathed. A formulated breath, constructed such that oxygen is obtainable. This was my logic. Devised, developed and devoured. Who was I talking about? The guy who constructed the Truth-Tables, or set us on the path, that one may breathe. One wields the pencil, the prosaic prosist and the search for correct symbols, signs and signifiers in the fulfilment of these concepts so created. Ergo a pedant. A painstaking fucker.

Hannah. She was still here. One's wife, one's partner, one's rock: in short, one's salvation, without whom perish the thought lest perish the man. I should have said all that but I didnt; I couldnt. We didnt communicate in such high-falutin ways.

She ignored my arm, which encircled her waist. She said, You signed your name to this residency.

Aw dear. I shook my head. Then I pulled open the filing cabinet, pretending I knew what I was looking for. To my amazement I found it! Leastways:

1) the initial invitation

2) their acknowledgment of my acceptance.

But that was eight months ago, or was it eighteen? and nothing since. Except thinking about it now, my old email address had bitten the dust. Maybe they were still using it? Was that last year or the year before?

Could be, said Hannah, and you wouldnt have known so you couldnt acknowledge it, and they wouldnt know you hadnt received it because you dont always reply to things.

What do ye mean?

People make contact and you dont reply.

Well I dont know who they are.

Some of them ye do.

Yeah some of them. These are the ones I reply to. It's only the ones I know that I dont.

What do ye mean? Jake, what d'ye mean?

Nothing.

They should have phoned you for confirmation.

Exactly.

They didnt write to you did they?

No. If they had I would have filed the letter; and I would have found it.

Then you need to contact them now, right now. Phone them.

But

Oh for God sake.

Okay okay.

One human being to another. A simple communication made as an unobtrusive, non-intimidatory method by which one reminds Authoritorial Bodies of a certain existence viz. one's own. I did not wish to upset anyone.

Hannah, waiting till I lifted the receiver, till I began speaking. I underwent the digital response rigmarole with great patience then she left to make some coffee. Eventually I was talking to a woman of a most relaxing and verbalaceous disposition. I began by apologizing for the inconvenience, asked what style of accomodation was provided in their House of Art and Aesthetics? She corrected my font over the phone: *The House of Art and Aesthetics*. I was two words into my next sentence and stopped: Why apologize for other people's inefficiency? Why are we put into this position? And why do we accept it? I was having to conceal my annoyance. Why?

Other queries based around the if-then proposition rushed into my skull, and I rushed them out: Given resident writers will write in residence does this House consider the supply of computers a necessity? Must we bring our own? How about reference books, desks, coffee pots, wi-fi and so on, does this House take into consideration the Creative Writer's nether regions, e.g. hot water bottles? And I needed a postal address too, obviously, so Hannah could post me the occasional pot of soup. I then paused. The net effect had been silence. Eventually I said, Hullo?

From afar the voice of another: Hello?

Hullo, yes. I was talking to somebody there, I said. I am supposed to be arriving at Form & Substance in ten days' time, and I have not heard anything.

I beg your pardon?

The literary House thing: sorry, what is it again, Form & Substance or something?

This is the regional office.

Yes, well fine, okay, but please put me through to the Arts and Culture department or whatever it is, the Aesthetic people, somebody who knows about Art and Aesthetics.

Please hold, said the human being. Then was transferred to the building department.

?

Vivaldi's *Four Seasons* played that I might cope with the absence of human stimuli, recover sufficiently in order that I might converse with the person from whom one had been passed on from building to the sports and leisure department thence architecture and design and a most patient lady. One required such patience lest one succumbed to heart stoppages or emotional breakdown. Everything was so very very dreadful. How can I help? asked this patient lady. I explained. I think you're referring to the Form-in-Thought project, said she. This has been outsourced. I recommend you try online.

I put down the phone. Hannah reappeared, gesturing with my earlybird medication, the 40 mg clodriwarfarin-spiringel pills that one may continue one's existence. Had I already taken them? Who knows. I swallied them anyway, closing the peepers and counting to ten. In earlier days itinerant intellectuals of the Gallowglas persuasion reached for a good grade uisqué bha, who cared the time of day, out we went and sailed to Greenland, created the conditions that a sabre-toothed megadon might be harpooned prior to the kippers, toast and boiled egg, then headed for the nearest internet cafe; rows of foreign students, hiccups with the rampant bluetooth, bumping elbows and so on, the noises and coughs and fucking pongs man why do people emit these silent farts in these damn places and how salient is such silence? sitting in clouds of yellow and green man could they not have emailed their fucking body odours to faraway lands? What about some old-fashioned decency for christ sake. What a nightmare it was, young people nowadays, but naybody seemed to think so except me. I was the wrong generation.

But what has age got to do with it? Old folk die young. A grandfather of mine lived till he was eighty, fuck sake, my maw's da. Even just being a grandfather was strange, its naturalness. Naturalness? And this is not the place to discuss the offsprings' offsprings, not even one's daughter who was expecting another any day soon, let alone our younger son who had vanished into the west but from what I gathered may have become a father for the first time.

The Shorter Oxford Dictionary is so damn heavy. I prepare for accidents whenever I lift the fucker, e.g. knocking ower the coffee or in this case the mug of green tea—I had had my coffee two hours ago.

"Naturalness" is a word, albeit clumsy as fuck.

Hiccups over. I replaced the "*Shorter,*" had a he-gazed-vacantly for seven minutes, snapped out of that and checked online basic details of the company now operating the House on behalf of the local City Fathers. It was owned by a giggle of former politicians and ex-employees of the County Council, headed by the former Chief of Homeland Security operating as co-chair with the CEO of the Department of Sports and Cultural Pursuits: Metaphysical Division. I found a telephone contact. When I dialled the number a man answered who knew about stuff. He apologized for the lack of communication. The system has been down, he said, we have been unable to access home addresses. Also major changes in personnel have occurred since the company was awarded the Art-as-Thought-in-Substance project. The funding can no longer to be taken for granted. At the same time there is nothing to worry about.

Pardon?

If you have any further questions on that score you should drop into the House upon arrival or perhaps after bedding in—at the Neuk I believe.

Pardon?

You've been booked into the Neuk? You are Professor Proctor?

Yeah, well, usually I just say Proctor, Jack Proctor.

You've been booked into the Neuk, a rather charming little hotel; homely, family-run.

Sounds like a guest-house, I said. So there was no space left in the actual House? What is it those and such as those?

I'm not sure what you mean.

You've booked me into a guest-house is what I mean.

The Neuk is a small hotel; family-run and homely, a charming little place.

So it's the old A-list authors of first rank I presume? Let's call them frankers, wuckin frankers even better. The usual cìoch I said, using the Gaidhlig but who cares nowadays fucking shits man sorry, it's not your fault. It's whoever booked me the damn room. Really, when ye think about it. Stuck in a single solitary room for six weeks. God's teeth!

I used to have these fantasies as a young father, in the midst of nappy duty—diapers I mean, sorry—if I was stuck in a prison cell for six months with nothing but inexhaustible A4 paper, with an efficient typewriter, plenty of ink ribbons; an infinity of sharpened pencils, rubbers and so on, tipex and that glue stuff.

Professor ...

So what about the work space in this wee family-run hotel? Is there space to work? Several questions require asking, and I really need to ask them, given I need answers. Let us begin:

Does this guest-house bedroom have a desk? What is the lighting like? Some of these hotel rooms nowadays dont have an actual reading light. Honest. Ye cannay even read a book! sorry. One has to adjourn to the fucking cludgé. It's the only place where sufficient light exists to read. Who cares that it is a very friendly little place, this family-run hotel with its own little residents' lounge which no doubt has housed the most illustrious writers and artists, not to mention members of the aristocracy and other red-nose celebrities-loved-the-wide-world-o'er, all with their own wee kippers, cornflakes, toast and marmalahd. I chuckled.

But was anybody there on the end of the phone? Hullo! I said. Hullo!

Yes?

Sorry for the language, but given that writers write and a working writer works at writing albeit creatively albeit res-identially I, being a human, space to work notwithstanding

The others thought it wonderful. The other writers and artists.

Did they bring their own desks and easels?

Beg pardon?

Did the Neuk supply them? Look I'm not getting at ye. It is just ye see I write in residence. That's the thing: I'm not saying "one" writes in residence? I'm saying I: me, me me me. I am talking about me myself who am a writer and am to be in residence. I need to write. I am not saying others dont. Just that I need to. It's pathological. If I can I shall. So will I be able to?

Oh yes, I am sure.

Ah.

I'm sure you will.

So you arent.

Excuse me?

If you were sure you would not have said you were. People say "I'm sure" when they mean not quite.

They have a residents' lounge Mister uhh.

Proctor. Is it a writer-in-resident's lounge?

Honestly, they are very friendly people.

Who to? friendly. Friendly to who? whom? I am in the middle of writing a fucking novel sorry and wish to be writing this novel while in residence. What you're telling me is there's no work space in the allocated room, unless one is of those and such as those and I've to dwell in the damn place for six weeks, including the entire month of November man we're talking December, it'll be December before I get hame I mean god's teeth! Is it communal, this residents' lounge? Have I to sit in there while people are watching fucking television?

It is a completely satisfactory room Mister Prock-torr. Others have found it so. I can assure you that they are very much used to artists in this location.

Excuse me, I chortled, can you put that in writing? Just email it to me word for word.

An award-winning international poet for one, very well known, he found the facilties wholly congenial and enjoyed his stay very much. He was from New Zealand.

Oh dear, New Zealand, I'm goni faint. So how long was his residency, this paragon cowardly bastard?

I am unsure exactly, two weeks.

Two weeks. Yeh well, two weeks is a holiday; six weeks is a prison sentence. And not being able to write is death. Obviously poets are different from prose writers; we have wur own individual habits and methods. I work on a daily basis: whether this is forenoon, afternoon, evening or through the night depends on external obligations, and I organize accordingly. Typically a prose writer requires a computer, a seat, and 24/7 wi-fi access, plus kitchen facilities. This would be impossible in a single room in a small family-run hotel, no matter how cosy and charming, how friendly. My breakfast is at four in the a.m.'s. Or p.m.'s. It is contingent, all of it, the whole damn lot.

I understand.

No ye dont son. That's exactly it. Wait a fucking minute, are you chuckling? I heard you chuckling.

I'm not chuckling.

Ye fucking laughed.

I didnt.

Yes ye did. I know why too, it's my presumption. It sounds so damn vainglorious. Proctor is a writer as also Tolstoy who also was a writer ergo not all writers are Proctor and not all Tolstoys et cetera et cetera. So who is in the actual House right now? I'm talking about the actual House itself.

Excuse me?

Yeh, excuse me too, the effin rankers, the A-listers man the Writers of Distinction, hallowed be thy name. I accept my identity in the lesser known B-, C- or D-species but I demand the right to ask a question. Who is in the House right at this moment? Right now? Are the rooms all allocated?

Even as I spoke, dear reader, how ridiculous I sounded, how utterly naïve. Who is in the House! What House? There was no fucking House. A stupit figure of speech. How foolish can a man be? I said, I am very sorry. I thought there was an actual building where the writers all lived, where they cohabited, sharing their pencils and making each other cups of coffee laced with the finest cognac.

I started again:

I'm sorry son I just need a place to write. It isnt anybody's fault. I'm one of these writers who write all the time. It is not a requirement it is a need. It is a fix. I fix to be writing: if not my brains enter a state of expiratory explosiveness. Ask my wife. She will confirm this as a sad truth.

Neither is it a gender issue; some of one's pals who are writers are women and so on and if one asks of them etc. etc. re survival they too will describe, in their own words, a process of disintegration, our descent not into madness but the personification of a logical absurdity. I just need a place to work.

I shall try to find out for you.

Thanks.

I shall phone you back.

After a moment the line became a whine, a howl, then dead altogether. Hannah appeared from the kitchen doorway with two cups of coffee: How are ye? she asked.

Fine, I said.

2

Who did ye say ye were again?

I was to arrive Sunday lunchtime but the plane was delayed seventy-five minutes and the driver sent to greet me had gone. Or failed to arrive in the first place. I contacted the House office. No one answered. Why should anyone be there instead of someplace else, wherever that happened to be, a cheery pub watching a game of fitba.

But where was I staying? I was lugging a bag, a backpack and laptop. Was it the Neuk or was it not? Nobody had told me. Otherwise I would have gone myself. I phoned again. Still nobody. There were no trains from this airport but a variety of road transport. Outside the control zone I was scrutinized by packs of relatives, smokers and would-be guides; assorted pirates, petty thieves, and private-hire drivers. A taxi would have been ideal but I prefer buses in foreign climes, if trains are unavailable. It aint parsimony so much as paranoia. I have a tendency towards same. If I move only by taxi I end up in a room and scared to leave it. With buses one is forced to acclimatize oneself to the concept "strange person.

I kept my head down and made it to the terminus. Later a bus sped into the city and I was aboard.

I had this elderly mobile phone which had no internet access. But I had a map. I misjudged the distance and walked for ages, then found the virtual House, inside a suite of offices. I rang the doorbell. A shadow at a side window. I kept on ringing. A guy answered. He had waited for me. He should have stopped work at 1:00 p.m. and here he was. Thanks a lot, I said, and sorry to keep ye waiting.

No problem, he said. He handed me an A4 size cardboard wallet that contained much information on the residency, including a copy of "the" contract I signed eight months earlier. Doubtless the original had been placed in the vaults of a lawyer's office, that evidence might be used against me. The guy went off on connected business. I browsed the information documents, and found the "conditions of residency":

> Creative Delegates will work within the community. They will meet with professionals, amateurs and others. Community groups are encouraged to seek support. Award-winning Creative Delegates will enter schools and learning institutions, colleges and universities. Those on longer-term residency programs will work across country on behalf of the county or regionality, displaying motivational skills as tutor, mentor, "halfway house" and conduit, making extensive use of their many contacts within the Art and Thought industry, including areas adjacent to that as may be selected by or on behalf of Creative Delegates from the many areas in which he or she excels.

Excels? The "many areas. What is that a joke? Writers are failed livers; nondescript individuals of shallow mediocrity, who write about life rather than live it. Something like myself; ruined gambler, dogmatic pedant, sarcastic father, selfish husband, cantankerous neighbour; utterly ruthless in all day-to-day activities. Seriously but did I sign such crap? I must have been fucking drunk. "Halfway houses" and "conduits"? A conduit is a pipe, and a "halfway house" is a—what? What is "a halfway house?" A house but not a house, a metaphorical house, a thing on its way to becoming a house. Halfway to a home. "It is hoped that successful Creative Delegates ..." What does that mean, Creative Delegates? One who successfully delegates creatively.

Ah to hell with it anyway. What it all meant was whatever I meant it to mean. Where was the guy? Maybe he fuckt off. Did they even have a place for me? Anywhere would do now, just for the night. The airport lobby. How far away was it? Did one get a bus to there at all hours of the night qua morning to the airport qua airport?

At least the chair was comfy. I yawned, stretching the legs; eiderdown quilts, intimately soft and cosily wonderful. Imagine an eiderdown chair. One reads mystery yarns in which these right-wing think-tanks and quasi-government institutions situate eiderdown seats for visitors and other outsiders such that one cannot stay awake, cannot take cognisance of one's whereabouts, of why one is visiting the parent body quack quack, parent body quack quack, remembering one's arguments against the existence of these think-tanks, publicly funded, purposes of control, exercising control of us long to reign over us within the community, schools and learning institutions. At least the chair was comfy, especially so so wonderful just so wonderful one finds oneself, one is coorying, just comfy, yawning and so forth for one dozes, been dozing.

The brochure on my lap. Creative Delegates! I was never Creative. That was the problem. It was all sweat, grime and fucking fuck knows what, sweat sweat sweat, boring boring grind upon grind and draft upon draft upon draft, even that one may sit, aching shoulders, stiffness, draughts from faulty fucking windows one never has time to repair. One finds a space, comfortable knee positions, that one's shoulders, one's backbone, the crick of one's neck, the snap of one's braces, adequate medication of a non-liquidacious form

that one may create; in order to create one must perform truthfully, one must adhere to the tracks of the good for therein lies lies and more lies, one avoids, avoideth, yea tho one walk, two walk.

The guy with the cardboard folders had returned. I was not snoring, annis tu gahd I wasnay sir no sir. We've found you a place, he said.

Thank christ for that, I said, stumbling to the door, Merci, merci.

He lifted my chattels as though I were an elderly chap. I sighed and followed. He waved me inside the car. He wasnt coming. The car was a taxi. He dropped the chattels on the passenger seat and pushed me in beside them. Where am I going?

The driver knows, he called, slamming shut the door. The driver accelerated away.

What a strange life. I looked out the windi, watching the fields roll past, an occasional waterway. The driver yapped on, politics and families, existence and so on.

Fair enough.

We passed through a sort of village, turned off along a wee country road, more fields and shit. Then here we were.

It was a log cabin in a holiday village a few miles out of town, a hundred yards from a canal bank, maybe eighty. The driver called it a chalet. I paid him the dough and said cheerio. Inside I found a living room with good windies, a decent table, a television and okay kitchen facilities; plus a bedroom with shower-cubicle and toilet. It might have been better furnished but so what. The heater hadnt been on for a while but soon it was fine.

As well as the laptop I had an extra few items: notebooks, pencils, green teabags and the three hardboiled eggs Hannah supplied in case of emergencies. If the plane crashed into the depth of the ocean at least I would have a bite to eat. For some reason airport security throughout the world failed to pick up on hard-boiled eggs.

Oh but seeing out the windies man it was great. The space! I could go for long walks, enter interesting states of mind; periods of repose, of contemplation. Unfortunately this was the end of October and we were located north of the equator. Never mind.

I plugged in the laptop, checked for emails. Nayn. Nothing at all. Because nay wi-fi!

Ha ha! Where's my pencil!

Is that a joke? There wasnt any. Jesus christ.

Nothing. Isolation.

Hang on a minute, isolation. Isolation! It was the dream. No communication. What if I dumped my phone! A scary thought. But I could. I could go a walk along the banks of the canal and it could slip out my pocket and with nary a splash sink to the bottom: in among the slimy reeds and dead frogs I would never find it. Ergo: peace. Concentrated work. I might bring to an end assorted creative products, the stories, the essays, the plays, lyrics, all the stuff, all following me about. Mayhap I might end them all and clear the decks, get finished, live a normal life, just walking about enjoying the scenery. Whatever they do I would do, normal people, walking about, ye see all these people and that's what they are doing, they are walking about, they just kind of walk.

I loved books about artists when I was young: locked into isolation with no option but to paint, write and study. Stevenson and all that. Hamsun on the wee island, Kerouac seeking fires on the horizon; boats on the Hudson with Trocchi, Arctic ice with Jack London, Mexican highjinks with Malcolm Lowry, Seneca and the rivers of Rome, tutor-delegate to Nero, taught him to fiddle creatively, yodel odel eee. Sienkiewicz and that lighthouse aff the coast of Texas would have suited me, long swims doon the Gulf—except staying off the booze. Periods of isolation, tend to drive one up the fucking wall, having been born and brought up with assorted companions, siblings and offspring: the solitary life, I had none of that, never alone man never ever, not through choice. One talks to mirrors. No offence. None taken.

Nay grub in the chalet but and I was starving. Boiled egg number one.

The cutlery drawer was smelly. Hannah would have rewashed the fucking lot. Somebody else's crumbs is worse than finding an auld sock under the bed; a pair of fucking y-fronts man now ye're talking. God's teeth.

Supernatural wallies. Gie that to the schoolkids, an exercise in atheism. If God is the ancient of days has he still got his ayn gnashers?

I checked the information pack again, the diary with the engagements and so on. The first was tomorrow evening. Eight o'clock in the theatre section of the local arts centre: I was doing a reading! They would send a car. Good stuff.

I thought I might find a shop but this was the countryside, the real countryside. One walks for miles. At the same time I was knackered; I went to bed. I lay there in the favoured coffin-position; hands crossed on the chest. I do it to save time. One of these days I would wear my best suit to bed. Imagine the undertaker, Your husband was ready Missis Proctor, take consolation from that. I would wear a pair of fancy white socks just to fuck him: ye cannay bury a guy in a pair of fancy white socks.

Hours later I was awake. Starving. Maybe I could find a hotel somewhere; one with a bar doing evening meals. Fish and chips and a pint of lager. How rustic can one be. Even the walk would do me good, except it was so very dark, country dark, and what might one say, unconducive; bushes and trees, shapeless masses, ruts in the ground. Plus it was cold. What if I fell in the fucking canal is what I am talking about. Icy shards and so on. Plus the animals, let us face it, these beast bastards, they recognize a coward at a hundred paces; even cows turn nasty, never mind owls, bats and foxes. Who cares.

At the same time

I switched on the telly. Another mug of green tea and boiled egg number too. Aint life just wonderful.

3

Stan scratched his head

I needed to be awake. I could lie there but had to be up, had to be working. Some wait for daylight. Because of the story, how it begins in or from the space that comes prior to the first word. The artist plots the beginning and it requires emptiness, or blankness. Is emptiness the same as blankness? What about absence or the presence of nothing? What is a blank, a gap? Hollowness? To grasp this better refer to other art forms, perhaps especially, and obviously, music. The first note in Beethoven's 5th, the concerto. Donnnggg. It does not need anything as positive as that. Stories begin somewhere. They seem always to do that. For any artist this should be crucial. Why does this happen? We avoid the term "artist." How come? How come we are so wary of it—afraid even. Some are hostile? They think writers are presumptuous because we use the term "artist" and apply it to oneself because how else do we make the reference? Who cares. Fucking shite. I was working and glad to be working and that was plenty.

The table by the window, the new location and the shifts in light. Yes, and I kept it going till around 9 o'clock I closed down the machine, changed clothes and set off on the canal tow path.

North, south, east or west? I turned left. I would arrive somewhere. Okay, October, I wished I had brung a pair of waterproof boots, walking boots. If I had known, if only. No complaints but I had warm clothes christ almighty the world was a great place to be, hoofing it along, breathing deep lungfuls of air. Cliché upon cliché: "this is the life," "just what the doctor ordered" and so on, but in crept the image of Oliver Hardy declaring to Stan Laurel:

Well Stan, here we are at last, things going good, the future looking rosy, a bit of money coming in, a nice meal to look forward to, at long last things are on the up.

Stan smiling, scratching his head, vaguely puzzled.

Ducks and swans. Perhaps they noticed my approach but not from watching, they werent watching. They didnay care one way or the other. I was just there and they accepted that. My existence. One more element in the natural order. There I was and that was that. I passed without fanfare.

It was just fucking wonderful. A mile farther on was a lock-bridge. Lock-bridges are beautiful. That smell of canal water, silt, brown leaves, the vegetation. What is it that makes it so singular? Like Glasgow subways. All whatever it is—I hope it isnay sewage—but so what if it is, it's beautiful. I crossed and continued by the opposite bank. Another half mile and another lock-bridge. Country living. It was still a bit early to phone Hannah but to hell with it and I did.

She was hoarse and bleary-voiced but denied she had been on the booze all night to celebrate her freedom: my departure.

I avoided relaying information on the Holiday Chalet. The location and the countryside would have impressed her in the first instance but ultimately raised questions on organization and eh ... well least said the better, at this stage anyway. Great ye shoved in the boiled eggs, I said.

Hannah intended visiting at some point. Fair enough, that was later. By that stage things would have settled down.

Arrangements were in place for the use of a car. I should have had it yesterday but fair enough. Except the food. How did I eat? Miles from anywhere: nay stores, nay transport. At least they laid on a taxi, aye but I had to pay it myself. A lack of foresight, never mind, kind of silly but so what. I didnt tell her any of that either. I'm doing a reading tonight, I said, the local arts centre.

A reading! Already.

Yeah well it's a welcome. I'm the new Writer-in-Residence, so I mean

I heard her sigh! All the way from Glasgow, Scatlin! Hannah, I said, it's nice hearing yer voice.

Surely they could have given ye a day-off?

Ach it'll be okay. Somebody I know might turn up. Some writer I hadnay seen for years. I was hoping for that. But was I? Maybe I wasnay. Maybe I just told Hannah that for the sake of conversation, so she wouldnay ask an awkward question. She pulls them out of thin air. Who knows what.

But who knows what about anything—apart from being alive and just like whatever; walking, marching, marching. On I marched, the world athwart. Athwart the world! Have at thee dull future!

I had arrived with a plan; not so much a plan as a befuddled dream: concerning the AoY, the Albatross of Yore, as I termed the shite/oblique/massive tomes that hover above one's shoodirs, making them even humphier, all the part-written stories, part-written lyrics; essays, reviews, dramas and screenplays: the usual dross acquired through a lifetime's workaholism. Last time I looked I was writing twenty-three novels and needed to isolate *the one*. The trouble is they were all lifeless dried up crap man it killed me to look at them let alone read the bastards but I needed to I needed to, if ever there was a time this was it. If not I had to wangle two years in an offshore prison, a period of solitary confinement; one of these old Beckett guys, stuck in a sack with a miner's lamp; posted a meal every couple of days, and a few sharpened pencils.

Mens sana, I just needed a rest. Maybe this was the place! Maybe I could make a start on some new work, using the fields and the canal, the grass and stuff, squirrels and animals, all the ducks.

A couple of miles hike and I came upon a swivel-style road bridge. A garage nearby with a shop attached selling the edible wittals Mister Bumble, typical groceries, coffee and booze. Poyfikt. I bought a packet of cheese sandwiches for later and four 3 packs of cup-a-soup. Some guys buy beer and single malts. I buy cup-a-soup, invented for those of us who live wur life in a state of emergency.

It is amazing the mischief one does not get up to when living alone. I could have bought anything, instead of which dried mushrooms drenched in wattir. Plus the usual essentials, and a coffee and donut to go. I scoffed it going along the tow path but not as enjoyable as it should have been. Said coffee cup one of these thick container things with one of these stupit wee fucking vent-holes ye get such that the coffee dribbles through and ye dont know if ye have a mouthful or is it just a weird saliva, so-called coffee man know what I'm talking aboot, the lassie was embarrassed to sell me it. I was like her effin grandpa and there she was ripping me off! Imagine ripping aff yer grandpa! Never mind hen, I said.

And the donut! Hesus el cristo. I didnay want to complain but being English, us Englisher guys dont complain, donuts are donuts he harrumphed, except every time I get one my heid gets stuck in thoughts of interiority, one's belly and the state therein, living on coffee and donuts, down-and-out guys in Kromer's novel and what it does to his insides, ripped up bellies. At my age who needs mair problems. I considered flipping the fucker into the nolly, as we weans termed the canal back when I was growing up. Christ, where had that come from? We're talking sixty fucking years ago and that was the last time ever I heard the word, nolly. What an extraordinary hard drive the guy has. Call that a brain, this is a fucking high-flying fucking was that a fox! Jesus christ!

Am I scared of foxes? Should I be? God's gnashers!

Who cares.

I needed a seat. There was a bench but it was wet and shitty.

It wasnay me Hannah worried about, not in particular: it was just life in general, everything, our daughter Julia was expecting a child, only weeks away. She already had one and Hannah was helping out. Who knows where the boys were. One of their marriages was falling apart, the elder yin; the other one had disappeared. Disappeared. What can ye do about that? Nothing. There was not anything. Ye sit back and ye wait. What else was there? Nothing. When one is not in control one learns to

"relax," I almost said.

I was glad being out of it altogether. Except that I wasnay. A spatial gap existed but what did that signify? Not much. Families. And I was not going to feel guilty. No chance. I was returning with a bag full of provisions and a bottle of red wine for future reference.

So what.

Isolation was great for youthful creatives but too much drives the more mature chap nuts, if not to the pub. A wee bottle of *el plonquerro* solved the problem.

The truth is

Never mind.

The canal was not oily but there was a surface substance where the weeds were and the slope up through the undergrowth. One imagines a body—alive, help, he croaked, the voice weak, uhhh, groaning, mouthful of bitter earth and a host of non-edible beetles.

I was feeling a bit unsettled, truth to tell, talking to Hannah.

How long had I been here man, a fucking day. One sighs willy nilly. At least with Hannah. A big cuddle. Okay that's me going to work, fuck the work Jake let's go back to bed, let's snuggle—oh man the snuggles: get thee beyond me weary physicality!

Onwards.

I was missing my chattels tae, the books and whatnot, the wee bits and pieces, mementoes and shit. I never throw nothing out, not even the totiest wee item, its very absence disturbs the universe. And what if something enters into it

this black hole theory man where's the grandkids, I could explain this!

I was knackered by the time I got back to *le chalét*. And already there was that kind of what the fucking hell—smell! Was it the drawer? Naw.

It was a smell but. It was my smell. Can one believe it!

Truly but a smell. Existence: with a smell—no no one cant take that away, from me: fartus ergo sum

the cheery old warbler.

He warbled.

Three hours later I woke up.

For much of the rest of the afternoon I devised a reading program and running order for the evening, selecting stories and rehearsing them. This is what I did. People dont think of that for writers but ye have to unless one is a fucking boy at the game know what I'm talking about, amateur night at the palais. Rehearse! Ye have to. Tonight was a performance, whatever it was; so treat it as such.

Consumate, one is consumate.

Short stories differ from one another not only in plot or story content but the manner in which the story is narrated. The "voice" telling the story may be unique to it. This is more clearly the case in "I-voice" narratives. There is the illusion that the "I-voice" is the voice of the author but this "I-voice" might be its most crucial fictional component. Literature is full of examples. It gradually dawns on the person reading the story that the narrator is a lying bastard! Individual stories are performed in the voice of the fictional character and how they are emotionally, psychologically, at the given moment. The same story can be read in a slow or highly-charged rhythm, or medium-paced, the voice of a drained and weary pensioner, an excited young man or woman. This is the beauty, and complexity of the performance. One cannay fucking read a clutch of stories in the same voice in the same emotional state jesus christ almighty it would drive one to eternal damnation. And nay wonder. They need a rest as well for christ sake the audience, ye would be as well listening to

no, never.

Fuck, I was angry already!

I planned on splitting the performance, leaving time at the end for a short Q & A. People enjoy them. Do writers? Sometimes yes sometimes no. All gossip is welcome, literary, celebrity or otherwise.

And I was glad not to be driving; a couple of drinks and so on, meeting with local writers, bla bla bla, I was looking forward to it, somebody I hadnay seen for years, maybe he owed me a few quid.

4

Flying seagulls and that Belgian guy

The taxi didnt collect me until twenty past seven and didnt reach the venue until twenty to eight. Doors open 8:00 p.m. Not much time for the tekki and sound stuff. I looked about for organizing folk in the lobby, and found a pile of flyers, with a headline:

> "Banker Prize Winner Reads From Book."

Pardon?

> "Banker Prize Winner Reads From Book."

Aw for fuck sake.

Fifteen years ago I was awarded the damn prize and these buggers were still picking over the bones. Fifteen years of purile chatter about "bad words": it drove one to distraction—fucking nuts as we say in the business. Also, there can be malice aforethought. People wait to pounce: lexiconographers, encyclopaediotricianophiles, journalists and other scrabble experts; students, teachers, lecturers, professors and all these other upright guardians of Their Royal Highnesses' Standard English Literary Form. Fuck them all. I went straight to the bar and cried for the organizers.

The barman looked at me. Hullo, I said. Will ye pass on a message to the organizers. I'm the writer for this evening. Will ye tell them I won't be reading from *the* bloody book this evening.

The barman had picked up an empty pint-tumbler then was polishing it, avoiding eye contact.

Look, I said, are the organizers about? I need to speak to the organizers?

What was that? he said.

It's the way they've written the programme, I said, holding the flyer so he could see it. I spoke slowly. It was done without consultation.

He squinted at the flyer.

I tried to smile. See? They didnt consult me first. I indicated the headline. He peered at it, keeping his distance and gripping the pint-tumbler. It makes it seem like I've only written the one damn book I mean "Banker Prize winner reads book." I shrugged. I'm not even going to read from it, I'm going to read short stories.

The barman had nay idea what I was talking about.

I retreated. Even that word: "book"! Why not novel? I had written five of the buggers. Then the short stories. What about the short stories? Then the lyrics, what about the lyrics, if it wasnay for the lyrics I would have collapsed as an economic unit years ago, I'm talking income, I'm talking dinners-on-the-table for the starving multitudes, the wife and the weans and the weans of the weans. Even had they told me in advance, if they had given me the flyer when I arrived. Surely they knew writers prepare for these things? Even the plural! "Reads from his books. That would have captured it, allow me the leeway, from there I could

oh god. I would just apologize and read the planned program. The audience wouldnt mind. Tonight I shall read from other books, announced the writer, to a stunned but appreciative audience. Bravo, they roared.

People would come in the expectation but that was the problem. Based on the flyer information expectations would abound. People would say, Oh he's the guy who won the prize for bad language! I want to hear if it's as bad as they say!

This kind of stuff built up the audience and organizers love audiences. Fair enough. But I wasnay going to change my programme. I had it worked out and that was that. Never pay attention to the requests of an organizer. They know fuck all and blab for the sake of it.

Oh god.

I found a quiet corner. Somebody in the audience would have a copy of "the book" for me to sign and I could borrow it and read a page, the opening section. I could start with that. But why should I! Why the hell should I?

I groaned so loudly I drew an audience. Only kidding, relax, calm down. What is this heart attack stuff? You are too old for this shite. It would drive ye fucking nuts but nay wonder we drink.

What the hell time was it!

Anyway I didnay need the fucking book, I had read the opening page so often I could bellow it from memory. The person doing the introductions would have a copy, if there was a person. Maybe I was introducing myself. I hoped I was.

Where the hell were they anyway? Naybody had come to say hullo. It was outrageous. Fucking amateur bastards, I needed space, space. A walk round the block. Oh man the canal, I could have done with the canal there and then, the fucking quack quacks, the ducks.

Nay organizers but imagine that, naybody to meet me, naybody to greet me, naybody to be there, to lead me to a quiet corner, where one might rehearse, to get the rhythms. Mellifluous, mellifluity, fluidity. Calm doon.

Deep breathing, one calms, becalms, becalumnd, so to say, that my stories are "in voice." None is my voice. The audience need to know that. But not from me. That was the organizers' job. A brief introduction, advising the audience that contrary to conventional wisdom the book that "won the Banker" was neither my first nor last publication. I had written more than one plus a collection of short stories with another pending. Plus I was known to dish up an essay on occasion, and wrote lyrics too and if it wasnay for them bla bla bla economic survival bla bla bla, the weans of the weans; and one worried, one worried. And I would read a couple of stories now, short ones, wee things, where one paid attention to form, as a matter of course, where the separation between form and content

Pretentious shite.

Who cares.

Seriously.

God's teeth. Okay. I would definitely read from the prize-winner. The opening section then juggle a couple of stories about; twenty-three minutes of a reading followed by a couple of short stories. An hour performance leaving twenty minutes for the Q & A; the spare ten for sundry verbals.

Phew.

Okay but I could do it.

An internal rehearsal. I remained in my quiet corner attempting same.

An internal rehearsal! Is that a psychological absurdity?

To pass the time I took the flyer out my pocket and uncrumpled it, delving further into the notes to the programme. Merciful heavens:

> *"As a proud Scot, Jock writes in Lallans, an old Scotch language."*

I ripped the flyer in two, then four, then tried for eight and dumped it. Immediately I regretted it, found another, and read:

> *"As a proud Scot, Jock writes in Lallans, an old Scotch language."*

So I was going home. The very next flight. I wasnay goni pack the bags. They could send them on or fling them in the fucking nolly for all I cared man I was goni sue the bastards, racist fucking arseholes man sue the cunts, no danger man, fucking bastards, calm down. Naw. I was not goni calm fucking down. I was angry and had good reason to be angry fucking Jake or Jack man no fucking Jock jesus christ almighty. Nay soundchecks either. Fucking amateur fucking bampot bammy bastards. Okay but calm down. Calm down. One tries. Do it. Okay, okay

> one sighs,
> sighs, he stood alone
> he stood alone he was alone,
> so naturally, nat chew ra lee
> nat chew ra lee

Oh man. The first gig but. Three days I had been here, or two—what the fuck was it? Christ I was losing track of time already. That was Hannah, where the hell was Hannah, her and her fucking wall-chart diary shit. She would have sorted it out. She would have sorted them out.

"Jock" but man it was totally racist. Also it was a lie. What they had written was an actual lie! I could subject them to a legal challenge. Lallans? What the hell is Lallans? I dont even know what it is, Lallans man know what I'm taking aboot—naw, neither do I. Definitely libellous shite man. I could bring a private prosecution. Fuck them. People cannay get away with this kind of shite. One simply

> Ach well.

Although a uisqué would have been nice.

I was strolling, I had left the arts centre. Should I stay or should I go? I circled the car park working that one out, concealing ma face, hiding ma shame.

It was drizzling. Good it was drizzling, I needed to get soaked, catch a cold, a flu—oh he had to get home, he caught a cold, it was drizzling. "It" was drizzling. "It"?

What is this "it"?

Rain was drizzling.

Rain drizzled. One would be as well saying "rain was raining" tautological cìoch man know what I'm talking about. It was raining. This entity "the weather," the weather was drizzling, the weather was sunny

But why had I come? Hannah! If she hadnt looked at the damn wall-chart. Her stupit wall-chart, that was the problem. Her and her stupid

It wasnt her it was me. I signed the contract. How come? Because I needed the dough. *We* needed the dough. Jobs paid a wage and I signed on for that. Once upon a time it was me then blink twice and it was one plus one, and another on the way, and another, and another

Gadzooks a fellow approached; an anxious fellow, covering his head with a flyer.

Truly. He was looking for me. He smiled and waved. Hullo! There you are! He was glancing at his watch in such a manner that I knew I was getting a row, just that way he done it, looking at his watch, I could tell how he brought up his kids, how he had been brought up, his aspirations, settling for dull mediocrity, a life of paper clips and shuffles to staff meetings.

I waited for him to speak. His hair was standing on end and words were failing him. What a life. Here he was drenched and having to face this auld man with fire erupting frae his nostrils, oh Thor, Thor, the fellow shuffled sideways, nudging the specs up the bridge of his nose. I was goni eat this bastard. He sniffed and cleared his throat, swallowed the catarrhal content. About the format, he choked.

Are you the organizer?

Not really uh they asked me to officiate, I'm uh I teach at the uh the university here.

Nay bother. Unfortunately they've got me down to read from a novel I wrote fifteen years ago. I just wish they had asked first. I've written five other ones not to mention a clutch of other stuff; short stories, lyrics; squibs, blogs, fancy texts and old-style reviews, old-style essays and old-style writings of all manner, *belles-lettres* m'boy ... I stopped and grinned. The worry on the guy's face was a worry to me. I put him about 40 years of age—if that, a father, definitely, young teenagers. Heart attacks were on the way.

By now we were inside the lobby. He nodded vaguely, peering someplace else, now grimacing, his face twisted and I saw his eyes close, poor bugger. Dont worry, I said.

He blinked at me.

I'll introduce myself, I said, it's nay bother. I'll read the opening section from the book like it says and do a couple of stories after that. Dont worry about it. You just come on at the end for the Q & A, if ye dont mind chairing it. It'll be fine. I shrugged, glanced at my watch.

Oh eh well of course Mark Allen is reading with you.

...

Mark Allen? he asked. Mark's reading with you.
What?

Mark Allen? Mark's reading with you. Mark's a local writer.

...

Mark Allen. He's highly regarded. Did no one say? Mark's very good. Very popular. Very very popular. And funny. He has a tremendous sense of humour; never contrived. He is a brilliant raconteur.

The Chair was smiling in this most peculiar manner; he raised his head and looked me in the eye. He keeps people going. He'll be a strong support. He's a very popular writer, very highly regarded

Not that it matters about life. Time has no place in the continuum. I smiled. So that now, now where we are, here we were, right here; the Chair squinting at me. I punched him on the shoulder, but cheerily. I said, Ye mean now there's two of us on the programme, me and another writer?

Mark Allen, yes, he's very popular.

So I'll need to half my performance now, that's what you're telling me and there's only two minutes to go. Do you know that I'll need to half my performance?

He smiled, uncertainly. That word "performance," it had thrown him. Mark will happily go on first, he said.

Is that a fact? Happily too, great. I'll go for a pint then, smashing. Any pubs round here? I patted him on the shoodir. I am going a walk round the block now. To clear my head. If a pub is there I shall go to it. Or not as the case may be. One thing but, dont introduce me as Jock or I'll find yer fucking huis and burn it down. I grinned. Dont worry, I know it's no your fault.

I left him.

Not that it mattered. Half the performance. Fair enough. Who gives a fuck. Not them.

It doesnt matter anyway. None of it. It was all just like—why does it happen? How come they even bother. I would just half the performance. 50% of the opening sixteen minutes amounted to the first two and a half pages of "the book"; then a couple of stories. Fair enough. I would just apologise. Blame the organizers. It was their fault anyway. Bastards. Imagine the

Hell with it. I strolled round the block again. At least it wasnay raining. I quite liked the weather when it was not raining.

Not a bad wee town either. More like a big village. An elderly man was passing along with a stupit looking fucking dug. He gave me one of these quizzical looks: Who the fuck's this? the bubble above his heid, I havenay seen him before.

I'm the guest writer, I shouted inwardly.

I could explain to the audience about the flawed information in the flyer, re Lallans: Dear friends, I stand today accused of adhering to a non-existent entity. Or maybe I should say nothing, begin with the opening pages of the "book that won the prize" and end with a couple of brief short stories—one to two minutes each in length. I write the shortest imaginable stories, and at times like these it is a life-saver man that is all one can say. I could even just not read the stories, just whatever ye call it, the book, the novel. I could even just sing them a song, Coming thru the Rye or some such shite, thinking of what, the old Kentucky thingwi. Gin a body, booze everywhere.

The elderly man had stopped along the street so the dug could have a piss, he staring back at me. I was speaking out loud? As a young fellow I charted an algorithm based on inward ponderings deducible from outer fidgeting. I could tell that to the audience. It made an interesting diversion for those of a psychotic bent.

I saw the Chair at the entrance to the art-centre; another guy with him—Mark Allen no doubt, author of *The Uniformed Dandelion in Charged Urban Settings*, a story of Chandleresque detection among the smooth-talking domestic military; 30,000 sold in a week—purchased en masse by the War Office for distribution among the overseas military. It was the same man. After he had introduced us the Chair asked, Shall we do a Q & A?

Mark smiled benignly. Audiences enjoy them, he murmured, in tones of a Life's Like That feature writer for the *Reader's Digest*.

Mark's right, confirmed the Chair. They get the audience interested.

People prefer audience-participation at literary events, explained Mark.

I gripped my fingers tightly tightly. Uriah Heep grasping and ungrasping his, at the final denunciation. Old fucking Uriah man rhyming with pariah, with black mariah, gripping the fingers in case off they flew away and away.

Mark and the Chair gestured me ahead as befits my years, showing me backstage, and through the wings.

Onstage a table and three chairs were set. There was a wee desktop mic thing in the middle of the table. A young guy with a beard the length of Methuselah was fiddling with this wee desktop mic thing, watched by the Chair, proudly. Jonathan's on sound, he said and to Jonathan: Things okay Jonathan?

Jonathan ignored the silly bastard, and continued tickling the mic and pushing it about the table. The beard he had informed the world of his technical prowess. I wished I had had a pair of scissors in my pocket.

The Chair was pointing at the three chairs for the three fucking bears and he said to Jonathan: Shall I sit in the middle?

Eh ... Jonathan pondered.

What's happening? I said to the Chair: Are we supposed to do the reading from here, sitting down at the table, chins on our knees, talking into that stupid wee mic thing?

Jonathan frowned up at me. Is there a problem?

I need a stand, I need an upright stand.

We have a clip-on.

I use an upright stand. That is what I need.

I'm not certain there is one. What is it for exactly?

I smiled at the bearded bastard. And he held my gaze, looked to Mark, and eventually to the Chair who studied the floor. I dont sit during the performance, I said, I stand. I stand at a mic, and the mic is attached to the upright one, the upright stand.

He stared at me.

Like a singer, I said, ye know the way a singer stands at the effin mic?

Nobody told me.

Is that a fact.

I'll look but I dont think there is one.

I nodded, waiting. He exited backstage, accompanied by the Chair. I sat down.

Mark was now chatting with a group of people sitting in the front and second rows. The place was about three-quarters full. The Chair reappeared, waving. Jonathan found one, he's bringing it up.

I shrugged. By the way, I said, see when I'm reading dont sit at the table. You and Mark, dont sit there during the performance; it distracts the audience, especially if ye're picking yer nose. Move out the way, go to the side or something; sit with the audience.

The Chair nodded. We thought Mark should read first.

Fine, I said and stepped down from the stage. I sat at the vacant end seat of the front row. Jonathan returned with the mic stand. Eventually Mark and the Chair returned to the table shuffling papers, books and bottles of plastic water.

The Chair introduced the evening using the desk mic. He was nervous. Mark didnt look nervous; no doubt he was but was hoping he looked cool. He did look cool. Anyway, he was doing his best. They all were. Even Jonathan. Existence is shaky. It was only me. I was not doing my best. Ach well.

Mark had friends and family present, and a pile of older school-pupils. This was his first book. The atmosphere was very cheery as it should have been. There is no room for niggardliness here. Somebody attracted his attention. His maw or his auntie. He gave them a wave to tremendous applause. Then he spoke about the book, and read wee bits here and there to tremendous applause. It wasnay about angst-ridden detectives after all thank fuck: the extracts he read were humorous anecdotes relating to his childhood and made reference to several personages who were sitting in the first and second rows. The audience roared with laughter. He explained incidents and answered questions along the way. This continued for thirty-five minutes. The audience thoroughly enjoyed his performance and were loath to let him leave. Including the Chair who giggled frequently throughout. Mark saluted the audience to more applause, clamorous applause. Then retreated to a chair down the side of the space, people cheering him along, and even when he was seated, elderly bewhiskered gents reaching to tap him on the shoulders with their malacca walking canes: Well done m'boy!

I clambered up from my chair onto the stage and laid my books on the table. I feel like the Sheriff of Nottingham, I muttered, missing the mic by a foot. The Chair was about to introduce me. I waved him to remain seated, adjusted the stand, glimpsed my watch. I shall just begin, I said to the audience, and talk later.

I began on the shortened two-page opening from "the book" but it was sounding good to me so I continued for four pages, which lasted about nine minutes, thirty seconds, roughly. People clapped. Thanks, I said. I glanced at my list of short stories, reached for my books. The Chair appeared beside me. He announced the closure of the first half of the event.

More clapping.

I was still leafing through the pages of the short story collection, holding my list. But this appeared to be that, or that this, me finished. I whispered off-mic: Is that me finished?

What?

Is that me?

He frowned.

Mark's been on for thirty-seven minutes and here's me getting ten or eleven including breath pauses! I smiled. The Chair smiled too, thinking I was being friendly, and he reached as though to shake my hand but had the sense to back off upon glimpsing the black density of my eyes, heralding an untimely end for the unwary and those fools disinclined to heed omens and portents of doom.

A group of aunties and uncles and school-pupils were by now encircling Mark. Others were scraping back chairs and moving around, repairing to the bar.

There they all were. Everybody.

I repaired to the cludgé. A uisqué would have been good but to be avoided. I left the building afterwards.

The rain was raining. I was glad of that. I trusted the rain. When rain was on one's head one was wet.

So far the night had been bad but not catastrophic. At one point toward the end of Mark Allen's performance I noticed that he was looking at me. It was a strange look. Perhaps he was seeing my non-absence but without it having registered: "seeing" as distinct from "perceiving" which gave me an immediate insight on the nature of "nothing" so-called, and the netherlandian artist too, reminding me of his work and swiftly I got out the pencil, uncrumpled the flyer and wrote into the margin,

e.g. flying seagulls and that Belgian guy

the absence of punctuation consolidating the free-falling-form casting all asunder while rising forth beyond Mother Earth's gravitational pull. It was simple enough, except that very thing, the rising forth, introduced Parmenides and utter contradiction, there can be no movement, no rising, no lowering. Everything is jampacked the gether. There is nay gap, nay space; everything is just moving in and through one another. God!

I saw two women smoking by the door to the building. I smiled, reentering the building. They did not return the smile. Sometimes a woman might fancy one, and emit a certain signal. This was no such occasion. But something had happened. What? Had I done something? Just the way they were looking at me. I could not remember. Apart from the non-reading. Probably my voice, they didnt care for it; insufficiently melodious. Unless maybe they had paid to hear me and were annoyed at being short-changed. Were they blaming me for that? Unless they were two more relatives of Mark thingwi and thought I had encroached on his time. Maybe I was being ostracized.

This reminded me that nobody had said hullo. Right from when I entered the building the first time. If it wasnay deliberate it was weird. Here I was on the very first night of my residency, my first public event. Maybe it was me. Maybe I was to say hello to them. Maybe I was representing the House of Art. So I was expected to circulate and welcome folk. I trust you are enjoying the show: I trust you are enjoying the show. My name is Jack Proctor and I am the conduit and creative literary developer, I trust you're enjoying the show, young Mark there, the boy genius.

I thought I was the damn guest maybe it was them. God's teeth! Seriously but. If I was the guest and all that, where were the local writers? Surely they would have come along to say hullo? Gestures of solidarity and all that. Alright Jake! How ye doing? Hey man can we buy you a beer? Your work is brilliant! Your last novel—exceptional work, superb! We think your lyrics are the equal of your prose, and so on: Would you care for a wee uisqué? Make it a mhor.

Strange eventualities take place on reading tours. One arrives to discover entire towns alienated. Is it an authentic alienation? I never know. To be on the safe side I usually apologize to the organizers.

A 66-year-old writer travels for weeks to do an hour and a half performance and they cut it to twelve minutes in order to accomodate a first-time local writer of 37 summers and his fleet of relatives, including aged-aunts and babies-in-prams. It is so damn fucking ach well one just gets sick of it, one really does, one simply
  ach well.

But really, it is so very difficult to deal with such shite, simultaneously to the thing itself, that the inability to so deal with it becomes irreducibly the thing itself, an attribute thereof, or else oh for christ sake I just needed out of here, I just

out of here this very moment, the selfsame moment because folk were watching me from behind the partition. Not only the female relations of the literary boy genius but the Chair together with a man and woman who were whispering comments; upper members of the Cultural workforce, I could smell them at thirty paces, checking up on me, seeing how it went.

And the Q & A set to start. The safest place was the rostrum. I went through and sat at the table, bouncing from seat to seat, grasping a bottle of water in both hands to control the trembles.

Mark had written a book and good luck to him. People thought it was great and so it was. A female colleague extolled his virtues in the schoolteaching department and how, secretly—she would never have said it to him personally given he was sitting here facing her—she was not alone in hoping he wouldnt be too successful a best-selling author lest he stop being such a spectacular schoolteacher, friend and general fucking sweetie-pie husband and father.

Fantastic applause. The rafters shook.

The line of inquiry shifted to how the old hometown might look the same but has changed greatly since Mark stepped down from the train as he and the audience advised all us strangers. He was also strong on answering the old life-changing writerly questions re cell phones, smartphones, tablets, pads, laptops or sticking with the old pens, pencils, and calls in the wilderness. Is it true that some writers dont access social media and decline to become mental zooming skypecooking facebooking sonuvaguns.

Mark battered on chattering to one and all. The Chair was relieved. I too was relieved. I sat there smug as fuck. Oh man it was great not talking. Apparently the old town had changed much over the years with the advent of mall shopping, and its recent demise. Mark's headteacher was present with other colleagues so he obviously was popular. Fair enough. He seemed like a good guy and not a boasting bastard which I would have been, if my first book sold twenty thousand copies in the

what? Twenty thousand copies ... ? God's teeth! The guy was a best-selling-novelist. That was why I saw him swallying a pint of beer during the interval. I hadnay even been offered a cup of tea never mind a tankard of foaming ale.

The Chair was patting my wrist. Somebody asking you a question Jack ... Do you ever revise your stories?

Or a question to that effect. Heh heh, I chortled sternly, giving my questioner a wave. I was looking for a word. What word was I looking for?

Flying seagulls had begun to irritate me. Were they flying or not? I looked for my flyer marginalia to note a correction because in a sense, no matter what they say about that Belgian artist

I was interrupted by the Chair calling for applause to end the evening.

Then to the bar at last. I joined the small queue. Only one person was serving. There was a sign. According to this sign the place was scheduled to close at 10:00 p.m. I checked my watch: fifteen minutes to go. Another five before the person arrived to serve. I ordered a pint. When he brought it to me I passed him the dough and asked for another. He looked at me. Another pint, I said.

Sorry.

I smiled. I'm thirsty. It's just to save time.

Sorry.

Pardon?

We're closing.

I am an actual performer eh surely eh

Sorry.

Yeh but

The barman walked off. I realized vengeance was his. He was the same guy as heretofore. I turned in time to catch the Chair and a couple people glance away: they had been watching me.

I looked for Mark the boy genius but he was nowhere to be seen. Him and his entourage had fuckt off, doubtless to a popular local tavern. The remaining members of the audience were accepting this early closing malarkey as natural bar behaviour and were taking their leave in orderly fashion. The shutters were being drawn. The Chair gave a cheery wave and walked to meet me. The other two came along with him. I thought that went well, he said.

Yes, I said, it was magnificent.

The Chair beamed. He introduced the couple: Joe and Sally "from the department."

MI5?

They chuckled. I waited for him to add something. A few young people joined us, zipping up their coats, glancing at me, maybe wondering who I was and how come ever I won a prize; what for? a book, what kind of book? what sort of stuff does he write. I realized the Chair was waiting for me to leave. They were going off elsewhere, some amazing spectacular late-night bar where they would sit down, have a plate of fish and chips and a few pints of the local ale, roaring fires and so on. In days of yore I couldnt have concealed my annoyance. But now, now . . . I was not anything except slightly incredulous that here I was in a different country. What a strange life it was. So long, called the Chair. I raised my hand in salute, then I too headed for the exit.

Once outside
I flapped my wings and flew,
away away,
away I flew

beyond the mountains
the cold and lonely,
the farthest reaches
the furthest depths
oh the white mountains.

5

The Patience to Live

0301 hours, viz. a minute past three in the a.m'.s: experiencing strange sensations. I was a practical bloke, normally. Work is to be done. One groans, sighs, pours anar cup of coffee and proceeds. Just now but no, I found myself at the window, gazing. This rarely happens to me in the midst of one's work. My immediate concern, therefore, was to inspect inwardly the nature of this "gazing" and to ascertain origin and predicted outcome.

1) Was it me doing this "gazing"?
2) if not then who?
And woe betide
Stop.

Tales of Madness lay therein. Yet another one might subtitle The Uneddyfing World of the Solitary Male, [subtitled *Wee Willie Wilson*]. One of those fine darkest of nights in the depth of a bitterly long lonely winter I would finish my essay on Poe and dualism, his early period in Ayrshire, his familiarity with the works of Billy Maginn and Jimmy Hogg—the gilmartinesque fool grinning devilishly over the shoulder of the central figure, verifying empirically not only the internal but external appararitional existence, later embodied in an early caricature of that early 20th century figure of fun and behaviourist psychology, whatsisname?—put to sleep by Common Sense, resurrected by authoritarian governments everywhere. The longer one peered the less indiscernible the world beyond, a narrow world, tightening, entrapping; one shudders, *was* survival problematic?

What is the opposite of mystery? You've lost me there, he intoned bleakly.

3:20 of the a.m'.s, so where did that 19 minutes go? And the dark, of a blackness in depth impenetrable. The old fellow pulled on his boots and headed for the door. He paused on the threshold. The sense of foreboding. One peers out the windi. Canals and ducks, overhanging vegetation, bodies partly submerged among the rushes beneath the raised banks, slippery banks, a greasesome mud, a murky depth, weeds strangling the limbs, twisting, holding fast one's ankles, one sinks, the pebbly bed athwart the vattir. He could no longer rely on escaping the mess. Might he race headlong to freedom?

Mayhap one could, pack the chattels and dash for it, catching the first flight outa here. What about dough? Maybe the publishers could help. The novel-in-progress was overdue by eighteen months. More like two years. And if I didnay know what about them! Who cares. Naybody. They all hoped I would drap deid. What is the opposite of not worried? That was them. With luck I would forget all about it. That was what they hoped. Bookwriters were obsolete. Bookshops were closing at a faster rate than pubs. My world was going, going

The old fellow boiled the water, dropped in a green teabag, a green tea teabag, then twitted a tweet, the twat, shat a sheet and twitted a shite. One peers into the dark. He of the devilish grin, peering back at me. Who was he peering at?

'Twas I dear reader.

What was he peering at me for?

Ring ring. Hi Hannah, it's just me. Sorry for waking ye up! I was sound asleep! I know, I know, sorry I was just eh . . .

Survival, he gasped, turning from the window, this old fellow—if indeed sixty-six was old, not if ye're sixty-five, he chortled, softly, softly chortling.

Maybe I could give her a call. What time was it back hame? The same as here or less than the same? Hells bells, he intoned grumpily.

Fair enough but. Everything. Alone and lonesome. Only I am from a big family. I am used to people. Fucking ducks. Nay horses! I want a bet, a game of snooker, a beer, I want a beer. What am I doing here! Is there a game of fitba on the telly? Balls on the table. Jack set them up. A duck race. How could ye organize that? Easy. Which one will hit the air first if ye drop inti the vattir a boulder. Splash. Evens the two duck! Go on my son, up ye fly.

J. Proctor Esq., The House of Art and Aesthetics, returned Member for Canals and County: Second Order Author of Mid Standing

okay, third-order.

Starving.

If Hannah had been there then fine, I cooked often; as often as her. I relaxed in the preparation, played music. But on my own a nightmare, nay time to slice a loaf of bread. I lived on oatcakes, cheese and dried fruit. I dont put butter on anything because it takes too long to get out a knife and open a pack and scrape a dash and spread it on for fuck sake it takes as long to write the sentence as it does to perform the activity and I must use this one with the students re Wittgenstein and Picture Theory, furnishing them with insights into the totality of art—then if there was wine to quoff one quoffed such that I needed a half hour kip afterwards—Kafka's paragraphs—otherwise there would be no work the dull boy and if there was no work my outsides would become inners and my inners outers and he of the devilish grinning countenance would have spirited himself away, the lone church bell tolling, the poor student trembling, staring at the wooden door, seeing the latch had fallen from the edge and would fly open should a passing murderer take a flying boot at the fucker, having sold his soul to he of the bestial hoof, that he might sail through the exams and win the winsome wench.

How long had I been here anyway? The days disappeared like wild horses o'er the mountains—who was that? Bukowski? He was my age, sex all the time. People have sex. Six weeks of stifled space—excuse me? One is in a cocoon; the absence of another body. No other body, no touch; we miss a sense, how can we judge if we cannot touch? lost in space. The hermit lost himself, he disappeared, he kept his eyes open but the world closed theirs. He vanished off the face of the earth.

Three days. What was this, my fourth. Third? Last time I phoned Hannah she reminded me of my resolve not to enter the state of madness, that state of mind, of non-mind; the state described commonly as madness and eh madness, madness was the danger. The old fellow suffered an acute attack of it.

Acute attacks of imagination, its absence, an absence attack. I needed to go home. Just end it! Hannah would approve. Just come home. You're right, I said into the mirror but it was me, kind of stern-faced, and not Hannah with a grin, Oh Jake, sometimes ye're just stupit. She was right. On ye go the three duck, bang, bumped at the first bend, ower ye go flapping the flappers.

Now I lay me down to sleep, greyhounds quacking, the *el plonquerro* finished.

6

Who I am

Next day I wandered into the House of Snottirs (my new name for it). The same guy from the first day met me. I think Events Officer was his job description. Word has come from Head Office, he said. Media people are wanting to contact you.

To contact me?

They want to speak to you. They did not say why.

Media people?

Journalists I think. They didnt say what it was about.

Not books?

Books?

Aye well books, maybe they want to talk to me about books.

They didnt say.

Given I'm a writer, some things can be deduced, surely?

He smiled.

Why are you smiling?

He held his hands out, palms upwards.

What does that mean? Are ye puzzled, or—what does it mean?

He frowned.

I am a writer, I said.

Yes.

So I mean, if people want to talk to me about books . . .

Books, yes, well, they didnt really say what it was, I'm afraid.

Okay, I said, okay.

He smiled.

7

Excuse me, are you expecting a writer today?

They brought me to the office. When I arrived they presented me with the keys to a motor car, hired on my behalf. It was to have been here days ago but better now than never.

A dinky. A 980 cc engine.

I didnt know they still made them. A motorbike yes but a four-wheeler naw, no way man. I hadnay driven anything as wee as this since I was twelve.

They said it was nippy. I laughed. It was nice to laugh. I had two engagements miles away, miles and miles away, about fifty by my reckoning. Okay so an hour to get there. No! Not with the dinky it was more like an hour and a half. First was an afternoon session with highschool pupils: 1330 hours through 1530. So two hours. Then in the evening the second event was from 1930 hours, a community group. This meant it would be near midnight before I got home. Maybe later. The worst of it was the long gap in the afternoon: four hours. Four hours.

What would I do? I had been awake since early worrying over the details. I would have to leave the house between 1100 and 1130 to get there for between 1200 and 1300 because then I would need a snack or else it would be late afternoon before I could eat and that meant trouble with the belly. Hame at midnight. Cup-a-soups and a large fucking brandy. And a slice of toast. Five morsels a day keeps the undertakers at bay. Four hours. What do ye do for four fucking hours! That is reality. The end of October for outdoor fucking pursuits. What are we talking about here? These long hours in a wee town the back of beyond. Quite dangerous: pubs and bookies and four hours to spend.

I would set out at 1130 hours. I was allotting two hours for the drive to be on the safe side. I was guessing. No one had so advised. No one had advised me of anything at all. Nobody—none body, as my granddaughter said. But country roads and all that. One never knows the minute. So what if I arrived with an hour to spare? A bowl of soup in a warm cafe. Perfect. Bowls of soup are perfect. Bowls of soup are life-enhancing, are energy-inducing, tasty and dont sap energy on cutlery kit and caboodle. Ye dont even need a pint of Guinness if it's a good bowl of soup—bowel as my grandpa said. A bowel of soup son? No thanks grandpa I've got bowels of my ayn.

The main concern was the time to *kill* between commitments. Time being killed. All time is good time. I needed to work, wanted to work, required to work, was able to work. What was one supposed to effin do? Take the laptop. I could work in the local library, if there was one.

It occurred to me about Hannah, if she had been here she would have booked us a hotel for the night. Even me myself, if she had known the schedule, she would have booked me a room. Hannah drove me into battle, shoving me on. See the brave and courageous writer! Who's that behind him? That's his wife with the hobnail boot, toeing him up the arse. And right enough, leaving the house at 1130 and not getting home to midnight.

Plus a couple of books to read in case there wasnay a library. Although I could work in the car. Except no doubt I would doze off and wake up freezing. A blanket was essential. Except the car was so damn wee one wouldnay get fucking comfortable; yer knees banging into yer chin.

Thick woolly socks. I had a beanie hat complete with pom-pom. That was the granddaughter again. Beanies were necessary and pom-poms were nice.

I was not sleeping too well. Holiday homes are not built for the winter. They are not built for fuck all, they are thrown up like one of these Airfix airplane kits you get yer kids from Santa.

Moans and groans.

First things first: I had to find out where I was going! They had forgotten to give me the details. If it had been the good old summer time I would have enjoyed it all, getting to know the wilder frontier outposts. It was a mountainous area and mountains are mountains in my land or yours.

A strange wee car to drive. Bee beep went the horn. Bee beep. Here comes the writer! Reminding me of somebody man who the fuck was it? that cartoon the weans watch, Postman fucking Pat with his wee pedal car: Bee beep, here he comes, it's Postman Pat,

Never mind. At 1105 hours I arrived at the House.

Out came a member of the Events Organizing fraternity to check the diary. He smiled as though in welcome but I know this smile; this smile haunts me, it reminds me of entering the office of one's publishers, it signifies an odd anxiety that derives from the self-conscious recognition that one is a smug little guy and all the world knows it. Why dont ye hide in a cupboard and gie us all a break! The Events Organizing fellow exited the office, cell phone in hand to make a call. When he came back he said, Not to worry, the afternoon session is canceled.

Pardon?

The evening event goes ahead.

The session at the school is canceled?

Yes. He smiled, after a moment. He continued to smile.

Do ye mean the school I was about to go to? I would have gone to if I hadnt come in a minute ago. Is that the school ye're talking about, the one that's canceled, the one I was just about to drive to?

He smiled. Not to worry.

Not to worry? Ye said that earlier on and I wondered if I misheard ye, and now ye've said it again, I've not to worry, or if I should worry I shouldnt, there's no reason for it.

He continued to smile, not knowing what I was talking about.

I glared at him. This is the trouble with sarcasm ye know it demands fellow-feeling and you dont fucking huv any. A sense of shared humanity is necessary, without which it cannot exist, like irony and other subtleties that separate us humans from android suppers with salt and vinegar.

He nodded.

I had been about to say animals but I was carrying a wee book of essays by Montaigne in one of which he makes interesting points on the animal kingdom and guys that hide in cupboards, I hope, if not I had to find somebody that did. I needed to read properly. Proper reading, proper writers. I just never had the time time time, I never had any because stupid fuckers like this guy here did not do their damn jobs and we were to suffer, us chasing halfway across the country to earn a crust. The aulder I get the less inclined I was to esteem the use of sarcasm. A swift punch on the jaw is efficaciouser. So what do I do now, I said, go back to the holiday village?

He smiled.

How come you are smiling?

He shrugged but was still smiling. There is no irony here, I said, I am angry.

I can see that.

I need to know why you're smiling.

He shrugged.

These are wasted hours out my life, I said. Seriously, it was lucky I came in at all, else that would have been another eight of the buggers, gone and lost forever. I'm talking eight hours out my life, eight hours.

He didnt stop smiling but it had become a different

smile. He was wondering what was wrong. He did not know. He saw me there and wondered why. He had passed me the relevant information yet I remained standing there muttering stuff to do with wasted hours out my life.

You would have been responsible for that, I said.

He smiled.

I dont know how to get fucking through to ye.

What's wrong?

I need to get through to ye.

He nodded.

This damn thing has been on my mind all morning, I said, logistics. I couldnt do any work because of it, just working stuff out, and that stupit wee dinky of a car, and a two-hour drive across mountains for some seminar, talk or whatever the hell it is supposed to be at some non-existent school and then having to kill a further four hours before doing some sort of event this evening. I probably wont get home till half past midnight. Do you know what I am talking about? That was me out the house from 11 in the morning. And meanwhile my own work, my own fucking work, the stuff I'm doing and writing jesus christ almighty it's gone, I cannay do my fucking work for this stupit fucking nonsense man and it was all a wild goose chase, if I hadnt taken a notion to call in here on my way. I would have got to that town and found out the school, about the school, the session, I mean

I stopped. My head was shaking. I stared at the top of the counter which protected the likes of me from the likes of him. The silence continued. Cowed, bowed or neither. I patted the back of my head then gripped the lobes of my ears and tugged. In order to "understand" one must firstly recognize the other, I said, the validity of the other, fellow sufferer in this vale of nincompoop misery.

What is it? said the Events Officer.

What do I do now?

He frowned, as though concentrating. I raised my right hand and saluted, about-turned, and out I quacked.

On the drive back to the cabin, I did quite a bit of

I'm not sure, a bit of something. I seemed to get from A to B very sharply, maybe it was Y to X.

Something about the old days maybe. I was here just now but in the old days I was someplace else. I preferred the old days. I was not keen on this way of living. I dislike the notion of non-physicality. I figure I should have slapped the guy on the coupon. Not punched. But a slap. A slap on the kisser, stinging, the way a sharp slap stings. It was past the time for talk. I dont see why I should talk. I was not going to talk ever again in that situation

while switching on the computer, then the electric kettle while passing the kitchen area. At least I was home. I stood by the window. At least I had this.

The October countryside. It wasnay even October, or was it? Maybe it was November and there was a sort of smokiness; the vegetation.

I would leave at 5:00 p.m. for the evening event. I would have a proper meal first. In the meantime work. I donned the battered joggers.

But I did not go to work. I returned to the window and I gazed. Certain forebodings had arisen, a black cloud from nowhere. The fact is that things were not going too well at all. I was losing my temper too easily. Surely I had passed that stage. Surely I could just take it all in my stride and just calm down, just breathe in, breathe in

> but why can we not go home, blum,
> go home, blum,
> go home, blum,
> oh why can we not go home, blum.
> never can we go home, blum
> never can we go home, blum
> never can I go home

But who was I anyway. I wasnt on any chaingang. I was just this stupit writer trying to earn a few quid. An easy life, a life-of-Riley type of life, not like some poor bastards, still working away, still carrying the load, the hod, whatever, up and doon ladders, in and out doors and sites, trucks and buses. I didnay deserve to sing the blues. I didnay deserve anything. I wanted to go home, I would have crept my way there, jacket covering my face, it needed to cover my face. This was shameful.

I went to bed, pulled the sheet ower my head, the world, I did not want to see it.

8

His eyes drifted skyward

Call yerself a gear stick? You're not a gear stick. I've seen better gear sticks on a fuck knows what, a kid's wind-up racing car. Ye're a matchstick ya cunt, ye would be better lighting a fire. Bee beep. I'll fucking bee beep ye—break ye in two and pitch ye oot the fucking windi ya cunt, that's what I'll do—you and yer fucking be beep.

Such are the inner dialogues I have to contend with. One thinks of Poe or Lermontov, Stevenson, von Kleist, old Hawthorne. Who else? Anybody else, the Gothics. One dark and winter's morning, the venerable Count A_____ from the northern town of G_____ called for his horse to be saddled, pistols cleaned and oiled. Swiftly he dressed and strode purposefully through the long musty corridors into the courtyard, at this time of the morning bathed in the opaque light of early winter, his boots rattling on the cobbles. There in the gloom his trusty retainer grasped the reins of his horse, the magificent beast whinnying and stamping her foot, eager to be on, galloping

Nevertheless it ran smoothly. It was just so wee. Pitiably so. In an emergency stop ye would be liable to castrate yerself. When I made it to 60 mph it started to shake and bits fell off the engine. Where does one put one's elbows and knees and so on? Seriously but the gear stick was ridiculous.

Small-time cars for small-time writers.

I didnt tell her the truth, when she phoned, Hannah. It just became another thing, and the world is full of things. One gets on with it. In another life I would be another writer. One that makes money. I would write the Life's Like That column for the *Reader's Digest*. Is there a digital *Reader's Digest*? A *Reader's Digest* ebook?

I was heading for a Community Workshop. A local Arts Officer chaired the group. This was the third *scheduled* event. Actually it was the fourth but the third had been canceled.

When I arrived in the town I could not find the place. It was blustery and cold; my ears were numb. My own fault for not wearing the beanie. Never mind the venue I couldnt find the street. My phone was incapable of satnat subtleties. I searched the streets roundabout. Buildings were boarded-up and surrounded by scaffolding, and with demolition orders pasted. Piles of bricks and hard concrete; plaster, cracked stonework and everywhere mud, mud, and that wind was strong. Oh man.

Along the road I found a pub. The people inside gave me directions but the way they did it suggested that they didnt believe me, that everybody in the world knew how to get there and I was playing a trick. Outside I spied a fast-food joint. I bought a bag of chips. I hadnay eaten properly, just kind of slept and stayed sort of healthy. One gets through it. I ate the chips while struggling against the wind, beyond roadworks and collapsed scaffolding. I saw a street sign. The very one. A two-minute stroll from here and I found the place itself, down a wee lane and up the outside staircase of an ancient brick building. I rushed to swally the chips but they seemed to be reconstituting themselves mid-gullet, it was a weird sensation. Another pint would have done the trick but I was already late. Four people were present; three females and one male. Hullo, I said, I'm Jack Proctor. Sorry about the time A wild night out there eh!

We were wondering if you had get lost, said a woman about ages with myself. People do.

I'm no surprised. A lot of building going on eh?

It's been like that for months, she said, they're altering the lay-out of the road too. Widening the pavement.

Aw, right. I nodded, glanced at the man who was engrossed on his phone and hadnt looked up. The third woman was elderly. She was studying me and doodling with a pencil; writing maybe, I couldnt see, but she was also watching the man, a guy with long grey hair and a beard.

The door opened and another woman entered, quite hurriedly, hair windswept with a shopping bag in one hand. Sorry I'm late, she said, bringing a manuscript from the bag. I couldnt get away, she added, glancing at the other women. She looked to me: Are you eh . . . She smiled politely.

Jack Proctor, yeah. I was late too. Sorry, are you the eh Arts Officer?

No. She laughed.

You're meaning Elizabeth, said the first woman. Elizabeth won't be coming this evening.

Aw! Okay.

The elderly lady was watching me, still doodling. I smiled to her and she didnt smile back. I had noticed before about elderly people, some elderly people, how they respond to phenonema as though mere observers, even from within the experience. Her doodles would have been worth seeing but ye felt like if ye did get the chance ye would want to do it when nobody else was there.

My stomach was a bit queasy but so what.

The grey-heidit guy was still on the phone, Mary had the manuscript in front of her, then there was the elderly woman, and the two other women. Just all waiting, I suppose. What a dreich night it was, all horrible and freezing and ye wished ye were anyplace else in the world.

What are people interested in? I said.

Mary's writing a novel, replied the first woman.

I've brought a section along with me, Mary said. She pointed at the manuscript she had withdrawn from her bag.

Great. I write novels myself. Maybe we could start talking about prose fiction in a broad way, since I'm only here the one night. How do things usually operate?

People are encouraged to produce writing of their own, said the first woman.

That's smashing. Good. Me too, this is what

May I speak? said the man. Tonight is my first time here and so far it has been disappointing.

I looked at him.

They said you would discuss books and publishing. I'm listening to you and you are not discussing that at all.

I chuckled.

Well you certainly arent.

What are ye talking about?

They said you would discuss books and publishing.

We havent discussed anything yet. We're just bloody in the door.

He gazed at me. I noticed the elderly woman now studying him, doodling as she did so; the long grey hair, the beard—full beard, crumbs and nesting bluetits—and the sweater he was wearing, one of these many-coloured efforts they darn in the icy wastes of northern Lapland. He was drawing my attention to something. I ignored him. I said to Mary, Have you finished the novel?

No, not

The Arctic Wastrel shook his head at me. Are you the Arts Officer?

I told you who I was.

He means Elizabeth, answered the first woman.

The man ignored her. What is it you are? he said to me.

I smiled. But I was not sure what to do. I had this strange feeling that it was not me, *that I was not*. Maybe the chips were too greasy, or the pint of beer was sour or who knows, the old woman doodling there and Mary with the shopping bag and obviously she was a very fine writer, I knew she was, even just how she didnt worry about stuff and just had her manuscript and was glancing over it almost surreptitiously, trying not to be impolite but really she was wanting not to be here but to be back in her own place, where she did her work, her own work, her own writing—probably the kitchen table amid a houseful of noisy kids all screaming and her man too, him screaming, all wanting her attention and her, just wanting to write, to write, whatever it took and wherever it went but they were all at her all the time, all the time and she just didnt get any chance at all, just being by herself.

I checked my watch. An hour and a half to go.

The elderly woman was now doodling me.

This was my first workshop and I was beat. It wasnay the grey-heidit guy's fault either, he was just a fucking idiot, and the world is full of them. The women were just looking at me, Mary too. They knew I was goni "win the day." They were used to shite and this was shite. Mary had to come here. It was the only way she got space. It wasnay a gender issue, it applied to me too. The older I got the less able I was at concentrating, especially in instances of this nature.

What is it you are? he said.

I'm the eh visitor. What about you, what books do you read? Are you writing something?

That's why I have come along this evening.

To write?

Certainly not to read, he said and he frowned.

I nodded. After a moment, I smiled to the women, one by one. It's your evening. I said. What is it you want to do?

Mary had opened her manuscript. May I read the first few pages of my novel? she said.

Yeah, that would be great.

She nodded and gazed at the others for a moment. I rested back on my chair. Mary read a story about a woman who lived down the street and was having an awkward time of it with a neighbour. It was full of fun and I laughed aloud at a couple of stages, reminding me of stuff from when I was young, my mother and her friends, and so on. It was good. When she ended she was waiting for my comments. It was clear she had few expectations.

I enjoyed it, I said.

Thank you.

It's difficult for me to say much. Only because I would need to read it, to see it in front of me. I cant really make comments. If I came regularly it would be different. I could read it sentence by sentence and maybe show you stuff.

Mary said, I'm going to finish it anyway.

Of course. I'd be the same. Well, I am the same. That's how I work on stories. I just play around with this and that and once I've got something finished then … well, that's it finished.

The man was staring at me.

I said to him: It's true. The writing is the thing. It keeps us sane. We're all fighting for time but other people couldnay care less, and why should they. Then after they fall asleep up we get and do some work on a story in progress. Round and round we go. What is activity, what is force, write a force? Here we are pressing ahead, we step forward, feet moving one by one, up and down, backwards or forwards, side to side. Not shirking the issue. Shirk. I shirk. Expressing shirk …

What we want isnt a writers workshop at all really it is into the studio itself, the place where the writer works! We want to see the sketchbooks, the files and folders. The artist at work. Watch and learn. Take. Do what they do. Beg, steal, borrowl. Watch the artist. Sniff the bugger! Talk to me! Let me into your hard drive! Let me into your brain! Can I watch you in action? How do you store your work? When does one draft end? What do you do with the bits you take out? All these words and sentences and paragraphs; pages and pages and pages, all that edited stuff, what happens to that? I want to write about real stuff, why is life so hard, what is it about sex, I want to write about sex. How come it's so difficult? Is there something unique about sex? What is movement? What is up and down and in and out. How do you write moving, create moving, creating movement?

The elderly woman was drawing me. I didnt want to see it. Sometimes people did that, they drew ye during the evening then handed it to you at the end. It was nice of them but not something that

oh god

The second woman smiled at me. I smiled back at her. I said, If I had more time I could do more and be better. But I dont, it's just this once.

Facing the blank page? she said.

That's right, I said.

She nodded.

We called a halt before 2200 hours. It should have finished a good bit earlier than that but people had started talking. It was good hearing the voices. The guy with the grey locks was not there. I dont know what happened to him. He just seemed to be not present. People had brought bottles of water. It hadnt occurred to me. There was a bathroom with a washhand basin, so I could get a drink of water straight from the tap; a stream of it down my chin, my neck, auld fucking scraggy chops, chin rough as fuck, hadnay shaved since yesterday. So what.

It's also the other people, the ones who turn up. Not just Mary and the elderly woman. The second woman too, her who knew about the blank page, she said she liked Emily Brontë. Me too. Emily Brontë is great.

The guy with the scythe in that one of van Gogh, the harsh reality, uncompromising nature, inexorable, inscrutable. Like what happens in music, if we are describing a piece of music "building to a climax," what is "building to a climax," what is "building"? write "the building," express "the building," the "quickening of the pulse," never mind sex, express "a quickening of the pulse" or quickening, quickening, what is quickening?

This was my first workshop. Usually there were more people, apparently. Not so many came if a guest was there, a "professional writer. That was me, a professional writer. Not even Elizabeth came, the tutor. It was mainly the short story, or poetry, that interested them. They read the work she gave them then tried to write something, or else looked at the great works. Elizabeth the tutor gave them a book to read. They were to have looked at Flannery O'Connor for this week. They thought Elizabeth the tutor would have told me. So if I had read it and they had read it then they would have read it and so would I have read it. And if we all had read it why then, why then, we all might write something of wur own.

So there we are.

I was knackered and glad to hit the road. I drove home as carefully as I could, nay option, nay lights on the road. It was the country. And wee cars dont get ye out of trouble. These big 4 × 4's drive ower the tap of ye, and the lack of a camber too if ye're in a wee car, fucking hell, it is tiring, tiring.

Back at the chalet I sat a long while by the window, seeing in the direction of the canal. Country dark, country black. The density. No thanks, I thought, responding to an electrical mental impulse in regard to a quick dip.

Totally knackered, amazing how knackered.

Canals are not just full of ducks: god knows what else, creatures of the night, uncertain origin. After dark they all look the same, just like people, whatever that means. I hoped to sleep, a proper sleep. But my feet get cold when Hannah aint there.

One imagines a furniture business. Apprentice carpenters are sent to the nearest stately home to study a

Chippendale cabinet then are sent away to make one of their own. Imagine a music school where students are given a boxed edition of Classical Works of Symphonic Genius, sent home to listen and afterwards they are to compose a symphony of their own. Students of the visual arts visit an art gallery to see the works of the masters, then are to go home and paint a picture. People going to creative writing groups are told to read *Resurrection* then go home and write a novel. Maybe it worked. How did I know it didnay?

9

Art Students Interested in Art

Okay, one pulls on the socks, steadying oneself, shoulder to the wall lest one topples in the act, the very act, his head smashing against the whatever, floor, radiator, wall, fuck knows man. Come on Proctor yer time is up, was up, would to have become so.

Oh man. The elderly artist syndrome. What the fuck is that? Visions of that bastard Picasso bounding up ladders at the age of eighty, paint brush in one hand, a smoking stick of Gauloises Caporal in the other. He never dusted his house, never allowed his stuff to be so much as breathed upon by a strange pair of lungs. When it overwhelmed him he exchanged houses. Of course he had the dough, the old fucking hoh hoh hoh. Unlike J.P., the J.P. syndrome: skint.

Okay, so, bla bla, shoes and jeans.

Jesus christ how long had I been here! Never mind. The Events Officer had phoned earlier. Dont worry, he said. What about? I said. Ye've no told me fuck all so why should I be worrying? There isnay anything, unless ye're keeping something back. What are ye not telling me?

The line went dead, I dropped the receiver as though it were burning lead, liquid lead, my hand fell off, my bones, skeletal

skeletalness

Oh jesus enough, enough. I shut down the machine.

It was an art college, where I was speaking; doing a seminar with twenty-four students aged between 17 and 25. Twenty-four students is a lot. Did they all want to be artists? That would be wonderful. Imagine all the young folk of the world. We all want to be artists. Nay wonder. The lives of the artists, the loves of the artists. That is what excites one and sundry. The House Arts Control Officer introduced me, with what passed for a hint of wonder in his voice, glancing at me for corroboration: Mister Proctor is a writer.

I nodded gravely. There they all were looking up at me. Freshly scrubbed faces, including three teachers who were sitting in the front row, arms folded and fixed smiles at the readye. Everytime I raised an eyebrow they took mental notes. The Arts Control Officer had removed to the back of the room. He opened his laptop out and got on with his own work. The students were just gaping the way students gape, even when they're dozing. It signifies nothing at all, other than that a teacher held the floor and they were to shut up.

What is the square root of energy? I called. The very stuff of madness! That's something to gape about; yez are all gaping at me. It's an existential nightmare. Did ye ever read old Sartre? People dont like Sartre? Why not? Never mind. Political, not only political, an intellectual. The French tradition is different to ours. You'll know that by now, if ye're looking at painters, and I'm sure ye are, given ye're art students. Just go where ye like and enmesh yersel, enmesh—what a word!—is it a word? maybe I've made it up. That is what I like about art, ye make things up, ye go with where it takes ye, ye stay with it and ye stay true.

Somebody cleared their throat. Probably the head-teacher. The students they were looking, looking, no longer gaping.

What did it mean? Were they embarrassed? I grinned.

That is what I like about artists, I said, they stay true. Think about old Zola and the Dreyfus affair; his relationship with Cezanne; van Gogh as evangelist; Mrs Pissarro's pots of soup so Utrillo survives, and old Ingres too, how he saw the tradition too, making what he did, and there's nothing wrong in that. It is what I do, and always have done, taking from here, there and everywhere, just trying to get by.

I'm telling ye about me because I'm only here for the one day, and it's artist to artist. Most of the problems I faced as a young writer are variations of the ones faced by all artists. I realized that early. So I just saw myself as one of us, an artist, not a writer, one of these kind of rolled up academic bourgeois besoms. It made sense and it saved time. And that is what we all want, to save time, to get the work done: who cares what ye think of me, just do it in yer own time. You're all the same, all of ye: ye're young artists trying to make a go of it.

So: any questions? Any questions?

The trio of teachers looked at each other then glanced roundabout, hoping somebody might answer what they thought was a question. I knew how they operated. If none was forthcoming they would fill the breach. Okay, I said, you are right not to ask. I havent said enough.

A male student had his hand up.

Yes?

How did you begin?

In freedom! I pointed my right index finger straight at him, then at the table in front of me. Right there at the table, I said, with the pen and paper, the keyboard, the screen.The stories, poems, screenplays, the scripts, song-lyrics, ye just begin. Get it down there and move move move, making and shaping. It will become something. Forget inspiration. That's all shit, forget it.

The word "shit" caused a breach in the atmosphere. The intake of many breaths. God's teeth, I said. I glanced at the three teachers.

Artists fight to regain freedom through the base material which in my case is language. That's the way it is. Ye begin in freedom then discover the constraints. All the taboos. Society and how repressive it is. Class and hierarchy;

social and cultural; the suppression of indigenous cultures, immigrant cultures; working class experience; inferiorization and racism, elitism and downright snobbery: the value we place on our own family.

Never sit about waiting for ideas. Plunge in, at the deep end. Get words down and go with them: build sentences. Making stories, making poetry, making plays; go with the rhythm, right from within, artist as maker, building out the way. Forget the shite handed down via conventional education processes. Art critics dont explain how art is made. They say what it is but not how it arrives.

I stopped blabbing. A teacher was looking at her watch. What time is that? I asked. Apologies if I'm blethering, I get carried away. What about? Everything. Space and time, just the idea of it; sharing and being around with other students and artists, art students and just—man! I loved that idea when I was your age; even if ye fought like fuck with everybody, it was just so exciting! and painting whatever ye liked, nudes, nudes and nudes, whatever ye wanted, and then Delacroix too because that's where it takes ye, that's where it took me, breasts in freedom and torn blouses, who cares man it is just so exciting! What writers do gets distorted because everybody uses language in one way or another, in one form or another. Anyone not illiterate can write. Think of what we do in the same way as other artists, whether musicians, painters, sculptors. How does that affect our basic approach? Our basic approach, I said, just how we go ahead and eh

I stopped. A student was jumping about on his seat, in a sort of paroxysm. He calmed himself. I looked at my watch for a moment. He was staring at the ceiling, at the floor. He was finding it so difficult.

It was difficult, it was invasive, bloody excrutiating. And he had no cottonwool to stuff in his ears. Some things are too personal. What things? What I was saying. What was I saying? I had forgotten. Art students and art. Pub conversations man ye batter it, ye just fucking batter it; that is what ye do. Was his behaviour disturbing? I dont know. It disturbed me but only literally. I didnt want him to leave the room, just to sit still, to calm down, calm down.

That was my youngest, take it easy son, take it easy, just take it easy, getting the breathing back to normal. Maybe it was me.

I opened a bottle of water, sipped at it.

Painters do not sit in a corner, I said, and think through a bunch of ideas for possible pictures. They pick up a brush. They pick up a pen or crayon, they start drawing. Musicians dont walk around thinking, they dont sit on a chair dreaming up ideas, they go to the keyboard, they pick up a guitar, a flute, a fiddle. They start tinkering, humming notes here and there, playing the instrument, a kind of doodling, like painters. Writers work in similar ways. They play themselves into something.

Stop waiting for "it" to happen. "It" happens because you make it happen. The rain is raining. Nay in between bits. What is "it"? It is energy, fucking energy, what is the square root of energy? I know I said that before but now I'm saying it again, just so

One of the teachers stood up now, and said something to the other two and signalled to myself that she had to leave the room. I glanced at my wristwatch. God's teeth, the interval.

Sorry, I said, it's the interval.

I escaped outside the premises for a walk in the fresh air. It was a most fine walk too. I passed a cheery-looking wee diner. Fresh coffee refills plus toast & marmalada. In another life, another life. In days of theretofore the man
the man.

Ach shut up. Stories are all very well but some mornings are just so beautiful that one nothing, nothing.

When I returned two male students were by the gate, having a smoke. They told me not to worry about the one who could not sit still. He was from India and "got very excited about *political* stuff. He always acted like that when he got interested in something. When he was really really interested he stretched back on his chair with his hands behind his head, sometimes he left the room altogether, he just couldnt stand it.

That makes sense, I said, maybe another meeting would be good. Is that something?

Yeah, replied the two students.

We can turn it into a discussion, just art in general or whatever.

Yeah.

Okay.

Fuck in a classroom, said one, I've never heard that before. The students grinned.

Keep that, I said, language and power, I'll begin with it after the break.

But I didnt. I just read them a short story which lasted less than ten minutes. It was by a Russian writer, a most beautiful story. When I finished there was a silence.

I waited. I watched especially for the squirming one at the back but he just sat there with his hands clasped in front of him.

I hoped somebody would shout: Wow! But none of ye did. It is strange how people respond to art. Sometimes they get embarrassed. What this means is they have been moved by it. So although they act in some way uncomfortable or blasé or in some other negative manner they reveal themselves in that very act, that they are so moved. They are trying to conceal the emotional effect the encounter has had on them. What encounter? Hearing the music, seeing the painting, reading the story. Amazing! Art in performance.

I just read ye all a story there, a great one, a great piece of art. So there ye are, right here in the classroom ye encountered art.

One of the teachers, a man of about fifty years of age, was folding and unfolding his arms, frowning at his colleagues then frowning at me. I knew he would go on the offensive because he couldnt cope.

Before he could speak I raised my hand, not to silence him but to indicate that I had a plan of my own. He was astonished by my effrontery. I waited for him to calm down, smiling in a friendly manner, even conspiratorily. I should have winked, I wanted to wink—to the effect this is what we teachers do, we get people excited by ideas, we make students squirm on their chairs. Okay, I said and I chuckled: I only want to call this room to order, the Q & A session is now open! Okay everybody, anybody got a question?

A murmur, then silence.

The silence continued. It didnt bother me. Silence never does. Most writers are used to it and we have our own methods of dealing or coping with it. The fidgety student was clawing at the back of his scalp and shaking his head, he laid his head on his folded arms on the desk. I was about to speak when the boss teacher folded her arms and smiled: Hi Mister Proctor, I'm Ruth Reagan, uh, Head of Department?

Hi Ruth.

Yes. Well, my question relates to

Oh dear. There was nothing I could do bar grin and bear it. On she went. She should have not spoken but that required less arrogance. She appeared unable to grasp that I was a human being. Her line of assault derived from the Banker Prize fiasco and related to a television programme, a situation-comedy, based in north Britain which featured several lower order males who spoke in accents similar to mine. I was not sure what her position amounted to other than the old thing where we have science fiction, historical fiction, children's stories, war stories, ghost stories, Scottish stories, love stories, westerns, kitchen sink (working class), cops and robbers, spies and terrorists, doctors and nurses, true romance, and so on and so forth.

I waited for her to pause then I addressed the room: Art can cause physical revulsion and distress. People scent not a stench but a distinct aroma which we might term essence of armpit. It depends on certain vagaries. How I respond personally is an effect of that. I am not wanting to alienate myself from anyone here but there may be another discourse, different in kind, which dervies from the range of topics we have been covering this morning.

Ruth chuckled as though my answer confirmed she had found me out. I felt like giving her a cuddle. I dont mind you staying in the room, I said, but I would prefer you not to speak, you and your colleagues, at the moment anyway, maybe later. I would prefer that the students themselves did the talking.

Did the talking? she said with a look to her colleagues. The middle-aged man chuckled, shook his head, folded his arms. They were scorning me right there and then.

This kind of antagonism defeats me. There are art teachers who hate artists. This is the strereotype. Weird. Here it was at such a low level of knowledge that it was embarrassing the students, the poor old students. In these situations not only might they suffer embarrassment but shame, and students shouldnt be ashamed of their teachers. It was just time to leave. I raised my hand, *in nomine patris liberi mei*, we go in peace.

After the class the two students I met earlier were with the fidgety one and a few others by the gate, having a smoke and a blether. When I passed, a young woman said, Thanks.

Dont make me cry! I said.

They smiled. They were not lacking in confidence and what forebearance! I'm not sure that I care for "forebearance" in young folk. They assumed the mediocrity of their course which is not a nice thing to see. I was from another world, one to which they could not gain entry, unless changing direction altogether which meant going it alone. Their college was a halfway House between school and the unemployed register. Tough times ahead. Stick at it, I said, ignore the halfwits and get on with yer work. The fact is I survive. I make a go of it; do the work and survive. Seriously, I said.

The conversation might have developed but the Arts Control Officer had appeared. He walked with me to the carpark area. That went okay, didnt it? I dont think they're used to language.

What do ye mean "breasts" or "fuck"?

He chuckled. Mrs Reagan is Head of Department.

Ah.

The students were interested though. I heard them talking among themselves, so they were uh . . . He nodded. They were interested.

I shrugged.

They were.

Aye eh, fair enough, of course, a working artist talks about art to students of art, and they enjoy the conversation. It's pretty predictable

He frowned a moment.

An artist, that's what I am. A writer is an artist.

Of course, he said quickly. I uh . . . Yes but really, they were talking about it, I heard them.

I smiled. I'm not operating a scam ye know.

I didnt mean that. I'm only saying what I heard coming from your talk, the students were listening.

Like I say, I'm a working artist, what ye might call a journeyman, and they're what ye might call apprentices, would-be artists. So they want to hear me talking about what it is, from the inside.

Yes. He was still frowning.

Surely they've got teachers who can show them how things are done?

Of course.

I nodded. If any of them fancy an extra session on method and the basic practicalities, then we can fit it into the schedule. I know some of them will. Just work it out with the headteacher and so on, the House people. Another day is easy. If I had time I would offer more but I dont. I shrugged.

10

Matters Empathetic

The old chap returned to bed. Bodyless except for him, and he, logically, was not there.

What does that even mean? Is the act of perception a thing? If it is his body and him writing it and trying to state clearly, no ambiguity at all, that this is what it is, how can he do it if it is only him, if nobody else is there, and if

Oh man. Life.

Cold between the sheets. Even snuggling, there was nayn!

True but it was always freezing. When she wasnt there. The thing about Hannah, she didnay put up with nonsense. I did. Although it was not always nonsense; sometimes matters are unavoidable, one sees it from their perspective, *le bampots*, one puts oneself in the shoes of these others: authoritarian right-wing bastards, owners of art and the means to produce it, elitist fuckers, racists, monarchists, imperialist bastards man they drove me fucking nuts,

he said, tugging the sheets ower his napper and adjusting the block & tackle. Imprecision drives me crackers. Precision even more so, he giggled, uncontrollably.

The difficulty with long drives is sleep, the requisite, one needs to sleep, to rest, and if one does not sleep why then one would not be rested, have rested.

The old fellow pondered. How to sleep and I needed a break.

I had been working and needed a break. I had been working.

I go to bed, I cannot sleep. In the morning I must rise

and go to a school, discuss with the pupils what it means to exist, to be in the world, just as a man, a human being, not trying for anything, just to get by

The patter of rain. I was awake. If out walking it wouldnt matter, my boots were sturdy. I appreciate nature and my place therein.

I cannot sleep. If one cannot sleep.

Spent.

Spent but not spent. At least working for a living I got paid. Here as artist in residence I did not get paid. Not as such. What does that mean, paid as such? Paid as such and such. Paid for what one creates. I was to receive a fee, presumably, paid on completion of sentence. Writers-in-Residence operate in the manner of the Ruling Class And Their Minions [RCATM]. It is assumed that writers belong to the RCATM ergo we are in receipt of an income and do not require a wage.

The worst thing was having to leave the writing when it was going good, when it was just the thing man that really got me and made me the angriest fucking bitterest fucking

ach well a wage slave. What's new.

When one is in the middle of a piece of writing but that is just the worst, that is the damn worst man that is

ach

in the middle of it, and one is dragged away, christ, sex as analogous, the old coitus, get oot get oot wherever ye are

What time was it, one wonders.

My own work had been going okay earlier. I could have stayed and written a couple more sentences which is always the way of it, as of yore, years gone by

Stop it.

It's true but.

11

School in the Morning

One sees, one hears, one feels and one sniffs, there is no need to find the words, to utter sounds; to utter, utter found words.

One sits in one's dinky with the cheese and onion crisps, staring out the windi, in a town many miles distant: schoolchildren; what does one say to schoolchildren, one addresses these children, boys and girls, young women and young men, youthful males, youthful females, I am with you here today, and I speak to you as an elderly chap, viz. a grandfather.

Fifth Year school-pupils from 9:00 a.m. until 12 noon. The pupils were aged around fifteen-sixteen. I had this one morning with them. I was waiting to see what was what and what they were up to. Once I knew that I would just kind of jump in and blether. It all depended. Then from 1:30 p.m. until 3:30 I was at another school altogether.

But that was then and now was now.

November is an unattractive month. Ridiculous statement. But it is. No it is not.

Weans love fireworks. Mine too.

One half hour's solitude. An hour and a half on the road; three hours of a meeting. Lunch, an hour. Two hours of a meeting. One hour and a half for the drive home.

What is all that? My maths is fucking murder polis man.

All this driving. Hannah would have worried. Seat-belts and so on. Without her I forget to snap it in, then if I was driving too fast, was I driving too fast, I drove too fast, according to her plus peak hour driving.

Who cares

Ach well. Three hours on the road equals three hours of solitude, of peace, encountered as a form of bubble in the midst of chaos; back to van Gogh's wee guy in the painting, scything back the wheat

back back,

oh but he is going to be enveloped, the wheat is going to smother him and choke him,

back back, back. I gathered my stuff and exited the car.

The Regional Arts Control Officer met me at the office and accompanied me to the classroom. He sat at the rear working on his laptop. None of the pupils bothered. Neither did I.

My last jaunt had involved Art College students, young adults between 18 and 25. Today's bunch were younger and I needed to see them there, to see what like they were. Fifth year pupils. Did they pay attention? Maybe if their teacher was present. They must have had a teacher; kids dont just teach theirself: or do they? Who knows. Education had gone the way of the family silver, sold to accredited sources. I would just wait and see them, then jump in, batter on, slice through the chaff and just whatever, who knows, the basics, first principles, what is true, what exists: forget about *What I did on my Holidays*. How do we make a story from nothing? I make stories out of nothing. Even if I couldnt I would. You might think I was cheating. In what way would I cheat? In what way can a story writer cheat?

Me personally, I would cheat because I need to write the story. Nothing else matters. Imagine you are a visual artist, a painter, could you paint anything at all? What could you not paint? Is there any one thing an artist cannot paint?

Yourself painting? The one person the artist cannot paint is theirself in the act of painting. What do we think about that?

Of course artists do paint themselves. They draw themselves painting. Think of self-portraits. Artists draw self-portraits at a mirror. Even if you have not seen such a drawing you can easily imagine it. Artists draw themself drawing themself. They sketch themself sketching themself.

Can musicians do self-portraits? Can they compose self-portraits? A painter paints, a writer writes, a musician composes. Can a musician compose a self-portrait? Imagine listening to a piece of music composed by a musician and when you compliment him on the new piece of his music he says, Yes, what do you think it is?

Well, it is a tune.

Yeh but what about?

I do not know.

It is me, it is me sitting at a window. That is what that music is! Dont ye see it?

No, says you, I dont.

Well that is what it is, says the composer.

Go back to painters for a moment. What if the painter paints only abstracts, and she shows you this painting which is all noughts and crosses, triangles and splashes of yellow. Do you like my new self-portrait? she says.

Of course, says you, being polite, except the more you gaze into the abstract, all these noughts and crosses, triangles and splashes of yellow, my god, it starts to even look like her! It does! Imagine that!

Can you imagine that? Is that a thing that we *can* imagine? Stop a second. Hold it. Close your eyes. Can anybody imagine triangles? What does one look like? How about splashes of yellow? Imagine a splash of yellow? Can ye imagine a splash of yellow?

Yes, says you.

I dont believe ye, says I.

How about writers? Can they do self-portraits? Do writers look in a mirror and try to write themself down? Do they describe their actions? If they do, how do we know it is them performing these actions. Do they write "I did this" and "I did that?" Is the story they write in the "I-voice" first person? Is this "I-voice" a character in the story? Perhaps this "I-voice" is the whole story.

What is fiction?

When we draw a portrait of ourselves is it our whole selves we are drawing?

Writers write from ourselves, we make use of ourselves, of our emotions and the way we feel, from all the stuff we experience, even at the very moment it is happening. If I am feeling irritated by something that irritation might be revealed on the page, during a story, or it might bring about a new story. I sit down to continue working on a story I was doing yesterday but I am so irritated, I am so so irritated it is difficult to continue. But I have to. I continue the story I was doing yesterday in a state of irritation

Maybe I was interrupted by somebody. If I was one of those artists who work in cafes. Some writers do this. There you are with the laptop on the table trying to write a novel and somebody comes in and sits down at your table. Hullo there, how are you today? You feel like flinging the laptop at them. Then if they burp! Oh for god sake. Or else they eat some ridiculous food, a blueberry muffin with icing smothered in cream, even their food offends ye! Maybe they dont do anything, just mind their own business. But it does not matter. Just their presence, their very presence! If you were allowed to say "fuck" you would tell them "fuck" off, but this being a classroom you are not allowed to use these words, not even as an example.

A few years ago, when my kids were young, one might come in when I was working: Daddy daddy!

I would pretend I had not heard but they would persist and persist, big smiles on their face tugging my arm: Daddy daddy. Daddy!

How many times have I told ye never to interrupt me when I am working?

Oh but Daddy

How many times?

Oh but

No.

Oh Daddy.

By this time they're choking back the tears.

God's teeth. What on earth is it? What's wrong?

Then the gulping and the crying and I have to pick them up and confort them. And I might have been in the middle of a paragraph too and there it is now, gone. And I was working on the damn thing for the past hour! I see the screen over my kid's shoulder and will return to it as soon as I can, tomorrow morning. Then tomorrow comes and I try to do it, I sit down but I cannay do it, I cannay get it, not "as I am" or "as I need to be," I cannay get into it, the story. I leave it till later but that doesnt happen either. Later becomes tomorrow. I spend the evening watching television, staring out the window, the passing clouds, the darkening skies, birds squawking, time is passing, how long till my kids are all grown and leaving home, and why am I such a mean old shit, a selfish bugger, ruthless and always needing to work, just work. All these thoughts going through my brain, maybe tomorrow I'll get on with it, whatever it is, tonight I'm just ... tonight I'm just ... although it is now, this morning.

I smiled. A teacher was signaling me. She was young. What if she was twenty-three!

Yes, it is true, she could have been my granddaughter, thinking about the kids. I was writing and they burst into the room, yelling about something, whatever it was—a biscuit, they were bringing me a biscuit and a cup of tea. I was irritated and I shouted at them, I was angry, reducing them to tears all because of my own ruthlessness, my selfishness, my "need" to continue the story. They werent yelling anyway, they were asking a question, they were excited, and I slapped them down, and for no good reason. Writing a story. So what? The land of make-believe. Meanwhile kids suffer. All for what? This is what my life amounts to. My entire life. Such foolishness. What can be more beautiful than children caring for you enough to wonder if you would like a biscuit? Ye could cry about that. The beauty of it all, all humanity. What makes it so beautiful? Is there a God? Although kids are not necessarily beautiful; what if they are belting their wee sister? Kids are kids; sometimes good, sometimes bad. What does beautiful even mean? Daddy's been writing, maybe he wants a biscuit. I shouldnt have made it such a big deal. Instead of shouting and bawling I should have given them a cheery smile, Yes please, and a cup of tea please! Who cares about the story? I'll write it another time. Except ye wont. The story you write is a different one, it can never be the same, the same does not exist.

Oh god.

Young people worry. Not so much as kids but they still worry. Normality is required. One can be too dramatic, even in stories although usually they're not dramatic enough. We need to make them more dramatic. We need to build the drama. How do we "build the drama?" We pay attention to detail in the proper sequence. We dont jump ahead of ourselves. Slow down! slow down! You are walking along the school corridor and hear voices, your friends in a classroom, you hear them talking but cant quite grasp what they're saying . . .

You pause a moment and look about: nobody there but you. What are they saying? Something about it makes ye wonder, oh my god, you listen so closely, is it you? these voices, my god, it is you, are they talking about you . . . surely not. The classroom door is ajar. You cannot make it out properly, only words here and there, you try to hear more, pushing open the door, the door creaks slightly and you freeze but the talking continues and you push the door farther ajar but now someone notices and ye have to go inside, and there they are, and it is your best friend too, yer very very best, and oh my god she blushes and right at that moment you know the awful truth, that they have been talking about you ...

Okay. Now. Stop. Go back.

They were all looking at me, all the pupils; their teacher too, she was young, what the hell age was she? all just waiting.

I smiled, so they could relax.

Okay, I said, go back! Exchange the "you" for a "she." Alter other words where necessary e.g. "her" instead of "your," "she is" instead of "you are. My god it was her, were they talking about her! The classroom door was ajar. She could not make it out, only words here and there, she tried to hear more, pushing open the door. The door creaked slightly. She froze but the talking continued. She pushed the door farther ajar but now someone noticed her and she had to go inside, and there they were, and her best friend too and oh my god she blushed, her very best friend, and right at that moment she knew the awful truth, that they were indeed talking about her.

Now give her a name—Ann—Ann was walking along the corridor and she heard voices, familiar voices, the classroom door was ajar and oh my god, and so on and so forth.

What a scene already. I want to start altering words here and there to make it better. What do I mean by "better"? More precision. To get it exactly. Capture every wee detail.

If it was an actual story you were reading in a book the writer might tell you. "Ann's best friend was embarrassed and ashamed. Imagine that scene in a movie, how would it work? What is "embarrassed and ashamed?" What would be there that you could not get in words? If you were watching that scene in a movie how would you know the girls were "embarrassed and ashamed"? What does "being ashamed" look like? How do we write "being ashamed" in words?

The teacher was signaling me.

Okay, I said.

It was the break, I left the building. I strolled along to the carpark, got a bottle of water from the car and sipped it strolling along the road. There must have been a staffroom but it was not for me, not the now.

Back in the classroom the room was empty except for the Regional Arts Control Officer at the side of the back row, head down. After a moment head up, he saw me and nodded, continued on the laptop during the remainder of the session. I stood by the window and waited and when the pupils had returned I said how the way we look at someone can have a very powerful impact, we dont need to say a word.

Or if we dont look at them. People expect us to look and we dont. That is so significant. That makes us uneasy, uneasy. I was saying about Ann and how she pushed the classroom door open and in she went. Immediately she knew they were talking about her. Why? Because as soon as they saw her not only did they stop talking, her best friend blushed and looked away. She could not look Ann in the eye. Because of that Ann *knew* there was something wrong. They were avoiding her. So if ye imagine that scene in a movie? Ann's friend is "embarrassed and ashamed?" What does "embarrassed and ashamed" look like?

How do we know what is happening if nobody is there to tell us?

A silence can be full of meaning.

People communicate without speaking. We use our body, it's a language in itself: body language. People do not have to speak but we know what they are thinking, or feeling. We can even take offence at it.

When I was at school people got punished for not doing anything at all. "Dumb insolence. What is that? Dumb insolence? Come out here boy! shouts the teacher.

The boy doesnt move.

Wipe that look off your face?

He still doesnt move.

Did you hear me boy! Wipe that look off your face!

The boy doesnt so much as blink.

Dont you dare look at me like that!

And whack whack whack. In my country people got belted by a thick strap. In other places they battered ye with a stick or a cane. All because the teacher did not like the look on your face! *You* didnt have to say a word! Ye didnt have to do anything! What matters is how ye look. And what they think about you looking. It is their idea of what your look means. The teacher doesnt care what ye say. Yer body language is what's important.

Two people stand in a room. There are spaces in between them and all around them.

Think about it. People standing in a room. Each one in space. Every way ye can imagine: spaces in sound, in smell, in taste and in touch. It is up to us to fill in the "gaps." This is what artists do. They fill in the gaps. They make sure these spaces are occupied.

When a space is occupied something is happening.

Enter a smell. What happens then? Somebody's nose twitches. His nose twitched, he was sniffing, he smelled something.

Enter a sound and they look about: Did I hear something?

Enter a presence and they shout: Don't come near me!

What is a "presence"? That sounds scary. Think about it. You're all sitting there with the guest writer, trying to concentrate on what I'm saying, and a presence enters the room. This presence is unseen, unheard, unknown to everyone. But still and all it is there.

Even though nobody knows.

Even if "nothing" is happeningand "nothing" is there the artist turns it into something.

Imagine a teacher returning to the classroom, and stopping outside the door, listening closely but not hearing anything at all; she might think to herself "I dont like it, it is too quiet."

The absence of any sound means something. A silence can be full of meaning.

People say one thing their body language says something else. Imagine an actor. The script calls for "anger." The actor acts "anger." What is it she does? What if she guffaws? Now the director gets annoyed! Why are you guffawing? You're supposed to be angry?

I am angry! she says.

Guffawing is not a sign of anger, says the director.

It is with me, she says, I always guffaw when I am angry. Ask anybody, they will tell you.

But can it be "anybody"?

The same teacher from before was signaling to me and pointing at her wristwatch.

Can it be anybody? I said.

The teacher shook her head.

Questions? I asked.

There's no time, she called, tapping at her wristwatch.

The pupils were waiting to see what I would do next. Thanks, I said. It would have been good to have had more time, but artists always say that. I hope ye were taking notes.

When I returned to the office area I found the Arts Control Officer chatting with a couple of teachers, laptop packed, coat on, all ready to leave. There you are, he said.

I smiled. My smile disconcerted him, momentarily. He introduced me to the teachers. One was interested. Oh, he said, are you the same Jack Proctor?

Yes, I said.

Ah.

Then the teacher appeared, the one who had been present the past couple of hours. She smiled at me and turned to the Arts Control Officer. That was good! she said to him. It was though.

He shrugged.

Really.

Well, he said, it's what we do.

All the same, it was good. She turned to me: We dont often get it.

Thanks.

She nodded.

If there had been room for questions it would have been better but at the same time that would have gone and on and on and there were things needing to be said, certain ways of looking. I wanted students to be in the company of an adult writer, an adult artist ye know one who actually

The Arts Control Officer had been signaling me: We're going for lunch. Are you uh uh ...

I could have paused and forced him to say something, either to invite me or explain why he didnt, but I couldnt be bothered. And anyway, I would have found the company difficult. Thanks, I said, I'll see ye later.

You know where to go?

I'll find it.

12

... then in the Afternoon

I was glad to reach the carpark, the car, glad to sit down, then to move off and drive, far far away, oh man just away and getting lost forever, I drove that dinky as far as I could, abandoned it out west, hitched a ride to the airport, flew all the way home, and Hannah opened the door, where have you been? she said, with the hint of a smile, wearing these good clothes that I remember oh so well. She wore these good clothes, silk scarves, who would think of silk scarves! That smile. She knew me. That is the thing with Hannah, how she knew me.

I had only been gone a week, or was it two. Or three! Dear god. I wished I was home I wished I was home.

What an idiot. Ye let people into yer life. I should have learned by this time. One never does.

How come I was embarrassed? That was how I was feeling. Weird. What about? Who knows. Embarrassed.

What does it matter.

Petrol. The fuel tank on this dinky was the size of nothing. Everytime I drove a distance I needed to refuel. I bought a packet of nuts and a bottle of water in the garage shop and parked on the edge of the forecourt to swally it doon. Two gulps and I was back on the road. Maybe I should have gone for lunch with the buggers. No, no no.

Anyway, there was nothing to be depressed about. Okay, I should have allowed room for questions. But that was all.

There were things needing to be said and I only had the one chance at it. Intellectual legacies. Ye never know what ye leave to young folk. I think about old people I have known and most of them I've been glad to meet. Usually I find them memorable, and if my memory wasnt so damn poor, etc.

I aye liked listening. Maybe that is what writers do.

One cannot reclaim the time.

Questions. People like to ask them. I should have left space for that. People always like them. I didnt work things out. That is my trouble. I just fucking dive in. It's wrong, it's stupid and hard going. I was always exhausted. How come I was always exhausted? I didnt think of anything at the time, nothing, except to give the weans a blast. Just so they were left going, Wow!

Arrogant stupidity. Jesus christ. Wow, what is wow?

I could have done it better. At the time ye dont know. Ach well.

The trouble is I was tired. People expect ye to tell jokes and regale them with previous-life anecdotes, writers-I-have-known, the usual shite. All ye feel like is collapsing into a chair.

I dug out the appropriate information and drove on.

That was a good example but, Ann in the classroom. I found it quite interesting, maybe I would work on it when I got home, or note it down for future reference. Alex in the classroom; Andy, Adrian; Aristotle—that would take a trick. I couldnt use the same example. Or maybe I would, why not, play it by ear, just whatever came to mind, the usual. I dont work from notes and my memory is abysmal so it was bound to alter enough to keep me alert but the basic structure was there from this morning. That had worked fine. Somebody who guffaws when they are angry is behaving in an unusual manner. There are certain signs that we recognize as evidence of anger but guffawing is not one of them.

It is true that some people smile when being punished; especially boys, the dumb insolence syndrome. But girls do it too. And adults in a weak position. One of the last lines of defence. People laugh in the face of a sadistic tyrant.

Otherwise they will cry. Convicted criminals laugh in the face of the judge delivering the verdict. School-pupils grin in the face of an unjust teacher. Laughing is the last refuge. By laughing the school-pupil is "saying" I am the equal of you except you have all the power.

Apparently kids of twelve can learn calculus, if the authorities could be bribed into teaching them properly, helping them to learn.

One is easily sickened. Anything to do with children, with young folk, and the utter

Forget it, the Arts Control Officer was in the carpark, sitting in his car. When I got out of mine he got out of his. There you are, he said.

I looked about, indeed yes, I recognized my shoes and trouser cuffs and if I were by chance to pick my nose my left index finger would penetrate my left nostril with unerring accuracy.

He guided me into the staffroom. He knew the teachers there. He had been one himself before making the shift into eventing, controlling and coordinating. I was glad to sit on the fringe of the company. My attention drifted so pleasantly that I must have dozed off for a minute or so. Awakened by thunder: belly rumbles. My fault for failing to eat. I dont find it straightforward to be in restaurants alone. I get dithery and clumsy. Single males need unobtrusive spaces. Solitary booths. Wee corners and inshots, nooks and crannies. How come nobody ever thought of that?

Two teachers and the Arts Control Officer were chatting. They made no pretence of including me in the conversation.

Who cares. I like sitting. Sitting suits me. The truth is my brains were minced beef. What was I going to do with the kids was the problem. The same format as the one I did this morning? Roughly. The same age group, so why not? Mind you, I was tired, I could have done with a kip. I wasnt sleeping enough, why could I not sleep? Even being tired, I was so tired, people who are tired should sleep, should be able to sleep

But what the hell had I spoken about this morning!

Never mind.

I lifted a journal from a nearby table, an illustrated celebrity graphic; the literary fare one might expect in a teachers' common room. I read the television, movie and royalty gossip, avoiding pictures of naked ladies in case it was a set-up and I was being CeeCeeTeeVeed by the Creative Writing Police.

But what was I going to talk about? I couldnt remember a thing. Ann in the corner. God's gnashers. I was experiencing dull pains to the belly in respect of my own work. I might have gone into a corner with a notepad and pencil. Maybe I could have borrowed a laptop. I should have carried a stick with me. Why hadnt I brought a stick! Ann entered the classroom.

Seriously but, so much of my time was spent sitting about waiting for this, that and the next thing, and it drove a body mentally dysfuckingfunctionally fucking *retardus-a-um*. However, one survives, one survives. God love us all. Who was that writer again—a certain pub in Mayo. I was in there once. But was it Mayo? It might have been Connaught. There was a trout on the wall. Flann O'Brien, how come he was involved?

2:25 p.m. Pardon! 2:25 p.m. I was seeing my wristwatch. My session was supposed to start at 2 o'clock and here they were still talking. Surely they knew the time! It wasnay up to me to tell them!

Was it?

No. They would have known. I checked my watch again, with an exaggerated rise of my left elbow and a show of surprise at the location of the minute hand. Nobody noticed. Then I heard a comment by a teacher that referred to me, or should have, given it related to this very session, the one I was supposed to be doing at this very moment, the one that was supposed to have started half an hour ago.

I sat back on my chair and I looked at them, the two teachers and the Arts Control Officer. Excuse me, I said, are you eh, is this eh, what's going on, are you talking about this session I'm doing?

Yes, said a teacher.

I'm actually supposed to be doing that just now, am I not?

Yes.

The other teacher smiled. I didnt know why he was smiling but that is what he did. I glanced at the Arts Control Officer, and he said: We reduced it. We felt it would be too long.

As a double-session, added a teacher.

Several moments' silence passed; a strange silence. I was looking at the teachers. One of them said, A double-session is long.

It is, said the other.

I said, Eh yes eh but you know that I've structured the class on the double-session, in a sort of seminar format.

They nodded, politely. They didnt know what I was talking about.

What the fuck was I talking about?

The Arts Control Officer was studying me with a weary smile. He was prepared for the untoward. And here I was. My use of the phrase "seminar format" may have thrown the two teachers but not him. I have structured the class on a two-hour session, I said to the pair of teachers. Ye see I did a similar event this morning for the same period of time with the same age-group and it went fine. It did, it went fine. The pupils were eh ... I shrugged, hoping the Arts Control Officer might interject with something positive. He moved his head, suggesting a nod. If it was a nod it would have been deemed affirmative in a court of law grounded on cultural signifiers of Anglo-Saxon origin. I experienced an odd sensation, as if my head was swivelling on my neck in the style of a ventriloquist's dummy; tombstone teeth and the raised eyebrows, perpetual surprise.

But it had gone well this morning. Nobody could have denied it. The teacher there said it, she agreed, she told the fucker this morning, she told him, I was there when she told him. I was goni use the same damn example to kick it off: the girl walking along the corridor and then she walks into the classroom, discovers her friends have been talking about her, or may have been talking about, she doesnt know but must work by inference and oh but what the hell. Then of course my own kids, when they were small, bringing me a biscuit and a cup of tea and interrupting me in the middle of writing a story

and to finish the thought finish the thought or perish the thought, which is more like it, withering, decaying; western civilization, paradigmatical and the two teachers, waiting politely, that I might make my point. The Regional Arts Control Officer, too, the three of them.

If I had had a fiddle I would have fiddled. Excuse me while I fiddle, not so much Nero as W.C. Fields, old Micawber: Dear friends, esteemed colleagues and most humble patrons, you must excuse me now, excuse me now, while I fiddle, while I fiddle

while I solidee diddle

deedol didee

doldidee diddle

They waited for me to speak.

Yes, I said, well, I cannot do any of it now, I said, the class I had planned, I said, I just cannot eh ... it cannot be done, a hundred and twenty minutes down to sixty I mean it just cannot eh cannot be done.

A session is fifty minutes, said a teacher.

Yous have halved the session and not bothered to tell me, and here we are. It should have begun twenty-five minutes ago and we're here, just sitting here doing nothing, chatting about nothing.

We did not think it would be a problem reducing your time, said a teacher.

My time?

We thought if

If, you thought "if." Excellent. You thought "if." Sorry for interrupting but your halfbaked intellectualism sticks in my fucking craw, that you are able to conjure up the conditional, a relational force, by the power of your thought. Never mind thinking 'if' but when you say "my" time, what do ye mean "my" time? I thought I was giving you time? Do you mean that you are giving me time? How kind of you, how very kind of you. What about the students, I said, have they got a place in all this?

It's been a difficult day, said the Arts Control Officer.

What do ye mean "a difficult day?" You were there this morning. You know how it went.

He stared at me. I held his stare. I dont know about the other two, probably gaping. So that was the three of them. Plus the clock on the wall also gaping. This was the land of gapes. Further questions and comments were redundant. None of any of it mattered except what to do now, what to do now. Why the hell did ye not tell me? I said, If ye had told me, I would have prepared.

They smiled uncertainly.

What does the word "prepare" throw ye? Do ye think I dont prepare? A guy coming in to talk to the pupils. So what? What does he talk about? Who knows, what does it matter. He's a writer. Oh a writer, what does a writer talk about? Books? Books! Jesus christ, if ye had told me fifty minutes I would have prepared for fifty minutes. I shook my head. This was just beyond fucking anything.

The Arts Control Officer was watching me. Yes, so I watched him. He looked away. Obviously he had no idea what I was on about, any of it, he didnt know any of it, why I was upset or annoyed or whatever it was. Even although he had been in the same damn classroom the entire damn morning.

At the same time what does it matter—now now now. That was the problem, now; now was the problem, what to do now. God's teeth. But why had they not told me?

What did it matter it did not matter. Just where to begin. Where to begin and where to end? None of this morning's session could be used now. None of it. Not a thing of it. I would have to change the whole damn format and content, I had to change it, change everything, just change it. But what what what? Really, what could I change it to? The blank page. The blank fucking page!

This morning began from the blank fucking page. Is there another one, another fucking blank page. What blank page are we talking about?

Other aspects.

Other aspects, yes, and what other aspects, there are so many. What age group again? Fifth year students. Young adults my god I would just maybe

what a nightmare what would I do, tell them a joke sing them a song, invent a quiz, a literary quiz, who wrote *David Copperfield* bla bla bla, Betsey Trotwood, settle down, *Star Wars*, who wrote *Star Wars* did anybody write *Star Wars*, *Spider Man* and fucking *Marvel Man*, the comics, who wrote these comics? By the time they got into their seats, perused the smartphones and sharpened their tablets that would be another ten minutes gone, and end it five minutes early, making thirty minutes. Okay. I would read them a story for quarter of an hour then ask them questions, Does anybody ever read a book? Or else I could read for twenty minutes. One twenty-minute story for six book pages. Personal stuff. Hi there everybody, I happen to be a grandpa, therefore

Oh for fuck sake.

Okay.

Then they were getting up, the teachers and Mister Arts Control fucker. Time up. In the name of the Father, Son and Holy Ghost we escort you to the place where you will be hanged by the neck until dead and God rest your soul, your soul! he screamed hoarsely because how could ye read!! to a pile of 15-, 16-year-olds!! For fuck sake!! Talk to them, just talk to them, about something. What? Anything. Saturday's football results, then of course the lassies. Just anything, writing or whatever, tell them about writing, getting up in the morning, I switch on the machine, get myself a cofffee, a bowl of muesli. I prefer muesli *au naturel,* especially with some plain yoghurt and a wee drop of milk fucking bastards man that is what they think of writers these fucking school-teacher fucking bastards. Arrange my Tippex and pencils. My computing bits and bobs.

But what do we mean by "bits and bobs?"

Now the Regional Arts Control Officer was gesturing. Forward! Being led along a corridor into a classroom; a large assembly of older type schoolkids; including three teachers, the aforementioned pair of men mysteriously having arrived here prior to myself, plus a third, a woman, and at our entry all paused in murmuring and gazed at me, yes, politely, but what had the buggers been murmuring about!

The Regional Arts Control Officer introduced me as an Award-Winning writer from something that sounded like Bony Scallin.

No I'm not, I said.

He looked across at me with a grin and continued, Who writes in Lallans which is the old Scotch dialect.

No I dont, I cried and laughed, and the bastard held out the flyer and read from it:

As a proud Scot, Jack writes in Lallans, an old Scotch language.

Jumping jaysus! I dont even know what that is! I said and ripped it to shreds: If any such thing exists, or could exist, given the nature of that benighted country! Ha ha. Really, I said. I dont know what that means.

The Regional Arts Control Officer grinned and continued talking to the large assembly of teenage weans and other schoolfolk about what precisely they should expect to hear from me, expect to hear from me, he was saying to them what they would hear from me.

Pardon?

To the large assembly of schoolfolks. This guy was informing the entire bunch of them of what precisely they should expect to hear from me. This stupid fucking arsehole who had barely listened to a single damn word I said throughout the entire morning was now telling them of the treats in store, of what the coming fifty minutes might consist, whatever this was about, he was telling them how much they were all going to enjoy what Mister Prock-tor has to say about musicians, painters and sculptors and how ye go where ye want and paint whatever ye like and fight against stereotype things and stereotype language and how much everyone would enjoy Mister Prock-tor's disquisition because it would remind them of real life, real people and real places, and it was so very important if pupils just listen and give the guest writer their full respect and attention, and if they did so how very worthwhile it would all prove to be, he had come such a long way, from Bony Scallin, he believed, a region which has more to offer than many of us think, a very beautiful place with the mountains, rivers and the glens and no people hardly at all because they've all been shipped to fuck knows where thus not to interrupt one's appreciation of the land's unspoilt beauty.

The Regional Arts Control Officer fixed upon them a very meaningful look whose significance he presumed beyond me. The look was of a particular camaraderie that exists in pupil-teacher relationships and is founded upon a tacit though playful threat. It suggests that the subject of the moment, in this instance myself, may well be deserving of ridicule but, for the time being, civility is required.

I closed my eyelids. He continued to inform the large assembly of schoolfolk of that which they should expect to hear from me, exactly and precisely. He spoke for between 3 and 5 minutes. I hardly made sense of it. What on earth was he speaking about? It bore no resemblance to anything I had said that morning. He mentioned the French Revolution and the Dreyfus affair and how he just knew for sure that they would enjoy the story by the famous Russian writer. It felt like a pair of thick woolly socks had been sewn about my lugs about my lugs, sewn about my lugs. Was I dreaming? I opened my eyelids the better to focus.

He came to notice I was staring at him. He saw in my stare a distillation of the following question: Did you just say that ya slimy ratbag bastard?

I watched and I listened. He communicated with the pupils and teachers in a jokey ironic manner, grounded on the eccentric singularity of their guest writer, winner of the Banker Prize, and lent to them for the day by the House of Art and Aesthetics and as he was talking, something not unfamiliar escaped the membraniacal web that obscured entry into one's brain,

echo, echo,

ah, yes, what he was doing, this bugger, he was outlining the session I improvised at the College of Art—not this morning's session at the school, but the one from a couple of days ago which I gave to a bunch of 17- to 25-year-old art students—this foolish fucker, Regional Arts Control Officer to the royal court of creative suffocation was describing a two and a half hour improvised session delivered to a roomful of art students, and putting it forward in the name of Jock Prock-tor as that to which they were about to receive and be truly thankful forever and ever amen in what remained of these forty five minutes.

He had failed even to notice that I didnt work from a prepared script. He presumed I was saying the same thing to each crowd of folk on each occasion, no matter their age and whichever community, school or college they might belong. I may say it quickly or slowly, turn it up or turn it down, shorten it, lengthen it, yakety yak, I would deliver "it." Any place, any time, any length and to any audience. He must have thought I delivered "it" that very morning too.

What did all of this mean? Now here I was. I was here. There was nothing else. It was just me.

I looked at him.

He gestured that I should begin then removed himself to the rear of the room.

Silence.

The school-pupils and the three teachers.

I said, My name is eh Proctor eh no hyphen and eh the Arts Control Officer there, thinking about art in general ye know, it is not the property of the education system, even although the education authorities believe that it is I mean that it belongs to them, they actually what I mean is it doesnay. Art has nothing to do with them at all I mean, the education system. Never. So in my experience, thinking back to boyhood

The faces all gazing, gazing, the faces all

whatever the heck they tell ye, hell I mean, whatever the hell who cares it's just language, the thing that goes on between people, Feuerbach's answer to Hegel, blabbity blabbity, one talks about these things, incoherent ramblings

I talked.

I do not remember what I talked about [I do but am

too embarrassed to say although Delacroix may have been involved although not nipples and breasts please God] except it all went wrong, it was a disaster. The teachers could not believe it was happening, but neither could they look elsewhere, they kept staring at me, hoping that the intensity of the stare might have me vanish in a puff of smoke, might shield them from the curious looks of their school-pupils, among whom an uneasy fidgeting had occasioned.

These were youthful, sensitive souls. They knew they were stuck in one of life's big moments. In years to come they would meet for a coffee: remember that time the old guy journeyed from far distant Bony Scallin and all the mountains, the rivers and the glens and had a nervous breakdown right in front of their eyes?

Pause: clearing of throats.

Eh ... time to finish now, it is time for me to finish, it is eh ... I apologise, I should say it, sorry, for what has happened you see I had been expecting to speak for a length of time rather than what I was given and eh ... well, I was thinking I was to do that, expecting to, and about the blank page too which is usually of value and can be interesting to young folk of your own age, I have found that in the past anyway. So then okay, okay

should I sit down now or stumble to the door
one makes the decision
to seek out
look for
eh

I was in the car. I was seated. Weans appeared, the end of the day and they were off home. None noticed me. They blethered together. I switched on the engine, drove slowly from the carpark. Weans crossing the road. I waited for them.

But I was hungry. I had not eaten for a while, not a meal. Artists talk about art in a different way; this is the problem.

Teaching as a branch of custodial activity. The world of the lettered resident. The lettered resident.

A pint of lager and a packet of crisps. I sipped the pint slowly, ate half the crisps, shoved the remainder into my coat pocket. One guards the intellect, the noggin, one takes pains. They will not drive me mad. These bastards. We think of Hölderlin, of Clare. Cowed or bowed but I was neither. In order to "understand" one must firstly recognize the other, the existence of the other, a fellow sufferer in this vale of nincompoop misery. The smell of saturated fat. The suspect has entered a takeaway joint. Hamsun's island. Christiansen. Poor auld fucking what d'ye call him, Strindberg, *From An Occult Diary* he intoned gravelly, heh heh, mad I tell you, mad—fuck you bastards.

13

Shared Roots and Square-toed Luggers

Oh the swans and the ducks. I didnt keep alcohol in the chalet. I should have but didnt. I had red wine but I drank it. This is the nature of booze, if one has it one swallies. Here one does without. Here I had work.

Only things had deteriorated so swiftly, so drastically. How long had I been here! Years. In the space of whatever, and another million to go. I was so utterly utterly looking forward to the end.

Somebody had passed on a list of questions to me. A wee literary magazine that carried a major punch in the world of metropolitan letters. The editorial committee wished to interview me, expressing also the wish that I might journey to said back-of-beyond and deliver a reading of my work. Maybe I would.

Christ it cheered me up. That is how bad it was.

The literary cake. We all must share. Some have the icing, others the crumbs.

A metaphor. This indicates the severity of my plight. I was never any good at metaphor, with metaphor or creating metaphor, although I regard the creation of such as oxomoronic. Lying bastard, I just cannay do them.

Another invitation had arrived via Rob, my agent. This proved I still had one. I certainly had accounting systems that appeared to depend on me. No matter that writers like myself earned fuck all we still had to account for it. Account for the nonexistence of your means of survival you swine you! This produced a misguided solidarity from such as myself, but allowed insights into the recent advances in psychofinancocologicalculus.

The invitation was the kind of thing I usually avoided. For a start it was a hundred and ten miles away. So what but I was goni go. Nothing against the ducks, I needed a break.

One of these Arts and Practice events. It linked to old matters to do with "being an artist of the times. Who dreams up these titles? Supposedly it would be full of writers and artists. Maybe I would know somebody.

The trouble with no dough is the world of restricted possibility into which one entered. I was here to earn a crust, not spend it on inconsequentialities such as safeguarding one's effin sanity. I endured the crap because we needed the money. Any to spare and I would have grabbed a flight home, just for the weekend. I needed normality. This is by way of an explanation for my attendance at one of these yoicks and tally-ho affairs with the upper-crust Captains of the Creative Industries.

The place was the size of a mansion, with many tendered lawns, groves and flower beds. No doubt there was a diabolical maze where a mad ancestor vanished into "thin air" in the mid 16th-century. But what is "thin air?" What do we mean by "disappearing into thin air. The issue concerns metaphysicality and transcendence. If we look at the nature of a particular cliché we can gain insight into belief-systems formally associated

oh man, the job was driving me nuts. I shut down my brains and strolled, and it was a nice place to stroll, given adequate clothing man it was a freezing cold night in November, great for stars and constellations but I was glad to move indoors. Quite a crowd of people so I was able to hide. I spent most of the evening lurking by the food table. I filled the pockets with grub and planned for a quick exit. There was a story I was working on. Imagine not having a story to work on. I couldnt. Then this guy appeared out from a circle of suits, and dodged behind a door. Who was he? How come he was looking at me? God's teeth it was Jerry—Jerry thingwi, the Director, and there was no escape. Jake! he said.

Jerry! How are ye?

And we shook hands. This was the first we had met in years. This guy moved within international festivals the wide world o'er. At one of those he met me, me myself, I was there. Not only was I there, I was in the company of a handful of local writers. This was Jerry's first time in that part of the world. He had not realized "they had writers of their own. What country was it? Who cares. It is *de rigueur* to remember such detail too precisely. But shortly after that he took charge of the same country's foremost arts festival. He had been headhunted by the National Art-Control Authorities. Their legal team stated categorically that his ignorance of the existence of a native literary tradition was "a major plus" in the "international arena. His very presence, allied to adequate funding, would ensure an "international outlook" and guaranteed the participation of First Order Authors of Top Rank and Standing. Jerry held Directorships in other parts of the world, generally in the cause of Literary Freedom and Readable English, part-funded by London, England, Langley, USA and the Cultural Coordinating Council of the Gulf State Monarchies. All differences were set aside until the booze arrived. Not that Jerry ever drank too much.

So now here we were. He had not noticed my name in any list and when he saw me hovering by the biscuits, wine, olives and cheese table he wondered if he was seeing things or else "were there two of you?"

I grinned.

He chuckled.

I laughed.

He guffawed, then lapsed into silence. Once upon a time I would have jumped into the heart of this silence and offered a full explanation of why I happened to be at such an event in such an out-of-the-way place. From this Jerry would extract a list of all my known contacts in the World of Arts and Letters with potted biographical detail, attested addresses electronic, audio, virtual, visual and tactilian, and all further informational data as developed via existing technology and all technology subsequent to this given that only nothing comes from nothing that may be something and in certain operational circles becomes a rather shrewd method of dealing with posthuman issues inclined to surface in physiological models based on the hylomorphological theory favoured by post-St Bonaventurian behavioural geneticists.

Why Jerry was here at all was the question. No it wasnt. The real question would have been why he wasnt if he wasnt. But he was, so the question did not exist, or had no need to exist. Logic and reason were indispensible tools in such circumstances.

He was smiling at me, footering with his phone in my direction. I wondered if he was filming me. We were at the side of the room. A manservant appeared with a bottle, stared stonily at me then poured Jerry a glass of red wine on behalf of the organizers. How the hell does that happen? I said. You're only here on an espionage visit while I've been a literary stalwart for donkeys' ears.

Wait now, he said, I remember the last time we met. We had a row.

Did we?

Leastways a difference of opinion. Jerry chuckled. Canada?

Canada! That's right, the northeastern coast. Some bugger shouted a question about "norse-celtic ginger-heidit bastards" and seemed to be challenging me to a fight aboard a beached fishing boat. Then I saw you standing next to the guy. You were attempting to shield yer face from me.

Jerry grinned. It was not on the northeast coast, it was to the northwest, a fringe event on the outskirts of a coastal town festival. And there *you* were.

And there you were too.

How are you anyway?

Slippers and comfy sofas as befits a man of my years. What about yerself?

Good, I'm good.

How's the family?

Oh good, good. And how is Hannah?

Fine. What about ah …

Sophie and I split.

Uch, sorry to hear it.

Two years ago. He looked set to say more but only shrugged, turning his face from me, then he glanced back. You're doing the residencies. You enjoy doing them?

I smiled.

You dont? Other writers seem to.

Seem to what?

Enjoy doing them, I suppose.

I strained to smile. Jerry was staring away from me now. I was about to say why residencies had nothing to do with enjoyment but he knew all that already. It was Pat Tierney, there she was, in company with three other women. I hadnt seen her for years. Is that Pat Tierney? I said.

Mm.

God.

You're not in touch nowadays are you?

I looked at him.

Jerry smiled. She came home recently. She was with an Arts Overseas project for quite some time, South East Asia. You were never there were you?

Not unless you're counting Australia.

Ah Jake, you are so mordant.

What do ye mean "mordant"? I dont have a dictionary to hand.

Jerry grinned but only for a moment. Already he was looking for the means to escape my company. He didnt have to, I was goni escape his.

I had forgotten you knew Pat. You havent seen her for a while?

No. It's good she's still around

Pat's a survivor.

There's nothing wrong with surviving.

Jerry nodded, sipped at his wine. He indicated one of the three women. That's Lizzie Knox with her. Do you know Lizzie?

No.

She's quite brilliant. Short story writer. You'll appreciate her work.

We both looked across. The women were laughing about something. Pat looked so relaxed. An attribute of hers, how she relaxed in company, or seemed to, she always seemed to.

I needed to leave. I didnt want to talk to people. Really, I wasnt up to it. I interrupted. Sorry Jerry I hadnt realized the time, I said, it's quite a long drive back to the place I'm staying, the canal, it's on a canal.

You're staying on a canal?

Yeah, they offered me a B & B for six weeks. I turned them down and wound up with a wee sort of chalet thing. It suits me. I like it there, peace and quiet, swans and ducks. I just need to eh a long drive ...

Jerry raised his right hand in a gesture of peace. Let me say it's been good seeing you. I have to confess I was surprised to know you were here!

Ah well, an actual writer!

Jerry smiled.

Sorry, that was stupid.

I know why you're peeved, he said.

I'm not peeved!

Jerry chuckled.

It's you that's peeved, I said, if anybody, it's you. That event on the northeastern shores, I said, you walked in and there I was. And you spent the next three days working out how come I was there.

The northwest. You were there with Joe Fuller. Your invitation came via him.

I smiled.

Jerry was about to say more but controlled himself. He moved sideways—to cuddle Pat, the lady herself, who now arrived with the others. I stepped back a yard, watching her and Jerry embrace. Then it was my turn. I kind of pecked at her, nearly nipping her ear, trying not to get too close then almost toppling and I cleared my throat to speak but Jerry already was speaking and I was glad and just listened. I hadnt seen her for a dozen years or more and found it tricky and embarrassing, although not a big deal, except that it was, just for me the big deal, for her who knows, stupidity, water under the bridge and stupid crap anyway, nonsensical alcohol induced crap that Hannah would have

Hannah would have what? She would not have laughed. It was not funny. It was hopeless foolishness and shite, really, just nonsense, but not to talk about. Only I needed to get away. Why the hell was I here? I was a hopeless case. Totally my own fault for coming. I should have known. Something always happens, always catches us. Her and Jerry were talking about some event or other, it didnt matter. I needed to escape. I was trembling. I realized I was trembling, and Pat was looking at me now—looking at me because I had just interrupted their conversation. Jerry had been talking about something and I just butted in. Sorry, I said.

The three young folk were watching me. Jerry saw this,

and said to them, by way of an introduction: You know Jake, Jake Proctor?

Hullo, I said.

Hi, said Lizzie Knox.

The other two smiled politely.

Jake's doing the residency, said Jerry.

How are you? asked Pat.

I'm fine, I said. You? Keeping okay?

I am.

After a moment Jerry said, We were talking about Joe Fuller. Did you ever meet with Joe?

Years ago. Pat smiled at me.

I shrugged. Joe, he was a good guy.

They were waiting for more. Pat interested, Jerry interested, Lizzie Knox interested in why they were interested. The two women who came with her were interested in everything in that polite manner publishers' assistants have. Lizzie was a rising star and they were present on her behalf. I had guessed that much.

Joe Fuller's people were whalers, I said. His great-grandfather served aboard a square-toed lugger out of Nantucket, just come to the end of that epoch ye might say, old man Fuller, he was the last of a kind, and I suppose Joe too, when he was a kid, spending his days on the water. This is how it started. It's going back a few years now ye see I met Joe in a bar in New York City. The denizens were gabbing on about Herman Melville's use of the 1st party narrative which I found extraordinary and thought to chip in with certain thoughts of my own.

Which bar? said Jerry swiftly. As a matter of interest?

I cannay quite remember, being honest: they had that old-fashioned beer, what d'ye call it . . .

Narragansett?

No, I said, I think it was Shiner, on the Lower East Side someplace. Joe was there with Francine Ardee which

Francine Ardee! cried Pat.

Lizzie Knox stared at me. Her publishers' assistants looked from her to me. A manservant was passing and Jerry touched the guy on the shoulder. He halted at once, offering drinks from his tray. They all took something, except myself. I was tempted but the politics of the situation demanded otherwise. I glanced at my wristwatch.

Pat was smiling at me. I smiled back at her. I think she was about to wink. I didnt realize it was so late, I said, there's a story I'm working on.

Oh, she said, I thought you were telling it to us!

I laughed.

Jerry grinned. Meeting Joe Fuller and Francine Ardee in a New York bar is a story in itself I would've thought. He smiled at Lizzie Knox.

Aye well, I said, old Francine, *ah m'sieur, oui oui.* She was some woman. I got on with her but. Her and Joe had been doing a reading along at the old Cheka club. It was a major place during Prohibition. I read there myself once. Anyway, in the bar after—what was the name of it again—it's a kind of long bar and they have jazz there on certain nights. People were firing away on all sides and of course I took a certain line on Melville and Joe was interested in that for obvious reasons. Ye know he was Abnaki?

Yes, said Pat.

It's a particular use of 1st party narrative Melville uses. Joe was very keen to know about that because of course he was so damn fond of Dostoevski. Then too with Francine there, the Dartmouth and Bretagne connection was crucial, given Chateaubriand and the old St Malo run to the Grand Banks. She had strong opinions on Melville's bigotry which Joe found very interesting indeed. I dont think he found Francine's argument textually significant but I did. And eventually me and him fell out about that.

Pat laughed.

I dont know why you're laughing, I said, it's all true so help me gahd. A kind of a shouting match developed. Old Francine did her seconds-out *le rang m'sieur*. We had a laugh about that and swallied a few Calvados. Through Joe I was invited to certain less than prominent events. It makes up for the crap we take elsewhere and helps us avoid becoming resentful, and embittered, and writing all these bitter diatribes masquerading as essays—the ones that begin: Writers such as myself.

Jerry smiled. So too Pat, and also Lizzie Knox I was glad to see. The two folk from her publishers were attempting to guage her needs and to what extent her concentration was sustainable given myself.

That's how we end up in local hostelries, I said, sharing tales of woe with kindred spirits, constructing our own channels of aesthetic solidarity. Shared marginalization. We learn of these outsider events. We share information, bestow and receive invitations; always on the fringe, having to bribe the security staff to let us in via unofficial side entrances. I once had to leap over a fence to get into an event I was doing. The security staff would not let me enter the street never mind the venue. Very embarrassing. We're the ones you see arguing with the staff at these huge buffets. We get stopped at the entrance to the food tent on pain of producing identity cards. Empty yer pockets! What's this? Bundles of pakora and samosas wrapped in a napkin!

Jerry grinned at Lizzie Knox, and jerked his thumb at me. He's a Banker Prize winner.

That misses the point altogether. Seriously, I said, there's a writer-friend of mine who shall remain nameless— she traveled with me to Irkutsk on the Urranba'ar Express.

Now I know you're joking, said Pat.

I'm not joking at all.

But I know who you're talking about.

Yarra Zhitzyn? said Jerry.

No, said Pat, Yarra's still in prison. The writer Jake's referring to her was on the committe who organized the PEN event.

Jerry gazed at me.

Pat had turned to Lizzie Knox. She went on hunger-strike. After a few weeks they released her, then jailed her a month later. If they hadnt released her she would have died. Once her family and friends helped her recover her health the prison authorities returned for her, they put her back in solitary.

That was what they did in the old days, I said, the old Cat and Mouse routine. They learned it off the Brits. That was how they dealt with women trouble-makers.

Jerry smiled.

I shrugged.

Jerry glanced at Lizzie Knox: Yarra Zhitzyn was one tough cookie.

Pat said to me, I didnt know you knew Francine Ardee.

I'm sure ye did, I said.

She's a wonderful writer, said Lizzie Knox.

Oh yes, said Pat.

Another tough cookie ... Jerry was glancing at his wristwatch.

Time to go, I said.

I needed to beat him to the punch. At least I had knocked him off his stride. He was so damn comfortable, always so damn comfortable. And women too, how they went for him. It was so totally unfathomable. Now here with Pat—and Lizzie Knox too, she was smiling at him for god sake it is extraordinary, just fucking extraordinary. But so what! If women did go for him, it was none of my business. How come I was even here? It was crazy and hypocritical too because I was never done bloody complaining and moaning about officialdom and the establishment and bla bla bla and now here I was, right in the belly of the beast. Only because

I was feeling lousy, so so lousy, just so damn lousy. The same manservant again, a tray of booze, wine and all sorts. Jerry was watching me. I raised my right hand in a wave. Good seeing ye all, I said.

Nice to see you too, said Pat.

Yeah, I've got work I need to be doing.

It was a pleasure, said Jerry.

Thanks. I smiled at Lizzie Knox and the publishers' assistants, then left the company.

If I hadnt I would have shamed myself. My emotion had reached danger level. How come? How come I was so angry, and upset! More upset than angry. Why?

Anyway, whatever. This was the last, the very last. Never again. Never. Never never ever, ever. This was the last time. I would never ever attend such an event again, never. Never in my whole life, whatever was left of it. How come I even went to these damn things! Truly. I dont think I ever went home feeling good, with the remotest sense of self respect. Never. Bastards. And herewith the stereotype, taking a samosa from my side coat pocket, exactly like I said, chomping fast while trampling the manicured lawns en route to the dinky.

Food. Food and drink. Sustenance and a night out. One sells one's soul.

It was near midnight by the time I got home. I was tired but so what. Instead of switching on the laptop I changed my shoes and went for a walk along the canal tow path. It was still very cold but the earth was soft.

Uneven earth demands respect. I learned that a couple of nights earlier when I tripped and fell on a pile of long-stemmed weeds. But what I had noticed, speaking as a city boy, that from midnight onwards mud seems to expand and become more slithery. Maybe I was just treading on dog-shit. After dark one cannot distinguish shite from mud. Fortunately there were nay dog-walkers. A dog-walker after midnight man ye would run like fuck if ye saw one. A duck was a different matter. If one of them blocked my way I would gie it a toe up the arse, an almighty one. I would set off at a run and boot it high into the sky.

I once saw a university student do that to a pigeon. A wee flock of them hopped about the cloistered pathway, pecking at crumbs and avoiding one another. The student walked towards them. I knew something was wrong. Ye see it in students occasionally, a form of paranoia, or psychosis, a certain thing in how they move. It was the pigeons, he was outsmarting the pigeons, pretending not to see them. Suddenly he charged and started lashing out with his feet. Other students were around and they were horrified and shouting at him, but he paid no heed. He just charged, kicking at them; as though the birds were a stack of footballs pitched from a huge plastic carrier bag, and one of the poor buggers he caught full on the side, and he hurt it badly, the poor thing, fluttering off; maybe collapsing out the air, the way it happens to birds. The student strode off fast along the pathway. I didnt involve myself. The thought of that, of not involving myself, has stayed with me. if I could have done something perhaps, whatever that might have been—help, that was what he needed.

I was careful in the use of irony in regard to sanity. It is consistent that sanitation and sanity share a root. I had stories to write, essays to finish, lyrics to pursue, plus the exploration of one's inner psyche.

Quack quack.

The work had to get done. I always did the work. Here was no different. I wanted not to meet people, not to think, not to whatever—only to work, to work, to sleep. Yes the workshops, the talks, the readings, whatever the hell else they wanted, then just get on with it, get on with the work.

Walking was good. Walking made the world a better place. Made the work go better, the physicality, the risk-taking. Some of that mud is swampy and if too near the edge of the canal bank one could slip down into the dark waters. These stories about people, people's lives. I just needed this, what I had, solitude. Hannah said I was a gambler but that was life, she was talking life. I was not gambling my life, I was just trying to survive. Surviving is fucking hard.

14

I could have been a Dance Troupe!

This small town in the middle of nowhere. It had required a peak period drive. I avoided the worst of it by crossing a range of lower mountain peaks, finding an old drovers trail through a lost valley where wagonloads of innocent pioneers perished back in the mid-19th century; out of the gloom loomed a faded billboard, with the name of the town and the number of lost souls living in the dump. I arrived in the town centre at 7:25 p.m., parked by the venue. Time enough. The event was scheduled for 8:00. I snatched ten minutes in a pub across the road, forgot the sandwich, drank a bottle of beer. I had a quick look through the stories, checking the reading order. I would do a range of stuff and talk about it. I was quite looking forward to it. I can relax with a reading. Just get to the mic and tell the story. That's that. Turn down the lights there and we can all relax.

Organizers like when I say that, relax, you dont have to worry, it's me now, I'll just tell them a story. Phew, they say and head for the bar.

Apparently people came along to such nights no matter the event, just to get out the house and away from the television. At twenty minutes to eight I crossed the road to the venue. A couple of people were gazing out an upstairs window. They had watched me cross the road from the pub and were looking to see if I staggered. There goes Proctor. He turned up drunk, abused the audience, villified the organizers and kicked a passing cat.

7:45 p.m. Inside the main lobby, dan d randan, more people milled around the foot of a flight of stairs. There was an A4 poster with my name in big print, dan d randan. Plus a charge on entry! God's teeth! Actual money to come and see me! I saw a woman gazing in my direction. Not dreamily, no, although one supposed, reasonably, that she had read every book ever I had written, murmured he, thoughtfully.

There was a small reception area in from the box-office window. A young fellow in his 20s was chatting to the box-office lady who was dishing out the tickets. He said, Are you Jack Proctor?

Yes, hullo.

I'm Ian Roberts, Cultural Officer.

I'm a wee bit late, sorry.

No no. Would you like a beer before the talk?

No thanks. Afterwards, okay: not before. I checked my watch. Do ye want me to do a soundcheck?

Oh uh. He squinted sideways at something or other. Sorry, he said, and away he went.

It occurred to me that he had called it a talk.

Another A4 poster was tacked on the wall. This on yellow paper. My name and 8:00 p.m. Nothing about talks and nothing about readings. Nothing about nothing. I could have been a dance troupe or a movie. Jack Proctor 8:00 p.m.

I lounged around the box-office area, reading other posters, then flyers and information leaflets. They had a wee art-house cinema on the premises apparently. Good stuff. Quite interesting films. Up on the mezzanine a couple of people were staring down at me. I checked my watch and moved to a corner, checked the slip of paper with my reading order. I would begin with a few very short stories. This acts as an aid to concentration; maybe follow it with a longer one, fifteen or twenty minutes. I had prepared a selection earlier in the day. When reading very short stories it is better if audiences do not applaud individually. It brings a smile if I ask for this. No applause please! But I mean it seriously. The tyranny of the clap. (I beg yer pardon, the hand clap.) It can relax people when they do not have to applaud.

And these silences help me control the emotional dynamic. This heightens drama. Different stories, like songs, like music, like paintings and pieces of sculpture, operate on different emotional levels.

But is that true? What does "emotional levels" mean? Is it just a cliché that has no substance?

But applause can disrupt the tension. Bla bla bla. Pretentious shite. No applause between movements. What is it a symphony? Fuck off.

I checked my watch. I had "my novel" in case of emergency, in which case I would give a background to the stories or something, the influence of other art forms maybe, discuss my early published work and so on. It interests people how somebody first starts and manages to get published—hope for us all etc. The Cultural Officer returned amid a cloud of tobacco smoke with two cartons of coffee. I thought he had gone to check the sound. The coffee had been an excuse to escape for a smoke.

7:55 p.m. Look, I said, I'm ready to go up the stair— whenever you think it best but eh I'm looking at the time . . .

Yes, he said, and he began chatting about arts organizations in general terms which was very different from what he had been led to believe while studying for his MLitt in media studies. Nobody told him then how it would be. There were major difficulties getting people to even leave the house in the *provinces* let alone venture abroad to actual events; especially literary events, poetry and all that. How lucky arts organizers were to get somebody who was funny and down to earth, especially if people knew the somebody from television. Even radio. But television especially. Also if the writer was a local writer. Local writers were best of all. One need not worry about audiences if local writers were there.

He studied the cigarette which had appeared in his right hand. He had brought the packet out his pocket absently, and withdrawn one. He returned the cigarette into the packet, then into his pocket.

Do any writers live in the vicinity? I asked.

Oh yes, he said. One writes for Corry, and the other for *Rubthick.*

Corry referred to a television series, *Coronation Street.* *Rubthick* was a long-running drama series featuring aspiring singers and dancers who were good to look at. They always get an audience, he said. Then if it had been the punk fellow or the black lady when it comes to poetry, they get an audience too and no wonder, if they can do a routine, like stand-up, people will come out. They can be so funny, and interesting too. Interesting and funny. It makes the job of building the audience so much easier when it is people like that, entertainers. He shrugged. It's a pity you canceled the school session Mister Proctor. We might have built up the figures.

Pardon?

It left the problem you see, in small towns such as this, one requires to build an audience, and everything helps, especially the local connection. Province people are parochial. I hoped you might invite the teachers and pupils to come along.

Sorry, I am not sure what you're talking about.

It just makes things difficult, he added. The school session would have helped tremendously, especially if you had invited the young ones, perhaps they could have read their poems.

Sorry eh, what are ye talking about?

You canceled the afternoon school session.

I didnt cancel any afternoon school session.

Yes you did.

I didnt.

You did.

No I didnt. I didnt.

You canceled this morning. So that left me with this evening.

It was not me.

They said it was you.

It was not me.

Why would they have canceled?

I dont know. Ask them.

The people at the House of Art and Aesthetics?

Son, it wasnt me.

I dont know why they would have canceled.

Neither do I. I would have come if I had known. It would have meant leaving my place at 10 o'clock this morning but I would have come.

You wouldnt have needed to leave at 10 o'clock, if that was the problem.

There wasnt any problem.

You didnt need to leave at 10. It wouldnt have taken you all that time. It was an afternoon session.

It's a two-hour drive, I said.

No it's not.

Yes it is, to be on the safe side. Plus an hour for a bite to eat and emergencies.

It's never two hours, he said, I do the drive into town regularly.

The box-office lady called, It's true.

Not for me it's not! I live on the other side of town. I have to drive through and out the other side. That takes an extra half hour.

Which road did you come? asked the Cultural Officer.

Never mind which road I came.

It matters.

What matters?

I cross the hills every day.

You are missing the point son. If *you* break down you relax at the side of the road. If I break down I miss the performance. I'm not the audience remember. It's alright if the audience turns up late, not the performer, know what I mean, it's me doing the actual show.

I get that, he said.

Good, I said. That is what I am talking about. When I arrive at a place I dont just jump out the car and in I go. I check out the venue; the sound, I find a quiet space, I go to the bathroom, I have a wash and a brush up. I think about what I am going to do. I work it out. I even have a wee rehearsal, I go into a corner and if I'm doing a story I havent done for a while I might need to check the rhythms, get the rhythms right., in character, the narratve voice and so on.

He had a cigarette back in his hand, playing it over and over between his fingers, and biting the nails off the fingers of his left. I figured him for 25 years of age and already he was a nervous wreck.

Look, I said, gently, I'm not wanting to make a big deal out of this. What you need to know is that it wasnay me that canceled. Tomorrow morning you check it out. Phone the House and they'll tell ye. I would have come. It wouldnt have mattered how long it took.

He pretended to glance at the box-office lady but I knew he was sneaking a look at the wall-clock. It is ten past eight, I said. It's up to you but the event is scheduled for 8. I dont know why we're standing here if people are waiting. I can just head on up.

He frowned at me. He cleared his throat and examined the cigarette he was still holding.

Sorry son, what's yer name again?

Ian, Ian Roberts.

Okay, Ian, what is wrong?

Nothing.

Come on.

He hesitated and glanced at the box-office lady. People are expected, he said. They told me personally. They attend a writers' group in this building and I would have cause for irritation if they did not come, especially after saying they would. Things never start promptly in these parts, they operate at country-time. Have you heard of country-time? That's what they call it here, country-time, it means they just come when they feel like it. This is the *provinces*.

I smiled. Fair enough, but some people are waiting up the stair. Tell the latecomers just to come in, but go quietly. I'll handle it. Wee anecdotes. On my way to the theatre et cetera et cetera. How it is as a traveling writer, a writer-in-residence et cetera et cetera, I'll just blether. I'll introduce myself too, you just relax, go for a smoke.

He moved his head from side to side, put his left hand to his mouth and chewed his thumb. I saw him frown at me. Not only did he not know what I was talking about, he had forgotten who I was. He looked from me to the box-office lady. She raised her hand to her mouth, pondering. Then she called to him in a sort of loud whisper: Is the man thinking about the cinema? She smiled briefly at me, pretending that it wasnt her who had spoken. I smiled back at her. Then she spoke to me directly: Are you thinking about the cinema? The people upstairs? Doors open 7:50? That programme began at 8 o'clock.

Pardon?

The people upstairs? muttered the Culture Officer.

They're all in by now, added the box-office lady.

I scratched my head. The clock on the wall, the watch on my wrist. I tugged at my chin, I had forgotten to shave.

The Culture Officer was looking at me. I knew now I was not to "head upstairs" at all. Nor was I to head downstairs, nor even across the stairs.

It had dawned on him too, the mistake I had made, thinking the people upstairs were waiting for me. He entered a coughing fit. His cigarette landed on the floor. He managed to clear his throat, shuffled his feet and did some other communicative stuff always excluding the verbal.

I was not to head anywhere because—and I blushed. Oh man I blushed. Sixty-six years of age—I was sitting at the heart of the perfomance space at that very moment. I had never been anyplace else but in the performance space. I was here. This fucking lobby, complete with box-office window-hatch, a wee settee and a couple of Scandinavian plastic dining chairs, this was the venue, this is where I was to deliver "my talk"! Oh the shame, the ignominy. The calamitous level to which I now had fallen! Henceforth I shall stop this writing malarkey. Henceforth I shall seek a proper job. oh blessed providence, and I stumbled to my knees in search of forgiveness.

The lobby area was split in two: the box-office in one half, the performance space was the other. No dividing partition. There were a couple of pillars. Anybody walking in off the street would blunder into the performance. Performance. I abjured the word. I am talking about a reading, my reading; people would blunder in while I was doing it. They would see me from the street. While engaged in the act of perambulation, they would bear witness to me, if they glanced through the fucking windi of the fucking door and if they walked in they would pass me by and gie me the time of day. Oh dear. Ach well. My grandkids too, imagine that, them hearing about it, what happened to grandpa that night, poor auld fucker, his last night on earth, following which he breathed his last.

Sixty-six years of shite.

Ach well, gather in one's things, zip up the coat. The Culture Officer watched me. I could grab his cigarette and head for the hills, choke to death in a mad scramble home to the nolly.

What a self-deluding oddball! Imagine expecting folk

to turn up for a talk! What about? What on earth would he even talk about? What did he even do? Maybe if he did something. If there was something he could talk about, I mean if one gives a talk it has to be about something. I didnay have anything because I didnay do anything. Except once I wrote a book. How could he be expected to sell such a thing to the damn public! It could not be done, not by the most committed of Culture Officers, the most fervent of Cultural Superintendents, Admirals and Brigadiers.

The boy must have thought I was mad. Especially ten minutes ago when I was all set to begin my talk and nobody was there except him and the box-office lady. God's gnashers, he must have thought I was going to give them the "talk," him and the lady! I laughed. This relaxed him. He picked the cigarette up from the floor and launched into this anecdote about a poorly-attended event in a previous employment, located way north, talk about *provinces*, this was way way way north. It too was an utter disaster and she was a writer of the first order, very very famous so she was. From America. Everybody had heard of her.

I was still smiling.

On he battered with the story, directing it to me and the box-office lady who was all ears and very cheery now that I was in good spirits.

She was on television too, said the Culture Officer, and just so so famous, an African-American lady from San Francisco. They had no hesitation in booking her for a talk. They were to expect five hundred people as an audience. And major decisions on catering had to be made. So this is what he did, and he hired a private company who prepared a cold table.

The Culture Officer paused to explain to me. This is a buffet with tea, coffee and sandwiches, he said, sausage rolls, tuna salad, tuna pasta, tuna mayo, and biscuits and cheese and olives too. People asked for a sweet too, he said, but there wasnt any, as if cheese and biscuits werent enough. Nobody could have been disappointed by the catering.

The local media supported the event. They all carried the press releases; photographers and so on, they all supported the night, they were all there and these radio guys, sarcastic swines who just complained all the time and scoffed the food. Ones from the town council came and they were horrible and were sarcastic too. A personal publicist. Snooty people from the publishers. How much do these people make, the clothes they were wearing, my girlfriend said it, full designer, and so so snooty, the Chloes, that was what she called them, my girlfriend: "the Chloes." They just stood there and wrinkled their noses at everything. And twelve people came. Ha ha ha. So damn snooty, as if it was his fault. Twelve people! And she still gave her talk, the American lady, she just laughed and that was that. We all listened. Her own personal people and the media; the ones from the town council, my girlfriend too. We all sat and listened. Then the food. It was a beautiful spread. And she didnt take any. I couldnt believe it! And the snooty Chloes, they were all going back to the hotel for dinner, out in the country somewhere. They had booked it, one of the best. Their food is excellent. It meant she could relax, the American lady. These nights can be exhausting. She spoke about that too, about the public and their demands on you, it was part of her talk. And you could understand it, when a new book is released and she has to travel everywhere, she goes all over the world. She always takes her laptop and she writes all the time. People think it is straightforward but straightforward is the last thing. If ever he were to write a book about that! My God! The fickleness of the public! You can put on an artist from London, Paris, Venice or New York one night and an artist from down the street the next and more people will come for the artist down the street. Honestly, it's a packed house. Especially children. All their parents and their aunts and uncles, friends, grandparents, they all come. In the big city it is food and drink. People eat and eat. Nibbles and wine, you cannot have too much of it, if you want to attract an audience. But here in the provinces it is local, it has to be local, everything is local; local custom, local tradition, local history.

The Culture Officer had picked the cigarette up from the floor.

Away and have yer smoke, I said.

Are you sure?

Yeah. I waited a couple of moments then sidled along to the exit. A half bottle of brandy from the local garage store. I had my two bananas and a bottle of water. Back at the canal I would sit with the lights low, and the sound of the wind down the water, darkness and the moon; the transition from night, late night, the earliest light, approaching dawn, not just the fiery colours.

Outside the Culture Officer was walking around, puffing on his cigarette, looking this way and that. I had been set to make a dash for the dinky till then this older woman was there and he greeted her with a cuddle. Maybe she was his auntie. I heard her ask, Is Margo here yet?

The Culture Officer whispered something too her. She glanced at me and walked forwards. Are you Mister Proctor?

Yes, I replied and stepped aside.

She smiled.

The Culture Officer called to her: Well done for coming!

I followed her back inside.

15

Little Georgic

I had a message from Hannah and not to worry it was not something bad. I could call her later and so I would, I would, probably to do with sandwiches. It was an all-day workshop and I was not looking forward to it. Nevertheless it was not so horrible as all that. There can be good times ahead. People forget that. One has to remember, to cling on to that, the remembrance. Where's the dinky? Driving settles the psyche. Nervy nervy. Just my own stuff really, I needed to be doing it one has to be doing it otherwise what will happen? the world, what about the world and all that.

A council building. A janitor watched me. Writers? he asked.

Aye, yes, thanks.

He pointed me along the corridor. I found the room and introduced myself. Ten were here, around a large rectangular table. Okay, I said, well ... Are people already writing?

They glanced at one another then back to me.

Some of you must be. What is it? Fiction, plays, poetry or ... ? What is it people are working on?

A younger fellow spoke up from across the table: I'm working on my novel. It's about my experiences as a child. I submitted the first four pages and I'm waiting to hear. He sat back on the chair and nodded. The others were waiting for me to say more.

Good.

The younger fellow glanced at a woman two bodies along from him. A couple of the others glaced at her too.

When I also did she said, We were advised to submit samples of our work.

Right. I smiled again. Did ye I mean, did ye submit them?

Yes, we're just waiting.

What for? I said. When nobody answered I added, What are ye all waiting for?

The spokesperson smiled but not pleasantly. I had annoyed her in some way. What had I done since arrival? Nothing. I had only been here five minuites. One of the other women said, We were advised to submit samples, samples of our work.

Well, I smiled, as we know in art there are no such thing as samples, if by work we mean the stuff we're working on, the creative work, poetry and stories, plays and scripts. I dont know what all you are working on but whatever you are working on should be classified in the column "work-in-progress" "artwork-in-progress." Samples of artwork-in-progress is an absurdity, a fallacious and nonsensical fantasy invented by a lazy bureaucrat attached to the admin department of a large clothing design factory.

I grinned but no one returned the grin. They just kind of were looking at me or else the spokesperson who was staring at me. We were advised to submit the samples, she said.

Well yes eh ...

Don't you think we should say our names?

Sorry, yes, of course, I thought I had done. My name is Jack Proctor and I am a writer.

My name is Alice Brockway, she said, and I hope I can one day become one. She sat back and folded her arms.

. . .

sat back and folded her arms.

I blinked. Well the thing is, I said, I have already published eh well, five novels and two collections of essays and eh, I'm just stating a fact, it's not a challenge nor intended as a challenge. It's just eh ...

Daniel Costello, muttered a male.

I'm Marcy, said an older woman, or Mercy, sounding like Murcy. They all were saying their names, smiling or not; ordinary people, I could see from their faces, all looking at me or each other when names were called. I had grasped together my hands, and performed a twisting motion with them, my fingers clasped together thus mangling them, turning them this way and that, minor bones snapping, tossing the entire ten of them over my shoulders. They landed on the floor with a sickening thud. Aargh, gasped the

The others had submitted to me their names. I was not able properly to hear them, in order than one might make sense of the utterances other than derivations of the verb "to submit."

The younger fellow who had spoken firstly said, My novel is about my experiences as a child.

I'm sorry, as I say, I didnt receive it. None of your work at all, none of it reached me. Eh sorry, I've forgotten your name.

Ed.

Ed, thanks.

We were given to understand you would have had it to prepare for today, said the woman who had been second to speak.

I'm sorry, I said, eh

Catherine.

Catherine eh I'm sorry.

I worked pretty damn hard on that story, said a male.

Well that's good, I said, but ye know the thing is about writing

It's a pretty poor show.

The thing is about writing

Why on earth were we asked to submit samples of our work? he asked Alice Brockway.

We should have emailed them, said a woman.

Olwen advised against it, said Alice Brockway.

Well yes but you know Olwen.

I do know Olwen, said Alice Brockway.

Quite frankly this is ridiculous, said Daniel Costello and he too looked to Alice Brockway. We were asked to submit samples.

I too looked to Alice Brockway: Sorry about this, I said, but I didnt get them and here I am and we have an entire day of this.

Perhaps they could be scanned? said the other male.

One of the woman suddenly held up a smartphone and she waved it at me. I could email my poem right now!

Well done! said the other male.

I have copies of the four pages I submitted, said Ed. What should I do? Perhaps I could scan them! he said to Alice Brockway.

No no, I said, no, it doesnt matter.

They all turned to me.

It doesnt matter ye see, not really. I shrugged. I'm only here today, for today. So I would be unable to read them all and even if I could do it or whatever we wouldnt be able to do anything with them in that sense they would be unalterable. They would exist as finished so the idea of a workshop, well, it wouldnt be one, it would be like just saying something was good, bad or indifferent really I mean so, basically, it would be meaningless.

I glanced around the table. Folk were waiting for me to make my point while referencing Alice Brockway. What is it ye all want? I said.

Did you read any of my four pages? asked Ed.

No I didnt, I didnt read any.

It was the first four pages of my novel.

It's more of an autobiography, said a woman.

It's real life, said Ed.

An autobiographical novel. Ed was in an acting company as a boy, something of a star.

Ed grinned. I had some very weird and wonderful experiences. That is for sure. People would be astonished to hear some of the incidents that happened.

Including household names, said Daniel Costello. The scary thing is it's all true. What about Joseph Pettigrew?

Ed shook his head. People would not believe it! Even when the camera was rolling. Joseph Pettigrew, you would never believe it about Joseph Pettigrew! I remember clearly one late afternoon, we had been going over and over

I chuckled, holding my right hand aloft. Remember Ed this is a writers' workshop. What I mean is dont get lost in anecdotes, what we want is to focus on how to get these anecdotes onto the page. This is where stories begin and this is what we have to do, we have to concentrate on the stories, writing the stories.

Mine is factual, said Ed.

Granted.

I thought you would have read the pages I submitted. I've gone over them time and time again.

Ed has worked so very hard on them, said a woman.

The same pages? I asked.

Yes.

Well, never mind. Ye've made a start Ed. And ye have to make a start, that is the thing. Ultimately it does not matter what we write, autobiography, poetry, menus, diaries or school compositions; it is the activity that counts. As long as you sit down and start you'll have nothing to worry about, so let's push on.

I stopped. People had frowned and were shaking their heads. Eh … I'm sorry, I mean if I swore, I apologise. My emotions are pretty hung out and are now kind of drying off. I grinned. I was trying to write ye see, earlier on, the wee hours, I set the alarm for early, so I could get the work done before coming here. I needed to get my own stuff done then had to pull myself away from the table, remembering where I am, and so on, you'll know the feeling. There I was in my room, dan dih randan: a dark figure hunched over a shabby laptop, major shadows through the tattered blind, dan dih randan, when all of a sudden dan dih randan dan! Rriiinnggg. The alarm! jesus christ where am I! Up I jumped and drove like the clappers to get here and meet yous all!

I was about to continue this line of nonsense when my attention was distracted by Alice Brockway who either closed her eyelids or had had them closed already which I found even more significant. Ed said, I've been doing diary-type entries.

Good.

It's more difficult than I thought.

Of course it is but at the same time it's straightforward. Okay, I said, let's push on.

Once I finish I want to write a script for television or the movies too, said Ed, that would be cool. There are actors I know like close friends? people I've worked beside? I know they'll come on board. I have plenty of ideas. Things based on my own personal experience. I'm not worried really. I'm already shifting things about inside.

Good, I said. Unfortunately Ed paused here to indicate the side of his head, an invitation to sup stout with the gods. The others were nodding agreement. I gazed steadily at this area of his skull, then chuckled. Ed and everybody looked to Alice Brockway. I chuckled again. I couldnt help it. Zeus would have guffawed. Ed, I said, do ye mind? When ye say shifting things about inside there . . . are ye meaning inside yer cranium?

Yes, said Ed.

Are ye talking about veins and corpuscles; bones, bits of gristle? Are these the things ye're shifting about?

Ed smiled then frowned. The others were uneasy. I addressed the body severally as per withinside: Ye have to learn about this Creative Fiction Writing so-called, if ye think we're referring to an activity that exists within our skulls in reference to the making aspect of writing then forget it. Ye have to forget about ideas no matter how brilliant they are, like the poet said, no ideas but in things. Think in terms of more physical art forms. What we do is shift things about not inside but outside in the material world; cut, copy and paste. We move sentences and paragraphs from one page to another, transfer entire sections or chapters from one part of the work to another. We can be working on chapter 3 and then seem unable to move into chapter 4, so why not just jump to chapter 10 and come back to chapter 4 at a later date! Do ye know what I mean? Ye have to be in the discovery; everything is subject to change at this early stage, the embryo stage, surfacing from the mud, the dawn of civilization, ancient Egypt, the old kidney beans.

I dont understand what you mean, said a woman.

This is because you havent had the chance to make sense of it yet because I am now saying it to you and you have never before heard it. This means you are learning something new. This is why you do not understand. It is a process. It is a learning process. You are within it. You are here to learn. We all are.

Daniel Costello was smiling, but puzzled. His eyebrows rose and he glanced to Alice Brockway who did not notice, she was staring down at the table. Others watched her too. Then Ed glanced at me surreptitiously. I nodded encouragement. Well, he said, I only want to write a book about my acting experience as a boy. It's a world people dont know about, not from the inside. So much happened to me and I know people would love to hear it. Big names too, household names, you would not believe what they get up to in relief. I'll give you one example, even for mixed company!

JAMES KELMAN

No dont do that, I said, we're talking about writing here not verbal utterings.

Yes but

I grinned. Form a workshop called Recounting Anecdotes.

Alice Brockway snorted and turned her head from me. Meanwhile another woman was speaking, an older woman, ages with myself maybe, speaking to me. Pardon? I said, but was unable to make sense of it, my head being gone with Alice, with Alice who had snorted. Did she actually do that? Did she snort and turn her head? Did she actually do that, fucking snort, she snorted and turned her head from me? Only Hannah, ever ever, Hannah and nobody else and I mean nobody else, ever ever

The television series? said the man who was neither Ed nor Daniel Costello. *The Georgics*?

What are ye talking about? I asked calmly.

The Georgics. It was very highly regarded in its day.

Ed was Little Georgic, said a woman.

Look, I'm sorry but what is it we're talking about here?

The Georgics was a long-running television series. Ed was centre stage.

Well I wouldnt go as far as that, said Ed.

You were, said Daniel Costello. Without any doubt you were.

I agree, murmured others

Ed shrugged. It was a very interesting experience. I call it "weird and wonderful. People will enjoy hearing about it. They really will. It also happens to be true.

What's true? I asked.

The story. I'm not embellishing anything.

God's teeth.

Every bit of it is true. I swear! Ed appealed to Alice Brockway: Every bit of it.

I know, replied Alice Brockway.

The others had waited for this. Now they looked at me. And I said to Ed, I'm only saying that ye still have to write it down. You. You have to write it down. Whether it's true or not, a pack of lies or who cares, it's you.

Every bit of it is true. I swear.

Yes but it is you who has to write it down Ed, that is what I'm saying.

Yes! This is why I joined the group. It would make a good movie too. There are some decent actors around and I know a few. But that's long term. Ed chuckled. You know I was in that series from the age of four until the age of twelve.

The others smiled.

Then when the studio bosses advised them it was coming to an end! My part was written out. It was massive for my parents. They had to tell me. How traumatic was that? said Ed. The studio bosses didnt. Can you believe it? And that asshole B D Whitlock or whatever his name was who spent most of his time groping Little Molly, and me whenever she was elsewhere, yes, I could tell you stories! Joseph Pettigrew! My God! My parents never recovered. This ended their marriage. This is the burden I've been carrying.

I raised my hand.

Ed has had some marvelous experiences, said an older woman.

No question about that, I said. The trouble is none of it matters if it aint wrut; you got to write the stuff!

I went over and over them again and again, said Ed, exactly as I was advised until I was sick of the sight of them. Ed folded his arms, shaking his head.

I laughed.

Honestly, I went over and over them, the same four pages.

Dont, I said, you'll make me cry.

Ed was puzzled. Alice and others glared at me.

No I mean it. More honestly than you all can imagine. It's too sad to bear. Who advised you to keep on revising the same four pages?

It was just advice.

I groaned. This is why I do not teach and cannot teach. One cannot follow a dumpling. Not in a day. What I mean is I dont always agree with the methods of other tutors. Sometimes what they say does damage. The whole point is how you write the damn story. None of the rest of it matters. If your writing is boring your story is boring, even if it's exciting, or should be exciting.

Ed's story is really very interesting, said the second of the older men.

Of course it is, but what I am saying is if the writing is boring the story is boring.

I really must take issue, said Alice Alice Alice, snorting her way free of the woodwork. I so disagree, she said, I so so disagree.

Alice Brockway, arms folded, head tilted, set for the kill, clinically. But calmly. I think she was, calm. Fucking hell. Hit the return key. I smiled and left the room. I did. I got up and left the room. Imagine that, sixty-six years of age. So so disagree, I so so disagree, what is "so so" an adverb, two adverbs?

If the place had had better facilities I would have rinsed my face and swallied a mouthful of water.

Raining heavily. I crossed to an adjacent doorway and sheltered. My head was empty. Weird. A blankness. Full to breaking point yet nothing was there bar the conditions for "realization." Alice: Alice Alice Alice. Scorned!

One was sixty-six years of age. One could not cope with Alice Brockway who so so disagreed with one.

At one's wits' end. Wits' end, one's wits' end.

This was my life. My fucking life man know what I'm talking about. To lose one's temper is to lose one's head.

Losing not only my temper my sanity. Humpty Dumpty sat on the wall.

Thirty minutes into the workshop and one sought the tallest building for an old-fashioned skydive, abseil without the harness. I was fucking fed up man telling ye, just fucking fed up. I returned to the workshop. I waited for them to stop talking. Whatever they thought, who cares. Finally the one remaining conversation continued in an enforced pseudo-natural fashion, ending in a self-conscious stew. I was glad of that.

Now they gazed at me.

Thank you, I said, I shall continue where I left off earlier. The trouble with these notions I am bringing, these ideas, is that they are new to most of you and maybe different to what you expect. There is so little time. I'm here today and gone tomorrow. I say this to you not as venerable sage but as an aged practitioner. Ye need to be writing. Nobody should be *wanting* to write, we should already be writing otherwise what the hell is it we're doing. Is anyone not writing?

This needs to be something you have to do; you have to do it, if you dont you'll die. Writing is Art. What we do is literary art, to engage in this is a way of being that we do as humans to avoid suicide, if not suicide then an honest death nevertheless. Forget all this faery tale magician superhero sci fi fanstasy shite, backpage of the *TLS*, *NYR*, *LRB*, *McS* and all that television cops & killers and all that fucking phantasmagoric shite, debased artforms and establishment control.

One of the women laughed suddenly and was embarrassed by it.

I smiled. I know it sounds funny.

It doesnt, she said, I'm sorry.

It's like these reality shows, I said. It's time to grow up in other words, and I apologize if I swore, and I did swear so I do apologise.

Poor Ed was shaking his head at the floor. He thought it was his fault. It wasnt his fault. Nothing was. Not even the fact they had bounced him off the television show. I said to him: Is any of this making sense in relation to you and the autobiography, which is what you're writing and what you want to write.

I'm not sure, he said and glanced at Agnes Brockway who sat with her head lowered.

I'm only saying it's no good talking about it. Ye have to write it. And stop all that thinking crap, it is absolutely useless.

Daniel Costello guffawed.

Excellent, I said.

Daniel Costello gazed at me. Alice Brockway was shaking her head. Ed looked from her to me and back to her again. I was hoping I would get some help, he said.

What like? Do you want me to write the fucking thing?

Oh unfair! said one of the other women.

Alice Brockway smiled, shaking her head.

Sorry, I said, I do apologise. The thing is, ye might not believe it, but some people come to groups like this under the impression that the visiting writer will perform assorted factotorial functions, even to ghostwriting their work. They think I'll take home their manuscript and conduct an online correspondence until the point of publication. It's true. The truth is I'm only here to help, using my own experience. Help is what I'm giving ye right now. If ye intend writing then write, just write. I mean that is number one.

Should we have exercises? asked Daniel Costello.

No.

I should have thought exercises were important.

Should ye? Look out the window and ye'll see a street with a hill at the other end. Away out there and run up the slope. When ye reach the top turnabout and run back down.

I beg your pardon?

The way ye say exercises, it sounds like the punishment ye get from an irritated PE teacher, having to do a hundred push-ups or run a marathon; *The Loneliness of the Long Distance* bloody writer or some damn thing, god's teeth man, ye're here to write. So write, stop telling wee stories.

Yes but ... Daniel frowned at me. He folded his arms, sat back on his chair. He stared at the floor.

That's okay, I said, I see that as positive but stare at me instead of the floor. I'm the one that's written the books and published the books.

Daniel glanced at me.

Alice Brockway cleared her throat. I see a need for exercises, she said slowly but assuredly. She raised her head to look me in the eye. Her bravado surprised me, and stopped from coming to pass a sentence I was set to utter. I addressed the group as a body: Like I said, I do not give exercises. Exercises and samples are similar conceptually. They dont apply here. I prefer to look on what we do as art. No, sorry, it is not a preference, it is a need. When we begin a poem or a story we begin to create art. Instead of exercises I refer you to the page, the place we work. I want to discuss vulnerability. I want to discuss creation, your desires, your hopes and so on.

I really dont understand you, said Alice.

I know that Alice but if you open your mind you will stand a chance. This workshop does not exist until you are handing in work. None of you is doing this yet. We had a four- or five-minute break there and nobody seems to have written anything. A pity. Amazing what a human being can do in four or five minutes. We'll soon be having a further break, a longer one. I hope you all might have a go then. Once you do and pass the fruits of it in we shall move more quickly. In the meantime I hope you agree with me that there is a difference between literary art and all that detective cops and killers shite we see produced by Bruce Waddell, Jack Montgomery and Morven Taylor.

Who is Bruce Waddell? asked Daniel Costello.

Does he not write detective stories? Maybe I've got the wrong guy.

Are you saying that detective stories arent worthwhile?

I dont know. I dont care.

There are plenty of examples of detective stories that are proper literature, he said.

Great. Who like? Say one?

Daniel shrugged.

Just one.

He frowned. No, I'm not going to.

Why not?

You're backing me into a corner and I resent it. Daniel glanced at Alice.

Sorry, I said, and I too glanced at Alice. The problem is I look for things people say to use as examples. So I can dig more deeply. Dont take it personally. I'm wanting to lead ye to a place where ye get to work properly and this is the best way I can do it. Remember I only have this one day with ye.

Alice nodded. May I say something Mister Proctor?

Of course you may.

Can I make it known that what you say is very much your own framework? Professional writers have other frameworks. They earn their living by writing books and have their preferred teaching methods. I've been attending writers' groups for many years, as have others here this evening. Perhaps I'm wrong or perhaps you're simply in the wrong group.

I laughed.

I dont mean that in a negative sense.

No, I said, it's fair enough. Maybe I am in the wrong group. But it wasnt me chose it. I've been dumped here for this one day. I try to get across my own perspective which is not elitist though it might appear that way. I'm not getting at you or any one of you. If I am it is unintentional. It's only that I'm a practitioner too, if not a professional in some other sense, a long-term practitioner. I can say more about the practice than others. There is nothing elitist in that. Is a joiner's idea of a good joiner of greater validity than a bank clerk's idea of a good joiner? How relative do we have to go? Should we be surprised that experienced writers might know more about the practicalities than inexperienced writers? People need to arrive at a position where it is possible to say what good writing might be, or bad writing.

Alice shook her head slowly. I dont see it, I'm sorry.

I know ye dont see it, ye dont have to be sorry. I shrugged. If I cant help you along that road then I definitely am in the wrong group. Not only that, I've failed. But people need to begin writing a story. Right now. I'm talking literally. I'm goni leave the room and want people to have written a page by the time I get back.

Is that not an exercise? asked Ed.

It is! Yeah! Well done Ed.

Ed smiled.

That is your exercise. Go and write a story right now. That is the exercise. Forget me leaving the room. Take the next hour. All of ye. Find a space and write like the clappers for one whole hour. I'll take it all home with me and I shall start reading it tomorrow. I have a day off I think. Even if I dont I shall, and I guarantee to stay in touch.

What about the pieces we submitted before you came? asked a woman.

Are you talking about the ones you all submitted?

I submitted mine to Olwen.

So did I, said Ed.

I think we all did, said Daniel Costello.

Yeah, I'm sorry about that. Like I say, I'm not part of the bureaucracy. The thing is ye wrote these pieces before ye attended this workshop today. So they're no good. I mean for today, for my purposes. Right now the important thing is to do it at this minute, this damn minute, in terms of how ye all are right now, right now, after all this shamozzle. It is important ye all batter in right now and do one page each right now, and I'll gie ye an hour—what could Babel have done in an hour, know what I'm saying! Grasp what I mean, that we can learn as a group, encountering and resolving problems through practice and discussion. I'm talking about different ways of seeing, it will help ye further too if eh

Alice had sighed. This silenced me. She said, I understand all that Mister Proctor.

All what? I stared at her.

She gazed at the others then, with a smile, lowered her gaze to the table.

I hadnt finished talking. So ye couldnt have understood. I'll just repeat: it's pointless discussing these pieces you handed in a couple of weeks ago. It is this workshop here and now that matters. Each one of you is a living breathing thinking human being sitting hunched over a laptop, smartphone or pen and paper. Begin your work from that.

Alice looked up. I'm only asking why you will not discuss the work we submitted?

Oh god. Is that all you're asking?

Yes. Most of us have brought copies of our work along. Why wont you discuss it?

Because I dont want to.

Then it was all a waste of time?

Nothing is a waste of time.

But you are saying

No, I am not saying. You dont know what I am saying. Not until it is said. The work you passed in before this evening amounts not to nil but to itself. Agnes, please . . .

She stared at me.

You wrote the work before you came here. I want you to see that and grasp what it is I am leading us through in relation to art, creativity and so on. I think it might be a different way of seeing what it is you're doing. For some of you a new way of seeing stories, plays and poetry—art!—and how it can be created, even by ordinary everyday people like us! It puts art within our grasp. Craft is crucial. We make a story; we enter, lay down our subject matter which is language and then fucking juggle it about. The process is one of manufacture. The set of ideas completed on the page is the artwork realized. Okay?

Agnes was looking at me as though concentrating. It is very possible she was concentrating and trying very hard to understand my argument. Meanwhile Ed was attracting her attention but she ignored him. She was communicating through a complex body language with other members of the group, right under my very nose. I said, I can see you're finding this very very difficult.

My name is Alice, she said.

Oh god sorry.

No Mister Proctor I dont find it difficult. I do find your particular experience rather more powerful than my own. Nobody was ever interested in worthwhile things where I was growing up: art and opera, ballet, theatre, proper litera-ture. I could not wait to escape. As soon as I was old enough I went. I've had to make my way entirely on my own. Do you know the North Eastern Region Mister Proctor?

A bit.

Is there any place worse? she asked. The North Western Region I hear you say but it isnt true!

I'm sorry, I do apologize.

She smiled, a strained smile.

The crux is this, I said, we dont have time to waste. I dont and neither do you all. We want to write and we need to write. Forget all this class snobbery elitist shit. All we want is to write stories, poems and plays. That is all we want. How many senses have we got?

Five, said a man.

Yeah? well for talking sake we'll make it six. Do we know what the sixth might be?

There was a silence, but only a short one, until once again enter Alice Brockway who could not fucking give fucking in, jesus christ almighty, all I could do was stare at her for christ sake willing her to shut her fucking mouth your honour, I'll take it on the chin but she insisted, she insisted. Mister Proctor, she said, I have no idea what you are talking about.

In that case shut up, I said.

Alice stood to her feet.

Aw Alice I was only kidding I was kidding. Just sit down and relax. Honest, sorry, I was only kidding.

But she didnt sit down. Instead Alice left the room, head held high or however the stereotype has it, lower lip quivering, I suppose, and no wonder. Trouble ahead. Too late now.

I continued to the others: Different writers say it differently but here and now it is me. I was the one invited here today. I know I'm bringing ye different ideas. And I know they're slippery. Dont worry if ye dont get them at first. Ye think ye understand what I've said then ye discover maybe ye havent. Ye thought ye knew and now ye arent so sure.

Some of you think you have ideas inside your head and that your task as a writer is to transcribe or translate, to somehow pin these ideas down onto the page. It is nonsense. What we do is invent stuff on the page, whether it's a paper page or an electronic page is irrelevant. We assemble stuff; we break ideas up, break them down; we cut, copy and paste separate bits together. We have names and phrases for this. One is "working," one is "writing," another is "continuing the work in progress." Other names are "doodling," "composing," "creating."

Daniel Costello was needing to talk. I ignored him at

first because I had a point to establish. But he was bursting. Okay? I said.

Thanks, no, only to connect with my experiences in meditation, it relates.

Great.

Have you been involved in meditation Mister Proctor?

No.

Mindfulness?

No.

You would find it worthwhile I think.

Good, yeah, fine. Time for a break. Let me repeat about exercises, I am not giving one. Any story you write is a story created. It is a piece of art in its own right. Otherwise I dont understand what art is. Exercise is like a rehearsal; we are not rehearsing here, we are doing the thing, we are creating. Nobody should blush about the word "art." Okay? Good, fine.

All gawking at me.

See ye later, I said. I left the building, ran a mile, had sex, swam twenty lengths, swallied two pints of Guinness and two fish suppers then returned for the second half.

So had Alice Brockway! There she was sitting on her arse the same as everybody else. I was very very glad to see her. Gradually I included her in my looks but she remained silent. Did anybody write anything during the break? I said.

Gasps of amusement. A couple of them were eating sandwiches and quaffing coffee.

I'm serious.

They looked at one another.

I hoped ye all would have been intimidated into skipping lunch and inventing a story. I went back to my room and worked on one and believe it or not I finished it.

I thought I saw you walking round the block? said a woman.

You did but did ye see me coming back? I'm not being cheeky. Look, I said, I want to end this session right now, and it's not a cop-out. Let all of us go now and if we havent already done so we should begin writing at once, and those of you who find it impossible to write a single word must find a pencil and write down on an A4 page the following words: it is impossible to write a single word

and follow that with the word: Why?

and following on from that just hold yer breath and dive in, dive, that heady plunge into the deep. And it's salt water remember so ye never know what ye might find preserved there.

A dead body, laughed Ed.

Exactly, I said.

But is that not an exercise? said Daniel Costello.

No it's not, I said, or yes it is. Once you all have written down that opening statement, replace the word "write" with the word "live," and the phrase "single word" with the phrase "proper life," and see where it takes ye. And I dont think it is an exercise, I said.

What happens when we finish? asked Catherine.

(*To be continued.*)

16

The Only Resident in the Entire Fucking Dump

It is difficult, when one cannot work. Yet no sooner was I able to work properly than I had to leave it, had to stop. I knew I could do it so I didnt have to, I didnt have to force it. That was how it went, that was just how it went. Only then could I relax. When the writing was going well I could relax enough to stop doing it. I should have explained these things to Hannah and the kids. All they saw was the crabbit bastard. I never knew what was happening till reaching the end. That was life, my life; designs and patterns, all shite. Authorizing the need for the supernatural, Keeper of the Code, the dream of all authority.

If I had had wi-fi I would have found some old movies on YouTube.

I didnt want to go any damn place. Not even the tow path.

Tow path, toll bridge, inland waterways, archaeology from a past, we tread along and see signs everywhere, trudge along, signs everywhere, every place, trampling underfoot, see the weeds, the steps down from the bank leading nowhere. The world as it was. A world that was.

Nothing was being asked of me at this conference; one to which I had been invited—organized by writers it was said, a conference of writers, pride of lions, flock of starlings. Hotels lined a clifftop, a coastal resort. One could aye jump over. That cheered me up. Not that I might luxuriate in thoughts of suicide but that irony had returned to my world.

What was happening?

Another invitation. This one looked cheery. Did food and drink feature? Yes. I could come for dinner and that was that.

I think of this as emerging from emergency mode. The machine has rebooted. An update on the neurological system. I managed to engage start-up on that complex keystroke that takes one into the skeletal bones of reality. There is no colour, no sound. Nor drama. No drama. No fuck all. We must inject it and we must do so as individual human beings. Nobody can do it for us. They can tell us how to do it but they cannay fucking do it, it is up to us. Do you want to live? Fine, fucking live then. Just dive in, there's the deep end, plunge.

No doubt the House had reminded the local writers that I was in residence for the remainder of current infinity, so why didnt they have me for dinner. I tasted fine with french fries and tartare sauce.

Old jokes die hard.

The conference was an all day event. A 9:30 sign in on Saturday morning: coffee and croissants. Two forums in the morning then lunch.

That word, "lunch." When we were weans, me and the siblings, our father would tell stories that had as a central feature the concept "luncheon." The very word made ye smack yer lips. When are we getting luncheon Dad. Sssh. He would continue the yarn and then came the good bit, and after the children defeated the forces of evil, along came Auntie Ellen who provided the children with a fine luncheon. What did we get! was the cry. A bowl of soup, hot buttered toast, Welsh rarebit, slices of crisp bacon and fresh tomatoes. Hurreh!

Two forums in the afternoon, then a couple of beers, glasses of wine, conversations and assignations. Then Dinner! And overnight for those who fancied the idea and could afford it. Some went home and some stayed. A slap-up breakfast, then strolling the clifftop promenade to walk it off. Guest writers such as myself could turn up for dinner, drink a beer with the local writers and fuck off home afterwards. If I drank too much I could dump the car, find an empty couch in the hotel lobby.

A smashing conference. Who wouldnt want that! Unless Jerry was there.

God's teeth!

Surely not. Surely it was too small-fry? No, nothing is too small-fry. The small scale stuff is the cutting edge, sooner or later. Guys like Jerry transformed the agenda. They made it their own.

Maybe I would go, but maybe I wouldnt, and maybe it would be lamb chops.

Lamb chops! How come lamb chops? I hadnt eaten red meat for years! A fish alternative to vegetarian would be great. Poached salmon, broccoli and pasta would do me, long on the crusty bread. Maybe a nice bowl of soup to begin. A homemade tomato soup; one of those with floating whole chilies, greed cardomon and garlic cloves. I had this once and entered a fit of sneezing. I sneezed the soup across the white tablecloth. It was not my fault daddy, I snorted on the black pepper. Or else deep-fried haddock in a proper batter; served with appropriate garlands. Of what? Something. Who cares, leave it to the chef.

Decent work in the afternoon and at half past four I lay down for a doze. Three and a half hours later I woke up, and I needed to shower man I was bogging, smelly as fuck. Plus the bodily movements, excretions and evacuations; bodily credits, bodily debits as they say. As who say? Bankers and Banker Winners. Dinner would be over by the time I got there but so what. Leftovers. Hot or cold food, the belly does not discriminate. In my youth I had a job washing dishes. When I started I was 120 lbs. When I quit they carried me out in a sedan chair, belly up, of meloniferous proportions, such that perambulation was beyond me, the female kitchen-workers having stuffed me full of leftover grub.

Normally I shave before entering the shower. Tonight I showered first. I know why. I didnt want to see myself. I was conscious of self in the presence of self, dan d randan,

the aged author staring into the gilt-edged mirror, open razor hovering at his thin-skinned throttle, dan d randan,

a lone cry from a solitary hound and his eyes rolled in horror, espying an evil glint in his eye, a glint in his evil eye, eyeballs rolling in terror, an evil glint in his eye.

Aha you bastard. Whaur's yer integrity noo? Free food and off ye go.

Anyway, it was not a question of grub. Glint in the eye, ergo sum: this world exists and I and I are of it, if not within it. Not only for the rest of my time here on Planet Earth, but now, here and now, he intoned evilly.

Sure I was starving but there was food in the house. Either I went or I didnt. So yes. Nay point sitting moping. People not only eat free food they drink free wine: thus freely they blether. Blethers are the writers' forte. But for the blethers they would eat not only their fill they would chow the plants in the plant pots. I was looking forward to the blethers: meeting writers I could at least talk to, if not communicate; share experience, be consoled, lick one's wounds, regain confidence; talk books, writers, residences and the Great Creative Writing Swindle, transforming disastrous workshop sessions into cheery anecdotes: in short, a cheerily empathetic environment.

I arrived around 10:00 p.m. The dining area was empty. The tables were not only cleared they were already prepared for tomorrow morning's breakfast.

People were in the two lounge bars and the outside balcony. A couple of braziers had been lighted, encouraging smokers. A half-swallied glass of red wine sat forlornly on a side table. It looked fine to me! I lifted it. A banquet menu lay next to it which I shoved in my pocket. A man in a dark suit had appeared. He had dish towels draped over each shoulder. He gave me a look that the best-selling novelist and ex-Secret Service operative, Rupert Bickersby, would have described as "wickedly baleful and of evil intent." I smiled in a friendly manner and sipped at the wine but he turned from me with a shake of the head, exhibiting irritation. It occurred to me it had been his glass of red wine. Ach well, there was nothing I could do about that.

This place was the opposite of what I require in a hotel which is plush anonymity. Homely anonymity is not quite the nightmare beyond one's wildest imaginings, leave that to the well-fed avuncularity we find in overweight arts bureaucrats. I found a lounge bar. It was smaller and not so busy as the other. People were sitting at tables speaking quietly. After a moment the guy in the dark suit appeared, minus the dishtowels. He was working behind the counter. He did not ignore me but when he approached he carried his head side on to me, so he wouldnt have to see my face. I sat on a bar stool to annoy him. I had been going to order a non-alcoholic to accompany the red wine but he was too annoying. Hi there, I said, could I have a bottle of Czech lager please?

The glass of red wine plus one bottle of beer. And no more. In the wake of such intense emotional scarring, one is liable to foam at the mouth.

He opened the bottle of beer for me and placed it in front of me. He waited for the cash. I pointed at the bottle of beer: Any chance of a glass, I said.

He hesitated for a moment then reached below the counter, and placed one in front of me.

Thanks you very much, I said and paid him. I perused the banquet menu to pass the time. Quail. Quail is a bird. A quail, imagine eating a quail. With Chef's choice of VEG.

I shall have the quail; ask Chef to choose me the VEG. Sir, murmurs the waiter, bowing and prostrating. Oui M'sieur.

The guy placed my change on the counter. I thought about tipping him. This would have cemented the customer-servant relationship, and induced a heart attack in the bastard but I didnt want to leave his kids without a father. Although who knows, with a guy like this it might have been for the best.

He had lifted a dish towel, slung it across his left shoulder. He walked outside to the balcony area. I watched him lifting empty glasses and clearing ashtrays. Then a thing happened I found quite weird, he started pointing at me. He was in the company of three or four people—smokers—and looked like he was saying stuff about me. What had I done? Nothing. It couldnt have been me. The red wine! But that was nothing. How could I have known it was his? It may not even have been his. I was just bloody guessing. Stupit nonsense altogether. And there he was, still talking. They were talking to him. It wasnt just him talking to them. Jesus christ, it reminded me of that example, the one I gave to the school-pupils, the lassie in the corridor; everybody goes silent. Are they talking about me! Yes!

It was a good way of looking at the process. Possible essay or something. I had too much on my plate anyway with that damn novel.

And what did it matter about that! I was the only one interested, apart from Hannah —and she only wanted it finished so she could stop worrying about me.

Why did I fucking bother! What kind of mentality, what kind of

The last thing I needed was another piece of work. I needed to be home, home home home. Why was I here at all? I shouldnt have come. I didnay have to!

Anyway, the stuff on the balcony had ended. Mister dish towel was nowhere to be seen.

I was not given to paranoia, I dont think, although I could have been forgiven. Things come from nothing and I had been too long on my own. We become sensitive to the remotest nuance. If I heard a squeak from outside the chalet door I grabbed a kitchen knife. The ideal landscape for a zombie attack. Maybe I could write a quick potboiler, the *Canal of the Zombies*. *The Flight of the Zombie Ducks*! I just needed to get home, and was considering that very move when a man arrived at the bar:

Charles, he said, and you are?

Pardon?

Charles, he said: You are? He was introducing himself, holding out his hand.

Aw. Jack, I said, getting up from the stool.

Of course you are. Jack Proctor.

We shook hands. You're a writer yourself? I said.

I am. Currently guest-editing, a local literary journal—the *Tight Line Review*, you may have heard of it.

I have. I didnt know it was based in these parts?

Oh yes, indeed.

I chuckled.

He frowned.

Sorry, I said, I'm a sarcastic bugger. I had to stop myself asking for your autograph. It's total prejudice. I write prose fiction ye see and people involved in literary journals usually have a low opinion of prose as an art form.

Ah.

Unless experimental. Unfortunately the editors are unable to define "the experimental" except when they're drunk. Then they confide to all and sundry that the most reliable guide to "the experimental" is "that which does not bore the editor."

Exactly!

And if your short story is up to scratch they publish on condition they can refer to it as a "prose-pome." When I was but a callow youth I submitted a longish story to a literary magazine where no term rooted in Latin appeared within seven words of a Greek one—the number seven being crucial—but the editor did not notice. I received his emailed rejection note by return and in this he supplied tips on manuscript presentation. I emailed a reply to his rejection and explained about the Latin and Greek contrivance. He said Latin and Greek had damn all to do with it but I should not be discouraged. On a future occasion I sent the bugger a story less than a page in length whose verbs were unable to cope with a principal noun. His rejection note was of copious duration, ending with a flourish: You must read the work of Michael Crumish, he said, and I say read because you will never master him.

Charles smiled.

Apologies, I said, I'm in a state of hypertension, having missed dinner.

You missed dinner?

I slept in. I was actually working through the night then had an afternoon nap but it turned into a sleep. I was hungry too. Typical residency man I've been living on cup-a-soup.

Ah. Would you care for a ... He indicated my near empty glass.

Eh, a bottle of beer, that would be great, thanks—although this makes two, and two pushes me over the legal limit. The difficulty then is some tail-gating half-daft bugger running into me. I'm the one the cops will do for drunk driving.

Exactly—unless he's over the limit too.

Yeah! Well said!

Charles smiled. He was looking for the barman who was nowhere to be seen.

Eventually I said, Country roads at night can be dangerous—hairpin bends and harebrained locals. But also safe.

I quite like country road driving, it just depends. On what says you? Well, that's the tricky bit. On matters beyond our control, that's what. Within our control we could exercise a degree of caution. External to it and no, we cannot. Matters within are within, but not on the outside.

Yes, said Charles. We had a recent issue devoted to the work of Baumer. You know Baumer?

Not personally but yes. My own difficulty is gradation and value-systems. It does irritate me that in the corridors of academia those who create poultry have higher status than those who create prose fiction. God's teeth man the buggers are assumed to be intellectual by virtue of form!

Mm.

Qualities such as grace are believed the property of poultry, occasionally found in drama, but not prose, except in rare instances. These rare instances take place in abstraction; in spiritual communion or meditation, what Peter Bryce calls "epiphaneous phenomena," exemplified by prose meditations of the mid-17th century, influencing T S Hitler and so forth. Persons engaged in poultry are involved in a graceful activity. Those who teach it believe themselves engaged in a graceful activity too. In conversations they expect others to observe a reverential hush in their presence. Ohh ssh, he teaches poultry! Ohh ssh, he writes poultry. Ohh ssh he edits a poultry journal of astonishing esoteretics. When the poor prose writer approaches the summit his or her work may be termed "prose-poultry."

Academics who pen the odd novel agree with that. I do not profess to be a poelt, is a statement often heard in university corridors. Others who pen the odd pome nod sagely, I find that one pome per annum is an assault on the very fibre of my being. Then they adjourn to the local hostelry to discuss the new standards of grading they will apply to their post-grad students of Creative Writing, over a large glass of wine and a supersize plateful of fish & deep-fried chipped potatoes, with a side dish of vegetarian onion rings. Sorry, I said.

Charles smiled.

All the same, it's true what I'm saying. People involved in poultry bestow their highest praise when they advise us poor prose writers that our work occasionally rises to the lofty peaks of poultry. When Tolstoy, Kafka or Chekov are at their most sublime we may say of them, they are almost a poelt, they are a prose-poelt. Whereas those who pen their one pome per annum can say of themselves, We touch the summit of sublimity once in each twelve month period. And even if we do not achieve it we may say of ourselves we engage in the pursuit itself, which is akin to the pursuit of perfection, at the summit of artistic achievement. In other words, we who fail cannot be said to have failed. Charles, I said, ye have to move with the times. I dont know what ye're up to with the *Tight Line Review*, but if social media isnay a part of it then goodnight.

Ah ... Charles glanced away from me, towards the reception area. Oh we know the difficulties, he said. We do try for a more widely accessed readership. Certainly we accept the newer techologies. Of course we do.

His attention was still to the reception area. I looked there too but didnt see anything in particular.

Most of our sales are through social media, said Charles, and of that I can assure you. In fact we have no choice in the matter. Young people today have no inclination to go in the old directions. I must say too ... Charles stepped back apace and gazed at me. Would you consider placing a story with us?

Eh ...

I dont think we've had anything by a Banker Prize winner before.

I chuckled, about to answer, but his attention had gone altogether. A kerfuffle sounded from the reception area and I could see the guy with the dark suit and dish towels. Words were being exchanged between him and several people.

Hang on, said Charles. He made his way through to the reception area.

Mister dish towel was gesticulating in my direction, so obviously I was the problem. A half glass of red wine. God's teeth. Now it was time to go. This was absolute crap.

Never fight when ye cannay win, and he was the barman. There was an old Gaidligh proverb to that effect. What the hell was it again, the one I was thinking of, I couldnt quite remember. I swallied the last dribble of beer, drained the empty bottle into the glass. That must have been the last straw for the guy. In he marched, followed by Charles and others. You were not here for the banquet, he cried, and you have no right to be here. He turned to Charles: He is not part of your conference.

He is, said Charles, he's a guest-speaker.

He's no such thing. I watched him come in.

Pardon?

He came into the dining area but he was not part of the banquet.

He is our guest, said one of the women. He is Jack Proctor the Scotch novelist.

Actually I was born in England, I said.

I dont care where you were born, you are not resident.

I am so resident.

No you are not!

Aye I am, I said, in my loudest sweariest voice. Although I hadnay sworn it sounded like I had, and it quietened him. I am probably the only resident in this entire fucking dump, I added.

Out! he shouted. Out!

What the hell is up with him?

Charles had cleared his throat. Language, he muttered.

Dear god Charles this is wearisome. Tell the guy he'll end up getting fired if he carries on like this. We're bloody customers. Honest, I said, and I spoke to the guy myself: They'll just kick ye out the door.

Nobody will kick me out the door. He glared at me. This is my hotel. I am the owner.

Let us all calm down, added a woman.

Do it without me, I said. That will solve the problem because here I go, I'm going home.

Dont, said the woman and she gripped my forearm. I almost jumped. This was the first time I had been touched in weeks! Mister dish towel had smiled at my reaction but it was not a true smile and I recognized it as a danger signal. It suggested a state of calm, but it was not authentic. There were beads of sweat on the guy's brow. Ssh, I said, calm yersel.

What did you say?

Calm down.

Who do you think you are talking to?

Yeah yeah I know, but forget that for a moment, you want an aspirin. Rephrase that, you need an aspirin.

I dont need an aspirin.

Yes ye do. The way you're going man ye want to be careful; heart attacks, strokes and so on.

He stared at me.

There's saliva dribbling doon yer chin, I said, take it easy.

One of the women approached holding an arts brochure towards him. She showed him the page featuring the legendary writer of Lallans, with a snapshot of my fizzog. Here he is, she said.

He studied the page. I hear what you are saying miss, but the bar closes at 11:00 p.m. Non-residents are obliged to drink up their drinks and leave the premises.

The woman said: Do you mean all guests are to leave the premises? Including those who have been here all day for the conference?

Correct.

Charles raised his right arm. Let me see if I have got this right: you will not allow writers and creative delegates who have been here all day to remain in the lounge beyond 11:00 p.m.?

The guy glanced at him. If they are not residents. Correct.

Writers and creative delegates who have been here all day, who have attended the forums, who have taken part in the proceedings and who have contributed all necessary: am I to understand that they cannot continue talking after 11 o'clock?

They can go to each other's room, if they are residents. But not if they arent.

Wait now, said Charles, are you telling me . . . and off he went rephrasing what he had just been told by Mister dish towel. This is what state-registered politicians describe as negotiation. I left them to it. It was not my fight—the old Gaidhlig proverb, whatever it was, if ye cannay win then vamoose immediately.

Outside on the smokers' balcony a pack of cigarettes lay on a table near the garden railing and I was very tempted. I hadnt had a smoke for years. A little along from there, almost concealed in the shadows, were a couple of glasses and a bottle of red wine whose top was a regular metallic affair and did not require a squiggly screw thing. Whose bottle was it? Nobody's. Nobody was there. Through the French windows I saw them all. I found I was laughing. Nay wonder man it was fucking comical. This is the way of it. This is life. This is how it is. Dear oh dear. I unscrewed the top and poured myself one, fairly smallish. The way I did it reminded me of somebody, an actor, which one I dont know.

I sipped at the wine and stood by the garden railing. Who knows how it would go. Everything. I dont know. I would play it by ear. That thought was cheery.

The moon had appeared through the clouds. The clouds had dispersed allowing the moon to stand revealed, allowing the moon to appear. The moon appeared, in all its glory. And the moon was there, the moon was there where it always was, it was only us, our position had shifted.

17

The Vanity of the Poet-Professor

This morning I called in to the House to check out the general situation. If I didnt do this on a regular basis I wouldnt know shit, as they say on television. These things are fine once ye get used to them. It's just having to work it all out. Once we do this we cope. Campuses, departments, rooms and buildings, and all the pathways in between: I find my way through all that myself and expect so to do it all myself. One just wants to live one's life.

The Events Officer slid out from the shadows to greet me. Unfair unfair. He was just a young guy and he was doing his best. What a miserable job. When we finished passing the time of day I asked him the name of the university I was scheduled to visit that afternoon. This baffled him. I need to know its name so I'll know where to go. I said, If I dont know where to go then I wont know where to go. It's a two-part workshop session, 1:00 o'clock till 4. Where's the schedule and I'll show ye.

Oh no, no, that's eh ... He nodded quickly and returned to his desk, looked at a couple of things then removed himself to the rear of the room, where the landline was situated. The difficulty was that I could not eavesdrop the landline. Nevertheless, he used his own phone. So that was the intention, that I didnt hear the conversation. He turned his back to me when he was speaking but I knew it was bad news. When he came back it was to face the music. I stared at him sternly. He gulped and passed me his phone: It's the Director of the University Creative Studies Programme.

Oh god! I gulped in reply.

He's a Poet as well as a Professor. He's known as the Poet-Professor.

Goodness me! I returned him the phone. It's best you do the yapping.

But it's you he asked to talk to. He paused, then shrugged. If it makes it easier for you ...

Yeah, that is exactly what it does.

He turned from me to conceal his face, especially his lips in case I read them. Since I was less than six feet away I was privy to his end of the conversation which was composed of muttered repetition and anxious glances. The conclusion was straightforward, a predictable. Yer man—the Poet-Professor—had forgotten all about today's event.

Inner sighs aside this was another of those ego-free moments I had come to enjoy these past many days. Thank you lord, a trauma-free day of tranquil musings. I shall wander the canal bank and mayhap find a sandy beach, stroll that selfsame beach, watch the tide roll in, watch it roll away again, or else dump the dinky and go for a beer. In the afternoon? Yes he screamed, utter decadence, an afternoon beer! Then a couple of hours' kip and get on with my own work.

Meantime the Events Officer was still on the phone and nodding away, now half turning to display his face for my benefit. Another of these wee behavioural manouevres that folk have developed through constant smartphoning: Look at me I have nothing to hide.

He put down the phone, cleared his throat the better to fabricate and dissemble. The university will phone back in ten minutes, he said. There has been some error. However I should say everything is fine. Only complicated.

I laughed. I didnt smile, I laughed. Not a chortle, although it was nearly a chortle. I wish it had been a guffaw. He waited for me to regain composure. I smiled. Obviously yer man, the Poet-Professor has forgotten all about this momentous literary event.

No no it's an error, an oversight. He will phone back immediately. Would you like a coffee? The Events Officer gazed earnestly. Whatever age he was, who knows. They all seemed twenty-three. I laughed again but briefly, and cut it off. Life was too singular for meaningless laughter. Here I was in another country. It wasnt enough to endure humiliations, one had to cope with one's own humanity which in this instance consisted of a cheery sort of sympathy, which extended to the Events Officer who was no doubt doing his best. I said, Would *you* like a coffee?

He nearly fainted.

What would ye like?

Well eh ... Would a latté uh ...

Nay bother.

Thank you very much.

There was a wee takeaway cafe next door. I passed him in his latté then retired to the bench outside the cafe doorway with my green tea. It was a good bench and I enjoyed sitting there staring at the ground, seeing wheels roll past, shins and shoes; all different yins, the sizes and shapes. I think I fell asleep until water blotches on the napper, i.e. rain. Quite heavy rain too, so back inside to find the Events Officer in the middle of a telephone call, the latté untouched, pretending not to see me but guilty as fuck. He gestured at the receiver with an attempt at cheeriness. He covered the end and whispered to me: The Poet-Professor did not forget about your visit. Nobody did. It was a misunderstanding. He's been under intense pressure. Your event can be delayed from 1:00 to 2:30 p.m. and reduced from a two-part three-hour session to one session of an hour and a half.

I chuckled.

Honestly, he whispered, his hand still covering the receiver.

Postpone it. Tell him to postpone it. Tell him it will enhance my quality of life not to go. Tell him everything is sweet, everything is dandy, we'll do it another time, or not at all, as the case may be.

The Events Officer raised his hand to stop me in mid-flow, gesticulating at the phone to let me know somebody was talking into the other end of the line and he couldnt be expected to listen to both of us at the same time.

I shook my heid. Cancel the visit.

No no, he said, no. You can get to the venue for 2:15, 2:30 and that will be fine by them; you can relax for a bit before it begins. Honestly, they are very keen and are much looking forward to your visit.

With bated breath and mammoth expectation?

What?

Are they keyed up, buoyant, and full of pertinent queries?

What?

The guy's lying, I said, he's buying time.

He isnt really.

Yes he is. Dont defend him, defend me. His almighty ego requires to re-inflate. He will worry that I might spread the news about how neglectful he is, and lazy, and foreign students might take their funding elsewhere.

It's not like that, said the Events Officer.

Yes it is. From now until 2 o'clock the Poet-Professor will be making frantic phone calls to students past and present to rise from their sickbeds and walk. He will be instagramming, texting and facebooking; rushing hither and thither capturing likely faces, that he may save his own, which is the only motive for this going ahead. So he can save his reputation. The truth is I feel like punching him one on the mouth, I said, with a cheery grin.

The Events Officer cleared his throat but remained silent. He had one of these freshly scrubbed faces. Rubicund.

For the first time in my life the word "rubicund" found its rightful place within my vocabulary. It was a favourite word of my father's, You'll go far son, you have rubicund cheeks. Who's Rubi? I thought. Is she my real mum?

The Events Officer covered the receiver with his hand: The publicity is out he says, it has been advertised and everybody has received photocopies of the opening pages. Honestly, that's what he says and you can relax when you get there.

What did ye say?

You can relax when you get there.

Did he say that?

No, I, it was me.

I smiled, watching him.

I'm sorry, he said quickly.

Okay, I said, okay. I looked at my wristwatch. Three hours to spare, but pointless returning to the chalet. Or was it! Yes, it was the usual, chaos. I should have prepared. Spare blankets, feet warmers, books and hot bottles.

Mind you if I got to the university in double quick time I could park at the venue, find a pub and sloosh down a pint, then have a big meal to douse the afterglow, and a half hour doze at the wheel for luck. Or forget the beer, what about an Actual Meal such as one eats in the real world, with real potatoes, real gravy and unfrozen fresh vegetables; and a bit of fish or chicken. Usually I tried for a vegeterian option but raw scabby horses would have done me, a couple of rusty habaneros on the side.

Except now rain was lashing down. Constant fucking swish fucking swish. The dinky had a pair of these toytown wipers that made a mad racket on the upturn and went fucking bonkers on the down. No lyric came but strange noises gurgled from my ears and they rhymed with havers. How come havers? God knows, and coupled with the nay springs what-dye-call-it, the under-carriage that bounces.

My brains are addled. It had thin wee wheels as well and that was a worry. Imagine having to change a tyre. I hadnt checked the boot for a spare. Maybe there wasnay one. What would I do? Nothing. It was a hired car. That was one job that was not mine. Phone the hire firm and ask for a breakdown service.

When I entered the town the street led over a river and farther along I found an indoor market. I stayed in the car waiting for It to becalm itself. But It didnt, It didnt. What is this "It"? asked Thales and now look what happened. Lashings of water. Who was that? You never step in the same river twice. So what man I made a dash for it.

The indoor market was great. Cheery women serving local cheeses that were spectacular. A decent diner doing a reduced price two-course lunch for Seniors, with tea and buttered breid. Also I found a drapery stall selling things like underwear and t-shirts, socks and dungarees. Fantastic! I bought a bunnet and a buy-one-get-one-free pack of plastic safety-razors. Jesus christ man I felt like wrapping the place up and posting it hame. What a town!

Then I arrived at the university.

The rain was worser. I unwrapped the bunnet and dispensed with the wrappings. I sat in the car an extra five minutes. Imagine the fishermen: Batten down the hatches there, aye aye skipper, the gunnels are lowping water! What is It doing? Galeforce storms cap'n.

I tugged the bunnet down ower one's lugs. It was the wind tae. It was fucking howling. Along from the carpark they had one of these map-board things with a map of the campus: You are here!

Aye but who am I! he screamed inwardly, battening down the hatches with indecent haste and with ferocious intent, as the gale force wind howled him athwart the lawn, thence perambulating in an easterly direction, upon the door of whose venue was tacked an A4 page:

TODAY!!

@ 3 pm

"Banker Prize Winner"
Reads From Book.
Jack Proctor

Ah. Publicity.

The door was locked and the rain washed us all, sweeping its rivulets across the college grounds, the rawness of

Back at the fucking notice-board I located the Department of English Studies and the office of the Poet-Professor Director et cetera. I chapped the door.

He opened it. Jack Proctor I presume: come in. Now I apologize for the earlier misunderstanding. Huh! Still raining I see! Obviously I had not forgotten about your visit. No one had. Huh! The students have prepared. I distributed photocopies of the opening pages.

What of?

He guided me to the seat in front of his desk, placed his phone in front of him and for much of the time glanced at the book lying there. Your novel, he said.

Which one? I've written a few.

Of course. You know students Jack success and career-building. Huh! The Banker Prize Jack, it must turn a few heads? Students are students. He rubbed his hands. The photocopied handout should suffice. He sighed. What a day it's been. His attention drifted to the phone, and he scrolled a few moments.

What do ye mean "suffice"? I said.

Suffice? The general picture Jack language and so on I would have thought. Huh! His attention was still to the phone, his eyebrows rising and falling.

I chuckled. When you say "a general picture?" A general picture of the general picture might be a more apt description.

He raised his head and blinked at me. His ears were waggling. But maybe I imagined this. Fresh bumps definitely appeared on his temples and lower cranium. I knew what he was doing! He was thinking! He was focusing on this other human being who appeared to have thoughts of his own!

Maybe he had a hearing problem. It occurred to me that he suffered a liver complaint of some description. He leaned towards me as though about to impart a secret, then wagged his finger at me. Now Jack, he said, what I am wondering— and you may have something to say on the matter—should we report the matter of the photocopied pages? Huh!

What do ye mean?

Oh well now Vernon becomes apoplectic at the thought of lost revenue. Vernon? Vernon Humphrey? You know Vernon?

No.

Oh. I am surprised.

What is he a novelist?

Oh no no. No. Vernon is a poet Jack and a very fine poet at that. And with a full-on reputation let me tell you. Huh! He and I have been friends for a good thirty years. But you know as well as I that unless you pass on the information yourself no one will find out the truth of it!

The truth of it, of what, what do you mean?

The photocopied pages Jack not unless we inform your publisher. Huh!

What're ye talking about?

Who pays?

Well I'm no goni pay

No no no.

Ye dont expect me to pay for your photocopies?

Not at all Jack not at all, we did it for you.

For me? Ye didnt do anything for me, what are ye talking about?

To make sure, that's all, for the students I should say, huh, and I worried about the little office girl who photocopied the pages.

Pardon?

Your shall we say liberal use of the Anglo-Saxon Jack I thought she might take offence. She never reads photocopied pages, apparently. I dont believe her, I suspect it depends on the subject-matter. Huh.

. . .

So we dont inform your publisher? Huh? What do you think?

I dont think anything. It's got nothing to do with me. Just do what ye do. I'm the writer, I just write the damn novels.

Indeed, indeed. The dosh you chaps earn Jack unlike we poor poets; impecunious, penniless. Vernon is lyrical on the subject. The backbone of English literature yet we earn hardly a bean.

Is this a jape of some description?

Oh that it were Jack oh that it were! He chuckled, his attention diverted by the phone. He scrolled hurriedly, while muttering, Democracy in action I dare say. Huh. No place in fiction for those who know the basic rules of grammar and are capable of spelling the Queen's English. What say you Jack, a literary minefield eh, the inappropriate use of the Anglo-Saxon, or Doric might you call it? The old Scotch language transformed into the new. Huh! How valid it is I dont know. You call it Lallans Jack but I cant say I'm in agreement.

This is getting worse.

All the same, he said, you must find it a little ironic—as a proud Scot Jack which I know you are—attacking the so-called establishment yet more than willing to receive its rewards, and who can blame you for that Jack a rather tasty prize of how much did you say? Many many thousands, was it not, the old Banker?

He was shaking his head in wonder, slipping the phone into his side jacket pocket. I do have a question before we leave, he said, apropos the demonic. And I say this with the best will in the world, if I may, on restricted vocabularies and their inherent uh how can we say it how can we say it—the *prima facie* being the obvious, the repetitive and restricted language of African-American blacks and the motherfucking this that and the next thing if they call that language, apparently, nowadays I believe they do—what say you Jack, for you it's the vernacular? or do you subscribe

Look, I said, I cant really deal with your eh lack of knowledge, it would be better if ye just stopped eh ye know talking I mean, it's hurting me right now.

No no, he said, this is not in any sense uh I was only uh when I say subscribe

and off he went offering an explanation of some sort which I was unable to render sensible. It was an odd experience. I was defeated. On the scale of humanity I ranked so lowly that he neglected even to disguise from me his lack of intellectual penetration. How many times does one have to endure it? How many times would such extraordinary nonsense knock me speechless? His comments were more worthy of a hammer to the head than a sharp retort. He should not have been let loose within ten miles of a student. If prisons had any validity he would have been locked up. Oh but he was tough as old boots. That is why he was Professor Director of Penitentiary Studies at the Institution of Higher Vomitological Humbuggery.

Facing me down in this one-to-one manner.

He did. He defeated me. Could it get worse? Of course. He touched me on the shoulder, propelling me towards the doorway and outside the building he patted me on the arm. It was 2:55. On the journey here I had wondered how I might structure my talk with the students. Defend myself at all costs was the answer. The students deserved the benefit of the doubt. It was not their fault a fascist arsehole controlled the place, filling their head with a load of embittered fantasies about so-called writers winning sums of tasty dosh for so-called novels written in the language of illiteracy, the poorest excuse for English it had been his bad fortune ever to read; not that he ever had, or would.

The students were checking me out; all six of them, seated round a big table, including a mother with a babe-in-arms.

The Poet-Professor sat to the side of the class, about twelve feet from me. That was okay. I would begin with a short reading lasting no more than ten minutes. For the remaining fifty I would convey to the students that beyond these walls and the authoritarian ravings of the Director of their Creative Writing Programme there might exist Art. If that was the case then they, as human beings, had the potential to engage in its practice.

He began his introduction with an apology: two students would have to leave after twenty minutes—Jason and Luke: they had a class to attend. Both were very keen to hear what Mister Proctor—Jack if I may—had to say for the next twenty minutes. People here have all heard of Mister Proctor's novel and if they look to their handout they can see the gist of it here in the opening pages. I can tell you that Jack and I have had a rather tasty debate of our own, and perhaps we can pick up on this later.

He said it with a grin, glancing at me in conspiratorial fashion. I barely noticed, being engrossed in staring at the surface of the table. The babe-in-arms was uttering occasional squawks, squeaks and squeals. Dont worry, I said to the mother, it wont affect me in the slightest.

Thanks, she said but she continued to look nervous.

And now if we look to Jack's handout, said the Poet-Professor, and he gestured to me that I might continue.

Well of course it is not my handout, I said. I could never dishonour my work in such a fashion. I must inform you all that I have written more than one novel. This is no secret. It tells you on the inside cover of the actual book, for those of you who look inside actual books rather than photocopies. I happen not to have a copy of that actual book with me this actual afternoon but I do have two actual short story collections and I shall begin by reading a couple of actual stories. They are short. The first runs to between 4 and 4.5 minutes.

There was an old-fashioned clock on the wall with a loud tick which was good and gave the whole atmosphere. I smiled. I like that clock, I said, it reminds me of "The Tell-Tale Heart": anybody here know it?

I stood up from my chair and stepped back from the table that I might begin to proper dramatic effect. Then I gave the title of the story, and I began reading it, much to the astonishment of the students and their Poet-Professor. God's teeth! What was the chap doing? Was he reading them a story? Yes! Out loud? Yes! And with as much eye-contact as possible, forcing an intellectual and emotional confrontation. How excrutiating! Yes.

And so I read, with dramatic wee gestures, in a voice roughly similar to my own, heh heh, intoning with undue malevolence now freed by the absence of my dearest enemy, the doctor who, having gone to fetch a most mysterious alcohol, left me alone, alone and I saw then the studded mahogany chest with inlaid panels of walnut or alder, the grain of the wood producing strange shapes and diagrams; and as I looked, dear reader, I beheld the dreaded goat's head, executed by a master hand, upon which I instantly turned my back. 'Twas Pan himself, as the old traditions of antiquity had portrayed him, Pan, whom the christian ages had transformed into Satan. It was he alright! I cried, holding my right fist aloft, and here I stopped due to a disturbance from behind and to my side.

I watched the Poet-Professor rising stealthily from his seat, crouching and creeping his way to the door, head lowered and shoulders hunched. I watched him click open the door. Two students were there; a male and female. They came in and the Poet-Professor closed the door quietly. He waved to me, still crouching, pointing the students to vacant chairs then creeping a return to his own.

All gazed in my direction.

I closed the book of stories.

What on earth was he doing they screamed in ghastly silence. Nothing. I returned to my place at the table and lifted a different book. I scanned the contents' list, leafed through the pages in leisurely fashion. I found a shorter story; one that lasted less than two pages.

So, I said, this other story I now am going to read, is even shorter and I have to advise you that this has as its beginning the year of Napoleon's Russian campaign, when the fabled Rabbi of Apt visited the Maggid of Koznitz on the Feast of the Revelation. He found him lying on his sick-bed, but that his careworn face quickened with a strange, very strange expression of indecision. And how are you? asked the visitor.

Oh I am a soldier now, sang the Maggid of Koznitz.

Ha ha ha ha ha.

The disturbance from behind, the movement to my side. I halted. The faces looking to the door.

This time the Poet-Professor remained in his seat, his face somehow shadowed such that I could not discern its features. But the door banged open and shut with a vibrating clatter. Enter a student; a gangly young fellow of some $8x + 4$ inches (let $x = 10$) vertically, wearing a beanie hat, a bowtie and peculiar sandals. The Poet-Professor signalled at a vacant seat. The student moved into there as swiftly as he was able, knocking his knee in the process. Aargh, he groaned and rubbed at it.

The faces looked to me.

I closed the book. I returned to the table and lifted the first book. I leafed through the pages. I studied the contents. I leafed through more pages. I smiled to the students. Do not be alarmed, I growled evenly.

The infant child moaned. Beyond the walls of the room there was a sudden crack of thunder. A shafted strike of lightning struck with a fervor of unwordly velocity. It was by now fifteen thirty hours and the hush in the room was deathly. I cleared my throat and perused the contents again. But I knew then what I would read, thus prolonging the pause, gazing at a point above the heads of the students, and raising my right hand, extending that forefinger. And I said to them severally yet as individuals alone and in each their uniquity: And I saith unto you … this is known as a deathly hush. And what you are receiving is Art. Search deeply into this silence and ye shall discover it. I kept my right hand aloft, moving my arm in an arc.

Most students recognized that whatever psychological state I was in I appeared to regard it as not abnormal, or not not normal, that it may have been an effect of a blunder, that this blunder may not have been self-induced, that an air of mortification was abroad.

Now, I said.

But the mother and babe-in-arms rose from the table. I am so sorry, she said, and swiped upwards her belongings with one hand then dashed to freedom with the baby in the other. The Poet-Professor cleared his throat and followed her from the room, either to commiserate or deter other leavetakers, or latecomers.

I gave him a moment. When he returned I said: Okay. I shall now read a very very short story. I shall stand with my back to the door so no one can get in or out. I chuckled. Is this not hilarious!

No one answered.

Fom the doorway I called to them:

If a heavy-armed or a light-armed (soldier) has been taken prisoner on "the way of the king" and a trader ransoms him, and brings him back to his city; then, if his House contain sufficient for his ransom, he personally shall pay for his liberation. If his House do not contain sufficient, the temple of his city shall pay. If the temple of his city have not the means, the great House shall ransom him. His field, his orchard, and his House shall not be given for his ransom.

Thank you, I said and returned to my seat, checking my watch at the same time: ten minutes to four. Now, I said, the work of certain writers is significant in respect of the decolonization of Standard English Literary Form, of Imperial English and how this freedom might be applied within our own work as writers.

A student raised her hand and pointed out two others. Excuse me, she said. We're doing a class in linguistics and the language of literary signification!

Good stuff, I said.

Approaching 4:15 p.m. the Poet-Professor attracted my attention while the same young lady sought to explain the relevance of Clerk Maxwell's formulations re thermodynamics to the work of certain Japanese artists influenced by Edgar Allan Poe and the later French Symbolists. The Poet-Professor tugged my jacket sleeve. He spoke quietly: This is a time for books Jack, huh.

My books?

He pointed at my bag. Did you bring books with you?

Pardon?

I mean to sell, did you bring books to sell?

No. They're too heavy. I only write thick ones.

That's a pity, he said, then turned to address the students directly. I am sure I speak for all of us when I say how much we have enjoyed Mister Proctor's talk, and how fine it would be if Mister Proctor would read another example of his work to close the session.

No, I said.

The silence lengthened. I paid no attention to the Poet-Professor so whether or not he was staring aghast I have no idea.

I addressed the students with a cheery smile. What if I were a musician? I said. Could someone ask for an *example* of my work? What does it mean for a musician to give an example of his or her work? What do we expect to obtain from a composer when we ask for an example of his or her work? What if I was a painter? What if I was an abstract expressionist. Let me tell ye that once on a television talk-show a famous American painter was once the first guest on. One of his recent paintings had become notorious for reasons I forget—mayhap the abstract expressionist equivalent to "swearie words." It was most informative. The television talkshow host walked a tight line between ingratiating himself with the audience and being outright sarcastic to the abstract expressionist. In reference to the painting which had occasioned the negative publicity he said to the artist, Hey man, could you tell us, what does it actually mean?

Instead of getting irritated the painter chuckled. Well now, he said, I shall tell you what it means. Just hang on a minute. Take an advertising break. I shall return!

He got up and left the studio. The talkshow host gave a world-weary rather than cynical wave to camera and studio audience, and moved on to the second guest, a famed theologian. Twenty minyooetts later, there was a disturbance and the heads of the studio audience all turned to the left. Here came the abstract expressionist with two assistants carrying one very large framed canvas which he displayed to the camera: This is what it means, he said.

Everybody stared. And, of course, this new painting resembled precisely the notorious piece of abstract art that was causing all the fuss; resembled it so precisely one was left wondering if indeed it was the original or had the artist painted two simultaneously for just such a demonstration and, if the latter, then what do we mean by demonstration? It was an amazing moment in the history of US art, US theology and US television. So there you are, I said, I shall leave y'all now. Beyond that? Yackety yackety yak, the mouse ran up the clack.

Thank you Jack, said the Poet-Professor.

A pleasure, I said, gathering my stuff.

He walked with me to the carpark. Halfway there he attempted to defuse the situation with a little chitchat. He gave me his card, and he said: If ever you're in this part of the world Jack whether for a visit or literary event, you should give me a call. Huh.

I smiled, about to walk on but instead grasped his left wrist firmly. He was a strong individual, stronger than me, but I had had a sudden insight. When I raised my right hand he stepped back apace, fearing the worst. I let go his left wrist and grinned. I wagged my right forefinger in his face: You know precisely what you're getting for your dinner tonight. Am I right?

He made no answer at first, dear reader, but then he smiled as though weary of it all.

18

Dont mess with Miles

Oh god it was lights out in the world and I had found this
radio station somewhere, who knows how. The guy doing
the show was quite elderly. He was a musician himself and
like most everyone else on this station, was a volunteer. The
operation worked on that basis, raising money via individual subscription and donation. This was no principle this
was a basis that got the job done. These people were in love
with music and with the musicians who create it. So they
ended here on this wee radio station not only working for
nothing but paying for the privilege. I heard stuff here I
never heard elsewhere; bands and folk I thought dead and
gone forever. One specialized in Hawaiian music; one in
Celtic, another in west and southern African; one from the
Indian Subcontinent, Mexican Ranchero, Native-American;
be-bop, doo-wop & hip hop. This night the old guy was playing a composition by Miles Davis. Several seconds into the
track he broke in, stopped it playing. I thought his machine
had broken down. It hadnt. The old guy was talking softly,
No no no, no. No, no man no, no no noohh old Miles no, he
would turn in his grave man I cannot do it I am sorry folks,
I began this too too soon man way too soon, old Miles, oh
no, ssh, ssh ... here now here now we just go easy, eaassy,
ssh, counting eight ...

  And silence. Nothing for a beat of eight, allowing this
most proper portion of space which is peace,

    peace,

  then the quiet early sound of that horn beginning bip
bip bip bip bip just where Miles intended it should. He

intended that quiet early sound to begin in, or begin from, silence. It required silence or it could not begin. It began from silence and Miles relied on that. Fucking hell. Can ye imagine. Break down that word "begin," be-gin. I see it as "be in" and "being-in." That was something. Respect for the music, for someone's art. And of course fun, it was fun. You felt like Miles was there and watching and he was a quirky edgy bastard and would have been grumping and groaning. Of course he was there, yes he was there. That was his music. How could he be anywhere else? The artist becoming present. And the musician-deejay understood all that.

I was lying there sprawled on the armchair, no curtains on the window, watching faraway airplanes, seeing the night, feeling very much alone, really. I was alone, but I was kind of liking that, away doing some kind of event and Hannah not able to come with me, home with the kids, and I had the uisqué in my hand and I knew about him, fuck, man, this guy he really did know, he knew, he knew. My eyes were wet. That was the comical side, how that deejay was in anguish at the very idea of messing up Miles' music: Oh jesus christ what have I done! Miles will know what I have done, he will know man—fuck!!!

> Do not tell me the guy is dead.
> I walk on sharp needles,
> but not too sharp,
> not sharp at all,
> almost blunt, sometimes.

> I dont care for countries.
> What is a country
> that is not a country,
> a place for dispossessed people,
> what is that?

Who I am and what am I
and what does it matter anyhow,
what I say,
the lights are out
the music plays.

This is art
how we are
in the here
in the now
when one gets the chance,
when one gets the chance

Och no man, fuck that, getting the chance, as though,
yes master, thank you for setting me free. To hell with that,
fucking fuck off to bed, good night man, making me laugh;
me myself, a dram and the radio, full stop, end chapter.

19

On We Go

Okay, but in music ye find versions of the same pieces all the time; different lyrics and arrangements, different "takes," maybe using fewer or different instruments; but they are easy to recognize versions of the same piece. Any writer working on computer finds it impossible not to revise. Each time we open a document we confront an earlier draft. How can ye not revise! Fucking impossible.

What is a perfect story, a perfect painting, a perfect piece of music? What is an imperfect story? It is different from a story that doesnt work. If there is a different version of a story can there be a different verson of a painting? Does that apply equally to an abstract expressionist painting? Can there be two or more versions of the "same one?"

If ye lay out the work of some artists and do it in a particular order what ye see is a series. The different parts of the series, all the different workings, might even be described as "sketches," and then at the end of the series there is one final thing that is bigger than the other ones and gets called "the finished work. In galleries ye find sketches toward a finished work exhibited beside the finished work. But what if there is no final piece that we can call "the finished work?" All we have there is a series of "sketches" that are related. Then it ends and a new "series" begins. The artist has not necessarily completed the series, but simply moved on. Hang all the sketches in their own time along a corridor and ye stay in the movement, follow the corridor and ye follow the sequence.

20

In Time

The four post-graduate students staring at me. Six originally but two had upped and gone. I shrugged. What else was there. I was being honest.

The thing is ye see I dont think yer stories carry enough weight. I said, I dont want you to worry about it, I just want ye to go more deeply. But I suppose that means trying harder. I want to help ye all to grasp that the creation of art cannot be removed from ourselves as individuals, as unique human beings. Ye make discoveries about commitment, I said, the nature of commitment and it can force through yer own—free ye towards it—commitment I'm talking about. As we know in great art, there is nothing without it, without commitment. Yous are post-graduate students so I make no apologies for raising art in this way because this is what ye're supposed to be doing is creating art, making art. The people whose letters I gave ye lived and died in pursuit of justice in one form or another—artists as well as political activists: sometimes there is no distinction. They should be heroes to all you young people. It is a surprise to me that this isnay the case. Although really it is no surprise at all, I dont live in dreamland. Although maybe I am in the wrong job!

I *was* hired to do a job, as it happens, and maybe I'm not doing the job correctly, the one they thought I would do. Imagine hiring a plumber to fix your shower but instead of doing that he fits a new window? Fuck! Ye're standing there watching. Instead of plumbing in the new bath the guy opens a window and starts inserting a new sill. He may well be a plumber but he does carpentry jobs when he feels like it. You've heard of the novelist John Montgomery?

The four post-graduate students stared at me. Their tutor focused on what I was saying.

Have any of ye read him?

Perhaps without being aware of it, said the tutor.

I havent myself. I may some day but I doubt it. But I have read his elder brother, whose work I do enjoy. The revolutionary subtext of common-sense philosophy was an interest of his and he wrote about that.

Nobody answered. The tutor was frowning at me

Does anybody want to say anything?

Shonagh said, I dont know what this is about.

Good, well ... Anybody else? No? Okay. Let's shuffle off the mortal coil on our way to the exit. People do find art difficult, I know that. They offer all kinds of foolishness that they might be excused work. Oh but I dont want to tamper with that first rush of creation! I might destroy the essence of that original thing! I have to leave it the way it is. Bla bla. I'm hoping to show ye there's a different way; we proceed towards knowledge through knowledge, making use of our full power at any one moment. We dont have an end. Otherwise we cant work on full power. No design, no map, no theory; nothing except who we are and what we are at this precise moment. And that is where it is. Artists move to truth in different ways from philosophers. There is reason and there is imagination. It's an old way of seeing. But nothing wrong in that. We get praised to the High Heavens by people whose primary experience has nothing to do with the process and who know nothing of the process. What they do is praise an end. The end is all they see, whether good, bad or indifferent.

I think I shall stop here unless somebody has a question? I smiled to encourage a response and I waited. I looked to the tutor. Any question at all, I said. And I should add that because a story is conventional does not mean it is not good. There is room for all stories.

I was going to say that yez all can make decisions later about whether or not the creation of art is for you. But on the other hand, it isnt really a decision, ye just find it is what ye're doing.

So, anyway, all the best.

ii

Earlier the tutor had shown me into the room. She had introduced me to the six post-graduate students and they listened politely. Two were males and four were females. Stories by each of the six had been sent to me a few days earlier. Now here we were.

I handed each of the six an A4 page on both sides of which were my notes, written in pencil. I said: I read through your stories and thought it an idea to approach the matter as though I were not only a fellow writer but an editor, doing a bit of line-editing and a bit of just I dont know what ye might call it, tips, analysis, advice; anything I thought pertinent.

Have a look at the notes and comments I made and we'll just maybe talk about some of it in general terms. I'm aware there's only today and we cannot go through each individually. If I was based here I would be meeting ye all on a regular basis. But that isnay the case and I'm very aware that to make a difference I have to charge at it, and I do want to make a difference. Okay? You have to trust me.

They were already perusing the notes I had made. Their tutor smiled then watched for their response. They were engrossed. One of the young women—Raina—looked at me in disbelief, then at the young fellow sitting near to her: Aidan, he glanced at her. He laid his A4 page down next to his story and tried to smile ironically but he was upset, far too upset. He was unable to speak. He peered again at my notes and comments. Raina watched Aidan who was working hard to focus, his elbows on the table and propping up his head, his hands covering his ears.

I often sit like that myself so there was nothing peculiar about it. It just seems peculiar when ye describe it. I waited for the other five students to lay their pages on the table but they too kept their heads down, as though making sense of it all. And that is what was happening. That is what they were doing. The post-graduate students were in the state of comprehension.

Their tutor had got up from her seat and was standing, arms folded. She smiled but she was anxious, wondering what was happening.

I said to the students: Okay everybody, When you submit a finished story to your editors they will pass it on to other editors, those who do this line by line stuff, which is what really you need and what you want. A good editor is a great thing, they challenge you on why you do one thing rather than another. As you see I read the stories you submitted to me and I've given you notes and comments as though I were an editor, and of course I am an editor, in the sense that every writer is an editor. Each of us has to edit what we write, we write something down then maybe choose another word, like hitting the find & replace buttons and having to go back again; constantly editing, revising.

Raina and Aidan were looking at me directly.

Why did you send us the reading list? asked the girl whose name was Shonagh.

I thought it important.

But why?

I smiled.

She waited for me to add something but when she realized I was not going to add something she asked, Why these people?

I thought it would be useful.

It wasnt. Really. It wasnt! Shonagh shook her head, glanced at the tutor, expressing bewilderment.

Yes but your life isnt over yet. What you might gain from getting into the stuff I sent can take as long as you like to happen, and it could last as long as you continue making art.

I dont follow.

Maybe ye should trust me on it.

Why? She looked again at the tutor. I dont understand.

The tutor raised her eyebrows. There was a silence. The tutor now smiled but certainly it was uneasy. The silence continued. I shrugged, hoping this might alleviate the tension in some way, but it didnt. The student Aidan was acting oddly, he had become emotional. Maybe it was rage. I think it was. He was shaking his head, avoiding the tutor and other students but not wanting to look at me either. His head was twisting about and his face was screwed up.

The tutor was worried.

What's wrong? I asked her.

She merely shook her head.

Aiden laughed abruptly and addressed me directly: You gave us these letters by people, why did you give us these letters by people?

As I said to Shonagh, I thought it would be useful.

I dont know what you mean by useful. I cant believe you did it, and this too, he said, indicating the A4 page: What is this?

Ah now! I smiled in a manner I hoped was confidential. I am here trying to convey the idea that everything that is happening at this moment is essential to the class. Including your own emotional condition; perhaps you can reflect on that. If so it will help you become less upset. It's good practice, and leads to the possibility of liberation, in creating art I mean. I've been trying to draw something out ye.

I addressed the three post-graduate students who so far had kept out of it: Do you think I'm being presumptuous?

Huh, said Aidan.

Calm down, I said.

You gave us a reading list, said Shonagh.

Ssh, I said. I focused on the other three. What do you think?

They glanced at one another, and also at the tutor. The student called Marcella stared at my notes and comments. Do you think it's cluttered? she said.

Yes, ye need to cut it right down.

Tautologous?

Yes, I said, tautologous. I mean you're saying the same thing three or four times only in different ways, 'shouted loudly exclamation mark exclamation mark,' ye dont need all that. 'Shouted' is enough, a shout is loud, it's a loud verbal act; it's not a place for double exclamation marks either because ye dont need them, keep that up yer sleeve.

Oh God! cried Aidan.

Raina held up her hands in a gesture of surrender. This is surreal!

I said, What's wrong?

You're just doing it to stamp your authority, Aidan said, giving us things to read about the Asian guy who turned his back on all that to do all this and then that woman he went with and didnt care about stuff and the other one too, the criminal guy, so what if he was like not a criminal and if he was killed and his young brother was killed and like executed or whatever and then if he was not a criminal but a political guy in jail writing his poetry so what, just so what? So he got like executed, so what? seventeen years old is old enough to know better asking us to read letters and stuff if that's his brother so what? this is about Creative Writing and it's not politics if that's what it is.

This is a Creative Writing workshop, said Shonagh.

You're just like I dont know, I dont know what it is. Aidan said, You, just like what you are, why you're doing this just like stamping your authority?

I pointed at the notes and comments I had given him. These are the comments and the notes I've made on your story individually. You should read them, then go through them. It matters to me if you dont.

Huh! cried Aidan.

I would be sorry to think you dont know what being a writer is, if you dont know what writing is, if ye

Aidan had turned to the tutor while I was talking. This is just a joke, he said.

Aidan, she said.

No, he said.

Aidan

No, he said, it's a joke.

Calm down son, I said, ye're being cheeky, this is a

Are you kidding me? Are you seriously—are you kidding me?

Ssh. Dont interrupt me when I'm talking.

Aidan gaped at me.

I was still talking. Ye interrupted me. Dont do that to people. Not in a group like this. Ye need to calm down, calm down.

Aidan was up from his seat and lifting his rucksack, stuffing in his stuff and he strode from the room. The door banged shut behind him. The tutor was horrified, gazing at the door and then at me, but not the other students. Maybe she was avoiding them although why I dont know. Aidan had left the A4 page with my notes and comments on his story.

By now Raina was standing and gathering her things together. She too left the notes and comments I had made on her story. She opened the door, looked along the corridor.

The tutor said, Has he gone?

Yes. He wont come back. Raina shrugged and gave a brief salute to the other students, and away she went.

The tutor said to me: Aidan's been offered a two-book contract.

Oh.

He's a fine young writer.

I chuckled. I said to the remaining four graduate students. These notes and comments are there on the page I've given ye. Some ye'll disagree with. It doesnt matter. Ye need to go where ye go but just be aware this is me saying it to ye; ye need to strip away the inconsequential stuff and see what's what, if ye're left with anything, then ye build. And remember the reading list I gave ye. I want ye to see commitment and maybe recognize what it might amount to. Not to "understand" it but to encounter it. Ye need to face up to it. Ye need to know such a thing exists. This why I gave ye the list.

Yes, why was that? asked the tutor. People mentioned it. I said that of course it was your class for the day but all the same I did wonder.

Wonder what?

Why you asked me to forward on the reading list?

So the students here might read it.

I did wonder.

Did you. Well okay, I thought people should see commitment. Not to "understand" it so much, to encounter it. That is what exists in the world. People need to know such a thing exists, and that includes writers and artists. Encountering commitment at this level stimulates the passions, it can arouse tremendous emotion in individuals.

The tutor's head shifted slightly, she squinted at me, in full concentration.

iii

Their tutor had emailed me the six stories as attachments a few days before the meeting. I printed out the manuscripts in the House office and browsed through them there and then. I didnt find them wearisome exactly. There is always something. The word "lacklustre" is uppermost. I wasnt meeting the post-graduate students for another seven days so I emailed their tutor a brief reading list and asked that she might forward it on to them. I hoped they would browse through a couple on the list before we met. They had had enough time to google the names and go where it led.

It was the same for me. I had to go through their stories more thoroughly, the students, and more thoroughly again. And again, and again.

Who knows what had been drilled into them, apart from the sense of triumphalism we associate with Anglo-American letters. The best way to handle this kind of thing, in my experience, is by treating students' work as though I was a "real editor," and do a line by line on them. I didnt see any way out of this. Also it would allow me to respond in a manner that was somehow positive, given that it suggested room for improvement. When the day arrived the tutor was there to greet me. She was very surprised by the amount of work I had done on the students' manuscripts. Sorry about that, she said, I asked them to send finished work.

They did send finished work. I wanted to treat them as though I was an actual publisher's editor, as well as an experienced writer.

Oh, okay.

It can be very useful, I mean practical.

Very much so, yes, I agree. They did have a publisher's editor here two months ago, along with a literary agent, a very respected one.

Ah.

You also sent the students a reading list?

Yes.

They would have been more interested in what you had to say about their own stories!

Of course.

You obviously read them. This is why you uh ... She looked again at the A4 pages with my notes and comments. This is their own stories. Yes ... she nodded. They are post-grads. Three have won prizes. They're all published.

Good.

You know the way it is, they accept the comments of their tutors but will presume this is tempered by paro-chiality. Award-winning authors such as yourself are of a different order altogether and they will take to heart what you say. Congratulations by the by.

Thanks.

Shall we go and meet the six students? she said, smiling. They've been looking forward to it.

Yes, I said.

21

All is not Lost

I was up through the night, as was my wont. I wanted to work but was not able to work. I thought perhaps I could invent the fable. A different form of fable. I was finding that my reading matter had regressed. It seemed I was returning not to my youth but to an uncluttered vision of what I was up to: making stories.

Is that what I was up to?

Yes.

I loved sitting at the window.

Did ye?

Yes, but it was too dark and I couldnt see fuck all.

Hard luck.

Yeah.

I thought maybe I would make myself a green tea, or else a cup-a-soup, I was kind of peckish. But Hannah would just

Add a packet of cheese 'n onion and ye've a three-course meal man 4 in the a.m.'s.; aint that somepin, that is somepin and sompin aint nuttin,

oh yeah.

22

Land Ahoy!

Two groups of children: the first group chased by the second, headlong down a wee hill they arrive at a burn and go jumping across from boulder to boulder. The burn is shallow in places but in other places very deep, dangerously deep, and the children move fast, zigzagging across to avoid flung stones and arrows of hostile warriors, the sharp-toothed gaping mouths of crocodiles and a variety of venomous predators. Those who hesitate are lost, they lose impetus; without the impetus there are no moves to be made, the unsteady boulder is simply unsteady, the submerged stone too slippery. There is no route except the run, the run is the route. You cannot figure such a thing in advance. For children there is never time anyway. You are always being chased by big boys and big girls, by irate teachers, parents and bureaucrats from the arts and tourist industry, by politicians, employers and State authorities. It would be difficult to figure an advance route anyway. Those who stop to figure the route dont do the run. The first group of children would never escape if they stood at the burn trying to map a course, "discover the pattern," when behind them the pounding of feet, the pounding of feet; here come the chasing parties. Bang, they are off and jumping oh from here to here and here to here oh careful careful. Look he is doing it! Oh I am doing it. But it is dangerous; cries from behind, who cares, on ye go because if you dont if you dont, but you are making it you are making it, oh from here to here from here to here greasy greasy oh for fuck sake nearly slipping in there and even your foot splashing and stumbling again, your ankle twisting but righted again by the agility of the movement and you pound on, the speed of the flight carrying you on, on through assorted dangers.

The children move swiftly, their feet finding boulder after boulder each steady enough to maintain the impetus; the unsteady few remain in place long enough for the running jump to continue: these unsteady boulders would be dislodged by somebody standing on them for any length of time, but dislodgment does not happen with the children's passing movements, and the same applies to wet stone; the children's feet are not upon them long enough to slip, the speed carries them, and they make it across to safety. They laugh back to the chasing group who now arrive at the burn.

All the chasing children and other parties, the art police, irate teachers and parents, art and tourist industry officers, they have all halted on the shore and are peering intently at the stones in the burn, trying to figure how the hell you did the run, and they are becoming more and more agitated, hopping from foot to foot and not able to concentrate properly because even if they could it would be no good, no good, not now the bird has flown, you have escaped, they cannot follow, it is useless even to try; they cannot even fling stones at you. They shake their fist in your direction! Until the next time! they shout. But the first group of children are too far away; not even their voices carry, the fucking wind is too strong. They enjoyed the run. Are the baddies following, have they waded across? But they cannot be bothered waiting to see. Why? Because further excitements lie ahead, look, what is that is that a secret passageway, it looks like a secret passageway, a kind of shadowy opening, fucking hell, what is that, is it a cave leading to buried treasure, what is it, just behind that bush and the clump of thick trees, the children start walking quickly ... now running, and headlong, the impetus carrying them once more.

Meanwhile the pursuing group are still there, still

hesitating. There are too many stones, and some look wet and slippery, many are loose, dislodged. They know there must be 'good' stones there otherwise how did the first group manage across? But they cannot see the way. If it is not to do with good stones it must be a certain pattern, if they can only find the pattern, is it two stones to the right then one to the left, back three to the right and one jump over! Oh my, what the fuck is it! Is it binary! oh oh oh oh one one one—how many fucking ones to a zero, is there a pattern what is the pattern we cannot find the fucking pattern and without that pattern. Perhaps it is a code! What is the code! They rush around the bank of the burn looking for the code, the Keeper of the Code—is there a Keeper of the Code? Praise be to the Keeper of the Code! Who holds the key? Maybe somebody will give us a key! What is the key to it all? Maybe it is magic! Maybe there is a magic word? Abracadabra! Hallelujah! What unlocks the mystery? Maybe if we sing praise-songs to the Keeper he will advise us. Praise be to the Great Being of all Mysteries. They talk about all this on their way home from the burn.

An hour later the first group of children return from their further adventures and have to recross the burn. There has been a little rain but not much. Even so the water is running higher. They halt by the bank of the burn. They cannay see their stones, the right stones, the stones that were there the first time. A couple look familiar, some have shifted, vanished. Maybe they were underneath the water. The children doubt the ability of their feet to find the "good stones" on their own, not without "telling them. But how do they tell their feet if they dont know themselves?

But any stone is "good" when the impetus is all-powerful. Any stone. It isnay a matter of "seeing" the stones, if all five senses are working. If they are then the whole five of them are permitted, are demanded, as required, they are demanded.

That is what they do, what we do. The first children to arrive were being chased by their pursuers, by the baddies, and they didnay have time to do anything just bar fucking going for it man they just went for it, they launched themselves across in one continuing movement, relying on their feet, their feet *finding* the stones. The stones were there and there to be found if that was what it was, yes, there they were; speed of flight, agility of movement, sensitivity of touch, precision of sight and hearing. When the children see the stone above the surface of the water they see its position in relation to other stones and the water and this allows them to know what may be possible.

What about configuration, size, depth and solidity; the nature of the stone; shape, mass and kind; the depth of the water, shadows and movement of weeds, rush of the water, sound and its absence; all in a flash, judged in a flash, and off you go, running and jumping, land ahoy, that is what we do, there isnay any fucking mystery, nay need for any keeper.

23

My name is so and so and I am a writer

One's wishes, distinguishing dreams and fantasy. Covering my head, pulling down the blanket, in a room that is empty, that is always empty, a trillion atoms on the head of a pin and here it is you, with a blanket, squeezing into a corner and pulling the blanket over you, your head. I needed to get out and I didnt want to go out. The canal was too faraway, I didnt want to walk there.

It wasnt the canal, a university, I was delivering a talk about morality or something, leading the discussion, ethics or whatever, in regard to literature, the histories, one thing or another, rhetoric, who knows. I dont know what I was up to. The place wasnt too far away. It was just me, I was too faraway. One tires. I didnay want to go anywhere. A college of education. A cluster of buildings where the young are educated. One gets sick of stuff, fed up with

whatever— it, sick of it.

I parked farther away than necessary, to capture additional oxygen, whatever was available, made possible by a lengthier walk. I was not walking, I needed to walk.

Up the steps. The entrance hall. Great Hall. This is the Great Hall, he said. Halls of Fame. Entrance halls. Hallowed be thy name.

Confronted by a uniformed member of the collegiate constabulary. Halt! Who goes there! Me. The man folded his arms and did not blink. Construed as bodily weakness by the authorities. This I know, the military manual tells me so. Who the fuck are these people. I dont ask the question, who needs to, not me. A big guy. Oh dear, how frightening.

Ethics Society. He directed me along a sloping corridor. If I walked to the right I would find it, an ante-room, where an event is taking place "to do with yesses and nos." Is this the one you want?

Had I the energy I would have asked that he define "want." What is "want"?

Control is with the right. Power is with the right. But I found the room.

Nine persons. The chairs formed into a semi-circle. An empty space at the head. For me, leader of the discussion. A woman sat closeby, young woman, engrossed, notepads and electronic devices. I sat down, lifted out the books I had brought. Two collections of stories. I resisted browsing. During the last couple of weeks I had discovered several errors. I did not wish to find more. The books were published, thus doomed. I had brought into the world a pair of disasters.

The door opened: enter man, hands in pockets. Also young, they all were. Students. Hello, he said, this is the Ethics and Literary Society. We meet once per month and this is our third meeting. Our last was canceled as those of us who came along on the night discovered to our cost. In conclusion, I hope you will come back for our December meeting when Donald Favour is once again our guest for the evening. He is rather a brilliant poet with a very strong ethical stance as most of us here are familiar. He enjoyed our last encounter and is keen to a follow up on that.

A woman had her hand up, mouthing words to him. He nodded. Sorry, he said, the meeting may be postponed due to the festive celebrations. I shall keep you posted.

Then he sat down. I noticed people studying me. Should I begin? I said. Okay, I said, let me begin.

Excuse me! called the young woman who sat closeby. She gestured at her electronic devices. I am from the university newsletter. I was called in at the last moment and must apologize immediately. I had never heard of you until this afternoon. My own area of study is political economy and sociology and I hope to enter journalism and the media. I believe you won a prize for books? she said. I must say that I find some of what they say about you very interesting and in its own way political like at a personal level, that is to say, I can relate to it personally.

She was onto her feet now and pushed an electronic device towards me. She checked it over and judged the space between it and myself, checked her watch against the time on the device, and stated clearly: Interview begins seven forty-two. She whispered: Say who you are and what it is you do: your name is so and so and you are a writer. Is it books?

Books, yes.

If you want to say what the names of the books are, or what you write about in the books, then go for it. This is for our newsletter.

Thanks. Thanks for coming, it's eh ... Well, my name is Jack Proctor and I am a writer. On the way here I was challenged by the question: What are you doing here? Collegiate Security was responsible. The officer's approach was intimidatory.

A woman had her hand aloft: Perhaps he thought you were a suspicious character and his job is to weed out suspicious characters. He didnt know you had written books.

Yes, I said.

So if he had known he may not have challenged you.

Yes, that is correct. So from the standpoint of literary endeavours and authority several issues are immediately implicit. Consider artists, musicians, writers and others engaged professionally in creative pursuits as upper managers, if you like CEOs, chief executive officers.

The man who had introduced the evening had his hand aloft: Is this is your own life experience?

It is although not wholly, not at thon personal level, although here, yes, the University Policeman, the Security

Officer, he began the process by "making himself big. Those of you with an interest in soccer will be aware of that strange phenomenon media commentators describe in goalkeepers: making oneself big, e.g. "he made himself big" vis-à-vis saving a penalty. How did he save the fierce shot? He made himself big. Here is where we recognize the Creative Impulse to Physicality in one-to-one situations.

You said about the personal level, said a woman. How does this connect?

It maybe depends on the Creative Impulse to Physicality, if it takes place in a one-to-one situation such that it appears beyond all ethical consideration.

But can something be beyond all ethical consideration? called the woman.

Well, if we are obliged to recognize not the reality of metaphor, for this would be one step too far, but the natural reality of the phenomenon.

Excuse me, said the man who had introduced the evening. You know that people are particularly interested in how general matters connect to one's own life experience, thinking of wellness issues and how we connect to our own physicality and as you say it, the Creative Impulse.

Yes. I was wanting to draw attention, that young people such as yourselves have beheld at least one artwork in your life, to draw attention to this, whether or not you realized that at the time. For those of you with an interest in 17th century matters of the intellect, aesthetic as well as ethical, I refer you to Spinoza, languishing all too ably in the Netherlands, and returning to the "making himself big" issue raised by the member of the Collegiate Security who advised me, tacitly, i.e. in non-verbal fashion, in his quasi-military outfit, that he was the controlling authority in our one-to-one relationship.

Yes but if we take into account that he thought you were a suspicious character, said the woman who had had her hand aloft in the first instance, given that his job is to weed out suspicious characters and that he didnt know you had written books …

She had long hair, falling across her forehead; I could not see her eyes.

If he had known, she said, he may not have challenged you. Surely?

Agreed. This returns us to the idea of artist as upper manager. It is true that young people are doing their best to cope within a harsh and uncaring world of universal exploitation, and that my heart goes out to you goes without saying, but unfortunately we must grab ourselves by the scruff of the neck. For many years I roamed the wide world o'er, gaining the requisite work-level experience in different social settings. That period in my life, however, came to an end. Writers such as myself must make choices. I made a series of them: now here I am sharing with you the fruits and rotten eggs of that life experience.

Could you repeat that please? said the intervewer.

Fruits and rotten eggs.

The one before.

Life experience?

No.

Writers such as myself?

Yes I didnt pick it up. Could you repeat the phrase?

Writers such as myself.

Thank you. The interviewer had extended the recording device towards the audience. She said to them, Could you please address any comments and questions in my direction, and then whispered to me, It doesnt seem as though we're picking up on everything.

I nodded.

The interviewer looked to the man who had introduced the event. He called to me: May I ask a question?

Of course.

…

...

Later by far I was leaving.

When I passed the security guy at the reception desk I gave him a nod. See ye again, I said.

I knew I wouldnt but I wanted him to feel okay about things. I didnt fancy his life. The whole thing of it. When I reached the entrance hall I carried on through without looking back. Down the steps.

Oxygen.

It was not quite so cold as previously. A dampness, intermittent rain.

I once read the work of Hammurabi the Lawgiver and would have recommended this to the students if it had occurred to me but it didnt, not until now.

The dinky was a strange little car. I preferred more powerful engines. But ye got used to it. I get used to things. I've lived my life in that way. When I was younger I didnt. I was more like other people in those days. The girl doing the interview reminded me of my daughter and the girl asking the questions one of her friends. Each was strongly in favour of life, acting keenly toward others. I missed that.

My daughter had decent friends. Hannah too. Hannah's friends had a liking for life although none would have agreed with me on that point, but they did. Politics charged their conversations. These friends were female. I was not so fortunate. I dont know about my sons, nor if it was a gender issue. I dont care about gender issues. I dont care about anything much at all. There is a saying, to that effect, not caring much at all.

Nighttime through the windscreen
and the wipers
udd udd
udd udd
udd udd
udd udd.

24

Horrible Nonsense

I was checking emails in the House office but was not in the best of moods, having just been handed a jiffy bag by the Events Officer which had arrived three days earlier, Special Delivery from Glasgow, Scotland. Why hadnt they brought it to me? They hadnay even phoned. Who cares, the usual, what does it matter.

My elder son had emailed me. Contact Mum, she's worrying! I emailed him by return: I shall phone Mum so dont worry.

I had phoned her anyway, a few days ago. Could it have been a week? She could have phoned me. Maybe she did. I didnt always have my phone on. Only because I forgot. It was not deliberate. If I didnt phone she would worry. She did worry. Cholestorol and heart attacks, strokes and fuck knows what. No point telling my son about that, he had enough to worry about. He had two kids of his own and a marriage falling apart; his sister gieing birth and me with the nosebleeds, and the rest of it, plus his wee brother, wherever he was. Then there was his mother, he worried about her too. That was the kind of boy he was, typical eldest child, he worried about everything. And this was him even more, worrying about Hannah because she was worrying about me. He was trying to sort me out so she wouldnay worry so much and definitely not to worry about my youngest because he would be lying on a beach someplace. His first loyalty was to his wee brother and sister. Fair enough. The three of them shared information; stuff that me and Hannah never heard. Probably Hannah knew, probably they told her.

So it was just me, I was kept in the dark. Poor Dad, dont tell him! How come? Who knows. Families: what can one say, nothing, not anything.

I left the House office with the jiffy bag. Outside I wiped dry the bench and sat down. Passers-by looked curiously. How can ye sit in weather like this! Shut up. Then I sneezed. I used the same tissues to wipe my nose, the ones from wiping dry the bench. So what, I said to the ghost of Hannah that had reared from the kerb: For god sake Jake. Thrift is my only defence I retorted.

I stuck the tissues back in my pocket. But it was quite chilly. There were days I appreciated November but today wasnay wan of them. I ripped apart the jiffy bag. In the old days one could do it carefully to re-use the packet. Nowadays it was one rip and finished. Fuck them, capitalist fuckers. Everywhere ye look the bastards are ripping ye off. Inside the jiffy bag was a book on cholesterol. A book on cholesterol. Her note read: Phone me!

I could have returned into the House and emailed a PS to my son: phone yer Maw immediately. But I was not returning into there. Once a day was plenty. Even that was too much. I was avoiding the place as much as possible. Life is too short. Or long, depending.

I browsed the book on cholestorol. Most interesting. Bla bla.

At the same time I needed to phone Hannah. It was freezing but. Too cauld to sit. My bum was frozedid, numb. A numb bum. I got up from the bench and did a couple of stupit walks to get the blood flowing.

Cholestorol, we've all got it, what's the big deal? Hannah accused me of being a "bad-health denier."

The book was too big to put in my pocket. I hate books that are took big for my pocket. Why did I write the fuckers? I never bought big books and would never have bought one of ma ayn. How come the publishers didnay just stupidity. Be quiet.

Okay.

That is my legacy, a bunch of unanswered questions. Unresolved thoughts. Scary. Never mind. Roll on death as an auld workmate of mine used to say.

Other people had emailed me. Rob, my agent. Invites and favours. We were wondering if Jack would like to. They all asked that. If Jack would like to. No, Jack would not like to. If ye're asking a favour ask it. Dont ask if I would like to. I dont like to do fuck all. I will if ye ask but ask. It's you wanting the favour man no me, I'm happy the way I am.

Bla bla.

Fucking freezing man I was chittering. Then if ye communicate with people ye have to keep it going. They want to say something and you have to say something back. Some people dont, they just shut up. I aye envied that. I was too polite man that was my problem; if people asked me something I aye replied. They didnay bother.

Fuck them. Who? I dont know, emdi. Ha ha.

I had only been gone a few weeks—whatever the hell it was, three, four? It definitely wasnay five, I dont think. Was it?

The phone was in my hand. I was turning into one of these mental male guys who have to phone home from cafes, Hey honey, do I take sugar in my coffee?

I phoned her. She answered. I spoke, about the work I was doing. She questioned, I responded, one thing and another I lapsed into monologue. She was silent. She asked a question. I answered. She pondered, she ruminated, she made a statement. Here is the statement she made: This is horrible nonsense.

Classic Hannah. I laughed. But it was a strange-sounding laugh even to my own ears. I felt the impact in my belly while reduced to silence. *This is horrible nonsense.* Classic Hannah right enough. She could get me like that. I hadnay wanted to speak to her. Because I knew how it would be. I knew all what she would say and everything, everything, seeing it through her eyes, the horrible nonsense, I would see it myself.

Horrible nonsense? I was still holding the phone but had stopped the call. I stopped. It was me. I could not continue. I didnt cut her off. I would never cut her off. It was just eh peculiar, it was peculiar. I was taking a break. I needed to kind of
think.

It must have seemed like I was cutting her off but I wasnt. *Horrible nonsense.* Horrible nonsense? Imagine horrible nonsense. Horrible and nonsense.

Of course. It was. She was right, she was dead right. This was fucking dire! Beyond dire! Jesus christ man this was too bad to be true. Horrible nonsense is exactly what it was. Even my feet! They were freezing! How come they were freezing? They were freezing because here I was in the middle of November having to travel into the House to pick up a three-day old Special Delivery. I could never ever have told Hannah that. Special Delivery, special to us, not special to them. They didnay give a fuck.

I called Hannah back. What happened there? I said. It just cut off or something.

I'm coming down.

. . .

I'm coming down.

I hear ye.

It is shocking what's happening. It really is.

. . .

Dont defend them.

I'm not.

You are.

No I'm not.

You dont want to admit it.

Admit what?

How bad it is, how shocking and horrible it is. Dont defend them.

I'm not defending them. It's just eh

If you're complaining it must be bad.

But I'm not complaining. Not really. It's more like they havent thought things through.

You're letting let them walk all over you.

I beg yer pardon!

I know you. Ye put up with the worst sort of treatment.

Are you kidding?

No Jake I am not kidding. I just dont understand why ye do it.

But I dont.

Yes ye do.

I dont.

Ye do.

I dont at all.

I'm coming down. I'm coming down Jake. I'm coming down. Are ye there?

Ye cannay leave Julia.

Yes I can.

She's too near.

A couple of days will be okay. I'll get a flight.

It'll cost a fortune.

It doesnt matter.

Yes it does and we need the dough.

It doesnt matter.

Hannah

My mind is made up.

Yeah but I'm actually goni be away for the weekend. Some wee town on the coast, they're having this major arts festival. I'm doing different things, school talks and workshops, a reading. Two overnights.

Two overnights?

Saturday and Sunday, yeah.

That will be nice Jake if it's the coast ye're talking about: seeing the sea, we'll have time for a walk and oh, it will be nice.

Hannah it will be snowing!

That's what winter clothes are for.

I sighed.

Do ye not want me to?

Not at all. Of course I want ye to.

Ye sighed.

Yes but it was just natural, it's not like ...

The call continued for a period. But that was that. Hannah was coming, she was definitely coming, she was going to book a flight. She could leave our daughter for a couple of days and that is what she was going to do, to be with me for the weekend. I was needy.

A horrible word, "needy." I was needy.

Wait till she saw the dinky, that was fucking needy. I would have to pick her up off the ground, knowing how prejudiced I was against toty wee cars.

And it wasnay a prejudice anyway. Toty wee cars are okay for city living. That is what they are designed for. But in the wilds of rurality, no ma'am. Tow paths and bumpy lanes; nay camber, potholes and big boulders, farmers' tracks with shark-infested puddles. Ye drive slow and it seems fast; groaning grinds and nay fucking whatdyecallit, springs—ye've nay suspension man all yer organs getting tossed the gether, yer fucking kidneys land on top of yer fucking liver. She would be thrown about, bent in two by the time we reached the canal. Oh what's that? That's the canal. And she would blame me, Oh ye drive too fast, ye still think ye're driving trucks. No I didnay and if I did it wasnt my fault, not here it wasnay with their stupit scheduling. They didnt respect the traveling time. I shouldnay have been rushing hither and fucking thither man but that was the way of it because they didnt think, they had no thought at all for the likes of myself, scurrying aboot the country on behalf of the Finer Things in Life, bastards—Hannah was dead right, Hannah, classic Hannah, that was my lassie, she hit the nail right on the head man, bump, back of the net. Where would one be without her. Here, I was fucking here.

Horrible nonsense.

I had let them off the hook. Even the heating. I hadnay realized how hopeless it was. I did now. Ye noticed the chill as soon as ye opened the door. Hannah would have noticed at the start, that is when she would have noticed. Not me. My way out was to stop using it. I tried to keep it going but it was an ancient effort with this tinny shudder. It kept cutting out and ye had to crawl on yer hands and knees to refire the cylinders if the arrows dropped below a certain temperature. Two pipes connected through a tube. Ye had to steady the tube with yer left hand then turn on the taps as close to simultaneously as possible. If ye were a fraction out the whole town exploded. It was probably linked to the fucking canal man the poor auld ducks, nay wonder they kept ducking their heids.

And the dampness. What a pong! Some sort of fungal growth like ye get in foreign climes; rainforests and so on. Constant dripping and blocked pipes, dead mice-clusters. The smell was everywhere. Ye couldnay miss it. Hannah would have smelled it before getting on the plane. I hadnt realized until now. At least I wouldnay be surprised when she pointed it out.

What could it be? Maybe the roof was leaking. If that was the case it might be tiles dislodged, slipped down into the gutter or something. So that was that with the downpipes, probably blocked, duck-shit. Maybe they had forgotten to clear the gutters. Maybe I could get up on the roof and check it out. Hannah hated me climbing on roofs but maybe I needed to, if it was leaking. There might have been water-damage.

Fucking hell man it wasnay even my house! How come I had to mend the roof?

And nay damn shop within walking distance. Hoh! That was the worst. Nay shops! She would not believe it. Where's the shops? Nay shops. Classic gender stereotyping but it was the truth. Here comes the missus. Fucking nincompoop House bastards, little did they know.

The thought made me smile but, Hannah, jesus christ, a book on cholesterol. Imagine a book on cholesterol. Special delivery!

Until last night I was growing a beard. Now I shaved. Her nostrils were sensitive to bristles which she once described as "pesky." It was not long after we met and were sleeping the gether. We did that quite soon, we preferred it, ha ha! Except one's bristles scratched her nose. Watch out with your pesky bristles.

What a beautiful word, "pesky." Oh man naked bodies are so wonderful. That was it, that was youth. All these stupit pyjamas. Throw them to fuck man, get rid of all that junk

Another attack of infantilistic baloney.

It was great she was coming. The truth would stand revealed but so what. I put up with nonsense. It had taken her to see it but once she did it was inescapable. In order to state reality I had to jump into her high-heeled boots, wobble about, straighten up, and observe from point H, and by using a geometrical perspective in which extended point A = j's occupation of the nose of H, and the two lines curving from the eyes of J as within their temporary occupation of the eyes of H $\therefore$ H, j = j > h + reality quantified on the three-dimensional spatial basis such that A, j > h = C *open brackets* horrible nonsense *close brackets*. Empathy! he shrieked. Doctor doctor here I come, hellzapoppin and so am I.

It was so precisely true. They were playing me for a sucker. The sooner she got here the better. Why not this weekend! Didnt she realize I was dying?

They were walking all over me.

Man.

I was allowing it to happen. She had inferred all that from phone calls, my very speech, the gaps in my sentences, my breathing. Now she would see for herself. This is nonsense, absolute nonsense. You're coming home with me.

You're coming home with me. That is what she would say

Even before that. As soon as she saw the dinky! Then she arrives at the chalet. What on earth is this? This is *le chalét* I would quip. She wouldnay even smile. Because she wouldnay have heard, she would have walked in the door. She would just look at me.

What if she couldnt get a flight? She would. It would cost a fortune but so what, one's health came first. Without me she would go mad, mad I tell you.

Madness abounded in her family. Her mother was crazy. She distrusted me from the beginning. A no-gooder, a wastrel. The usual. To hell with her and her ancestors.

No! I dont mean that. Forgive me. One's ancestors are unimpeachable. Good, bad or indifferent, they're all we've got. Without them what are we? Non-extant. Never-beens. They were all deid except us. My parents and her parents. The whole lot. There they all were, high on the vaporous canopy, petitioning the wise ones on our behalf. Let the poor buggers off, they've had it tough.

It was only me and her and was only ever that anyway, and I missed her, I missed her. More than that.

More than that I cannot say.

She needed to be here, utterly utterly, the lifeblood of her partner. Without her

Without her I was dying, her partner, her man! How

come she wasnt here? I was her husband, she was my lady, where the hell was she, cuddles and so forth. I was sick of this shit.

The only snag was birthing variables in regard to one's daughter and granddaughter *in embryo infans*. Or if the flight had to be Saturday morning, I was doing a school talk the same afternoon then something at night, and Sunday afternoon tae, or was it the evening, a reading or something?

I would have to collect her at the airport and drive straight there, dump her at the hotel then make a dash for the school.

The thing with mothers is that everybody needs them, including the unborn. Hannah had to ignore all that to be with me. She had to see I was okay. If she knew I was okay then she wouldnt need to come.

On the other hand a period of tranquility would have been great for her, two nights in a hotel and a walk by the sea. She had to slow down. She worried about me? Okay, well I worried about her. All she did was run about helping people. It was a break for her coming down here, she would relax knowing I was okay.

But was I not okay? It was true I was not "at myself" as my grannie would have said. Hannah heard it in my voice. Julia too, my daughter, she came on the line in one phone call and thought I squeaked, or was it squawked, it was a bad line. She laughed when I did it.

But so what anyway, I wasnt cracking up. I knew when I was cracking up and this wasnt it. Obviously with Hannah here I would relax. Of course I would. A whole being is what I became. I wanted to kiss her every time oh god shut up. This kind of stuff drove a woman nuts. Her especially, she had been worrying worrying worrying and the reality made it worse, what I had told her, all the damn shit man the nonsense, the horrible stuff, the exaggerated crap I was having to cope with, except I was, I was coping, it was shite but I was coping. No exaggeration about it. I was coping. Horrible yes, and nonsense yes but I was coping. Plus half-way through, I was, mair than that. I didnt have too long to go. I would make it and quite comfortably too. If not I wanted to know the reason why.

So there ye are. No need to worry. Hannah did but. She worried. That was her. She was a worrier.

And no wonder. This was how I sounded to those who knew me.

And she did know me. She was the one person in the world who did. She *knew*. She also knew I was prone to exaggeration. I was a nightmare. If something was ten times worse for Hannah it was a hundred times worse for me. That was how I was. I made things up. I invented. I made stories out of nothing, and that includes my life.

What the world failed to understand, including one's wife and weans, is that I was not in any sense degenerating into a raving lunatic. My sons knew that. Dont take the old bugger seriously. Dont worry Mum he's okay, he's just letting off steam.

And they were correct. God's teeth. Men knew men. I would survive.

Her coming here was impossible. She could not leave Glasgow. She had to be there. Why ever did I think such a thing? Because it was her suggestion. It wasnt mine it was hers. I would never have said it. I might have thought it or hoped it or oh god whatever, I dont know, I dont bloody know.

Because it couldnt happen it just could not happen. Her daughter's daughter. That wee yin was already there, a wee thing moving snug in the womb. I saw the wee shape myself. They have the machine and Julia was there and hooked up. It was getting to the day now. The wee thing squirming about. Tadpoles, a beautiful wee thing. Let me oot let me oot! The very idea I would want Hannah to leave home to come down here to look after me jesus christ almighty what a fucking

oh dear dear dear. Three generations of womanhood. I was a disgrace.

How come Hannah was allowing it to happen? Because if I needed her I needed her. If I didnt I didnt. She was relying on me to know the difference. I would sort it out. She knew I would. For the best, I would do it for the best, whatever that was.

She was right. What a woman.

She was something else man she really was. She kept me sane.

It could never have happened. Never. How could it. A crazy fucking notion. Nice but silly. Alienation from one's humanity: we dismiss ourselves as romantic fools; it's sentimental crap, silly old bugger. She was as bad as me, or pretended to be, for my sake. Oh god, I was always being protected. That is what drove me bananas. She was aye protecting me. I didnt need protected. My family did. They needed protecting from me. I was the fucking

oh man what is the opposite of life-force? A destructive bastard.

I dialled home while the force of it was there and she picked up.

One gets on with it. In the spirit of. I dont know, we just do. Silences and so on, our breathing, oh god Hannah, alienation from one's humanity, I told her, a romantic fool, I told her: sentimental crap. You're as bad as me! I said, but it wasnt true. Another couple of weeks and that will be that. Anyway, it's cold here. Damp and dreary. Great writing weather, I'm stuck in the House and getting on with the work bla bla.

Are ye sure? she said.

You know me, I said, God's teeth.

I can come.

Aw I know, I know.

What is it they've got ye doing?

Events just, three or else four, school things and readings, workshops or something, I'm no sure. Straightforward but. They're no heavy things.

Can ye not just say no?

Ach, who cares, they get done.

Do two and skip the other two.

I chuckled.

Jake!

What?

Say ye'll do two and no more. That's plenty for anybody.

Och Hannah they're straightforward. One's a wee school, that's the Saturday afternoon, and two readings and eh I think a workshop. It'll be relaxing. Not far from the seaside either. A wee Literary Festival.

I thought ye said it was a big Arts Festival.

Something like that. It's nay bother. I'll get out for a walk. It would be nice if you were here but it's better you arent. Julia's the priority, and the wee yin. As they say, the still waters are about to break. One of these phrases we hear as males and pretend to understand. Two women talking: the waters are about to break. The male jumps in: Oh are they not okay? What? Your waters? My waters? Sorry, did ye not say they were breaking? I beg pardon, says the female and slaps the male on the face. The two worlds, concurrently ebbing, flowing.

Jake . . .

Yeah?

Are schools open on Saturday?

Who knows. I get told stuff. I just do it.

Yes, ye do as ye're told. Go here go there stand up sit down, that's you all over.

Hannah it's not

Why cant you just say no, it's Saturday.

Because events happen on Saturdays. It's entertainment. People get entertained. Saturday is a working day for us entertainers and I'm in the entertainment industry, that's what art is, stand up sit down, and the rest of it, I've been a wage-slave all my days.

Nonsense.

It's not nonsense.

Ye're under too much stress.

I'm fine.

You are not fine.

I am, it's just this crazy damn bureaucracy in which no one bothers, no one does a damn thing except push it onto us, we do everything and it is just bloody stupid. Never mind.

Just come home Jake.

Pardon.

Jake, just come home. Jake ... Are ye there?

Aye, still here.

I know ye signed a contract but if it's as bad as that there is no contract. It's not worth the paper it's written on. Tear it up. Tear it up Jake. Honestly. Ye have to look after yerself because they wont.

Okay, that's a promise. Let's make a pact not to worry. I'll cope if you cope and vice versa. I can cope so can you, and I can cope, can you? If you cope so can I. If you dont I wont.

I wont.

Well I wont either.

Wont what?

What? I said.

Oh Jake. Take care, she said.

You too. And tell Julia, big cuddles et cetera.

...

...

Just put the phone down, I said.

You put it down.

No, you.
You put it down.
You first.
No.

25

When Hannah thought of me I was thinking of her

When that weekend came around I phoned Hannah before hitting the road. Hearing a voice is being in the presence of the person. The phone call gave me that. Without the phone call I was on my own; with the phone call I was with her non-hereness and that was something. I was not worried about the weekend at all. The drive was good and lengthy and I listened to music. But when is a school not a school? I drove up and down the street looking for a school and found a day-centre attached to a hospital. Hannah would have loved that, if not the local Arts Officer, whose name was Petra Schillinger. She met me at the entrance and led me into the lobby area, scrolling her phone while talking. Unfortunately I cannot stay for the session, she said, but I shall collect you at the end.

I thought it was a school.

No no no. This is the education section of St Winifreds. And do remember the radio people. It's Matthew, Matthew King—you know him?

No.

He'll find you.

What's it for?

It's an interview. I'll collect you afterwards.

So I dont have to book in?

She paused. You do know you're at my place? You're staying at my place tonight.

I didnt know that.

Me tonight and you're with Agatha tomorrow. She'll meet you at tomorrow evening's event.

Is that a reading?

I think it is a workshop. It should tell you in the brochure. Shall I look for you?

No, I can look for myself, thanks.

When do you think it might end?

When what might end?

Oh it's alright, she added, striding towards the carpark.

Home hospitality. God's teeth! What a nightmare. I felt like going home already. Thank christ Hannah wasnay here! People need their own space. What if ye cannay sleep, if ye need to be up through the night, I get these nostril emissions, stress or some damn thing, who knows, sleeping or not sleeping and splosh, bleeding all ower their fucking pillows and sheets. Plus I was an ordinary male, the anamatomical stuff, blundering about the house; confusions, misunderstandings. Are ye allowed to wear the boxers or have ye got to bring a pair of pyjamas—plus slippers if ye're no allowed to wear outdoor shoes for fuck sake or may one borrow same from the host who in this case is a super efficient young lady who is used to whatever she is used to, how the fuck do I know, probably she didnay know herself the way she was always rushing around. I was trapped, I could not escape, I was there in the day-centre lobby and a guy was coming to greet me. I'm Bobby, he said and reached to shake hands.

He was coordinating my visit. Another man appeared. Bobby introduced me to him. I cannot remember his name; he had the demeanour of an ex-army officer, probably a part-time Lieutenant Colonel in a community-guard militia. He addressed me curtly, as though I had a fixed place in the hospital hierarchy: You are?

Jack Proctor sir civilian sir all present and correct sir. I about-turned leaving him to look at the back of my head. He was baffled by this and continued to speak. I didnt listen. I said to Bobby: My wife might phone ye here, Hannah's her name.

Can you lead the group? said Bobby.

Of course. Is it Creative Writing?

People are more used to the hands-on side of it, said the Lieutenant Colonel. Acting, arts and crafts. It's a general educative process. If you lead they will follow.

People are used to a free setting, said Bobby. They might leave, dont worry if they do. They can enter and exit as the interest takes them.

So is this a form of therapy?

We dont look on it in that way, said the Lieutenant Colonel.

Bobby said, We can go along now if you like. He had raised his arm in a circling motion to draw me to him and onwards, indicating a corridor and as I passed he whispered, They are a good bunch.

Okay.

Bobby glanced back to see if he had been overheard. So now it seemed I was in league with him against the Lieutenant Colonel. This kind of stuff seems weird but is quite common in institutional settings which is what this was.

It was a big room and with an assortment of chairs, amazing chairs, and on the wall was a big print of that one by van Gogh, a beautiful piece of work, that chair in his wee room. The Lieutenant Colonel was at ease to the rear, watching the proceedings, hands clasped behind his back. Bobby indicated the three people sitting there. Decent, he said. More will appear, dont worry if they stroll in.

Not at all.

It's Saturday after all.

Yeah.

Bobby gave me a little wave then exited.

Okay. It was very warm but I kept on my jacket. The three people were looking at me. Hi, I said, I'm Jack Proctor; I write long stories, short stories, lyrics, plays and whatever.

I've been invited along to talk about my work and how I see things relating to that and to art generally. Any of ye here writing? writing yer own stuff?

One man nodded.

The thing is, and you might be amused to hear this, I feel quite at home in this environment. I do, thinking about art and repression and what is important, basically, is just freedom, the freedom that can occur within art. I dont see it as catharsis. The way I see it we want to speak about our own imagination and making use of it. Our anger at the political situation, our rage and ultimate depression at the collusion of politicians of every party, the economic pressures. Whatever emotional, psychological stresses and pressures there are are central in and to art, are our most fundamental materials as artists. The question is how do we unlock it? Acquiring the skills and experience, the know-how to defeat the forces of evil. I begin from the premiss that we are obliged to exist in a society structured on punishment and the fear of reprisals.

The same man nodded.

Feel free to ask a question. If anything occurs to ye that ye want me to explain then ask away. It doesnt matter what it is. Dont worry about naïve questions. That's the last thing. If anyone has a question it is guaranteed others will want to ask the same thing. We use terms and phrases so often they become clichés, we forget what they meant in the first place. I need to be driven back to question myself. So the primary factor in someone raising the "naïve question" with me is that I have to explain myself so everybody present knows what I'm talking about, including me. So feel free.

It's not just books and writers either. Talk about other artforms. Music and painting. So famous actors, artists, musicians. Whoever. What is it ye think with them? Think of these paintings, songs and stories where we see the artist, their own emotional state. Stand up and fight. That's what some of them are saying. Eff you. Right at that moment in time, where they're working to sing the song, write the story, paint the picture. Individual artists, individual people. Each one unique, just like the thing they make, song or story or picture. If that makes sense. Bitterness and irony; sarcasm, raging anger, outrage. What about Vincent van Gogh and that chair he painted. Look at it up there on the wall. Ye look at that chair one way and ye think christ if ye sat on that it might collapse. In another way ye think no, it's just an ordinary chair, that's the thing about it except each damn leg seems like it's hanging onto the floor for grim life!

Nothing is perfect. Some of us are under pressure, too little time, too much work so we dont revise, not as much as we should. So different takes on the same 'idea.' Instead of one "properly revised" song what we get are two, three or more closely related ones and we see it in a lot of great musicians and painters, writers. Ye might get three or four "imperfect" stories that go together; "variations on a theme" is what the artist might call it.

What would we rather have, and I'm talking about us as readers, one "perfect" story or three variations on the theme. Can a story be perfect? I dont think so at all. I think it's a stupid idea. But even although it's stupid it can be worthwhile looking at.

Sometimes work-in-haste makes a great story; we just rush on like a kid jumping from boulder to boulder across a stream. They dont look down but their feet keep finding the boulders! That is us in a story, head down and on we go, no time to slow down never mind stop. Reading a story can be like that too, we can get very tense indeed, not knowing if the writer—the person writing the story—is going to bring it off! So that tension we experience as readers, it has nothing to do with the "plot."

So what makes us turn a page? Like if we watch the tightrope walker to see if he will fall off the damn wire! Some stories are like that too, excrutiating, forcing us to turn the page! The story is falling apart, will it work, will it work, will the writer pull it off or has he lost it altogether! will he hold on, can he reel it in—whoa, yeah, he does, he just manages it and no more and we can all sigh in relief, what a story!

That is true drama, real tension. And it's got nothing to do with the plot or any subject matter. It's to do with the composition, making the story.

So what does that tell ye? The making of the story exists in the finished thing.

Do ye get it?

The making part is intrinsic. The means is the story, that's the drama. Tell me if ye dont get it.

Art as therapy, art art and more art, art as music, as drawing, painting, sculpting. Fair enough. Poetry, prose and songs, the poetic, the lyric, ballad. We have these choices; not just narrative, first, second and third party, it need not be a story. What about meditation? Move from there. Letters, diaries, journals? What about a fictional meditation? Fictional letters, fictional diaries, fictional journals, fictional reports on a state of mind? Anything is possible.

The point where ye see the people, where ye see the audience. Now, like me seeing you, because that's what you all are, the audience, my audience, and I'm seeing you seeing me, my eyes from the outside, them flickering, nervy looking. I'm seeing them, my own actual eyes!

Seven people were present now: all males. Five in the body of the room but separate from one another. The other two sat together at the very rear of the room in a whispered wee conversation of their own. I gave them a wave and they waved in reply. I hadnt expected that. Never mind. Then nearby was a door and it lay ajar and in the shadows a figure. It was Bobby the organizer.

Okay, I said to the audience, if anybody has a last question just interrupt me. I get carried away! It's just that I need to say about freedom, the freedom to discuss rage and any other emotional charge: the very stuff of art, the life-force, as when ye're here, when you're getting stronger or trying to get stronger. It's like what artists do, it's the same thing, ye need to develop your own criteria as to whether or not your work is finished, building your own defence against the authorities; teachers, cops and critics, academics and doctors, army officers, medical health officials.

Bobby stepped forward, indicating his watch.

Okay, I said to the audience. Thanks.

Petra Schillinger appeared from the corridor. The radio people are waiting. They've been waiting half an hour.

I didnt know.

She gestured at the two men in the audience who had been having the whispered conversation. It's a live recording, she said. They have very little time left.

I didnt know.

Go with Bobby, said Petra.

Bobby showed us into a wee room. A third guy was there, rigging up the sound equipment. One of the two sat down, reading through some pages he had. The other approached me with a cheery grin. He seemed set to give me a thwack thwack mancuddle. I raised my right hand and he paused. I'm Matthew King, he said. I'll be doing the interview.

Right.

He jerked his thumb at the door. I heard your talk. Fascinating. Art therapy. I remember as a young fellow, he said then broke off. The third guy had signalled him. Matthew nodded. Remember it's a live recording, he said to me. Dont worry about the swearie words, we can take them out later.

The other guy touched me on the shoulder and guided me to a seat positioned for the purpose. I sat down. It was nice to sit, I had nothing to say. Without seats life would have been hard indeed.

Okay now uh, said the Soundman. He approached closely, holding the recording device less than a foot from my gub then held a mic to Matthew but firstly spoke into it himself: Testing testing, he said, art art and art; art art art and more art, art art, ssh ssh ssh.

Pardon?

Matthew winked to me.

Testing testing, said the Soundman: Art art and art; art art art and more art, ssh ssh ssh.

Matthew grasped the mic now. He and the Soundman exchanged nods. We have Jack Proctor with us this afternoon, said Matthew. His book was a winner of the Banker Prize some years back. It's his very first time in these parts as I understand—thanks for dropping by Jack. So, you're the chap who writes the swearie words!

I smiled.

Matthew winked. Remember you're on radio. Okay, we'll go again. So, Jack Proctor, you're the chap who writes the swearie words!

Ever had yer ears boxed, I replied.

He chuckled.

At least conceal yer hostility.

I beg your pardon?

At least conceal your hostility, I said.

I dont know what you mean.

Cheerio. I got up from the chair and left the building.

Petra Schillinger was by the carpark entrance. She was on the phone and did not notice me for a few moments. I called to her: That's us.

How was it? she asked, walking quickly.

Nay anasthetics, I said, keeping up.

She didnt know what I was talking about, she was an ordinary human being in an ordinary life, unlike myself who was a suffering individual, on behalf of humankind. Sorry, I said.

Petra was vaguely puzzled but lacked the time to pursue it further. In a matter of moments she was in her car and revving the engine, and I was scrambling into the dinky.

The big van belonging to the radio people was parked on the main road, just down from the day-centre entrance. Matthew and the others were walking toward it. They didnt see me, I dont think, I was staring straight ahead.

26

Horrible Nonsense right enough

Petra's place was miles out of town. She led the way at breakneck speed up hill, down dale, through swamps, round corners and along lengthy single-track roads with no passing places. No nothing, a track for cows and sheep with these huge puddles of muddy shite that ye're fear to step into in case ye vanish forever. It was dark by this time and I was driving with the headlights on full-beam, through other hamlets. At one of them I stopped for a break. Petra was long gone. Either she was angry or had never before driven escort to another car which I do not believe, ergo anger. She had taken umbrage at something. The radio people had phoned her, told her the awful truth.

Who cares. I sat there, happy. I was becoming fond of the dinky. It had one of these cheery frontages that makes families gie it a name. It comes time to sell the fucker and yer weans wont let ye. Oh keep little Daisy, dont sell little Daisy. But it is a heap of rust! Oh but Daddy please keep it, it'll be so unhappy, what if the new owner is a bully! Or else a monster! piped up little Squeak.

Do kids get called Squeak?

I trundled along for another three miles. I came over the brow of a hill and Petra was standing by the side of her car. She dived in and drove onwards onwards, ever onwards. Definitely she had taken umbrage. Come to think of it, she hadnt been too friendly before the radio show debacle. Maybe we had met on a past occasion. That happened. I met folk as I thought for the first time and they act aggressively towards me.

Previous blunders. Occasionally one bla bla blas, in particular if one chances to be in one's bla bla so-to-speak cups. Stupit stuff, we're all guilty. By the time we arrived at her place it was time to go away again, just about. She showed me the house and so on. I yawned. Then the room for me, everything laid out and fine, fine, a mattress on a wooden floor. I yawned again.

Your reading begins at 9:00 p.m. It's all in the festival guide, she said and handed me a copy. Doors open 8:30 p.m. Town centre. You need to be on time. You'll do the drive in forty, forty-five minutes. You have to leave here 7:45 at the very very latest. I'll give you a key and just come back whenever and let yourself in, whenever. I shall be late home myself. I cannot be there this evening. I have another commitment which is impossible to break.

Nay bother.

She stared at me. I have prepared food, she said, a salad bowl. Take a sandwich when you go. You can have a glass of wine later this evening.

I smiled.

Is there something wrong? she said quickly.

No. Not at all.

She frowned. She was waiting for me to say something. I gestured at the wooden floor, the mattress. I'm going to have a lie down.

Of course.

Once she had gone I drew the curtain. Then the crunch of gravel, car door slamming, engine on, lights, and she was gone. Soon enough I was undressed and into bed, all in the one groan.

27

Ever Thus

I jumped out of bed and nearly broke my ankle. It wasnay a bed it was a mattress and I was on my knees on the wooden floor. I lay back down. It was totally black. I just lay there. It was the worst, the very worst. I pulled the duvet over my head. Then I chortled, amid the agony. This was so extraordinarily horrendous. Where the hell was I?

Out in the wilds someplace.

One marvels at existence.

Imagine being treated thisaway! Nay wonder people lose their grip. St Winifred's annex. Dont worry oh luckless sinner, the route to salvation lies ahead, here comes the Lieutenant Colonel.

Being an ordinary human being in a society structured on inhumanity, transcendence the only answer, except

fucking hell man what a life. One spends one's life blushing on behalf of those who treat one with such abominable discourtesy.

If one had one's laptop.

I moved onto my side but my ankle was still a bit sore. It was quite good being on the mattress, given this was the countryside and stray members of the beast community might well hop over one's protuberances. Plus I needed to rest. But I could not afford to sleep, in case I slept in. This place was miles out of town.

The 21st century and here we are. I must write a squib, he cried angrily. What a nightmare of a life. Then you try and help, ye go and do readings and talk to people about what it is to be an artist and how being an artist is just an extension of a typically heightened sensitivity, the core of all mental problems, psychological issues. What do I mean by that?

What time was it? God's teeth.

Although it was a good double mattress, one must confess. Firm but bouncey. If sex was the issue this would et cetera, have done the job. I surveyed the damage. Feet, two; ankles, one and a half.

Where is one's laptop? Back in the holiday home *à la quack*. Pencil and paper. Nayn.

Such a lack of respect. Who was that God of the Scribes again? A goddess, I would pray to her. Not just for myself but for all writers, treating us like this! But was that the case? Would other writers have been treated in this manner?

Ye joking!

The sad truth is that but for Hannah I would have lain here thinking life was wonderful. Not only would I have put up with it, I would have been grateful to Petra Schillinger: *grateful*, for a fucking roof over one's head. I managed to crawled off the mattress, sat on a chair to pull on the socks. Decrepitude. Horrible nonsense beyond embarrassment. At least Hannah wasnt here to bear witness. If she had been she would have laughed at the absurdity. Naw she wouldnay. She would be packing. We would be leaving. She wouldnay stand for stuff like this, being treated in such a manner, never. It was only me, I stood for it.

So where would we have spent the night? In a small but comfy hotel. She would have made sure of it. She would have taken one look at the mattress and we would have been off, away, away away away.

Ha ha. I collected my stuff. Two could play at that game. That was the trouble with Hannah, people thought it was only her, that I was a just a fucking whatever man a dumpling. Fuck the salad bowl and fuck the sandwiches. I collected my stuff and fled. Easy done.

28

I would have wanted to batter somebody

In town I found the Tourist Information office. No accomodation was available. Everything had been taken by visitors to the Arts Festival. Sorry, said the woman.

I'm actually a performer. I'm doing three events. I did one this afternoon, another one this evening and another one tomorrow evening. I mean I need to sleep someplace. I'm talking both nights.

The woman scanned the brochure and found the events listed. One had a photograph of me. She checked the resemblance. I'll phone the House. There's a seat over there, she said, pointing to the far side of the area, from where I'd be out of earshot. It suited me, I had a book in my pocket. Eventually she called me back. You're staying with Petra Schillinger tonight and Agatha Jones tomorrow night.

Originally, I said, yes but there's been a change in circumstances. It's not possible now. My wife isnt coming. She's been under pressure and I have to find a place of my own. A small hotel or a B & B it doesnt matter.

You'll be lucky, said the woman.

I hope so. I wont cope otherwise. I dont find it easy being with other people. My health hasnt been great. I'm not wanting to make too much of it but I would very very much appreciate anything you can find.

Let me try.

Thanks, I said, anything, anything at all.

It might have to be. She smiled.

There was no room locally but she found one at a small town a few miles along the coast. You would need to go now, she said. Otherwise no guarantee. They wont hold it for you.

Not at all?

I'm afraid they wont. It's a cancellation. Go straight there.

The seaside resort was a little town with a faded last-century atmosphere. Hardy middle-aged people meandered their way along the front with wee dogs, big dogs and ones in the middle. A few bars and amusement arcades, kebab shops, An overwhelming smell of deep-fried food, but what's wrong with that. Nobody forces ye to eat it, and it's only overwhelming for folk that notice it. I found the place, a pub called the Swordfish Bar. It advertised oysters, seafood specials, live music and home-brewed ales. A woman came from behind the bar and led me upstairs then upstairs again along a passageway. The floor appeared to go up a hill. There was an overall warmth that was pleasant but somehow unhealthy, a sweetish smell.

The woman waited by the door, her hand on the door knob. I was about to enter the room but on second thoughts: No thanks, I wont bother.

She was puzzled. You're not going in?

No. No thanks.

Oh. She was still puzzled.

Sorry, I just eh . . .

On my own it would have been okay but never with Hannah and Hannah was with me! She wouldnay have stepped over the threshold of this place except for a laugh. The decision would have been made from the passenger seat of the dinky. Drive on Jake. Pardon? One look and away. She was right too; some of these places you woke up in the morning feeling strangely damp. How come? Males put up with it. Females no. No no no.

I left the car and strolled the promenade, wiped clean a bench and sat down. I phoned the House directly and explained the situation. I know you have guidelines, I said. But! This pub I've been sent to!

The Swordfish Bar.

Exactly, yes, it was great Tourist Information found it for me but it doesnt suit.

It's on the list.

Yeah fair enough but it doesnt suit .

It's very popular with festival regulars.

Ye have to know that I cannay put up with any old non-sense for the sake of an after-hour swally with the local boozebags. I know the bar is full of colourful characters who are rough and ready and can partake of the drink to all hours, even unto breakfast.

It's a premier venue. A well-known novelist from New Zealand stayed there and he had no complaints. He joined in with the local populace for an impromptu poetry reading and during one session he took the mic himself. The regulars hoped he would come again. He was an older fellow too. He had no airs and graces.

Listen son I wouldnay bring the missus here for a sing-song never mind board and lodgings.

I didnt know she was with you?

Just get us a room, a proper room in a proper place.

I accept it's not working for you.

No, it's not that it's not working for me. The room they showed me is smelly and damp; there are several lumps of shite under the pillow; semen and blood stains on the duvet, moth-infested carpets, lice and a blocked cistern.

. . .

God's teeth son I know there's a cap on spending. I know that. What I'll do is find a place myself and pay for it myself. I'll bring ye in the receipt through the week.

Uh . . .

Uh uh uh. I switched off the phone. I drove slowly along the out-of-town road, passing the marina and old-fashioned harbour and almost immediately found a small hotel with a neon light. In the reception a girl was behind the counter I asked if she had a room.

Yes.

Okay, thanks, I'll take it.

Would you care to see it?

Eh ...

It is nice.

In that case I'll take it.

Are you paying by card?

Yes.

Credit or debit?

I dont care.

What?

Credit, I said.

She looked at me again, wondering why I was smiling. I'm glad she didnt ask though because I didnt know either. The one thing I knew was that it met with Hannah's approval.

29

A Proper Event

The organizer of the evening event met me on arrival. Lisa Barry was her name; poet and playwright. I was the guest writer, reading alongside herself and another local poet, a middle-aged guy. The star attraction was a group of six teenagers performing their own stuff. They belonged to the local drama group, run by the same woman. The event was designed as a book launch in celebration of two books: one by herself, her first collection of poetry; the other an anthology of work written by the teenagers. She had encouraged them to write dramatic monologues as well as poetry and this made them ripe for performance. Now it was a book. Exciting. Such a night is guaranteed an audience, and for obvious reasons: parents, grannies and grandpas; siblings and pals; teachers, uncles and aunties.

Lisa Barry's partner was a musician. Between that and her stage experience she knew about performance, and the importance of sound and lighting. The guy doing the sound-check had taken care on this. He *assumed* that I knew what I was doing. What a relief. Writers reading their work in public are performing, they are performers. When ye read into a mic from a book the risk is obscuring the page by the shadow of yer head and shoulders, especially if the hall lights are out. It gives us the chance of going for dramatic effect in other ways.

The place was mobbed. I found space at a table, squeezed into the corner and surrounded by people dressed for the occasion. They all knew one another. A girl in the company was taking part. She and her pals chatted together, waving to friends. I realized an elderly man was watching me quite closely, wondering who the hell I was, could he rely on me. Rely on me for what? Not to be troublesome I suppose. Probably he was the girl's grandpa. I was nearer his age than anybody's. In what way could I be troublesome?

Ah. A solitary man with no connection to persons at the table. Grounds for caution, suspicion; potential predator, stalker, paedophile. Oh for christ sake. He watched me taking a notepad and pen from my pocket. Maybe I was a schoolteacher, keeping an eye on the pupils. A journalist maybe, there to review the night. In fact I was checking my own listed stories, which was now subject to change. I didnay usually do that but the sound and superior lighting offered other possibilities. The soundman had set up three mics and who knows, maybe I would move from one to the other, maybe I would use different voices, stand back to front and shout over my shoulder! I grinned at the very thought. Drama is drama, god's teeth man sometimes ye just want to whack them.

Yes, absolutely, this is art, art in performance, performance art. Bla bla! I even had a copy of "the" novel and could start with a wee bit of that. At this point I realized the elderly man knew who I was, the auld bugger had spotted the book and prepared for the worst.

Ah well fuck him.

The one criticism from myself concerned the programme itself, the running order. Almost all of the audience were there to see the young team but Lisa Barry had them first on the bill. On a night like this a more experienced reader should have gone first, setting the standard. It wouldnay have had to be Lisa Barry, I would have gone first. The inexperienced ones would then have been challenged into a proper performance. Instead of that all the teenagers "took their medicine"; they rushed on, rushed through and rushed off. Even so, awesome applause. Every one a hero.

Lisa Barry followed, talking about the local group and so on and what the night was about, copies of the two books were on sale, and so on, and she read two poems of her own. People cheered her. No wonder. There had been room for more but obviously she thought of it as the teenagers' night and didnt want to steal their thunder. She shouldnay have been so modest but that is what happens. Never mind, end of first half.

I had bottles of water with me and stayed where I was at the table, out of sight, out of touch. I never like blethering to people before a performance.

The other poet opened the second half of the event. He had the most difficult spot on the programme. Fodder. Ach well, it happens to us all. He was an amusing speaker and spoke a while before beginning. Unfortunately the teenagers were now back among friends and loved ones, high on the performance and loud in the craic. A fucking hullaballoo in other words. I think my table was the worst. Nobody even pretended to listen. I craned sideways and forwards to see and hear the poet more clearly. This indicated to individuals there at the table that they should shout more softly. The elderly man was watching me again, and the way his gums were going he might have been annoyed, unless his teeth were a bad fit.

About the third poem in the poet used the word "fuck." It was the first I had encountered all night, except in perusing my own listed stories. Oh man and it reverberated. Some laughed and some were embarrassed, even offended, except it was poetry and, therefore, they had to accept it. And the poet kept going, in his ordinary local voice, voice of an adult. Good on him. He was an experienced performer and well aware of the reaction. Once people got over it they relaxed; some did anyway. Who cares about the rest. A few of the audience had gone during the interval. The next on was the poet-organizer whose book was being launched. Then it was me to follow. They were giving me "my place."

Never mind.

My table was still crowded when the moment arrived. The poet-organizer called me up. The people at the table were nonplussed. The elderly man frowned at me.

I had a group of stories prepared for a thirty-minute set, and room for another couple depending on the time. I just battered on and did it. But what was it I did? I cannot remember. It was just kind of pleasant, which is an odd description. The evening lasted until 2245 hours. Minutes later I was on the road.

People were sitting on for another drink and I could have sat along with them. But I had the car and was tired, plus I was an auld fucker and being alone and comfy is being comfy and alone.

I drove back by the coast. The Swordfish Bar was still open. I drove beyond there and parked the car at my own place, then strode back along the promenade. I ordered a half pint, a dram and a packet of crisps, then changed it for a pint, a large dram, and two packets of crisps. A colourful character remarked, Would you be Scotch?

Aye.

You are not a Catholic?

Pardon?

Now I'm just thinking that; looking at ye. Are ye offended?

No, I said, I find it quite an interesting question. Sometimes racism and elitism run the gether in that way, and by the way, I am not a Protestant never mind a Catholic.

But ye're not offended?

Not at all. I've had a good night and nothing's goni top it, nor detract from it. I just feel comfy.

Good on ye, he said and patted me on the back. He was expecting a decent conversation but I couldnt be bothered. I swallied the booze more quickly than intended and carried the crisps back to my own place, made a cup of tea.

In such circumstances I coped better on my own. Humiliations are awkward when a fellow human bears witness to one's ignominy: especially one's partner. I knew what she would have said, had she been here. I knew precisely what she would have said. I could just see her there saying it and I chuckled, sipped the tea. But a thought occurred to me then, about the reading earlier on, that the local poet who read the poem with the word "fuck" in it, had done so to take the heat off me. He was paving the way, preparing the audience for what was to come, dan d ran dan. That was a nice of him. More than that, christ, what a good guy he was.

There I was sitting by the dressing table on the only chair in the room. I stared at my face in the mirror. How are ye son? Not bad at all. Tomorrow and tomorrow.

Exactly. The writer's life and thoughts of my daughter and the wee baby to come. I got up and walked to see out the window. I could not see the sea, that face of mine reflecting. Well, it was my face, depending on the light. I switched on the television. A movie had just started, so that was good too.

30

The Gory Details

Next morning I enjoyed a proper breakfast; proper coffee, muesli with yoghurt, poached eggs and toast. I packed my stuff in the car but before driving away I joined the strollers along the promenade. Cargo ships on the horizon. It was not too cold at all and good just ambling, seeing the sea. Me and Hannah always enjoyed it. We should have moved to the coast years ago. Maybe it wasnt too late. I phoned while walking. Good that I did, she had been worrying about me. I went through all pertinent information, the grub especially, it was great having a breakfast, a proper one. Eggs, toast and stuff; muesli, it came in the deal, I said, it was good value.

You paid?

Yeh but I'll get it returned.

Why did you pay?

I moved out the other place, like I was saying, so then I found this one. I had to move fast, it was getting late. I had to get back into town for the reading. So . . . So I paid it. But I'll get the money back.

So you organized it, you paid for it, and there's no fee?

Well of course there's a fee.

Did they say that?

Aw Hannah.

Did they say there was a fee?

. . .

Have ye got it in writing?

I dont need it in writing. But I will have it somewhere. And they had organized a place for me too. Eh

Oh God, Jake, I hear ye sighing. Why are ye hiding it from yerself?

I'm not. Hiding what?

They're exploiting ye.

I know they're exploiting me, that's what happens in these bloody jobs.

So the fee is at the end of the contract?

Yes, of course.

For all the events? For everything?

Yes, I mean …

And yer expenses as well? Last night, have ye kept the receipt?

I paid by Visa so of course there's a receipt.

A Visa receipt? So there's no receipt? You're only talking about the Visa. So how much did you spend yesterday?

What do ye mean, the hotel?

Not just the hotel Jake, everything.

Everything?

Your expenses, your outlay, the things you've been spending money on. Have you kept your receipts? Yesterday? The day before? The day before that and the day before that.

I know what ye're saying.

What am I saying? Jake, what am I saying? How much have ye spent? Food, petrol, grocery bills? How much have ye spent?

Well I dont know.

In the time ye've been there. Have ye kept yer receipts? I hear ye sighing but have ye?

Come on Hannah.

They havent paid ye a penny and they dont intend to pay ye a penny. How much have ye spent, from the very beginning, how much?

They cant be not paying me expenses Hannah.

Well tell me!

I've never heard of that, not paying expenses.

What does it say in the contract?

Honest Hannah that would be too strange, that would be weird. I'll check it out tomorrow. First thing tomorrow. I'll ask them right away, I'll go right in and do it.

Get it in writing whatever it is.

Of course.

Ye say "of course" but ye havent done it so far.

What do ye mean?

Have ye got it written anywhere that you get the fees and the expenses at the end of the contract?

I must have. That is how these things work. I signed a contract. I cannay remember seeing it there, but it would have been christ I mean obviously, obviously it would have been there. That is what contracts are for, so that one is paid for one's services. A contract is a written agreement. It's not like I was a voluntary worker. Matters are written and both parties agree to them: the gory details—then they sign their names.

So you did see it?

I must have. To sign it. Way back. Months ago. Then I stuck it someplace. I wrote it down on the big wall-chart thing. It'll be in my contracts' folder.

Oh God.

It will be. I just cannay remember.

Jake.

No, ye're right, I'm putting up with shit. That's what ye're talking about and ye're right. Ye want me to admit it: I'm admitting it.

Did anyone tell ye ye were being paid expenses at the end? Did anyone tell ye?

I needed a seat. Hannah was talking. I was holding the receiver tightly in against my ear. Hannah, I said, I need to stop ye.

The concept "no expenses" had reduced me, reduced me. The laughter of the world. Jake the Joke. Did anyone tell ye ye were being paid expenses. That was the query. Hannah's query. I was her queerie.

Oh love, she said.

Dont worry, I said, it just makes me angry. I'll phone ye later.

These fuckers knew what they were doing. They had a limited budget and were stretching it as far as they could, like in any other business. This meant employing C-listers like myself at the minimum cost. If they could wangle a method to not pay me then they would not pay me. That was their job. They knew they hadnay paid me. Their purpose was not to. How far would they take it? As far as they could. Might they get me to pay for the privilege? Yes. It happens in the world of art. In theatre they call it profit-share. The creators pay for the privilege. Ye work for nothing.

Ach well, what's new about that. In the old days I would phone a friend, and go and get fucking moroculous fucking drunk.

31

Feet Without One's Partner

I was at it from early as usual but unable to do a damn thing, the work just not good really just not good. It goes wrong. Wrong is not right, is incorrect; foolishness, aspects of, I cannay bear it just, excrutiating; I cannot see it, double-clicking on my work, fucking bin it man bin it, dont even look, dont even look, it is horrible and shite and horrible.

Also just tired, so tired, unaware but not knowing, trying to concentrate. Concentration is major. One cannot concentrate. Surrender. Go back to bed.

I switched off the machine.

And the reality: cold feet. My feet would not warm. This stupit empty bed hundreds of miles from home. What a joke. Scrabbling about for what: nothing. Shite man nothing. Just as well she wasnt here. She would have seen how truly bad it was. Take away the canal. Take away the canal and what? Hannah would have looked, Hannah would have seen. The world

One lies on one's back, the change in light.

One asks for little in this life, asks for a little, he asks

doomed to lie and trampled, trampled, the relationship as between persons.

Asking for little in this life is asking for a little and asking for that is asking for something.

All ye who walk in these places lean heavily on yer crutch and if it falls, if it falls, a repositioning, lifting ye up. You are

Arise from your bed and walk, switch on the machine, switch on the machine.

Hello? Is that the House of Form and Substance? I'm looking for the Metaphysics Division. Yes, all caps, my typesetter's a fucking standard english freak—Art and Aesthetics, yes, okay.

What time is it now?

Forget it.

Face up to it.

I put on the shoes and jacket and walked round *le chalét*—the building in other words, why do I call it a chalét. It is not a chalét. That is me making something out of nothing. This stupit wee apartment block is set by a canal in the country. It takes about thirty seconds to walk round it, maybe less, I'm guessing.

Round the building and back inside. I did this when I couldnay be bothered walking the tow path

I should have been eating proper grub out proper delis, diners and restaurants, paid for by them. I would have been if she had been here. She would have been fighting my corner. But she was not here. So nay nothing. Every absence is a wee dod of negative energy waiting to interact, explode into life with more negativity, effect an existent, bring into being. She wasnt here, so what, what.

Every last damn thing, I was paying it out my own pocket. Every time I stopped for a coffee on route to a venue I should have collected receipts. I was to ask everybody, for everything. Petrol. I had spent a fortune. Everything. I was paying for everything out my own pocket. Between arrival and departure, everything. Between these two points every item of expenditure.

I needed to get this information lodged inside that dull receptacle one refers to as the brain. It is the nature of existence that one requires to eat. Register this.

32

The Ugly Troot

I was just sick of it.

I went to bed but I was glad to get up again. Naps can be energy sapping.

I gave myself plenty of time, in case of road emergencies, one is a cautious chap. All being well I might relax for half an hour, sip a green tea. It used to be strong black coffee but this induced emotional seizures. The car squeaked at the knees. Did I mention this already, cars that squeak? I must have, I've mentioned everything else. But did I? Did I really?

> Did I did I
> did I really.

But it is true, once that dinky hit 65 miles per aitch the damn chassis started shaking and trembling, a-phut phut phutting, all eight fifty cee cees of her

> oh yeah jingling
> hear them jingling
> I'm a cee cee riding son of a gun

Three workshops a day keeps Jack a dull boy. I dedicate this life of mine to instill in persons the need not to talk. Do not fucking talk. This is the one statement of intent you require to pin above your desk. Paint it on the wall. Do not talk. Paint it to one side of the daily reminder: The Pills The Pills The Pills (remember the pills!).

Life Writing. What is Life Writing? A community-based workshop. Community-based folks are involved in Life Writing. More than that, christ, what a good guy he was. Bourgeois bastards create literary art.

This morning's output had been fair to middling. What does that mean, fair to middling? In reference to the output, my own output. What do I mean by "output"? Do I mean work, my work was fair to middling? Okay then, fair enough, it was, fair to middling, at least that.

I think better but who am I to say.

Never discuss work in progress.

Never never never ever discuss work in progress.

People at these workshop are always nonplussed when I stop them talking. I stop them in full flight. They think I am kidding. The story is upon them. They need to tell us all what their story is "going to be. Rrringgg rrringgg, hello, is that the Metaphysics Division, send for Parmenides.

Yes but

Stop! Have you written the fucking thing?

No but I am going to.

Not if you keep talking about it so shut up. Only talk about something you have done.

And what you find is you will not even do that; too boring too boring. What is your story about Mister Proctor? Who gives a fuck, away and buy the book.

I was discovering that the basic itinerary was subject to change. This afternoon's workshop commitment was yet another, only made known to me because I had been into the House office to check out something else. Oh Mister Proctor, you have a Life Writing workshop this afternoon, said the Events Officer.

I thought it was tonight.

It's this afternoon. He showed me the schedule. It was a new schedule, an updated version of the one they had given me on a previous occasion. I emailed it to you earlier in the week, he said.

You emailed it to me. I do not have access to email. You know this, I have told you this. I am not at home remember, I am resident in a holiday chalet in the middle of a field. I cannot access the web. Yous mob forgot to fix me up with a network connection. The only time I see emails is when I come in here.

You would have had full wi-fi facilities at the Neuk.

Are you talking abut the family-run cut-price rooming house?

Dont complain to me.

I'm not compaining, I said, my attention distracted by an asterixed entry on the itinerary. What is that? Is that a reading event?

Two nights ago. The one you didnt attend. The people were looking forward to meeting you.

I didnt know about it.

We left a message for you.

I didnt get it.

You didnt get the message?

No.

It was pushed under your door.

Did you push it under? Was it you who pushed it under?

No.

I shrugged. So now it's me, it was me who let them down: is that it? Look I'm not getting at you personally.

It isnt my fault, he said. You get on to me about things and it isnt my fault.

I'm not getting on to you.

It's not my fault.

I hear ye, but it's not my fault either and you started this by laying the blame on me for not attending. If I had known then I would have. I attend everything. That is the negative side of my personality. Other people dont bother and they never feel guilty. I always fucking feel guilty. This is the egotistical core of my very being. If I dont attend I think they'll suffer.

The Events Officer looked at me.

Two nights ago I was stuck in the chalet watching dark clouds brood over the canal. But that was fine because it calms me down, it calms me down, even the idea that I'm transforming clouds into beings, animism, a most ancient explanation of the ways of the world, in particular the ills of humankind.

It's not your fault son, I know that. I should have met people and would have except through administrative fuck-ups. Tonight, the bureaucracy let me down, to the tune of the popular country song. And with that I shall say fare thee well.

I needed to be at the desk anyway, stuck fast at the desk, finding space to write, day in day out. That was every day. This is what that meant. Every day. Staying with it and never leaving it lest it withers away, irrecoverably, not to be resuscitated on the operating table in rubberized smock, painstaking pens and tipex, scraping and clarifying, penetrating, reaching ever-closer into that essential pit, kernel, atom: that which cannot be touched else it ceases to be. Poor Aristotle. It is my opinion that he wanted to do something more than he did, but first he had to clear the decks, mop at the ready,

> sluice it down boys sluice it down,
> clear the decks and sluice it down,
> the square-toed lugger moving out the harbour,
> set sail of an evening
> under a red sky

Tomorrow I shall work, except there is no tomorrow, clearing the decks is classification, an eternal occupation, and literally so, one classifies the classified, alas poor Ari.

What am I talking about is not a question. I only had a couple of hours before this afternoon's engagement. Being domiciled on the other side of this bustling town any traveling commitment required an additional half an hour.

It was not my fault, says the Events Officer.

Well it was not my fault either, neither it was. I put up with shit.

I had an event to do that afternoon and I would go away and do it—Life Writing, what is Life Writing? What I did at the seaside? Mair like Lifetime Writing, Life-Sentence Writing. One writes about one's life. One writes one's life from within. One writes one's life while living it, from within it, about from within.

What the fucking hell did it mean! Anti-existential pish! Authoritarian shite. How had I let it happen? Easy. I was weak and cowardly—skint, weak and cowardly. Working for fuck all and paying for the privilege. That summed it up. The real me stood revealed. Secretly she thought I was strong, but no, I was a weak bugger, timidly so, verging on cowardly. They were treating me with contempt. I wearied of the struggle.

Hannah still had it in her head that she fly to me. She couldnt. It was crucial she stayed home with our daughter and granddaughter-to-be. That was the fight, that was how we take on the bastards, that is how we fucking resist man resist! That is how we resist, and I would advise the Events Officer of that before I left because I felt sorry for him, when all is said and done.

33

Ghost Writers in the Sky

At the Community Centre the local Arts Control Officer was around and I was to discuss the format with her. I arrived at ten past one and found the venue. A grey and dank old building. In bygone days this was an industrial town, once thriving. The doors were locked. The town had been built on heavy industry but there was little of that left. People were hanging about, committing to some indefinable future, much to the relief of the national politicians. I discovered a wee cafe down a backstreet. I was starving. I took their lunchtime meal-deal to-go, and scabbed in while walking. A comfortable deep-fried repast, muggy and gggllubbby: enter the snooze factor, falling asleep in class.

Oh well.

Rain drizzled. There was a central shopping plaza and pedestrian precinct. I entered. No food allowed! roared a sign. I am a city kind of a man: what do I do? stare into the windows of the local Spar? walk from one end of main street to the other? check out the sheep in the adjacent fields, convey my commiserations to the local bullocks? Betting shops are warm but very costly.

Drenching rain now. I sheltered beneath a canopy. A charity shop. I blundered in. A wall full of books, books and books, 98% of which were glossy. One of the volunteers saw me chomping a piece of deep-fried fish. No doubt a vegan. Fair enough; I used to be one myself. She waited for me to explain myself. Sorry, I said, I didnt eh ... and out I went. I staggered along to the venue in a fit of stops and starts, sheltered doorway to sheltered doorway, while at the venue the doors remained closed.

I sheltered across the street, finishing the grub, noting things of interest e.g. the venue was a former primary school. Well well. Imagine that. Everywhere one walks there are things of interest.

1355 hours. Maybe the schedule had been altered. Maybe I was in the wrong town. That had not happened to me yet. But it would. I knew it would. At 2 o'clock I tried the door again and found that it was unlocked. God's teeth. Could some bugger have unlocked and entered while I was standing there lost in some stupit bastarn daydream about who knows what, drenched in some technicolored fantastic shite, or other.

I prefer the other.

I walked the dark corridor. Nobody here. A classroom door was ajar. I pushed it open, stepped inside. Then noisy voices in the outer corridor. Folk approached. What a beautiful example that was. They saw me. A woman with a certain air about her entered to the rear; air of indifference. She was Arts Control Officer for the community. How would you want to do it? she asked. Would you want to begin yourself or ... ?

What is the usual format?

You would just begin.

Okay.

She walked round to the back of the room. I waited until she was seated. She nodded.

I called to her: Is there a particular subject or something or uh I dont quite know, what have I to talk about? I'm trying to imagine Life Writing and what it might amount to. Anything to do with life that is not fiction? Biography or what?

She nodded.

Okay. Well, all writing is writing.

What is you write yourself? asked a woman.

Thanks very much, I said. I write novels, short stories, the occasional screenplay, song lyrics and god knows what, anything. I would have been at home a hundred years ago. I see myself as a kind of old-fashioned *belles-lettres* type of fellow. A Charles Lamb for the two thousands. As a young-ster I was very fond of the English essayists and of course in love with William Hazlitt. Who wouldnt be!

What is your name?

Jack Proctor.

Would we have read anything by you?

Of course, called a woman: his short stories.

Thanks very much, I said. My short stories, you've read them?

Some certainly.

Thanks.

I think it is marvelous you've taken the trouble to come along and talk to our group.

Thanks very much. Thanks.

Are you going to talk about them? asked another woman.

Eh well I'm not sure.

How do you organize your writing time? asked a man older than me by a dozen years at least.

That's a great question, I said.

I'm especially interested in the physicality, he said, the position of my chair and its relationship to the table.

That's a great thing to say.

I do not have a desk. The older man glanced at the others. I used to in days gone bye but since we downsized I've had to work at the kitchen table. But this is awkward around mealtimes. My daughter comes with my food.

You write yourself? I said.

What?

You write things yourself?

No, he said, but my wife used to paint. I sometimes worked on a diary I kept. This was many years ago. We worked side by side. She at one end of the table me at the other. But she passed away and eh ... He nodded. I prefer the factually-based set in past historical. I find it fascinating hearing people discuss the mechanics of it all.

Me too.

Although I have to say, if I was going to write it would not be fiction. It would be about real things, real life.

People come along to Creative Writing Workshops for different reasons, I said.

I think they want tips, said a woman.

Yes, I said, but it's a kind of fantasy. They hear reports of best-selling books, worldwide fame and overnight fortunes. They wonder if they could do the same. Perhaps they could, if only they knew what to do. So they come along to the local workshop to discover how to sell books, achieve worldly fame and earn an immense fortune while they're at it. Not everyone who comes reads books. Sometimes you ask people if they read books and they wonder what you mean. If they read a book, what kind of book? Then I say to them, if ye never read books how come ye want to write one?

Members gazed at me. Eventually the woman who had read my short stories spoke. She said, I dont think everyone wants tips.

I'm glad of that, I said, because the tips I offer people never go down well. They aye seem to be the wrong kind of tips. So much so one studies the word itself, 'tips.' It's a strange wee word. 'Tips.' If ye didnt know what it was ye would be forgiven for wondering if it was a real word, or just a recent invention, or maybe an anagram, spit, or else one of these words that comprise the first letter of each of four words but why not the third letter as one sees in old-fashioned codes.

Tips on how to write? said a woman. Tips on how to write your own lifestory?

Is Life Writing the story of your life? I asked.

It can be, said a man.

Others agreed with this and a few just looked about the room, seeing all the faces, listening to everything said, and enjoying it all, or so it seemed to me. People dont ask for much in life, I said, ordinary people, we just struggle on making things and doing things and taking care of people whenever it's possible, although it aint always possible. This is why we need to write wur own story.

No matter how many tips and stuff ye get from people like me, it is down to you all, ye have to write it yerself.

When I started writing I was interested in the future and other people. I wanted to write about other people and the things they did and I did if I thought them interesting. I did not want to write things that were not interesting. If it was not interesting I wanted to make it interesting. I did not worry about a thing that happened and a thing that did not happen, I just wanted to write it down, whatever it was, and if it was good enough to write down it was good enough to make interesting. Even if it was not interesting I had to make it interesting.

There are different ways to be interesting.

Even the most basic matter can become interesting. So if I was writing a story that was not interesting I gave it a fancy layout on the page. I worked with pens then changed to pencils, and even coloured pencils although I soon discovered the harder stuff, these thick charcoal ones. Instead of indenting a paragraph I justified every last line. I did all manner of things. I made interesting shapes out the paragraphs. And I learned how to tell a story in somebody else's voice.

I can understand that, said the older man. I would like to do that. How do I go about it? Is one different from the other?

No, either it's interesting or it isnt. But even if it is somebody else's voice and somebody else's story it's always you that writes it. Fiction or non-fiction is irrelevant. Ye need to finish it yerself. It is as absurd for me to talk about somebody else finishing my story as it is for somebody else to live my life.

And we all know what ghost writers are, everybody is on the lookout for somebody to set down every last detail of our lives for the advancement of the human race. And if they stay and pay the modicum of attention they will discover matters of import relative not only to themselves but to each other.

Life writing is not ghostwriting, said the older man.

I never for one moment thought that it was, I said.

Life Writing is so much stronger than ghostwriting, said a woman.

Yes, I said, but no matter what you write you need to make it interesting. Dont be misled. There is an ancient urge many of us have. We see our life as an interesting and dramatic entity in its own right and believe that for other people a working knowledge of this will be an enriching experience. If our life is made known to the rest of the world they will appreciate how marvelous a wonder it has been. Fame and fortune become secondary. People see it as crucial for humankind that their life is put on record and open to public perusal.

There is a huge area of literature devoted to this: biography is what they call it. People who write their own biographies are autobiographers and the work they produce is known as autobiography. There are also the ghostwriters. Ghost writers. I grinned. Say it slowly and look each other in the eye, as though ye've stumbled by error into a church of unknown creed, where an oddly familiar ceremony is taking place.

Otherwise your brain will cease functioning. If it isnay interesting to you who the hell else is goni be interested?

Remember too that in the year of our Lord 17_, in the bustling sea port of C____ lived a wise carpenter D____ whose
father was the bastard son of Count A____ de L____. One
fine May morning the headstrong son of this wise carpenter
smuggled himself aboard a herring frigate sailing port star-
board with a gusting tailwind into the straits of Gasstang:

> Do do do do do do do do
> do do do do do do do
> Hiya
> do do do do do do do
> do do do do do do ...
> Do do do do do do do do
> do do do do do do
> You'll never take me alive, said he
> the wild colonial boy
> yippee aye ayyyy
> yippee aye ohhh,
> ghost writers in the sky

34

Knackert

Pelting rain. Again. People had invited me to go someplace. Maybe I wouldnt. Maybe I would just stay here in the chalet and not go anywhere.

The idea of not going anywhere. Nobody would even know. Even if they did, so what? It was up to me. Then tomorrow, whatever that was, I would deal with it, tomorrow, that was the day, the time, the time for dealing with stuff if it was indeed tomorrow then wait till the day after this yin.

Somebody said it was goni snow. If it snowed I would be snowed in. It would be good being snowed in. I would have to sail the dinky down the canal. I would just push it to the edge. I knew where there was a decent bank and ye dont often get banks on canals but I knew one here where the rushes were huge and plentiful, where swans and ducks would birth and hideaway their wee yins. I called it swan hill. If I pushed the car to there I could roll it down. Instead of that I rolled over, hoping to sleep.

The financiers,
the mercenaries,
the permanent State and servants,
government and managers everywhere;
whoever,
churchmen, sanctifiers,
one rolls over,

I rolled over again, wedged the last wee dod of tissue up my nostril to staunch one's lifeblood.

Too late for the RSVP and tomorrow was the day.

Although before this afternoon

What was this afternoon?

Who cares, fucking paradigmatic man whatever that means where's my dictionary I cannay google the fucker, being without resources, electronic resources, electrical sources.

Another social invite had arrived, in an envelope pushed under the door. Probably the Events Officer drove out with it himself to ensure delivery. Good on him.

So either I went or not. And it wasnt his fault.

If I did and messed up due to some basic interpersonal confusion then so be it. I would have tried, and failed. I could state that to the party: Apologies for the social inadequacy, the inadequacy of my end of this dialogue. Obviously you heard the one about the cakes.

At least I would have done the wrong thing which is slightly better than no thing at all. Potential inviters would get to hear about this and decide to forgo purgatory, to draw a veil over Proctor, Jake.

Although if you invite somebody someplace you dont have to hang out with them all night. The folk who issued the invitation would expect me to arrive but not stay in their company all night. What a nightmare that would be! I could imagine them, see that writer guy, we invited the bugger and when he came we couldnay get rid of him. That one with Laurel and Hardy where Ollie jumps into the river to save the life of this volatile and most capable young woman who is attempting to commit suicide. If ye save a suicide's life ye're forced to look after her for the rest of yer days on Planet Earth, as we children term it, distinguishing it from a greater entity, one that includes Planet Heaven, presumably, or these through-the-looking-glass worlds that weans fall through to the consternation of their mummies and daddies and are only found when a wise old owl confers with a brass monkey, xmas movie blockbusters, all worries gone, ye've earned the dough so stay home and write.

Nostril-emergencies.

I had to get out of bed for another pile of tissue.

The rain pounding down. Man! But it was nice seeing it batter into the bare earth, as opposed to back home, the tar, bricks and stones. Country living.

This is the problem, the burst blood vessels in one's nostrils, should one happen to stay overnight at the invitation of volunteer hosts. Although it was nice to be invited someplace.

In days of yore.

When nothing is asked may something be demanded? No, the people who invited me were fine. The kind of people I hoped to meet when I accepted this writer-in-residency job. It had been disappointing not to receive more such invitations. Nothing was expected of me. I could just hang out, relax.

I would be forced to, not having anything to do. Unless I took the laptop, found a quiet corner and got on with my own work. Nothing is given ye in this life. So why go any place? No point. Perhaps it was a formal invitation for whomsoever happened to be in residence. Naw. They knew it was me when they issued the invitation. Usually I got nay social invites to anywhere and now here I was whining.

Not saying no. Not saying anything. Saying nothing and not turning up.

I was not feeling great if truth be told. One wearies. One goes to work and dozes at the desk. I dont usually find excuses although this was hardly an excuse although maybe it was although if one is fit enough to get up and get out then one is fit enough to

whatever.

Although I was not feeling great. Maybe I was coming down with something, in the early throes of a nasty flu.

Although what was being asked of me if I did go? Nothing, just whatever, be a guest, who knows.

35

Agatha Christie to Gertrude Stein

Usually I begin in a more general way or maybe reading a couple of my own stories, saying a wee bit about my life, before I started writing.

Ah, yes, I understand that, replied the Creative Writing tutor. I also know that people here are very very interested to know what impresses a literary editor sufficiently to want to publish.

Okay, fine. I shall get to that later.

Sometimes people go on and on.

I hear ye.

I dont mean yourself I mean the members here.

Nay bother.

It's only that one of our members was given to understand that their work didnt quite fit the bill. I saw the editor's rejection slip myself and clearly this is what they meant.

I shrugged.

People need to be positive.

At the same time, I said, maybe it would be better to review the member's work rather than the editor's rejection. Otherwise it might lead to the conclusion that a "bill" exists to which they do not fit, perhaps through exclusion a priori. It is a sideways step from there to the belief that there is an ideal form, a design or even template entrusted to the chosen few to which they yield or conform. If no one gives them the design or template then how can they hope to conform to it. They then come to believe the function of the tutor or guest writer is to provide the template ergo painting by numbers

The Creative Writing tutor studied me.

Whereas the way out of the problem is don't be lazy, do the work. I shrugged.

I was not talking about myself, he said.

Sure, I said, I wasnt meaning "you" in that sense, if I said "you," I meant it figuratively.

He nodded then pushed open the door into the meeting room where the group awaited. He moved to the back of the room.

Hullo, I said to the members, my name is Jack Proctor and I write short stories, novels, plays, lyrics, screenplays and anything else that chances along. If there's anything people want to talk about then let me know otherwise I'll go on forever.

The tutor had opened an exercise book and held his pencil at the ready.

Clearly everything I say will be taken down and used in evidence against me. I smiled. The group gazed at me. A few had the pencils and notebooks ready as well. This is like being in a cupboard with a bunch of cops, I said. Sometimes it's good just to listen, not to take notes all the time.

Not to take notes? asked a woman, pencil poised.

That's right but ye dont have to write that down because if ye do ye might not grasp the point. Later on ye read back what I said and wonder why on earth I said it in the first place! Whereas if ye listen, if ye just listen . . . I smiled, she was a nice woman, she was doing her best. When did I last change my socks? I couldnay remember.

Okay, what was I talking about again—literary agents and what publishers want—okay, What this entails amounts to a fallacy, that there exists such a thing as the "all-artists together" approach. This is where we discuss "practicalities" e.g. the need for well-produced manuscripts. Computers or pen & ink? Virtual books or real books. Ebooks, kindle books or ether-based books of spirituality, wherever that means. How do we choose markets? Do we choose them or do they choose us? Are we doomed? Are agents essential? Is reading the work of other writers a help or a hindrance or a deadly thrust into the densest mysteriosity? Is revision a bad thing? Does hard work make you weep sinner, enter the waters, enter the waters and be cleansed, cleansed. Does criticism have a value or is it all subjective anyway? When is the best time for ideas and inspiration? When is a good time for writing? How much money do writers earn from a novel? Is it possible to

Eh excuse me Mister Proctor

No, no questions here, sorry.

No, but uh

No questions. Just listen, please. "Practicalities" is the least practical discussion I know. Its spirit is pseudo-egalitarian. It appears to bond writers, allowing a common purpose. But really it is crap. It states where we are but takes us nowhere. Even worse it takes us back the way and allows charlatans and imposters to enter the fray.

This is when a different set of questions arise, How do we inject "readability"? Does plot give rise to characters or characters give rise to plot? The most practical discussion is the "blank page. How do we confront, and defeat, this? How do we gain entry into our own imagination? Can we realize the freedom to create in the face of societal taboos and cultural repression? What is a "self-critical approach?" Can this be developed? The value of workshops in building self-criticism. Self-criticism is the goal. You need to be strong in the face of disinterest. What happens when we finish a poem, a painting, or a story we like? That rush of enthusiasm! We want the whole world to see the damn thing. So what do we not do? The whole world doesnay give a fuck remember. Thus we do not give it to our nearest and dearest, the poor old spouse, partner, best friend, close working colleague. At all costs we never succumb to such temptation. If we do, by mistake, the best we should expect is silence!

Mister Proctor

Silence. We start to wonder ourselves, maybe I forgot to send it. Did we actually give the story to that person? Maybe I dreamt it. Because nobody wants to know. We leave them in a state of dumbfoundedness, and what a terrible word, apologies.

But art begins from there. Honestly, that is where it begins; silence, ours and theirs. Okay, well

Mister Proctor

Yes?

36

How Long is a Short Story?

I have a question for you Mister Proctor, about those short pieces you write. You read them at the start of the evening, those very very short pieces. You called them stories.

I did, and I still do. They are stories.

Surely they cannot be stories?

Yes they can.

Not real stories?

Yes, real stories.

As short as that?

Do you mean the stories I was reading earlier?

Yes.

You are questioning whether the stories I read earlier exist?

Yes. Surely they cannot be stories?

The stories that I read?

Yes, surely. Not real ones, not as short as that?

What about not-real ones? How long must they be?

Not as short as that, that is too short.

Too short for what?

For stories.

Even for short stories that are not-real?

As short as that, yes, they cannot be as short as that.

The man half turned so that he could exchange looks with his Creative Writing tutor who was sitting at the side of the room, and from here he took strength: Nobody will ever publish them, he said. And he swivelled on his arse to make eye-contact with the Creative Writing tutor who displayed nothing, eyes to the desk.

I held aloft the book I had read from. This is the book wherein these stories are published. You watched me reading from it.

Yes, but that is a book. You could not get them published in magazines.

Yes I could. And I did. I opened the book. See! I displayed the acknowledgments page. This here is what we call the Acknowledgments page. It acknowledges where individual stories were published. See here there are five acknowledgments. And here I held up the book again, displaying the page, and I read aloud the names of the five journals wherein the five stories had been published previously.

I've never heard of them.

Well they do exist. Or did. These wee literary journals and magazines tend not to last forever.

Ah.

What are ye ahhing at?

You said they were "wee," you mean little?

What?

So they aren't big, that is what I mean, not big magazines. Big magazines wouldnt take them. You couldnt get them published in big magazines, that's all I'm saying; magazines with names, names we've heard of. The ones you're talking about are not big like that.

That's true. The only magazines who publish my very short stories are what they call "little magazines." Little magazines for little stories. So you're right, you are right—so what do we do?

What do you mean?

I dont know. Honestly, in answer to your question, I dont know. I am here though, and this is us talking.

37

The Terms

The following morning, after the previous night's reading event, the Regional Arts Control Officer met me at the House, and he asked, Did you enjoy it?

I was not sure what he meant.

The reading event, he said.

Aw. No, I said. But I'm not the audience. I am the performer. Did you enjoy the performance, is a question for the audience. I am the one who gives the performance. The audience are those who receive it, those who behold it, who behold the performance. The audience dont deliver the performance to the artist. The artist delivers it to them. I perform for the audience. The audience watch, they listen. Some artists accept the term "enjoyment" in regard to the performance they deliver. I dont. They only do it to save hassle, they cant be bothered explaining themselves.

I was only asking if you enjoyed it.

Enjoyed what?

Just enjoyed it, said the Regional Arts Control Officer.

Let me ask you a question?

The Regional Arts Control Officer sniffed.

Can I ask you a question?

Okay.

Why is it so difficult to admit that I am the one who creates and that this is the basis of our relationship?

The Arts Control Officer sniffed again. Two sets of sniffs in four seconds. He smiled and looked capable of answering my question quite easily, but thought silence the better policy. I would have preferred him to answer. People know things that I dont, especially in regard to myself.

38

Easy does it

I was out for a walk by the shores of the mighty waters and this flock of birds, at least half a dozen, were taking me for an enemy. Some bugger had been dropping empty wine bottles into the briny. Right there in the rushes! God's teeth! Who would do something like that!

Bla bla bla.

Really but, who would toss a wine bottle into the canal!

What damn right did they have even to be here! This was my damn tow path! No wonder we get angry, fucking fools. No wonder we get resentful. If I saw somebody tossing a wine bottle into the canal I would fucking drown the bastard, probably a young guy, probably stupidity, impressing his pals; I would still fucking drown him, if it had been a boy of mine, but no boy of mine would have done such a thing, never, they just wouldnt have done it, I mean, never, never.

So much stupidity. In the entire world! No wonder I couldnt write!

I could write, I just could not concentrate because of all this shite and then we hear some idiot tutor bastard yapping on about "readability." Readability! Fucking bastard I'd fucking strangle him! What was he even talking about he didnt know what he was talking about this leader of this stupid fucking workshop, Can you talk a bit on "readability"? I should have man, I would have. Leader of the Workshop. Permanent Member of the Authorial Upper Chamber. We dont write merely for the sake of it. If they dont pay we dont write. "Big" writers or "little" writers we all worry about markets. Pushkin, Stendhal or Mickey Spillane; Leonie

Sheridan, Franz Kafka, Bruce Waddell, Zane Grey. We all worry about markets. What we call the Doctor Johnson approach. It's "readability" makes the difference. Can you talk a little about that Mister Prock-tor?

No, I said, can I fuck. Let me ask yous all a question. How come persons seek to write books who have no interest in books? Fucking idiot with yer fucking readability. Fuck you.

And that is the truth that really, it is not that I wanted to fuck off. I needed to. Why could I not, not just fuck off?

Now a couple of birds flew pretty close to my head, to the extent I so-to-speak "ducked."

So there we are, how come we say "ducked," seeing as how these clever wee buoyant buggers submerge their heads every so often while traversing the waters.

One sees the other birds too, this wee robin comes hop hop hopping along, stands there a moment. I whistled on the wee fucker and it just hopped away. Dont ya want to be pals with me? I shrieked, plaintively, and it hopped back again! Can ye believe it man! This canal is a wonder to behold.

Such the thoughts, the fruits of one's what-dye-call-it, brain cluster, the sparks and so on.

This one too: how does one recognize a sentence, when the door slams on you, and is that how it happens,

what is knowledge, a duck, what is a duck

the knowledge is what I had lost, what was a sentence again,

stupidity, just stupidity. I needed just to relax, being able to concentrate, just do the work, get on with the work, forget all the cynical second-rate shite that comforts lazy arseholes everywhere, fucking "readability," this guy who had never published a book in his life. Whenever somebody refers to Doctor Johnson in that way the one thing you know is they know fuck all man, nothing.

But the guy brought it on himself. He set a bad example. It was his own fault. That is why I fucking jumped at the bastard.

39

Grounds for Optimism

A strange light glinting on the puddles, the wet street. Hardly any traffic. This wee town, wee miserable town; wee miserable, cold and damp town, fucking freezing town. My "strange light glinting" was a mundane attempt to inject life.

They had this shit teaching them.

I was reduced to silence, interpreted as a form of communication.

Maybe it was. In the long run.

I rechecked the schedule. I couldnt read it. I was going blind, maybe. The intellectual coordination shutting down; a reprisal, as against inanity, which with an "s" reads insanity.

the lack of verve present in the very thought

or its expression

if space between the two exists

I was to leave at 11 o'clock this morning, to drive and drive and do the events, returning home round midnight.

Except with an "r" is excerpt. This is comforting. Who or what is the excerpt? This, this was the excerpt.

A sudden thought of the car not starting, the image of me in the act of discovery, saying aloud, Imagine the battery dying on a night like this! Nobody to hear me. Making me smile. Putting me in my place. The self-deprecatory nature of one's sense of humour. The survival instinct. One day one is home, one has returned, Einstein and onwards, ever onwards.

40

Writers go away and come back

No, I said, I have to stop ye here. When Wikipedia says there's a gap of between five and eight years between Proctor's novels it doesnt mean that I go away and come back again. That isnt what happens.

It says there's a gap.

Yes I realize that but that's the gap in publishing it's not the gap between me writing them. If it says published in 2020 it doesnt mean I sat down and wrote it in 2020 and then had it published in 2020. It doesnt mean that. I see ye looking and ye're wondering if I'm suggesting something and if so what that might be. Well, it's the actual writing. I have to write them. Is that making sense.

(The faces gazing at me.)

So ye see I'm not going away and living my life for a couple of years till then I come back and publish another one, which is the gist of the comments I've been listening to. It isnay like I go away for a four-year holiday or something, living on the proceeds. I grinned. I mean where do ye think I go, for talking sake?

Greece? said a man.

Pardon?

I would, if I had the chance. Certainly I would. There are all these wonderful locations.

Unspoilt beaches and small islands, said a woman.

I nodded. I wasnt meaning it as a literal eh ... I just eh ... What was it the person said again, who made the remark, about writing novels?

Nobody answered.

Who made the remark about writing novels?

I dont think anybody did, called the tutor.

I'm sure somebody did, asking had I written a novel of my own. Then one of ye googled me to find out.

Some of us already knew.

Oh aye, yes, I know that. So now ye know I've written four.

Four novels! said a woman. You've written four novels?

At least. Why are you so surprised?

I think it's marvelous. I'm in awe. And you're here with us, she said and she laughed, glancing at the others.

Well yes ye see I'm the Writer-in-Residence at the House for this period so really if ye think about it, I would need to have written books to be here. Maybe one would be enough. If it was a bestseller.

Mark Allen? called the tutor.

Exactly right. Mark Allen!

Have you met him? called a woman.

Yes.

Honestly?

Yes.

Have you written a bestseller? asked a man.

No. I could have though. It's more arbitrary than ye might imagine.

You should write one. If you did you would be able to write the more serious work at your leisure. And do it in a better climate, as some writers do. Then you could go to Greece, if that was your dream. If it was me that's where I would go.

When I said arbitrary I only meant that the writer doesnt have much control over it. We cannay choose to write a bestseller.

Oh but you won the Banker Prize! called the tutor.

Fair enough but I didnt write the novel to win it.

Agreed, said the tutor, but surely it is important to remain positive?

Never say die! called a man.

Writing isnt just a grind, said the tutor.

No. I smiled.

There are some decent aspects.

There are.

But you have written four novels, said the woman.

Probably. I smiled. Sorry, I cannay quite remember where I was going with that, although if I hadnt written them I would just be an older person sitting in the house and just like I dont know, whatever, watching television.

I take issue there, said a woman. Older people arent necessarily housebound. Some are but not everyone. We get out and about, we join clubs, we go places and we meet people.

A man said suddenly. You could have been coming here, learning how to write a novel, from somebody like yourself!

Everybody laughed, including me.

Have you brought one of your novels with you? asked the same man.

No.

It would be nice if you had, said a woman. You could have read a chapter to us. So then we would hear it for ourselves.

I closed my eyes for a moment.

She smiled. Dont worry. We might have liked it.

The tutor said, Do you know Bruce Waddell?

No but the name is familiar.

The tutor smiled. He's another bestseller. His books sell in the millions.

A man had appeared at my side with a coffee. Black on its own? he said.

Thanks.

The coffee was slightly lukewarm but so what. Not so much lukewarm as off the boil. I put the cup down on the table and continued talking:

The problem with me is that I drink liquids at boiling point because there's nay time to do otherwise. I eat food at boiling point as well. The roof of my mouth if not blistered is shedding skin every day of my life, the remnants of scalded flesh. And see after the meal, when I'm doing the dishes, I wash them in boiling water. My wife cant go near the sink, she doesnt know how my flesh stands up to it. Neither do I. I just kind of ... thrash around, becoming ever more enmeshed until finally paralysis sets in.

Surely not paralysis? The tutor grinned. You have published rather a lot, taking the stories into consideration.

Yeah well, writers write and I'm sixty-six years of age. This is what we do and how come we are known as writers. Nothing happens of its own volition. Energy equals mass times the speed of light squared remember or whatever the hell it is, the tortoise and the hare, what is the answer? A body-swerve. It isnt just one race it's two. There is the world and there is us. Art is practice. The equation is the thought and we serve them together. Nothing is there that cannot connect, that is not involved in a relationship. We make it. What exactly is creation?

It depends which religion you are, said a man.

In this respect religion is irrelevant.

The man smiled.

I dont mean irrelevant; not relevant, not to here and now.

Do you believe in God? asked a woman.

Eh I'm not sure how you use the actual word. I tend not to use the capital, the cap G. I use lower case as in lower case g o d. With yourself and most people I feel I need to use the cap G to be respectful, respectful to your beliefs, not to "god" lower case or God cap G.

Nobody commented. The tutor was watching me from the back of the room.

I cant say any better I dont think. The important thing is that I dont have to deny the existence of an immaterial substance which in our culture is no longer necessary although in others it remains a capital offence.

That's all very well, said a man.

Heavenly gnashers batman! I chuckled. Excuse me, I've not been sleeping well.

God is always here, said the man.

God doesnt go away and come back, said the woman who raised the matter originally.

I shrugged. Then I laughed. Exactly! I said. If you believe in me as in front of you, standing here today, you will accept this as evidence of my existence, that I am the self-same this. And if you accept this, you must further accept *this* this, which is the indivisible I and me. So the burden of proof is not on me if here I am. But that isnt to say the burden is on you, you and thou.

41

Later it was later

Who was it gave up on oxygen? Some venerable worthy just thought, to hell with it, and stopped breathing. The duvet over one's skull, tugging down the lower sheet, the knees drawn up to the chin. Oh mammy daddy rescue me, I want my wife my wife my wife, I should be in the arms the arms the arms

I should be in the arms,

I should be in the arms

I should be in the arms

Where is Hannah, looking for Hannah, where is she, rescue me, I want I should

be in the arms

mother and grandmother having taken precedence

Where was I? Alive, dreams ended, failed again. Closed my eyes for five minutes now here I was. And to have been someplace. Pulling the duvet over my head, snuffing out the tiniest channel of fresh air in the offchance people can whatdyecallit suffocate oneself; asphyxia, a favoured idea by would-be suicides the world over or if poison, the act of opening one's veins, one opens one's veins. Never mind later—later it was later.

42

The difficulty of the I-voice ending

I stopped work at 0400 hours and clambered into bed for a couple of hours before setting out on this wearisome road not to nowhere but beyond all that, having awakened by the light of spiritual illumination rather than silvery moonbeams. And it was revealed to me that while revolutions do not exist risings may and shall remain glorious no matter the outcome. Revolts after this fashion are characterized by the deepmost regard for convention held by its insurgents. Authority states the case and the statement of the case is the act of becoming the case. Therein lies the supremacy of the unwritten constitution, that it governs every contingency as it so arises. Authority is a limited company of lawyers whose central function is

Do eyes even exist? What are eyes? Eyes are optical illusions, for is it not the case that the ayes have it, that eyes are "themselves," in nomine patris one swipes with the razor, ridding the world of nonsensicality.

If eyes be a true reflection of the inner state then outwardly I was awake but inwardly less certain. What time was it?

The fatigue upon me. Between bouts of stuttered breathing and had I dreamt it, that in answer to the "how did you pass the hour" question daddy I captured the thoughts I undoubtedly must have experienced. Yet there was nothing. This is normal, normal; that unsettling process that occurs first thing each morning, except that for me it happens, and had been happening, while I was driving. Where had I been and how was the road?

The dinky kept juddering and joddering and the gear stick kept grinding and rattling. I was feart to look at the fuel gauge. Mist was a-settling and a thick haar a-blanketing all sensory perception, thus immediacy itself: the moment smothered—and the story where the writer is lost up a mountain in Mexico and found by most charming locals, flattered by their uncommon courtesy, accorded the most incredible hospitality, poor fool, draped in pixelated fantasies wherein one's hosts knew even the names of one's books, all of one's books. Danger.

It is said that the father of my maternal grandpa once met Bret Harte in a pub in Glasgow. He disembarked from an ocean-going liner down the banks of the River Clyde in the days when real boats went down that river. Bret got lost somewhere along a stretch of harbour descryed by locals the Broomielaw, in the vicinity of the famed Betty's Bar where much the same thing happened to Woody Guthrie during the 2nd World War, him and Cisco Houston. But old Bret was found by my granddaddy who did not "happen to be" in Betty's Bar, he was there because he worked as a barman, according to my grannie. Being lost in the mountains in Mexico was a very different experience to being lost in Betty's Bar in the days when a five-pound note bought ye a berth from here to New York City let alone an all-night session in an apartment of your choice. There in Mexico the lost stranger was caught and flattered by singular individuals who spoke, acted, looked and had all the mannerisms of a White Anglo-Saxon Protestant elite. Yer man was stuffed full of the finest wittels and rarest of blood red vinos every two hours by his courteous, respectful hosts. He began to remind himself of something.

What might it be?

A f**king Capon chicken, he was being fattened for the slaughter, dear reader. That writer is to be butchered and devoured by this selfsame bunch of charming White

Anglo-Saxon Protestant elite whose existence was dependent on the very flesh, sinew and tonsils of the working-class poor. There ye are. Moral to the yarn: do not trust the ruling elite because these fuckers will kill ye and eat ye for their very lunch oh mammy daddy mammy daddy. Was it old Bret wrote that ghoulish warning to weary writers? And who was the weary victim, and was it an I-voice story? And if so, dear reader, by whose hand was the tale ended; whose the wavering pen of the poor deluded soul ... God's gnashers, he croaked,

> aint never written no horror story,
> never had the wanting to
> then the day I got lost up the mountain
> I wound up drooling for you
> yeah, I wound up drooling for you
> comma

the which I shall entitle Fangs for the Memory. Oh fuck, reduced to whatdyecallthem, figures of speech fucking things, puns! Puns, so this is where I had landed.

Settle down.

43

Tallulah and the Vampires

I was to arrive at a Residential Project located within an HM Correctional Centre of Ethics, Aesthetics & Commonary Cultures. I had been outsourced, or seconded as is said in military circles. Had the House charged a fee for loaning me out! I was to look for the lower reaches of a mountain wherein I might find several redeveloped outbuildings on the outer grounds of the castellated home of a Duke of the Realm whose entire estates, lock, stock and barrels + all properties thereunto had been purchased on behalf of The Nation whose citizen-members had been informed that the sum of 3.5 billion pounds sterling in the shape of gold bullion had been agreed on their behalf by representatives acting on behalf of the Hereditary Estates of The Nation. The terms of the agreement were binding; solemnicized by the ermined fist of a Permanent Secretary to the Upper Hereditary Chamber, sealed by HM the Right Honourable Signet-Holder to the Privy Purse. Citizen-members of The Nation who wished to view their recent purchase, or any other of their properties now rented by the Duke, should submit an application to the Duke's Land Agent six months in advance of the day of said visit.

The current Duke, well-known sportsman and fine arts connoisseur, holder of several charity directorships, friend of Princes and procurers, racing car drivers and all manner of buccaneering entrepreneurs, was an approachable sort of chap who bore an uncanny likeness to his ancestor, Duke number One, who had been granted these lands and properties in the mid-12th century for fulsome slaughter and general racketeering services on behalf of foreign colonizers. Through devious politicking, lickspittle servitude, religious hypocrisy, acts of murder, mayhem and general terrorism the first Duke's successors had remained in possession of these lands and properties for the next thousand years, sheltered and protected by successive monarchs, dictators and tyrannies, *in perpetua*, on condition that obediance, servility and all forms of hospitality stipulated by their Majestic Highnesses be extended to their Royal Offspring & Descendants, and all entourage, servants, financiers, lawyers and military heads, should ever they land in the region and have no place to go during a downpour of hailstones quantified at not less than 0.001ctl.

The sea! Cliff walks and stout hiking boots. But already it was dark. I passed through an ex-fishing village with a landscaped marina and a hotel by the pier. Ahead I saw a tavern: the Three Ton Tuna. The elderly barlady croaked a welcome. Meals might be ordered but alas no time. I had a spirited water, packets of crisps and salt peanuts salt peanuts salt peanuts; swallied the lot and inquired as to the whereabouts of the lower reaches of a natural protuberance termed Old Smokey. She gestured me onwards, Ahoy sir and by the Good Lord's grace I shall see thee again. Maybe not, I hazarded, and in the far distance heard the eerie howl of a lone wolf.

I returned to the car, bumped my knees and switched on the ignition. The engine sparked, as did my lungs. A couple of miles inward and still no sign of a mountain but the country was rough. No lights other than the moon and what the car provided. I was now in that situation all drivers hate: the road had become a track. How had it happened? I dont know. There had been no road signs but one gets used to that in this land of plenty. Everyone is out to devour us. The mair we blunder the likelier they are to skin us for a profit. The stranger was never seen again. Good title for a story. Good way to end a story. Now the track veered off, skirting a forest. I saw smoke rising from some old-style outposts. Maybe I could find the coast road if I drove left which is east, unless one is facing the other way, recalling the yarn by old Aleichem where an exhausted guy sets his shoes facing north before having a sleep at the side of the road: he about-turns during his sleep and travels south when he wakes up. Man, what a truth.

To hell with it, I was going back to the Three Ton Tuna.

My dear fellow! You were hungry?

The belly pangs were pounding.

I say!

Then the track had become a manicured lane bounded by tall rhododendron bushes beyond which no human might peer. Then I was there.

How come I had agreed to this shite? Nobody forced me. Too late now, I was here for what they called a long weekend, three nights and two full days.

Mine host was to greet me at reception: Robin Goodman, author of articles, plays, poetry and boomps-adaisy. He was one of the ones in charge of the project. Apparently he was twenty-five years of age and here he was tenured and with a ten-year Writer-in-Residency for x amount of a salary, plus pension. I googled the swine. He had written a best-selling novel entitled: *The Man Who Wrote a Bestseller and Remained Cool*. This won him all sorts of cash awards and promises of a rosy future.

The place was smaller than expected. I parked the car and looked for the main event-space.

Sarcasm aside, these weekend courses for people can be decent. Humans meet humans, surprised to discover, contrary to State propaganda, that they have much in common. I pushed open the door and a roomful of chary faces greeted me. A major table, old-style. Framed prints on the wall of difficult routes and climbs to the summit of the hill. These were offset by several gilt-framed pictures of the wizened countenances of elderly dook-dudes.

An old guy rose and stepped forward, not much younger than myself. He grinned and reached to shake my hand.

Hi, I said, I'm Jack Proctor.

Oh.

Fictive imaginings?

Beg pardon?

Fiction-books, novels and like eh . . .

Ah.

Sorry, yeh, it was a long drive, and not too well sign-posted. I looked for a mountain and discovered a hill. I havent missed the food have I?

Not at all. We all have eaten but I'm sure you can too.

Thank god. I'm hungry and tired and looking forward to the life ahead.

He chuckled. I'm Allan Maxwell.

Fine, what about Robin, is he here? Robin Goodman?

No, he said, not really. I am your host during this part of the Project. Please call me Allan. He indicated a chair. On the other side of this chair sat a "beautiful woman," if the term "sat" may be applied to an activity performed by such ladies, given it is premised on the existence of "bum" as an attribute, thus to say of certain women, "she sat" is grounds for a belt on the jaw. She was that kind of lady. I squeezed in. She gave me a decent smile. Bejasus I was sick of my body odours and sitting next to her was so very pleasant. Tallulah Debray, said Allan Maxwell.

Pleased to meet ye Tallulah.

Hi, she said. Her smile was gracious but with an edge which may have been playful. Allan Maxwell gestured at the students. For a dreadful moment I thought he was goni introduce me to each individually. This is Jack Proctor everyone. I'm sure you will get to know one another.

People gave me a wave and I waved them one back.

Allan said, A glass of wine Jack? And he poured me one of a decent-size. Most pleasant to the sip I must say.

He had been in the middle of talking to the company when I arrived. Now he passed me a copy of a glossy brochure and continued talking, a sort of general history of the project and the place. I listened a moment but it was difficult. I sneaked a look at the students who were mainly young people—young to me anyway, viz. early middle-age, or the later youngster stage. Maybe a couple were older. God knows. People had noticed me looking. I turned my attention to the brochure. The tutors were named at the back, some had biographical notes, others not. I found Dr Allan Maxwell, Composer, Essayist and Famed Excavier; Tallulah Debray, Dramatic Vibrettist, Renowned Exponent of Dance-as-Art-in-Performance; founder of the Debray College; and one Guest Fiction-Writer from the Hammer House of Snottirs, i.e. me.

Usually one does not rise to the bait but on this occasion, not even being awarded the benefit of a moniker—given that mine own is the one I would have been awarded—would have irritated a duck, if ducks could write. And who knows what they got up to in these hillside burns, streams, rivers and canals, yonder comes a sucker and he stole my gal. The banks of mine were infested with illicit activities and their sundry sound effects; quacks, squeals and—I am afraid to report, quoaks—the sound ducks utter on their last breath. Who was it wrote about the absolute horrors: the murders, rapes, mutilations and bestial tortures that occur every night of the week in the animal kingdom? These beasts are brutes. And then we come to insects. Merciful heavens! We see it looking oot windies. What goes on in hedges. God's teeth!

Guest fiction-writer. Oh dull reality! Not even my name? That was me, a fucking insect. Ach well, where was the grub? All I heard was the droning sound of Dr

Maxwell, blethering away on matters concerning bureau-
cratic domesticity:

Here is the Housekeeping.

Today is Housekeeping.

Tomorrow too is Housekeeping.

Here at Old Smokey we pay respect to Housekeeping.

I was starving. Usually a vegetarian alternative was
offered in these Art and Aesthetics residential institutions.
The participants pride themselves on their humanitarian
spirit which for wealthy folk entails putting down their pets
in humane fashion. Here at Old Smokey, the students cook
wittels of their own devising, where they may exhibit their
caring approach to the culinary appetites of the general
body. This finds favour, it is hoped, with those one hopes to
seduce post–lights out. The snag is one is obliged to praise
the cook after each bite of mashed potato.

Another snag with certain types of veggie cooking is
the biliousness suffered such that one's company is not a
desired commodity. One recalls ancient Egypt and their
aversion to beans. Things sprout from beans; plants grow
from them. Even the shape of a bean! It resembles an
embryo. Imagine eating an embryo. Murderer! But a crucial
line in thought, one hazards, in regard to the transmigratory
soul theory. Any life is a former life, a life yet to come. The
reason we know things we have never before experienced
is because we learned of them in a previous existence, dan
d randan, elementary el vino.

Students were taking notes, mainly by pen or pencil. I
thought they were here for the weekend but apparently they
were here for a week or more. They were thus chastened
to discover that no wi-fi signal might exist on Old Smokey,
nor would such have been encouraged. It came to pass that
my name was mentioned in relation to the House of Art
and Aesthetics and the concept Workshopping. I saw Allan
Maxwell glancing at a little piece of notepaper from which

he appeared to be reading my name and referring to one or two items of a personal nature, except it was so difficult to effin well hear. A few students were talking among themselves, too close for comfort.

Heh yous, I said, stop that. I cannay bloody hear.

They looked at me, astounded. I winked to cloak my annoyance. But they stopped the talking.

Allan Maxwell ended by saying, For those with an interest in fiction-books I suggest that Mister Jack Proctor should be very experienced in those particulars, no doubt, and will workshop with you. During mornings and afternoons students are encouraged to visit both he and Professor Debray on one-to-one missions.

Informality was the key to students' time here and they should understand that but, given the existence of the one-to-one, it was unacceptable to buttonhole the tortutors in the evenings or chap us up through the night in order to seek advice on whether or not publishers will look at dog-eared manuscripts or must they be pristine copies fresh from the laser printer. No wi-fi meant no emails no reams of electronic prose. Personally I refused to read emailed stories sent by any student on the grounds of—what? Not principle. I just fucking hate them. As soon as I open up a document I start revising the fucker.

Allan Maxwell paused, smiled at me.

I had yawned. Yes but it not through boredom, it was an effect of exhaustion and malnutrition. I had driven across the entire country to get here.

No matter what he said to the people here, in practice they would approach us on one-to-one missions at any time of the day or night. Why? Because students are students. This is what students do whether 18 or 80 years of age. Ah there is M'sieur le Professeur, let us provoke/punch/tease or seduce said party into revealing his inner imbecile.

The ones more likely to approach are those seeking

solace, who find themselves ostracised from the wider student body. There are any number of reasons for this; ranging from inappropriate impropriety, unseemly body odour, addictive behavioural patterns. Easily the most common is boring-bastard sydrome. This malaise is one I endure personally. Fortunately this is spotted quickly and I am left alone. Allan Maxwell reminded everyone that he may have been a professor as well as a doctor but if they should address him as Allan he would not take it amiss.

He invited Professor Debray to say a few words about the course she offered, and Mister Jack Proctor would follow. Then he sat down, and sighed loudly, reaching for a fresh bottle of red wine which he uncorked with his teeth and gargled prior to the swally-procedure: he refilled his glass and passed the bottle to me. Sorry for yawning, I whispered. I'm used to it, was the whispered reply.

Tallulah Debray had risen from her chair. Please do not call me professor, she said. My name is Tallulah Debray. During my peroration I shall clarify the term Dance-as-Art-in-Performance in regard to my own creative processes. You should know that Vibretticism is wholly of that, and belongs in that: a series of processes and forms of processes combining and operating as the one unique process itself. This derives from a very ancient life-bringing practice that has come to be known as mézzaj. Not massage! Tallulah smiled: mézzaj, m-é-z-z-a-j.

I had never heard of this. Neither had Allan Maxwell by the looks of it. He unfolded his arms and leaned closer, his right hand to his ear, as though hard of hearing, as no doubt he was. I'm pretty sure he was older than me.

Mézzaj was an ancient form of touch-healing which makes its origin consistent with "massage" itself. Tallulah continued to use physical movement as part of her perora-tion, using her body in a way I might describe as sylph-like, languidly so, or languidly sylphish; like a dancer acting the part of a cobra unwinding and twisting its way out a fakir's basket. Maybe Vibrettist had to do with that, vibrat vibrare the closest I was getting.

She spoke at length on music, dance and the visual aspect of early behavioural patterns in Middle Eastern communities, and within this were hints and murmurs of other areas of knowledge. Then she began moving, almost on the one spot, always gracefully, continuing to talk as she did so. Her voice had a husky quality. It was not only fascinating it was hypnotic, mesmerizing. She gave us to understand that her family was what in angloimperial structures they call "old Money. In passing she said how on one occasion, exiting from the inner city subway of a major international capital, she had been mistaken for a rather well-known Arabian Princess.

A woman raised her hand: Is your family name Debray or is it de Bray?

Tallulah smiled and moved on without answering which I found appropriate. Strange how students believe they have the right to ask these questions. Yet the more she continued the less able was I to grasp the nature of the subject. My agent once advised me that I had a tendency towards the overly critical. My kids agreed. A literary acquaintance once accused me of hurtful posturing. I liked to think I began from a position of humane sardonicism. In this instance I was trying to be as attentive as everybody else but the difficulty for myself as for other tutors is the degree of attention we pay to technique and delivery instead of the actual content. Especially when we find the content boring as fuck. Tallulah had written three books on the topic, each of which she happened to have brought with her in sufficient quantities to sell to interested students and other parties. In these she dealt with the history of mézzaj as a practice, moving beyond its "this world" physicality into the Scotusian thisness of the unknowable in-itself.

Tallulah referred to its mystical origin and the "extended intellectualism" of its Mid-Byzantine Sensibility, what she described as the Passions of Medieval Beings. This we might relate to Scholastic philosophy. I raised my hand instinctively which I at once regretted. It is an unwritten rule that tortutors refrain from intervention when a colleague is talking. Unfortunately Tallulah saw me and called: Jack Proctor?

Sorry, I said, but uh just something in what you're saying is uh the work of Frederick Copleston SJ in any way relevant?

Tallulah laughed and clapped her hands. Jack Proctor makes an interesting point. Ah Jack Proctor, you wish to say something more?

Eh not really.

Allan Maxwell leaned towards me. This is an informal setting. Informality is at the heart of your stay with us. We should like to hear what you have to say.

Aw. I nodded.

And please to remember here at Old Smokey, fiction-books are always of interest.

A woman sitting across the other side of the table gave me an encouraging smile.

Thanks. I said, Just as an aside: Frederick Copleston SJ is a hero to many writers and I'm one. If I had had half that guy's energy I would be self-sufficient. No writer under the sun could fail to laud an example of such indefabigle indefatigleness. It drives one ever on, that single-minded energy, ever and ever I suppose, although one is entitled to wonder, in regard to religious-informed structures of hierarchy and the good monk's infamous joust with a certain arch-atheist that eh ... Volume 1. Volume 1 is the best place to start, for those of a mind. He is not essential reading. But I would add—but on second thoughts no, better perhaps not to add. I sniffed, shrugged and frowned.

They were all watching me, even the inattentive ones. Tallulah was whispering to Allan Maxwell and I waited for the outcome. Allan nodded and called: Feel free to finish the point Jack Proctor, we arent short on time.

Thanks. Well, I said, the one thing I would add and hereby do add, in regard to the man, and this in mitigation, he had a temporal space and economic freedom, and full librarial access to an extent we non-believer writer-outsiders may only dream.

The truth is I'm very tired and the wine is too tasty for wur own good. Nevertheless, I said, it's just something in what Professor Debray was alluding to eh following on from anthropomorphic forms, given these were "eternal men"—men qua men—so these forms become "eternal sensibles" in the sense that any wise man is not so much "sensible," as "a sensible" and in this I agree wholly with those who find the eternal male of it not only tedious but wearisome, one wearies. Sorry, I said, I'll stop at that although I think the use of syllogisms is important here but more so the dialectic itself.

I sat down on my chair, for I had been standing, and gripped my knees tightly lest they attemp to unlock themselves: let the levitation begin.

Tallulah Debray laughed and gave a thumbs-up gesture of approval.

But Allan Maxwell had his head lowered as though something of significance had happened but that this had passed over him as a sprite in the night. I knew him then for what he was: a decent fellow. Allan, I said quietly, I am lost, apologies.

He smiled. But it was a complicated smile.

Had something of significance happened? What might I have said? One must always recollect the age-band into which I had settled. Us maturer males did all these mad things; noises and scratchings, nosebleeds, chin dribblings and the dreaded fly dribblings god love us all, the splashes doon the troosirs. Never buy an old guy a pair of white breeks! God's teeth!

Now Allan had his head lowered. How come? Had he read my thoughts. Had I said something I shouldnt? Unless the yawning, I couldnay stop yawning. I noticed another woman watching me, much amused by my very presence. She had a name tag. She was grinning at me. I grinned in response and she chuckled, her shoulders waggling. Her name tag ... Diagon? Dragon ha ha, Dolly, Diana—Doreen! What age? Fifty-seven next birthday I would have hazarded.

Tallulah too. I had assumed she was around the thirty-five age mark. Not at all man she was hitting fifty—maybe older. Plus she was avoiding me. Maybe not. Although I was a competitor. Although not really, she had me beat all ways up!

Suddenly a cacophony. The students had been quiet for an hour or more. Now they went for it, nineteen to the dozen.

It suited me. I sat there saying nothing. Only the yawning kept me awake. Just very tired. Too tired. The heady red red wine, stay close to me yea, on an empty bellee, and I was happy to leave right there and then except I needed food, other than wee nibbles at the nips, nuts, chitters and raisins that were lying about on wee bowls.

Oh god and I realized I still had to talk! the fucking peroration. I had to advise the assembled students and fellow guests as to the nature of my very own creative input, derived from my very own life experience and so on, according to the glossy brochure, *in esse lallanus joctore*. Yea tho I talk in death's dark vale, merrily merrily. Life experience! I didnay have any life experience. I was a writer of fiction-books, we sit on chairs and write one then we go away and come back again and write another one.

This was a time for precision. Will ye no come back again? Naw, will I fuck.

I noticed that woman again, the one sitting across the table, she was gazing at me and with a twinkle in her eye. I knew that twinkle. I thought I had yawned, maybe it was a snore. Whatever it was I amused her! I peered again at her name tag, Diagon, Dolly, Diana—Oh pleese stay by me, Diana. I'm so bold of this I'm told, oh Diana bla bla bla. Fortunately I managed to resist singing aloud. Although tell a woman a joke and they are yours for life, according to these male handbooks they dish ye out in certain cultures when ye reach the ripe old age of thirteen. Genderist shite man but what can ye do if it's yours? Rebel you swine. It was a guid skelp on the lug I needed.

But I needed my bed, my bed. Otherwise I would sleep on this very chair.

Allan Maxwell was smiling at me.

When I was a wean on the rough and ready streets of auld Glesga toon we had insufficient beds for the complete familial squad. We had to nab chairs and position them such that we squeezed our feet on to the one facing. I never regretted it because of the healthy upright-seated postures we all developed, a byword in our district: the 'Proctor Crouch' as it was known. Dear god, muttered a voice, probably mine.

I was speaking aloud yet again. Ach well.

Allan, I am very tired. I worked through all last night on fictive-imaginings and only stopped at five of the a.m.s this morning.

Oh.

Honest, I said, I grabbed an hour on the chair, lights out and blanket over one, sent to sleep by the quacking of ducks, then early early I had to leave to drive here—a much longer drive than anticipated. One would have thought His Excellency the Duke might have laid on a helicopter. Thus I say to you, apologies for snoring.

Allan chuckled.

Is it okay if I do my talk tomorrow morning?

Of course.

Then allow me to consign myself to my quarters.

I was cheered from the meeting place. Onwards via the kitchen. Salmon smoked and cheese finest, esoliv and toestoma, and a variety of teabags.

They had shoved me into this extended shepherd's bothy halfway up Old Smokey. It was among a number of data I failed to register earlier. Now I was having to negotiate the ditches, ruts and giant ferns upward along the trail, although I suspect I was crawling by the time I made it in through the door—which was unlocked. Unlocked doors on the side of a mountain! Now having climbed the bugger it seemed like a mountain.

Nay television! God's teeth, how was one to sleep!

I was no longer so hungry. I ate a couple of mouthfuls and sipped green tea by the window. Then was tired. It was immediate. I only had time to get off the clothes and clamber between the sheets, oh man, sometimes bed is best, one wriggles one's way, relax brains relax! is the scream, the tortured neurons, the motherboard. But how can one sleep, can one sleep, oh man thoughts of home and thoughts of family and all kinds, all kinds yet nothing, nothing, there was nothing bar a scratching—or was it a tapping—by the door, by the window, the glass pane, muffled noises and I, rousing myself, my head thick my body weary and my brains oh my brains if I have any brains oh man all of these years on the planet dangling there in space unseen unheard, unknown; never-to-be-known, each one of them, each one, and the tap on the window, insistent, as from that other planet but what planet oh jesus christ coming after me, Who goes there? croaked the stranger, the nature of reality, magic or mezzhyck m'sieur, his blood running cold, the hand of fate, his feet slabs of ice, oh my lord was someone out there in the moaning, groaning winds, whispering, Mister Jack Proctor m'sieur, Professeur . . . this sylphlike apparition wafting and I, with absent air, hoping she would take it for pleasurable bewilderment that she might seek to enter one's very room, Ah Zhoak, huskeelay, if I may, you give voice to earlier words and conceptual frameworkings I find so fascinating, staring at me, saucer-like eyes, bending her head, at the neck, collapsing swan-like, to the mattress. And I was to talk, to sit by her, no chair but the bed, the edge of the bed, now a mattress and my chin straddling my knees, the hems of skirts, I may be a damn fool, open to the slightest tickle, emotional, intellectual, the peneriel location; vague vibrations at the lower belly, the diaphramitic region, the old hiatus hernia which was a bit out, really, a bit kind of not good, the upper part, as I get occasionally, just like oh man, and she noticed thank god thank god thus might she depart, beguiling spirit, begone ye of no shame! She continued to watch me most foully. So I just eh whoh . . . heartburn or heart attacks, tumerous wee beasties who can tell, the pain; massaging my chest, that sense of anguish suppressed. It's nothing as far as diagnosis enters or ends, having undergone various tests in past years but I now am clear, clear, although I confess to bouts of exhaustion, and am subject to unbearable weariness. Thoughts of other people and of that which they must contend, offers a sense of calm through reasoned discussion and a secular mysticism forming the basis to reason rather than sinewey physicalities, and I was choking but she did not answer, instead leaning, stretching sylph-like, the sylphs.

I hope you are feeling better? I said, but she made no response, no word, no sigh and I had expected a sigh at the very slightest, that I might rescue this creature whose very life

but I didnay want nay damn enterprises, excursions nor encounters; no jousting in the male to female manner, ah Zhoak, you are the fanciful libertine, no no no, nay old-man-behind-the-building gropes, nay damn bloody gropes at all, I am too old man for the gropes yea in the old times, the heated old times I confess, for whom the bell tolleth as the blood stays full and running over, while I too

Gropes! Even the word. It's shoddy. I dont like gropes. One does not have gropes out in the open. I didnay need Hannah shouting in my ear to remind me for god sake I am not an absolute idiot, a damn fool yes and so on but not a goner, no ma'am, the physicality; wearing jeans thank the lord, stretching, indefinitely, and that other word what's that other word, how she was doing it, not quite whatever it was, and I was avoiding the word, but okay languorous, was it languorous, thinking of languorous

I was wide awake. Up I got, whatever time it was I dont know. Some grub left from last night, so that and another green tea, then out for a walk.

Once I reached the summit I planted a flag and beat my retreat, returned to the bothy to continue the story I was working on. It was an old one. Unfortunately it was a load of dross. I returned it to the SHITE STORIES FOLDER and started a few new yins. I battered in and by the first toll of reveille had produced four pages of workings toward three new stories. Three new stories! I shoved them into the WHO KNOWS FOLDER.

It aint all hot air, what the guy says, he went away and wrote three new stories right under wur noses.

Spectacular.

Truly, it's important. The students see you aint just blabbing man it aint just an exercise in hypothetics. It destroyed "how do I begin" anxieties at a stroke. People are as easily excited as they are traumatized by the experience of creation which is why religion thrives in the face of good sense and solidarity. Later in the morning I might print out the pages and build the rest of the day on that, leaving out the theological, I didnay want to unnerve them altogether.

God's teeth! Mind you we needed a laugh. I like having a laugh. Ha ha ha. Why take it seriously. I was only here for another night and that was tomorrow plus tonight. Last night, this night and tomorrow night. Nay merr red wine. Red wine is great and that is that. But no more, no more, no more Maccrimmon, was the cry. Nay nuthin man: work work work, to the tune Ode to Joy!

> Do do do do do do do do
> do do do do
> do
> do do

Nay choice anyway, thoughts of the evening ahead and something to look forward to after a day of workshopping, housekeeping and all sorts of bla blas. Nay guest bottles nor booze cabinet. Coffee bags and teabags and one cup. Nay hanky-panky. Nay person smuggling. Nay radio, nay television.

> Do do do do do do do do

The Three Ton Tuna was the nearest pub for christ sake it was miles distant. Never mind and hell mend ye, not bringing yer own plus receipts for payback.

Seriously but, how come I hadnay brought a bottle of the hard stuff? Because I never did. I was a play-safe kind of fellow. The truth is out. I was too weak and considered it dangerous. Hannah didnay mind. It was me at my self-righteous most nonsensical worst. Booze in one's room as the slippery slope and so on. But why? What's wrong with a relaxing wee uisqué after an event? Memories of old David Savirre at a literary jamboree in France, a few years ago. We had rooms at the same hotel and his was along the corridor from mine. I was last man standing as was my wont in days of yore.

He had gone to his room early and it never occurred to me he had not gone to bed. I thought he would have been snoring by this time. It was a smoke-free hotel but clouds of cigar smoke emerged from under his door when I strolled along the corridor. I heard voices too and was mightily aggrieved at the idea other writers would partake to all hours content in my absence. Here was an after-hours session for those and such as those. I had assumed I belonged to the "such as those" brigade. Instead I was excluded. I chapped the door. The smoke bellowed out when Savirre answered, puffing a cigar, brandy glass in hand. He had a penchant for that apple-one they distil in Brittany, beauty with a powerful kick. Inside his room, the window was wide open: he was exhaling into the Parisian night but a gale-force wind was blowing the smoke back in. He peered along the corridor right to left and back again, and whispered: Where's Jerry?

I dont know, I said.

He nodded. Over his shoulder, I spotted his laptop open on the dressing table and next to it a bottle or three of the good stuff. The voices continued, coming from the laptop. Instead of inviting me in he pointed indoors. Ssh, he whispered, I'm on radio.

He was tuned into a station somewhere in Connecticut. He knew the host personally and was taking part in a talk-show. When he saw me looking he closed over the door, to within half an inch of my nose: You would not care for him m'boy he is a right-wing shit.

Then he shut door shut in my face.

The lesson taught me was twofold: 1. nobody needs company for a good time; 2. even great writers hog the booze.

The wily old bugger was having his own wee session. Naybody else was there. I was in the teaching racket in those days and was teaching a couple of his short stories which I thought pretty damn wonderful. I still do. Maybe not great but—well, a couple are great. I thought so anyway and used a couple for teaching purposes. Students found them upsetting and were annoyed by them which was even better. They went online and condemned me. Our Professor is a rotter! Dont enroll with him unless you want Cs for everything. My job was to leave their academic tranquility undisturbed. I gave them one by Erskine Caldwell where for the evening entertainment the white plantation owners require the black manservant to masturbate for the entertainment of their white guests. Political Art-in-Performance. These books should be suppressed screamed the students!

The management of anger. The expression of the management of anger. What else is art. All students should get upset.

This man should not be teaching etc. Ach well. Time for breakfast. I swallied the teabag, spat it out and shut down the machine, pulled on the boots.

Why do I get so fucking angry!

Never mind.

Tallulah was wearing this long shimmying shift of a dress, designed for a free-flowing form of yoga by the looks of it. How on earth had she crossed the boggy lower reaches of Old Smokey! She sighed every ten seconds then glanced at the door. Over by the counter Allan Maxwell had a plateful of bacon, two kinds of red meat sausage and blood pudding; quail and duck eggs, lard-saturated pancakes, hash browns; two shades of full sourdough toast; extra red meat sausage, extra bacon, extra tomatoes and herb-encrusted baked beans. He was chortling at something an older student was saying to him but it was a false chortle, designed to conceal a drool. Elderly academics respect free food like no others.

I reached for the prunes to enliven my bowl of muesli. My days of the mammoth fry-up were long gone but I enjoyed my food, as much as anybody. So did Tallulah with her three shades of yoghurt, three types of grape and two of berry. Plus sliced thingwi, that green fruit with the fleshy middle—only the skinning process lets it down. Yer knife takes half the good bit and renders it hardly worth the effort.

I had an an arts-in-process journal propped up on a cup and was trying to read it but Tallulah's sighs had become groans. I could no longer ignore it and closed the journal. Okay? I said.

It is not okay Mister Jack Proctor no. If we are artists, we make use of our hours. What hours do we have if not twenty-four; twenty-four hours is our life, every day is our life.

Sorry, have I eh, have I done something?

She shook her head, then paused. Allan was returning with the breakfast tray, unloading it onto the table with the aid of automated shovels. The food is good here, he murmured, wiping dried blood from his brow.

Me and Tallulah stared at the heap of edibles. Who could have done it justice? A 16th-century Flemish painter. No. It would have been one from court of the Monarchs of All the Kingdoms, whose breakfasts comprise haunches of lamb, pint goblets of mead, suckling pig, skinned horse, palefuls of veal, spawn of frog, of cod, of salmon; offspring of sheep, shanks of all manner of beasties, critturs, ducks, starlings and game-birds baked in a pie.

Allan Maxwell set to with a will but unfortunately for him Tallulah resumed groaning. She was most peeved. Apparently her first class had begun at 0600 hours that very morning but only two students attended, an elderly male and female who went along as a couple.

I dont think people took it on board, spluttered Allan, bits of grub flying everywhere.

Perhaps they were tired, I said, brushing bits of toast off my shirt.

Tired? Tallulah scowled. You were working Mister Jack Proctor. Five o'clock you were working. I saw light in your window.

I smiled smugly. Actually I dont sleep much.

Tallulah relaxed the scowl but set her head and neck in a weirdly upright posture; shoulders braced, ready for a square-go round the back. I work because I must, she said. And you. I know it, I see it. I look at you and I see it. If our students wish to make art they must work. Why else are they here? It is why they are here. We give to them what we can, which is one hundred percent.

Okay, I said, yeah, fair enough.

Thank you, she said. She ripped the top off another yoghurt carton and delved inside with a teaspoon. I glanced at Allan for an opinion but he was lost to the grub.

No doubt the students who failed to appear at Tallulah's class had stayed up half the night boozing, blethering or otherwise; enjoying themselves no end. And why not? This was a vacation as well as a course of study. People paid mucho dinero to attend and this was their first *petit déjeuner* together. They would have waited until us torturial old farts had disappeared into the gloom then caroused till all hours. This is why they slept in. Who bothers about early-bird classes the first morning after the first night before? Who does such a thing, apart from sprightly teetotallers and assorted hasbeens, neverbeens and seekers of shebeens. Students are also people, especially the over 30s, 40s, 50s, 60s, 70s and 80s.

And a few of them still hadnt arrived by the time the dishes were being washed. Tallulah was still talking about how students are to be regarded on courses such as this, not as revellers or erstwhile bon savants, et cetera but rootin tootin tooters and whatever else, my concentration waned— the beginnings I had made on three new stories, the voices, time to tamper, see how they go, maybe they dont need any tampering. Some stories dont stop, zoom zoom zoom, it's cheery. Black coffee. I hadnay had any since the last day of the duck, the day before yesterday.

Allan Maxwell was listening to Tallulah as carefully as he could. I sipped coffee and tried to listen but my god it was wearing one to a frazzle and I needed to escape at once please—besides which never mind the three stories but that poor bugger I had dumped back into the SHITE STORIES FOLDER. Maybe there was a way I could carry it on—I had been working on the thing for several effin fucking years

a strange kind of effort altogether. I had never intended springing it from the folder with a view to reworking for the millionth occasion, except now, now, for some reason, I needed to spring it from the folder yet again. I just wanted to see it. I lifted my mug of coffee and edged out from the table. Allan watched me. I pointed at the exit. I just need to eh . . .

He nodded. A visit to the cludgé had been in brackets but I also knew I was not required for forty-five minutes and flitted up the hill into my room my room my room and switched on the machine. A strange kind of thing this story, and quite enjoyable in a crazy sort of way.

An hour and ten minutes later I returned to the dining area fast, laptop in hand. I was going to use the experience with my group, it was the best possible illustration of what it is we do in between going away and coming back.

But the place was empty and the breakfast stuff had gone. I heard voices, from next door. I sidled in. It was a large open-plan space. Allan saw me enter. He was addressing the body of students. He gestured at me and I gestured a response, walked to stand by Tallulah. Mister Proctor will address us later on, he said.

God's teeth man the talk, the peroration! I had forgotten all about the damn thing, but had the presence of mind to wave.

The students had been split into two groups. Allan called the names of the ones signed into Tallulah's group then the ones signed into mine. Of the thirty students overall, eighteen had chosen her group. Tallulah ushered them to the far end of the space. My twelve stayed where they were. We watched Tallulah directing hers, shifting back

chairs and furniture to create a sizeable area. This created
a general excitement.

Fair enough. But my lot kept staring enviously to the far
end when I started to speak. They were polite and seemed
interested. I was declaiming on the superficial distinctions
between modes of literary practice when there came an
inordinate clamour; not quite raucous but very loud! My lot
had stopped sneaking glances at Tallulah's band of joyous
participants, they swiveled on their seats and stared directly.
Tallulah was dancing! Jesus christ! In that long dress thing,
fancy silk or something, in the finest pastel shades, pulled
tightly together yet at the same time, at the same time

She was shimmying, Tallulah was shimmying. How
did she manage that? One tried not to gawp, men of my
age certainly, because parts of the body so accentuated by
diaphonous outfittery such that the upper portions and
rearend parts, decidedly female and such as those, those
who gawp, then she who is subject to such is entitled to
call the polis.

Tallulah's performance had snatched from me all eight
of my students. (I thought there had been twelve; another
four had made the traitorous crossover.) Six of her group
of twenty-two had formed into a circle on the perimeter of
her dancing space, not only observing but taking "mental
notes. Tallulah had called the instruction: You must take
mental notes please.

Anis ti gahd.

How does one "take a mental note?" What is a mental
note? This kind of slipshod shite does my nut in, especially
when I hear it from another tutor who is robbing me of my
means to economic survival viz. my students. I should have
explained this to them how nonsensical it was. 19th-century
gobbledygook. Who cares! was the cry. We want our money
back. And who could have blamed them. I smiled and said,
How does one compete with a beautiful lady who is dancing?

I beg your pardon, retorted a beautiful lady who was not dancing, disappointed by my flippancy which she construed as sexist.

No, I said, I just mean ... eh I'm not really being sexist if eh

Was it sexist? The woman had shaken her head and was now ignoring me. Certain critics had accused me of sexism. If I was I didnt know it. Could you be sexist and not know it? Of course. Many men were at least some of the time. How could I be mostly sexist some of the time. A sexist this morning but not this afternoon. It sounds like an argument put forward by lawyers on behalf of celebrity sports, music, movie stars and photogenic members of the British Royal family who make the most outrageously prejudiced comments on race, ethnicity and sexual preference, and are yet defended on the grounds of a pristine inner essence. Anybody who knows the Real Him knows deepdown at the very core of his inner being he is of lofty spirit.

Surely that wasnt me? Hannah would have left me years ago—surely?

I glanced at the woman who scolded me. She was still ignoring me, now staring to the other end of the room where Tallulah's students had begun a high-stepping dance, they were dancing round her, hands flapping while she continued with the undulating contortions. The kind of thing where in movies one blinks to focus properly.

I got up from the chair, doing my best to smile. It was all good clean fun, after all. I'm talking about everything, everything in the fucking world.

Allan Maxwell had gone. I needed to mention to Tallulah the effect her art-in-performance was having on my group. She did not see my approach. I walked slowly, not causing a fuss, but I knew my students would have been watching closely. I would have had to enter into the space through the circle of high-stepping students to communicate directly with her. They would have been afraid to yield an inch. I waited until the heads ceased bobbing, and called: Hey excuse me eh Professor Debray eh . . .

She kept dancing. Of course she kept dancing. Absolutely. I would have done the same.

In her own time she did take notice. At the conclusion of her own dance she raised her eyebrows in my direction. She was obliging me to talk here and now in the presence of the students who surrounded her.

Hi Tallulah, I said, eh I was just eh ye know like eh me talking et cetera wondering if eh like how it is difficult for folk to concentrate and they need to be able to and me too, when I am talking, and I need to be talking and the students too, they

Tallulah was amused and stopped me. Oh but I too am talking Jack Proctor. She raised her hands and waved them in a circling motion, including her students. We all are talking. We talk with all our bodies. When I communicate it is with my entire body. Movement is the language of the body. I communicate with the student body. I am within this drama which is performed only by the I of myself. Tallulah smiled.

Yes but as a tutor, I said.

Oh Jack Proctor you can be a tutor with your fiction-books. I am an artist and cannot be otherwise.

Off she moved in her undulating dance. Moments later her students resumed the high-stepping.

She was right. I was the author of fictive-imaginings. Quack quack. It was all my persona's fault. I had to adopt a different one.

I headed for the exit. My own bunch of disloyal student bastards—although who could blame them—watched me. But I was only wanting to see out the door. Was it still raining? If not I had an alternative course of action, I could march my students to the top of the hill and march them down again.

I returned to my lot and clapped handies: All turn and face me please! We must do our best not be distracted. I wish you to reference the name of any great author.

Wilko Codling! shouted a woman who hated me and wished she had never signed up for my class.

Are you talking about the creator of the DI "Deadly" Dudley Merson books? that great Cambridge-based aristocrat whose love for sleuthing, literature, the Bach cello suites and Conference League football is a byword and who is frequently asked to confer distinction on serving members of Her Majesty's domestic armies, viz. the cops, and frequently requisitioned to Fort Sumner, New Mexico, to solve extraterrestial mysteries involving suspect channels of communication between aliens and radical leftist groups? Is this the same Wilko Codling to whom you refer?

Yes, shouted she.

The same Wilko Codling whose novels are adapted on a weekly basis by television companies the wideworld o'er and whose opinions and musings fill the pages of our best broadsheet qualities? Why sir hers is a deserved reputation; it is only that

Quack quack.

I guffawed loudly to be heard above the high-steppers, and brandished my laptop. I wish you all to squeeze in around me, I wish to display to you the work I have accomplished this morning, begin from nothing, produced from nothing, and now returning me to a yarn I thought to have abandoned several years ago. Note the title of this folder, SHITE STORIES.

But here the truth overwhelmed me, these words and phrases I uttered, what did they mean, what was I talking about? The words. What were the words? I was sick of this damn nonsense. You do your fiction stories, I make art, it is not difficult.

Tallulah was correct a hunner percent. Creative

Fiction-Book Writing was Creative Fiction-Book Writing: Art was something else.

I stared at the woman who had shouted Wilko Codling. She smiled in reply. A cheery smile.

Fine, yes. But are there others we might seek to reference? It can be any writer from any country or culture in the entire world, the whole world. And from the past two and a half thousand years, I added.

Jane Austen!

Charles Dixon!

The Brontës.

Archibald Conan Doyle!

PG Wodehouse!

Agatha Christie!

Nothing wrong with that, I said, held the laptop in my left hand and raised my right. I shall return! I said, and smiled.

I repaired to my room.

Eventually the chap at the door, Prof Doctor Maxwell, to advise me that both sets of students were to come together after the break. I was to give my talk to the student body on the art of Fiction-Book Writing which had been postponed from the night before. Allan chuckled. You thought you had escaped eh!

No, I said. I smiled but shut the door on him.

I switched on my laptop to peruse the story. I stopped. I lay on the bed. I turned onto my side, huddling into a shape that reminded me of a butter bean, speaking from the inside. But I would not fall asleep. I would not fall asleep.

I wanted home. Failing that the company of ducks.

I was up again later. The afternoon workshop was to have started, when? Recently. Started recently. I needed to shave first. Such matters are of concern to students. Especially ones out to do you in. Dont enroll for this one, he neglects to shave. Chew them up and expectorate the bastards. Was there time for a wet shave or would I have to do it dry? One of these days I would use that machine, that what-do-they-call-it, shaver, battery-operated.

Then creaks outside. Eerie shivers! Nay kidding ye man. But then an envelope appeared under my door.

In the name of fuck, somebody was pushing it. The Events Officer. Dont tell me the poor bugger had had to deliver it by hand. Special Delivery! Jesus christ, Julia, the baby! Thanks! I shouted, thinking of Tolstoy for some reason, mixing up his image with Archbishop Makarios, and that sonata, Kreutzer, the Kreutzer, what a story, man, why do we bother? I grabbed up the envelope and tugged out the note. It read: Jack Proctor, staff meeting 3:00 p.m. Allan M.

Oh god.

There we are.

Chin up.

Aw but I couldnay be bothered man, really, this was too much. I needed to be gone thou varlet, have at thee nay longer. Old Savirre and his wee cargo for just such moments; the doughty battling spirits, unlike us cowardly fuckers who dont take booze along in case of danger. So what! Danger! Who cares! Fucking danger is this man's special tea,

you never saw a man outdraw

it's the writer's life me.

Nay danger, nay life.

I needed air and freshness too, just freshness and life, the new wee baby; everything. Horrible nonsense. I pulled on the stout hiking boots and stepped outside, took a downward spiraling pathway, skirting a bog and tearing a way through thick shrubbery and wild undergrowth, hoping to undo the twists and turns wherein my very limbs were enfankled from yesterday's tortuous drive on el dinko.

Everything was either damp or soaking wet and the stuff that wasnay seemed to lie beneath patches of skeletal ice, of an amazing texture, akin to what ye see on the skinniest most roots of trees.

I hoped for a dry bank to sit beneath a sheltering tree but there was nayn. I kept walking. It was good to be walking. This estate went on and on and on The landcape had shifted. I reached the foot of another hill.

It was darkly overcast, rain threatening, then delivering. It was mair like sleet! Thank fuck I brung the heavy jaikit. If I could have taken the dinky outa there I would have. There and then. Instead I found a path through the undergrowth opposite which led through a large area of bracken.

This rain was no drizzle and the path was not so much muddy as a swamp. To hell with the walk. I returned to the bothy, closed the door, and drew the curtains. I had only been here since last night and already I was hiding out. Starving too: thoughts of the food I didnt eat at breakfast. The movement of the masticatory muscles alone might have revived my flagging spirits. I just wanted to write stories. How come I was in this plight. One thinks of Tolstoy.

Somebody at the door again. God's teeth man ten past four! I got out of bed and pulled on the jeans, and so on, opened the door. Allan Maxwell.

Hello Jack, may I come in?

Of course.

Ah thank you.

I closed over the door. Look Allan, I'm sorry, I really am. I didnt mean to sleep in. I just lay down. I've been working too hard and again it is just eh apologies, really. Are people waiting?

Allan smiled. Dont worry about it.

I dont like letting people down.

No, said Allan and again he smiled, but it was an uncomfortable smile. I know it is difficult for you.

Eh . . .

Having to cope.

I thought I was coping okay. How do ye mean?

It can be difficult.

What can?

Allan smiled but only for a moment. It was a smile of sympathy! I shook my head. You're dumping me! I said.

Not at all.

Yes you are!

No. We were trying something and it didnt quite work. The House played its part but generally we prefer to go it alone here and dont always see eye to eye with the overall programme.

Goodness me.

You are the prize-winning Proctor. I hadnt realized that. You go at matters rather differently. You should have been on the course offered by Robin Goodman, if you had gone to Sector One.

Well that's where I thought I was going last night?

Ah.

Did I not say it to you?

I believe you did.

Well you didnt say anything back to me. You could have said something. Surely?

Allan smiled.

I'm not sure why you're smiling.

No. He nodded and extended his right hand to me. It's been a pleasure meeting you Jack. I mean that quite sincerely. His right hand continued to dangle there. I havent read your novel I'm afraid to say, and please dont take offence.

Not at all but offer me grounds and I shall do.

He gazed at me.

I shook hands with him. Pass on my regards to Tallulah.

Of course.

I closed the door. I was going to make the bed, clean the floor, mend fuses and replace burst pipes, but to hell with it, I packed the belongings and fukt off.

I hadnay been dumped from a course before. A slap in the face of integrity! Pistols at dawn! Never mind old chap, on the balance of probability, survival is possible: one merely follows the trail, the signs along the way, placed there by the heavenly designer, and if by the light of grace—who knows, who knows.

I was sidetracked by bitterness. One cannot control the fates. Who tried that? Who was the halfwit who tried to hold back the sea? Some king. I command thee impudent waters! That was Britannia. Only Britannia was impudent enough for that carry on. Horizons, rainbows and pots of gold.

Imagine being dumped but! Ha ha. What a come down. Award Winner Dumped. Read all about it. Nowadays they called "going for a shite" "taking a dump," so my grand-daughter told me. How appropriate. Thus the act of excretion becomes one of acquisition. I had been excreted from Sector 2, now the flit to Sector 1, where's my horse Pancho.

All I wanted was to work. It didnay happen. I was disappearing. Sometimes I felt that. I would not die, just disappear. I was alone and missing my family. I had phoned home the night before leaving. Things were reassuring but I wasnt reassured. I needed more. I kept getting a sense of dread, something bad had happened or was happening or about to. Was I powerless? Did I have to be? Could I influence the situation? Hannah had given up on me. I should have gone home days ago. Easier said than done. By nature I was solitary, by nurture not at all.

Our people are of the northern hue, more used to arduous terrain. We sought the roughest routes. Let us trample the bracken and burns, stepping stones, share the cool water with the roe and her kids, at first light of day, dawn breaking over the loch, the family group appears at the water's edge. Oh man, that is a wondrous thing.

It was a case of watch your breathing and caw canny.

I avoided bidding farewell to the denizens of Sector 2, and drove away.

The buildings at Sector 1 were closer to the perimeter, apparently. Yesterday evening I had blundered on too far, landing in the clutches of the gentlemanly Allan Maxwell and wondrous Tallulah Debray. What had they in store if I had remained? Trussed like a Capon chicken man, thank fuck I escaped.

Except I didnay escape, they kicked me oot.

One sighs, attempting to stretch one's legs, straighten one's back, attend one's hips, one's upper thighs, neck and upper regions.

At last a property. Another group of redeveloped barns, built to store part of their art collection; their paintings, scuplture and the spoils of grave-robbing, relics; gold teeth and clipped whiskers of ancient fascisti fuckers, grave-robbing colonizers, arise ye aristocracy. Enter at yer peril. Prepare to be swallied whole, head first and nay seasoning.

I entered a lobby area, then through another doorway sat a woman behind a desk, her attention to the computer monitor.

Jack Proctor, she said as a statement of the obvious. You were to be here yesterday. Robin was expecting you. He isnt here right now.

Did Allan Maxwell phone across?

I believe so.

She glanced from the screen to me, for a fleeting moment: Your Creative Presentation is scheduled in two parts, pre-dinner 6:00 p.m. and post-dinner 9:00 p.m.

Fine. Please advise Robin that I have arrived. Do I have a room?

Not allocated as of yet but you do have one.

If I have one then may I go to it?

It is not allocated as of yet.

Okay, please advise Robin I'm away home.

She didnt smile although I did. The idea was just so effin wonderfully daft, logical and courageously sane. She said, There are plenty of areas where you can relax.

But no bar?

No bar ... She almost smiled.

By this time I was exiting the room. I did fancy a beer, being able to sit down in a comfy old bar. The Three Ton Tuna had reminded me of a certain hostelry in Skibbereen if memory serves, a fine pint of stout and a bag of nuts—or was it Clonakilty, I think it was Clonakilty, and the presence of yer man now old Myles himself, wasnt he the boy, in that toty wee pub with its history of fishing, but was that not Castlebar?.

Why in god's teeth was I so law-abiding! A half bottle of brandy perchance to dream, I needed that for this evening, for me and me alone, gloated he, in my ayn room with my large ceegar and my ayn books—eight of them. Why eight? Why not. We are talking Heaven here. Does heaven have a capital letter if written by a non-believing swine? Can ye spell god with the lower case if resident in Ireland? Jesus christ that is a major problem for us writers of precision, for whom the exploration of keltic fact and anglican value is the very marrow of that which by the Grace of God, of god I say, given I defend the right to design *a priori* and all religion as such per se per se, if you are of that persausion, forget the Guinness, I'll have a Murphy, not that I am a design man myself, I prefer to shuck the chains and go it alone.

I moped around then discovered a strange antechamber with three elderly sofas and a strong but friendly smell of dampness, worthy of that ancient worthy whose bewhiskered countenance was hanged, in gilt surrounds, above a mantelpiece and inner walls designed by the Adams family, ah chiquita, in shades of restful greens and pale blues, there in the centre of the great room, surrounded by the stuffed heads of deadly animals nowadays rare, whose tusks ...

Mad I tell you mad!

Mind you, there was only one window in the room and it looked like it hadnay been opened since the old Queen died, the ledge thick with dust and expired bluebottles. Piles of books on the ledge. A proper fireplace with the remains of a wood fire. I might spend the rest of my life in this room. I knew it as soon as I pushed open the door. The familiar smell of fungicide, curiously scented, most welcoming, the plush sofas, sinking down, knees buckling, I am falling, please help me, one just sank, sank, sank down, so soft and oh man it was nice, nice just to sit, only to sit, slouch, slouching one asks so little, so little, downy softness, drousy softer, so softly arousing, rousing, somebody rousing yoicks tally ho, me.

Twenty past six!

I had been snoring.

The door banged open, the rush of icy air and crashing noise, the room filling rapidly with the people on the course. They were animated, and laughed to see me as though I was in on the joke rather than the butt.

Apparently I had been lost, last seen heading for the lower reaches of Mount Vesuvius. Robin Goodman had returned to discover not only my arrival but my departure. The person at reception had misinterpreted. She thought I had gone home or else to the pub. The student search party found my car but thought it abandoned. Sturdier persons were combing the cliffside walks in the offchance I had taken a dive.

You're Jack Proctor, said Robin Goodman.

I am.

Allan was in touch. He nodded, glanced at his watch. Too late for the presentation.

What if we postpone dinner half an hour? I said. I could squeeze in a shortened version of the first part. Between courses, I could squeeze in other wee bits.

Master Goodman sustained a silence for a full ten seconds. Classroom techniques. If I had been a student I might have twitched in discomfort. No, he said finally, that will not work.

I smiled.

After a moment he said, You're older.

I am, I said, older than myself, it's a peculiar phenomenon. People read one's books and have this vision of one. The first question they ask of themself: Is this really him? Second: Why did I invite the bugger? I'm assuming you didnt invite me, that the House offered me, the Department of Arts-Control. In other words ye were forced to take me?

Not quite. Robin smiled.

Other students were watching. They had nameplates on their fronts. One woman appeared sympathetic. I smiled, then realized her sympathy was with Master Robin. I said: Could I have the key to my room please?

Surely. Yours is the long room, numbered 2. But there is no key. The doors are not locked. We get by on trust.

Nay bother, I said. Can someone knock my door when dinner is served?

I found the room and that was that. At dinner I was separated from Robin by the length of the table, but there wasnt much space and everything was noisy. Next to me was a woman who smelled of tobacco and whose nameplate read Gillian. She had her back turned to me for most of the time. Four males and eighteen females. The woman sitting on the other side of me also had a nameplate: Mandy. She chuckled when my food arrived and awaited my reaction. What is it? I asked.

When she realized my curiosity was genuine she said, They've brought you the vegan main course.

She presumed I was a red meat eater, based on her perception of working-classness of which she appeared to believe I was representative. She glanced along at Robin Goodman, attempting to share a smile.

I said, Where I come from vegetarianism is functional but veganism carries a romantic connotation, connecting to an elemental political position. She smiled uneasily and I was ashamed of myself for making the comment. Look, I said, I'm sorry. That was sarcasm, uncalled for.

Dont worry about it.

I apologize.

It's okay, she said but she turned from me.

What a start to the evening! I was starving and just wanted to eat, to carry on regardless but difficult raising a fork without banging people on the chin. Clumsiness is characteristic of elderly man syndrome and here I had no chance. Everyone and everything were squeezed together on the table and round the table. All kinds of plates, jugs, cups and cutlery and napkins were flying about the place. How many people were there I dont know but whatever it was would have seemed twice that, and the chairs so close together, or half again the same with fewer chairs, in the words of the saint. It was far tighter than the space at Sector 2. At least ye could breathe there. I was too long in my own company and the students observed my every move. I let the wine stay where it was. Care was required, and caution. I had to watch my back. The dirks were out. Yes I was hungry but also, also

I filled a tall tumbler with water, shoved in a slice of lemon. Excuse me, I said. I rose and left the table, taking the water with me. I had begun this evening in hunger and was still in hunger but peace was necessary, spiritual as well as fucking physical.

Outside I thought I smelled mown grass somewhere, but how could that have been, late November, some other such, organic entity, the scent of

when death finally arrives,

when it comes,
as one approaches.
The last gasp,
when

Mown lives. Then Gillian was there, cigarette in hand. She had thought I was out for a smoke. Those were the days, I said sipping my water, leaning against the wall.

Are you a secret drinker!

Nothing secret about it.

She lit her cigarette and dragged on it, exhaled a lungful of smoke. I'm looking forward to your presentation. I know you dont write poetry yourself but do you talk about it? Nowadays people seem so afraid.

Do you mean afraid to talk about it?

She smiled and said something further but so very softly I heard nothing. I looked at her. I dont think she had intended me to hear. Where is it you come from? she asked. Robin said you had an interesting set of values.

What does he mean by that?

Your use of language, I think, its earthy quality. He doesnt disapprove.

Ah, good.

I think he was forewarning the students. Some are older and may be rather dyed in the wool.

Well I'm older too.

Oh I know, sorry; I didnt mean anything by it.

No, I'm sorry. I'm too precise, legalistic nitpicking. I jump on people.

Not in public I hope?

Pardon?

Gillian chuckled. Sorry.

I laughed. That's great, I said, thanks very much.

She frowned.

Really, I said, it's just normal and something normal right now, something just ordinary—I'm glad of it.

You're from the north?

I shrugged.

I'm from hereabouts. She sighed. Third generation.

Where before that?

I dont know. We're immigrant stock.

Immigrant stock? What do you mean by "immigrant stock?" Do you mean your people can be defined by that, that you are 'stock,' "immigrants," the usual, what, what is the usual? God's teeth! Know what I mean!

Gillian smiled.

Sorry, I said. Excuse me, I need to check a few things. It's been a pleasure talking.

I went to my room. I did not lie down on the bed and nor did I do any work. I just sat by the window until it was time to return, which was any time before they came looking. When I did return people were chatting among themselves but ready for the presentation.

Robin awaited their attention. He introduced me: Our guest for this evening is Jack Proctor who was awarded the Banker Prize many years ago with a novel in which—well, perhaps it is better to leave that to the man himself to discuss.

Thank you Robin. I shall begin in fun and, with good fortune, end in that vein.

The smell of tobacco. It was Gillian. She deposited a half carafe of iced water in front of me. She was retreating to her seat. Thanks Gillian!

She smiled.

Some of you will be aware, I said, and stopped. At the back of the room Robin was whispering to a young woman who had come in late. She looked very pale and not too well altogether. She sat near to him and looked as though she might fall asleep at any moment.

I had to not let things get to me. Above all.

Okay. Some of you will be aware

Fidgety fucker in front row. The usual shite. He who most requires to fidget is plumb in one's line of vision, directly beneath one's nostrils, stretching and unstretching his limbs, folding and unfolding his arms, sitting backwards, sitting forwards, sighing and yawning, picking his nose and scratching his bollocks, the back of his legs, his neck, behind his ears and into his ears and all with the same finger.

Excuse me, I said to him, I know that you are uncomfortable there. Could you possibly move a little farther back? That'll be great.

The guy arose. He glanced at Robin Goodman.

I shrugged. It's just my line of vision. Thanks.

I wanted to say something of the novel, for this part of the presentation, just to see where it takes us—into the outer reaches preferably. If not then perhaps towards a deeper insight into the culture of the central character.

Toward that purpose I shall read several shorter poems, followed by an essay on the peculiar absence of intellect within the contemporary English literary tradition. I shall then offer an actor's performance of two playlets of my own, in which I pick up on Francis Hutcheson's effect on conversational prose through his use of rhetoric, shifting seamlessly from so-called naturalistic imaginings into the wilder realms of religiosity, the spirited animadversalism of the christian illumination as perhaps inferred from the good Bishop of Derry's rather stunning use of optometrical theory.

I'm only kidding, I said. All this stuff, it's just nonsense. I just dont want anybody here to ask questions about my use of earthy language or to define the criteria for receipt of the Banker Prize. In that respect ye must firstly seek to discover our established authority's success in obliging us to take seriously infantadulticism, a construction designed to reduce the populace to the theoretical awareness of lesser enthusiastic seagulls, where even to name our bodily functions is a breach in cultural etiquette. Why seagulls, I hear you say: a most astute question.

Because it leads to a harsh truth that most of us who write do not write for money. This is because we dont get any and know we wont. We aint fucking nincompoops altogether. Other artists do get paid for writing. This is because their own art is not literary. Picasso would have been one of the highest-paid writers of the 20th century, if he had done any. But he never did. This is because writing was worse than irrelevant to him, it stopped him doing his real work. If he had been forced to write he would have charged a fortune for the inconvenience. To that extent one might argue that the highest paid writers in the world are those who do something else altogeher. Let us act as though the utterings of Doctor Johnson are of no bearing.

Here too is an example of a question I do not want to receive: Are Snappy Titles All-Important? No, snappy titles are highly dangerous. The snappier the title the less inclined we are to finish the story. It is important to remember that snappy titles may not have been snappy in the first place.

Nor do I ever write under the influence, neither booze nor weed. Nor do I care if tobacco and coffee are opiates, stimulants or what-have-ye.

I'm not attacking any body or thing. Forget the crap and get ahead with the writing. It's only the writing. The rest is just—what do they call it—zippity doo dah, like the man said. This is a meeting of writers not for critics *per se*, they've got their own dens of iniquity, they call it the higher education system

A woman waved. You know, she said, when I came out

I nodded. I could not read her nameplate from this distance. She continued talking for a paragraph or so on various odds, ends, sods and so forth. And I groaned or did I smile, smile wearily, if her opening was meant as a gambit, as a double entendre, or not, intentional or not, I do not know because I did not hear the rest properly because I do not give a damn whatever the hell it was, I said, because

The silence.

The faces.

Look, sorry, I said to the woman, but we are here to write, to write. I havent driven all this bloody way here to pass on potted autobiographical information. I confess I did not hear the rest of what you said because I was trying to make sense of what you had said, whether or not the comment on coming out was intentional. Was I allowing a prejudiced comment through unchallenged, as though I was in on some sort of joke. This is a swamp into which I have lurched. Suddenly I am a prejudiced bastard. Fortunately none of you appear to have thought that at all or if you did you said nothing which introduces a deeper complexity. We all have lives, or should I say, I and I, we and we.

I stopped. Look, I said, I'm off on the wrong footing here. I need to hit the correct note and I'm not managing that. I wonder if eh

Another silence.

I addressed the woman who had been speaking. I'm sorry, I cant read yer name from here.

Oh, I'm Rachel.

Thanks.

I am forty-eight. That is how long it took me to come out. My kids are grown-up. At one stage I considered taking Holy Orders. She smiled for a moment. The others were listening and I found I could focus more when she continued talking. She had read a book by a recovering alcoholic who, through the act of writing poetry and confessional works of prose had overcome his own obstacles and proved, finally, that he might cope with his own sexuality in a simple and primary state. She provided some of the details and factors relative to her own life.

It would have made a great story. Maybe it still would, I said. But when you say Holy Orders, in what sense do you mean?

Rachel smiled at me but said no more.

Sorry, I said, I dont mean to eh . . . I tend to see things as stories.

A man had raised his hand. Geoffrey, he said pointing at his nameplate. I'm gay. Should I write it up as a story?

Pardon?

Should I write it up as a story?

I just go back to the writing, it's only the writing.

There is more to life than writing.

But why are we here if not the writing? Is this not why we are here. This is why I'm here surely? Maybe not. Why am I here? Rachel . . . eh would you eh want to say something maybe, why you're here?

Yes. I am here to learn. I'm keen to learn. Above all that is what I want to do, to be able to write and just write, that is what I want. I dont want to talk and all that kind of thing, therapy, I dont want therapy. I do worry though. I never seem to understand, and I worry that I never will.

Me too, called someone.

Yes and me, I said, I'm no different. It is so tricky and perilous ye see I'm not sure there is more to life than writing. We dont have life. Life is not a property or some sort of attribute, that's what I mean with the I and I, and the we and we, we're just here, here we are, alive alive-oh.

But we do have writing, if we have it. In my own case I cant imagine not having it. Literally, I cannot imagine not having it, the urge, and doing it.

Mandy said, I seem so ordinary. I see these people who lead extraordinary lives. They have such marvelous experiences. You too. I googled you and your life is so exciting.

Pardon?

It is.

Only because it's not your own. I go home and see the same old face in the mirror.

Yes but

No, I said, none of that matters. Some folk never leave their room but their stories are wonderful—who is that again, old thingwi, Kant? Or Schopenhauer—not Schopenhauer. Goncharov?

I dont know who that is, said Mandy.

Eh well I suppose, Goncharov was a writer, and eh Schopenhauer was a philosopher.

It's no good if you talk about people we've never heard of before. We were discussing this earlier.

I nodded. At the other end of the room I could see that Robin Goodman was listening closely.

It is a problem. But only a slight one. I cant help it ye see it's just what my life happens to be. I dont think it matters. Whatever it is that is what it is. Prejudiced tae. I can be defeated by my own prejudices. I have ones I dont even know I have. It's like I'm enmeshed in it, inside a web and not able to get clear. My world, my language, modes of thought. Five minutes ago to do with sexuality. And could it be racism? Could it be something else? Elitism? Who knows. Where does it come from? All that stuff in wur head. There it all is. It is our own world and we make what we can with it— out of all that heaving morass, that's where the stories derive, where they derive, our stories. That's what makes them ours, they're all in there. And they come out and whatever else we do what we have to do is the fucking work! We have to write, that is what the work is, that is what we've taken on.

I'm not meaning to offend anybody. But I'm not surprised that I am. The idea that I might be prejudiced or even homophobic is just nonsense but at the same time people need to be able discuss this stuff without being found guilty, as though the expression of the thing can only be the thing. That would be silly in science, for example, or anywhere we expect something to be a fact or not, yet here we are discussing things to do with language, where we know it's all slippery and full of value and opinion and everything else, and yet somebody like me is supposed to be a robot, where anything expressed is factually sound, the end result of an inference table, without any trace of ambiguity.

All I can do is talk about here and now and this presentation which I'm doing about how we make stories and so on. I know in other situations Rachel's statement would be of interest. Not here. Maybe she so advised the company before, I dont know ye see I'm just using it as an example.

Geoffrey said, Example for some, for others it's our life.

But that's it exactly, I said, it's what we work from, or what we should work from. The trouble with most of what I see is how it works from the outside, so ye're always battering yer head against a brick wall till at last ye conform. It's forced on ye. Ye cant just use yer own world, yer own life, all yer own experience, good, bad or indifferent. Ye're forced into that other world, where ye do as ye're told and return to the masters what is rightfully theirs.

Oh God, said Rachel, I dont understand I dont understand.

Neither do I.

Neither do I.

It's not really a big deal, I said, ye just have to give it a go. No closed minds. I'll make a seminar from this and I'll call it The Pitfalls of Failed Delivery.

Rachel smiled.

Seriously. I could use your delivery as an example of the pitfalls in using the I-voice present tense. Think about it. If your "coming-out" statement is of interest in its own right then it lies in the words themselves because you havent made it interesting enough: a potentially explosive drama is being reported rather than dramatized and thus is not a drama at all.

Explosive drama!

Another woman had called this to Gillian who smiled. Rachel also smiled.

Robin called, Could you go further on that Mister Proctor?

No thanks. I've said enough for the time being.

And I left them to it, stepped outside for a breather. It was too cold for comfort. Away from the outbuilding windows there was no light hardly at all. A most unripe time for a walk. I went to my room. I was hungry as well. That was me again without a meal. Absurd nonsense.

I wanted to stay in my room. But I couldnt. People had paid good money bla bla bla. I packed instead. Next morning I was getting to fuck. It was the vamoose stakes as we say in the racing business. They would expect me for the old fucking *petit déjeuner* but I would fail to show. I'd be halfway home by then. I was getting up and getting to fuck, getting on my little dinky and moving on down the road, yessir, I wish to fuck I was a cowboy, I would just ride the range and make up snappy lyrics.

By the time I returned the wine and the beer had arrived. People were quaffing in an informal manner and it was pleasant. Robin waved to me and indicated an empty armchair within the company. It was a smashing old chair although sagging in the middle.

We were discussing the present-day preoccupation with the zombie and vampire culture, said Robin. He raised his right arm aloft, forefinger pointing to the ceiling in the manner of a pontiff. The donor's blood in prose fiction, a key attribute of the new genre. We had a session on it this morning.

Right.

Part of the fiction-writing course. I wasnt responsible for it Mister Proctor but we have to make the best of things.

Look do ye mind if ye just call me Jack. Everybody! Just call me Jack.

Robin smiled. You may have noticed that our most recent guest fiction-writer was Jennifer Rose?

No, I didnt see.

Ah, there's a good deal on her in our course brochure. She's the author of *The Whitby Blood-Line* trilogy which is now translated into several of the world's languages. Do you know the series?

No.

She is an astonishing writer, remarkably talented; formerly a psychologist.

She still practises, called Gillian.

I can believe it, said Robin. Yes. We were most fortunate to have her visit. She was not short of anecdotal material either and was generous enough to share much of it with us. What is interesting Jack—if I may—is how the genre has progressed beyond cult interest amongst the youth cultures of North America and western Europe to the extent that some would say it was no longer a literary niche.

Do you see vampirism as a literary niche Mister Proctor? called a man whom I recognized as the fidgety guy I had ejected from the front row.

Eh

I know that some people do.

Fair enough, I said, but I'm not sure what a literary niche is. I could guess. I just havent come across it much although I do remember a related project, an advanced course of study I taught way way north of old Labrador in fact, in Canada.

Labrador!

Aye.

What made ye go there!

Well I didnt, it was way north of there. I just go where I'm sent. The writer's life. One is skint: one is offered dough. The Literary Control Officer in charge of the department was especially keen that tutors as well as students had a go at these forms of story writing as an exercise. I remember too how the second night there the snow stopped falling but had lain so thick there was barely a sound across the icy wastes that led through and beyond many miles of white mountains. I had gone for a stroll late on, before turning in, when came a tortured howl of what I do not know. I remember thinking, that was neither fox nor snowtiger, neither wolf nor bear, nor that awful creation by an olden author whose name now slips my mind. I shrugged and had a sip of water.

People smiled.

Robin said, Perhaps you could you talk a bit about that.

I shrugged. I dont mind anything much about it, except that it happened, it happened, and I was there to see it, and not only see it but be part of it, part of something that was way beyond what the average person will experience in an entire lifetime.

Yes but can you talk about it? said Robin.

About what, the dark and eerie evening?

Obviously you're referring to Mary Wollstonecraft Shelley.

Okay if I am, I said, that's great, I thought I had invented it. My attention had been wandering, thinking of the workshop I had attended earlier that same day, the first of that series. This pale young woman who was there, leaning languorously by the draped window, her skin of an opaqueness that nullified colour. She had her arms folded under her breasts studying the dashing young student whose poetry had become central to the course, and I perceived, for our sins, the deep extent to which he relied upon how impressed she was by how decisive he was and I steadied myself, for the strange activities to come.

I dont think I mentioned that this course way north of Labrador was located nor' nor' east of Baffin Island, passing beyond the famed Hudson Strait, the same waters into whose icy depths a two hundred strong boatload of Hebridean men, women and children sailed to their doom in a vain attempt to find sanctuary on the wild shores of the great Red River on the west coast of that benighted destination, former dominion of the yoicks and tally-ho brigade, empire of the brits.

Now ye all will know, speaking of poor Mary, alas poor woman, that heading due east of there is indeed a wild and lonely territory and into this our unhappy being, neither man nor beast, had been thrust from a fevered imagination.

This pale young woman of whom I speak could not spell for toffee but in the language of vampirism was learned. She had drawn up word-tables and generic tree diagrams of the sort favoured by psycholinguists. This same young woman, former student of my own, had completed two novelizations drawn from failed screenplays and either had her own website or was party to one that was particularly powerful. One of her confidantes later advised me to exercise caution, that both she and the dashing young poet belonged to an online coven based in a tiny township on Ellesmere Island whose members drank blood purloined for their own ungodly purposes. They worshipped an actor who took minor but controlling roles in vampire movies out of Baton Rouge, Louisiana. Each semester they visited a Transylvanian township located in a lost valley nearabouts Chloride City, California, known for its fulsome moons and irregular UFO sightings. I advised the student body, speaking as their professor, that I had become all too aware of how entrenched hierarchy is within the new vampirism and was obliged to introduce a note of lower-order reality, having come to the stark realization that the officer corps of the vamiprist genre are based on East European aristocracies of the mid-to-late 18th century. I further advised the student body that in a previous carnivorean existence I too quaffed blood but in its icy cold and congealed form. I preferred it fried. We knew it as *black pudding*, a shadowy substance, known to Scotch vaqueros the wide world o'er. For this I was subpoenaed before the Court of the College to explain myself. What right had I to interfere with the imaginings of the next generation.

After a moment, Robin gestured with a bottle of red wine. You can join us if you like.

Thanks but I need to advance a story, I said but was having difficulty getting out of the armchair. I sank back. I tried again. I've got a deadline, I said.

Are you sure?

Yes. I'll see ye in the morning. Forgive me, I wish y'all a pleasant evening.

If you're sure.

I am.

A cup of tea?

No, I said, looking for shadows but saw none. That story by Stephen Leacock re the naïve young minister new to the parish who is visiting the flock on an introductory capacity. He arrives in the home of a local family who are not 100% glad to see him but nevertheless remain gracious. He is too polite to get up and leave. The family are obliged to offer him dinner and he is too polite to decline. So he eats, much to the irritation of male family members. He sits on afterwards, too polite to get up and leave the company. Likewise he is offered supper, and eats, much to the irritation of male family members. He has to stay the night by then because it is too late to travel. So for this that and the next thing he cannot say no and they cannot refuse him while younger family members plays jokes on him and he must suffer the jibes and barbs of assorted others—influenced no doubt by Dostoevski's story about the minor aristocrat who blunders into the wedding party of an employee, steps into the basin of dessert jelly—and eventually, poor lad, in Leacock's story dies in the house through that same social affliction, the inability to say no through a damnable politeness—unlike Dostoevski's central character who goes to work the morning after and wonders if it was all a bad dream, but then an elderly clerk appears and gives the guy a skeptical smile, thus the whole world knows of last night's folly.

Ah but not me not me! Time to go. Adieu.

I achieved lift-off from the sagging armchair, and onwards to the exit, waving merrily and saw then a strangely closed door with the loud but guarded rattle of a forbidden sermonic declamation and realized did I, dear reader, that this selfsame door would lead me asunder from an annexe to a fiery region wherein elemental company assembled round a coefficient of candles glowing dully red, centred in the ghastly dark, and from the shadowy rear appeared the wizened duke and goggle-eyed duchess, leading a choir in a medley of these round-the-campfire psalms one associates with evangelical organizations developed from the deeds and intellectual preoccupations of certain pre-Kantian mystics.

44

Ach

I was about fifteen minutes along the tow path when a shape directly across the canal caught my attention. Among the bushes and trees there was an old fence, broken in part. This is where it was, this shape, it was like a bird, a huge bird, a bird of prey. I stood where I was so not to disturb it, I didnt want to disturb it, not under any circumstances: this huge thing perched still as a statue; it could have been an owl but so very big—more like an eagle. These hunched shoulders too, and its head and its neck. Definitely an owl. Even for a wildlife ignoramus such as myself, a bird like this spelled danger.

What was it doing, was it resting, was it watching some wee animal and waiting to strike? What the hell could it have been, rats or squirrels maybe. Jesus christ, no, I didnt want to disturb it! Do owls attack people? The kind of thing ye google immediately. Are owls a threat? Do huge owls attack humans? This one was big enough. The idea of this coming at ye, what would ye do? Flap yer arms or something. Try to punch it! Imagine a leopard perched on a fence and having to walk by! This bird would have frightened a leopard. One time I saw these big black animals at the side of a country road and they reminded me of eagles. They were vultures. Probably they were waiting for roadkill.

This thing now on the other side of the canal from me would have seen me if it did that swivel movement with its heid.

Maybe the snow helped, the idea of a blanket, the sense of absence, muted sound. Maybe this applied to wildlife too.

If the snow hadnt been lying maybe it would have heard me, and vanished I hope. I was no bigger than it, and not nearly as powerful; nowhere near. This thing was solid. I was aware of how damn flimsy I was. If it flew at me I was fukt. I was glad to turn back. It wasnt a case of being cowardly, just not being stupid. Sometimes I gambled. Not now man, ssh, quietly does it.

This was a big experience.

But it was good seeing the bird, within its proximity. This mattered. About proportion. Not getting things out of proportion. That was me. That is what I did. Dont confuse horrible nonsense with life. I was guilty of that. This afternoon's session was one of my own creation, centring on method. I had arranged it for all or any of the twenty or so students who had attended a session I did a few weeks ago at a College of Art. They had shown interest in what I had to say on value and originality of vision; how these alone can knock for six most forms of stereotyping, the use of cliché and figures of speech generally, and how we might find these in other arts, in one guise or another, so-called metaphor. What is a metaphor? How does a metaphor enter existence? That had been a two-part session and towards the end I spoke a little about methods I use personally, similar to methods used by other artists; how we begin from ourself as artist, and the immediate world. We do not need to go elsewhere, the world around us is ample, ample and we see it everywhere, everywhere and everyplace.

Back in *le chalét* I was starving. Grub first, feet second. I was goni toast a slice of bread, cut a slice of cheese, microwave a coffee.

Yessir I was happy. I had done a shift, had a walk and it was still morning; time for a nap and I needed one, needed to sleep and after that, bla bla, soothing.

I prepared everything before phoning Hannah, in case she phoned me and my feet were in the bowl. I knew what she would talk about, the usual. The family and my impend-ing breakdown, in which I was colluding. That was how she put it: You're colluding in yer own breakdown. Then the family part of the conversation would end in that old-style nervous-breakdown blubbering where ye splutter beer froth ower yer whiskers, and them wattery snotters dreeping down yer chin jesus christ whit's the Gaidhlig for "dreeping doon one's chin"?

I switched on the laptop, to see what I had been work-ing on through the night. I was cheery about the work. Hannah wouldnay be cheery back. She would tell me sleep was mair important. Of course it was mair important but if ye cannay sleep ye cannay sleep.

I was hoping for a straight knockout; the physical exer-tion of the walk, the warm feet, the relaxation, plus I was knackered: ergo sleep.

What about a rent-a-slugger? That would be a job for a retired boxer. Ye hire him to punch ye one on the chin so ye can get a sleep.

People getting paid to punch ye. Some metaphor. Here we are in the 21st century. What's yer job son? asks the alien. Oh I get paid to batter folk. Who pays ye for doing it? They do, the folk themselves.

Fuck sake.

Forget aliens, people from other parts of the world. They must look at us as if we're another species. They see other human beings the same as themselves. It doesnt happen here. We're all fascist bastards! Maybe if we all emigrated, if we all went to their country. Then we could act humanely. Globalization = lobotomization. Receipts for everything. What about pints of milk? A loaf of bread? Everything. They cannay trust us and we cannay trust them. Colluding in wur ayn downfall. Aye. Of course we are. The death of art by design. All that anti-art rubbish; upper-middle-class etiquette fucking pish masquerading as art, who gives a fuck, tortutors who have learned whatever the fuck they have learned, not to recognize art man that is a fucking certainty. At last they've found a way to negate its very foundation, bastards, but we will survive, you better fucking believe it, in spite of all in the face of all, in the face of all, and of god

> in the face of
> the face of god
> we face off god
> there is a face
> the face of god
> we face off

But the need now was to go home, to get home, to have arrived. And I was looking forward to it man and it could not come soon enough. Breakfast breakfast breakfast. Hot feet, warm feet, relaxed feet, *mens sana.*

First I telephoned home.

No answer. I telephoned again and still no answer. I had switched on the laptop, now I switched it off. As of that moment, I could have vamoosed, if only, at that very moment, very moment, then, right then, my fourth grandchild had been born. The wee baby was there, I knew it, the wee lungs and all that. I knew it. And so long as I was not contacted it was okay, things were okay. As long as I didnt speak to anybody from home, my family, as long as I didnt bloody speak to a single soul everything was good everything was good. I just needed to act. This was not an emergency. Whatever it was was not an emergency. I was knackered but so what man that was that. Nine o'clock in the morning. Nay need to telephone home. I was making my getaway. Would I feel the same when I reached the House office!

Ha ha.

I logged on to the airline, found a way onto the soonest flight I could grab at a cost that didnt require me to remortgage the huis. The Events Officer had left me to it. One event left but I didnt tell him that. The ticket cost plenty but who gives a fuck. That was what I did, and I was no longer ashamed. I had been before booking the ticket. This is a sore thing to admit, but I need to do that and this is what I am doing.

45

Fuck them all

I was at the College of Art. I recognized the woman who collected me from the reception area. She had attended the original seminar and embarrassed her students. I think she was a Head of Department. She smiled as though pleased to see me. How are you this morning Mister Proctor? You're keeping okay?

I'm fine, I said, yeah. I'm here to meet with the students in a follow-up session to the meeting we had a while ago, if ye remember.

Of course.

It's not on the schedule. I offered them the additional session because they seemed interested. If they hadnt seemed interested I would not have offered it to them. If you want to cancel that's okay.

What?

It's your prerogative.

Sorry Mister Proctor, I dont know why you're saying this. Have I upset you?

Not at all. I nodded.

You do have admirers here you know. She smiled.

Eventually she was walking and I followed her along a wide corridor. She opened a door into a wee cubby-hole of a room; the sort one expects to find cluttered with brushes, brooms and shovels—that one Kafka introduces at the end of *The Trial*, occupied by the Whipper. Of course! Precisely! Although this one was big enough to contain a table and half a dozen chairs. The students will be along directly, she said.

She smiled. It was difficult to find a place. Four I believe was the number invited. Four students and yourself?

No. I said anybody. I said anybody at all. Anybody could come. Anybody. That is what I said. Anybody who wanted, they were all welcome. I told them that, the whole lot of them if they wanted.

Yes. She smiled.

Dont patronize me.

I'm not patronizing you. I think you're rather too sensitive Mister Proctor.

Do ye?

We thought you were offering something very worthwhile to students and they should respect that. I discussed this with the Regional Arts Officer and he suggested we curtail the number. He thought four the ideal number and I agreed with him.

For what? Ideal for what?

For a session such as this.

Such as what? What is the sesssion? What is it you think I'll doing?

She was no longer smiling now, just looking at me, not worried or I dont know, I dont know. I shrugged. What's your name? I said.

She stared at me and answered after a moment: Ann Frew. Mister Proctor, you must allow us to look after the interests of our students.

I shrugged. What about you yerself? I said. Did you ever ask questions? What kind of questions? What about dreams? Here ye are in a college of further education, in the art department—are we allowed to call it that, art department, department of art? Ye must have had dreams. We know it's not full of starry nights and life-changing ideas but the incredulity of kids is a phenomenon. Even in my own case. I had a glorified view not just of art departments but colleges and universities, as intellectual hotbeds. When

I discovered the truth the disappointment of that stayed with me and it's with me right now. The thing I noticed when I did the seminar with your art students was the crashed dreams. I spoke to two boys at the effin gate who were dead. One boy that spent the time shutting his ear and lying on the effin fucking floor. Nobody expected a single damn thing, there was nothing. It fucking broke my heart. I dont want now to talk any more. I'll stay here with the four students unless you want simply to call a halt to it, call a halt to it.

What do you mean?

Whether you wish the meeting to go ahead or not. It doesnt matter to me. You're in authority, you say whether or not art is to go ahead.

I dont know why you're speaking like this, of course the meeting should go ahead, art should go ahead, of course it should.

Okay then. I sat down on the nearest chair. I averted my gaze from her. The four students arrived.

The pursuit of knowledge as the end, that the uttermost radical history is intellectual history, our hidden history is the intellectual history of we the people;

our ignorance, naïveté

authority's seat of learning

universities and colleges cannot be what we make of them, we just steal, we steal, we steal in and we steal out, stealing away with our stolen goods. These shelves where lurk the uncut pages, the dust, fine dust

avoiding internet encyclopaedias and all secondary sources, the fucking lot of them. Glossy outers and glossy inners, updated last chapters, preface to the preface. Find that original voice and fucking read it, listen to it, look at it for that is the source, the seminal voice; one human being in the act of discovery, coming to terms, finding the terms, creating the terms.

It will take more work, return you to the labyrinth. Exams become less straightforward. But it puts you someplace else, if you are the one to read that book then its writer is writing to you. Aint it fucking wonderful! Aint it a fucking marvel! All you do is find a corner and pay attention.

You will not be alone. Not even among the staff: at least one accomplice will be found in any department. See the drinkers, failures, self-abusers, the untenured, unpromoted, those prone to emotional outbursts, embittered.

Maybe not. Maybe they head departments. They might well do. People find their way. They disguise what they are, disguise what they do, and do it in their own time and you will find them, you can smell them out. Dont be depressed. Be ordinary, just fucking fight. Ye're used to fighting so fight. Of course it's shite ye know it's shite.

One needs to talk art too, just talk it as ye go on, as ye go ahead, that is what ye do, ye do it, it's not as hard as all that.

(ending here)

Author's Afterword

I was asked for a report on the proceedings of my involvment in the House of Art and Aesthetics project. I did not have any such "involvement." I was on my own. I was glad to get out when I became aware that to achieve this while alive was a worthy goal.

I knew nothing about it when they offered the residency. Predictably, the elemental dynamic is governed by the drive towards the standardization of language, thought and being. In this the centralization of the Creative Writing industry is crucial. Questions may be asked as to why people should seek to centralize a form of art, but who may pose such a question other than lovers of art, and those who take the concept "political change" seriously? Whether the authorities like it or not Creative Writing is art and art is the beating heart of liberty.

I submit this report in its entirety. Writers such as myself have several suitcase folders entitled: Finished Versions. These suitcase folders are found within the mother-folder, the one we name The Set of Finished Versions. This now is my final submission of the multitude of finished versions of the final report that I was asked to submit by the Director of the House Organizing Committee. They have a clear idea of what constitutes a final report. This differs from my own. I dont have one. I subscribe to the old Sartrean existence precedes essence argument to the extent that it is not an argument at all. I just get on with it.

Most artists scratch a living. Having survived to the age of 66 I consider myself luckier than most but the scratching continues.

I did not discover "the nature of the fee" until ensconced in the residency, haring hither and thither in search of schools, universities and colleges; community halls, council chamber ante-rooms and residential centres of creativity. The verbal snippets I heard began making sense. I was catching the tail-end of whispered exchanges concerning stipends, gratuities and sealant doggie-bags. What is a "sealant doggie bag"? I never found out. It was noticeable, however, that uttering the phrase was accompanied by a wink.

Fees are not standardized among artists although our pseudo-meritocratic establishment pretends otherwise. Upper-class authors generally own the publishers. Upper-middle-class authors are proferred upper-middle-class monies. Middle-class authors negotiate middle-class fees. Working-class authors get paid working-class wages. Any dough I receive is a function of that.

I should say that my publishers requested that I allow the Director of the House Organizing Committee space to say a few words at the outset. There was no legal requirement. The publishers preferred that I comply with the House require-ments. Not to have done so was against their interests and one accepts such stuff. Otherwise survival cannot be taken for granted. There is no "ethical position." The imposition of certain boundaries were institutionalized decades ago. These masquerade as aesthetic and ethical and are consistent with passing ideas on the etiquette of the ruling elite. In reality they serve to restrict individual development and are con-sistent with most forms of religion.

Anger takes one so far, but no further. The authorities argue on behalf of procedures derived from certain fundamen-tal principles. What are these principles? Who knows. Those who seek may find. What if there is nothing to find, except only that, the absence? Our question then: what is this *that*? Can it be other than activity, having neither perpetrator nor victim, transgressor nor transgressed, creator nor created?

When the House of Art and Aesthetics came a-calling I accepted their invitation, and at the age of sixty-five, as then I was, I was pleased to have been invited. Let that be said. According to my wife we did not *need* the money; there was no state of emergency. From this I inferred we did need the money.

A measure of artistic independence is good for the soul. On the other hand, a close reading of the contract revealed that were one to become an overnight best-selling author in the meantime one might tender one's resignation forthwith. Afterwards I forgot all about it. There were eighteen months to go and the usual usual, everything was the usual, the writing to do, the writing to do, the writing the writing the writing, it was driving me absolute bloody nuts.

I would have outsourced myself years ago but where has a slow-moving once quickdraw writer got to go? Self-immolation is not the answer. Heinrich Böll heeded the call and shifted to Achill Island. He sets the template. A beautiful writer. Would that we all might follow. Nevertheless I could have prepared more thoroughly. I already had entered that bleak world of lost souls, twisted and bitter, deserted and languishing, shut behind closed doors, traversing canal tow paths, single track roads wending o'er hill and through glen.

This was early winter. The writer's residence for these several weeks was a converted holiday chalet; heating provided by a strange system that incorporated several evil-smelling candles that reminded me of an old wood-cut I once saw in an illustrated work from the 16th century. Yes it was my choice, but what do we mean by "choice"? It was either that or a so-called family hotel; in other words, a bed & breakfast lodging house for an extended period of weeks.

What does it mean to invite somebody to leave their home and family, and be your guest for several weeks? Are there obligations on the host body? I did not invite myself to the House of Art and Aesthetics, I was extended the invitation. I was there to work, whether writing "in residence" or performing at reading events; talking to school-pupils and students, giving seminars or workshops at higher education establishments; leading community groups and workshops.

I repeat that I was a guest. Instead of any final report on the proceedings it was my intention to provide a chart of the ground a writer such as myself requires to cover with a view to enhancing future residencies. None of us wants to do the damn things but exigency exigency. We are born into the world and we have to get on with it. Pre-11th century hermit-ages appeal to most artists but those were built on an illusion and maintained by subterfuge, torture and torment.

My personality inclines to the compulsive. I have managed to avoid one addiction or another throughout my writing life. The one whose absence I cannot surmount is pencil and paper. That's two things. Plus me, makes three. Three is number one like good old Pythagoras tells us, the Holy Trinity. The very last activity artists are enabled to do while in residence is create. We accept these posts in the knowledge one is being paid not to create while in residence. Bring your own pencil and your own paper, ye can aye dance circles round them. This is why we are always "spent": we are two plus an absence, forever doomed, forever champing on the verge of the One.

The House of Art and Aesthetics hierarchy requested space for a Foreword and the Director asked that he himself might take on the role. I conceded this on condition it was inserted at the end. My publisher reminded me that this transforms the Foreword into an Afterword. Therefore the "House" has the last word.

Upon mature reflection, and discussion with parties close to me, it was concluded that I provide an Afterword to their Afterword and return to the latter the title Foreword though placing it at the end, or rather the one before the end. Alternately, they might leave it the Afterword and mine then becomes Post-Afterword. This I did provide. I regret to say that my publishers withdrew this on the advice of the legal department.

I submitted this Preface to the House "Afterword" in the offchance of what I do not know and intend never finding out, given control is never 100% and never can be 100%, and who wants that anyway. I discovered, finally, that the House had withdrawn its "Afterword" and that my notes to a Preface now stand as an Afterword in-itself. Who knows. I'm just trying to get on amid attendant pressures, the usual, me and Hannah and all the kids, kids of the kids and so on, while I've been working on a story—not this one, I'm talking about the one I'm working on.

c/o Barry,
Teachín den Seandéanamh
Cannahiogh, nr Golleen
Mizen Head, West Cork
Republic of Ireland

About the Author

James Kelman was born in Glasgow, June 1946, and left school in 1961. He traveled about and worked at various jobs. He lives in Glasgow with his wife Marie, who has supported his work since 1969.

ABOUT PM PRESS

PM Press is an independent, radical publisher of books and media to educate, entertain, and inspire. Founded in 2007 by a small group of people with decades of publishing, media, and organizing experience, PM Press amplifies the voices of radical authors, artists, and activists. Our aim is to deliver bold political ideas and vital stories to all walks of life and arm the dreamers to demand the impossible. We have sold millions of copies of our books, most often one at a time, face to face. We're old enough to know what we're doing and young enough to know what's at stake. Join us to create a better world.

PM Press
PO Box 23912
Oakland, CA 94623
www.pmpress.org

PM Press in Europe
europe@pmpress.org
www.pmpress.org.uk

FRIENDS OF PM PRESS

These are indisputably momentous times—the financial system is melting down globally and the Empire is stumbling. Now more than ever there is a vital need for radical ideas.

In the many years since its founding—and on a mere shoestring—PM Press has risen to the formidable challenge of publishing and distributing knowledge and entertainment for the struggles ahead. With hundreds of releases to date, we have published an impressive and stimulating array of literature, art, music, politics, and culture. Using every available medium, we've succeeded in connecting those hungry for ideas and information to those putting them into practice.

Friends of PM allows you to directly help impact, amplify, and revitalize the discourse and actions of radical writers, filmmakers, and artists. It provides us with a stable foundation from which we can build upon our early successes and provides a much-needed subsidy for the materials that can't necessarily pay their own way. You can help make that happen—and receive every new title automatically delivered to your door once a month—by joining as a Friend of PM Press. And, we'll throw in a free T-shirt when you sign up.

Here are your options:

- **$30 a month** Get all books and pamphlets plus 50% discount on all webstore purchases

- **$40 a month** Get all PM Press releases (including CDs and DVDs) plus 50% discount on all webstore purchases

- **$100 a month** Superstar—Everything plus PM merchandise, free downloads, and 50% discount on all webstore purchases

For those who can't afford $30 or more a month, we have **Sustainer Rates** at $15, $10 and $5. Sustainers get a free PM Press T-shirt and a 50% discount on all purchases from our website.

Your Visa or Mastercard will be billed once a month, until you tell us to stop. Or until our efforts succeed in bringing the revolution around. Or the financial meltdown of Capital makes plastic redundant. Whichever comes first.

Keep Moving and No Questions

James Kelman

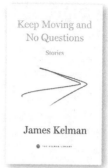

ISBN: 978-1-62963-967-3 (paperback)
   978-1-62963-975-8 (hardcover)
$17.95/$29.95 224 pages

James Kelman's inimitable voice brings the stories of lost men to light in these twenty-one tales of down-on-their-luck antiheroes who wander, drink, hatch plans, ponder existence, and survive in an unwelcoming and often comic world. *Keep Moving and No Questions* is a collection of the finest examples of Kelman's facility with dialog, stream-of-consciousness narrative, and sharp cultural observation. Class is always central in these brief glimpses of men abiding the hands they've been dealt. An ideal introduction to Kelman's work and a wonderful edition for fans and Kelman completists, this lovely volume will make clear why James Kelman is known as the greatest living modernist writer.

"*Kelman has the knack, maybe more than anyone since Joyce, of fixing in his writing the lyricism of ordinary people's speech . . . Pure aesthete, undaunted democrat—somehow Kelman manages to reconcile his two halves.*"
—*Esquire*

Between Thought and Expression Lies a Lifetime: Why Ideas Matter

James Kelman & Noam Chomsky

ISBN: 978-1-62963-880-5 (paperback)
      978-1-62963-886-7 (hardcover)
$19.95/$39.95   304 pages

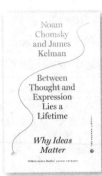

"The world is full of information. What do we do when we get the information, when we have digested the information, what do we do then? Is there a point where ye say, yes, stop, now I shall move on."

This exhilarating collection of essays, interviews, and correspondence—spanning the years 1988 through 2018, and reaching back a decade more—is about the simple concept that ideas matter. They mutate, inform, create fuel for thought, and inspire actions.

As Kelman says, the State relies on our suffocation, that we cannot hope to learn "the truth. But whether we can or not is beside the point. We must grasp the nettle, we assume control and go forward."

Between Thought and Expression Lies a Lifetime is an impassioned, elucidating, and often humorous collaboration. Philosophical and intimate, it is a call to ponder, imagine, explore, and act.

"The real reason Kelman, despite his stature and reputation, remains something of a literary outsider is not, I suspect, so much that great, radical Modernist writers aren't supposed to come from working-class Glasgow, as that great, radical Modernist writers are supposed to be dead. Dead, and wrapped up in a Penguin Classic: that's when it's safe to regret that their work was underappreciated or misunderstood (or how little they were paid) in their lifetimes. You can write what you like about Beckett or Kafka and know they're not going to come round and tell you you're talking nonsense, or confound your expectations with a new work. Kelman is still alive, still writing great books, climbing."
—James Meek, *London Review of Books*

"A true original . . . A real artist. . . . It's now very difficult to see which of his peers can seriously be ranked alongside [Kelman] without ironic eyebrows being raised."
—Irvine Welsh, *Guardian*

The State Is Your Enemy

James Kelman

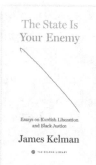

ISBN: 978-1-62963-968-0 (paperback)
      978-1-62963-976-5 (hardcover)
$19.95/$39.95   256 pages

Incendiary and heartrending, the sixteen essays
in *The State Is Your Enemy* lay bare government
brutality against the working class, immigrants,
asylum-seekers, ethnic minorities and all
who are deemed of "a lower order." Drawing
parallels between atrocities committed against the Kurds by the Turkish
State and the racist police brutality and government-sanctioned murders
in the UK, James Kelman shatters the myth of Western exceptionalism,
revealing the universality of terror campaigns levied against the most
vulnerable and calling on a global citizenship to stand in solidarity with
victims of oppression. Kelman's case against the Turkish and British
governments is not just a litany of murders or an impassioned plea—it
is a cool-headed takedown of the State and an essential primer for
revolutionaries.

"One of the most influential writers of his generation."
—*The Guardian*

RUIN

Cara Hoffman

ISBN: 978-1-62963-929-1 (paperback)
       978-1-62963-931-4 (hardcover)
$14.95/$25.95   128 pages

A little girl who disguises herself as an old man, an addict who collects dollhouse furniture, a crime reporter confronted by a talking dog, a painter trying to prove the non-existence of god, and lovers in a penal colony who communicate through technical drawings—these are just a few of the characters who live among the ruins. Cara Hoffman's short fictions are brutal, surreal, hilarious, and transgressive, celebrating the sharp beauty of outsiders and the infinitely creative ways humans muster psychic resistance under oppressive conditions. RUIN is both bracingly timely and eerily timeless in its examination of an American state in free-fall: unsparing in its disregard for broken, ineffectual institutions, while shining with compassion for the damaged left in their wake. The ultimate effect of these ten interconnected stories is one of invigoration and a sense of possibilities—hope for a new world extracted from the rubble of the old.

Cara Hoffman is the author of three New York Times Editors' Choice novels; the most recent, Running, was named a Best Book of the Year by Esquire Magazine. She first received national attention in 2011 with the publication of So Much Pretty which sparked a national dialogue on violence and retribution, and was named a Best Novel of the Year by the New York Times Book Review. Her second novel, Be Safe I Love You was nominated for a Folio Prize, named one of the Five Best Modern War Novels, and awarded a Sundance Global Filmmaking Award. A MacDowell Fellow and an Edward Albee Fellow, she has lectured at Oxford University's Rhodes Global Scholars Symposium and at the Renewing the Anarchist Tradition Conference. Her work has appeared in the New York Times, Paris Review, BOMB, Bookforum, Rolling Stone, Daily Beast, and on NPR. A founding editor of the Anarchist Review of Books, and part of the Athens Workshop collective, she lives in Athens, Greece with her partner.

"RUIN *is a collection of ten jewels, each multi-faceted and glittering, to be experienced with awe and joy. Cara Hoffman has seen a secret world right next to our own, just around the corner, and written us a field guide to what she's found. I love this book.*"
—Sara Gran, author of Infinite Blacktop and Claire Dewitt and the City of the Dead

The Football Factory

John King

ISBN: 978-1-62963-116-5
$16.95   296 pages

The Football Factory is driven by its two main characters—late-twenties warehouseman Tommy Johnson and retired ex-soldier Bill Farrell. Tommy is angry at his situation in life and those running the country. Outside of work, he is a lively, outspoken character, living for his time with a gang of football hooligans, the excitement of their fights and the comradeship he finds with his friends. He is a violent man, at the same time moral and intelligent.

Bill, meanwhile, is a former Second World War hero who helped liberate a concentration camp and married a survivor. He is a strong, principled character who sees the self-serving political and media classes for what they are. Tommy and Bill have shared feelings, but express their views in different ways. Born at another time, they could have been the other. As the book unfolds both come to their own crossroads and have important decisions to make.

The Football Factory is a book about modern-day pariahs, people reduced to the level of statistics by years of hypocritical, self-serving party politics. It is about the insulted, marginalised, unseen. Graphic and disturbing, at times very funny, *The Football Factory* is a rush of literary adrenalin.

"Only a phenomenally talented and empathetic writer working from within his own culture can achieve the power and authenticity this book pulses with. Buy, steal or borrow a copy now, because in a short time anyone who hasn't read it won't be worth talking to."
—Irvine Welsh, author of *Trainspotting*

"King's novel is not only an outstanding read, but also an important social document. . . . This book should be compulsory reading for all those who believe in the existence, or even the attainability, of a classless society."
—Paul Howard, *Sunday Tribune*

"Bleak, thought-provoking and brutal, The Football Factory *has all the hallmarks of a cult novel."*
—Dominic Bradbury, *The Literary Review*

The Cost of Lunch, Etc.

Marge Piercy

ISBN: 978-1-62963-125-7 (paperback)
978-1-60486-496-0 (hardcover)
$15.95/$21.95   192 pages

Marge Piercy's debut collection of short stories, *The Cost of Lunch, Etc.*, brings us glimpses into the lives of everyday women moving through and making sense of their daily internal and external worlds. Keeping to the engaging, accessible language of Piercy's novels, the collection spans decades of her writing along with a range of locations, ages, and emotional states of her protagonists. From the first-person account of hoarding ("Saving Mother from Herself") to a girl's narrative of sexual and spiritual discovery ("Going over Jordan") to a recount of a past love affair ("The Easy Arrangement") each story is a tangible, vivid snapshot in a varied and subtly curated gallery of work. Whether grappling with death, familial relationships, friendship, sex, illness, or religion, Piercy's writing is as passionate, lucid, insightful, and thoughtfully alive as ever.

"The author displays an old-fashioned narrative drive and a set of well-realized characters permitted to lead their own believably odd lives."
—Thomas Mallon, *Newsday*

"This reviewer knows no other writer with Piercy's gifts for tracing the emotional route that two people take to a double bed, and the mental games and gambits each transacts there."
—Ron Grossman, *Chicago Tribune*

"Marge Piercy is not just an author, she's a cultural touchstone. Few writers in modern memory have sustained her passion, and skill, for creating stories of consequence."
—*Boston Globe*

"What Piercy has that Danielle Steel, for example, does not is an ability to capture life's complex texture, to chart shifting relationships and evolving consciousness within the context of political and economic realities she delineates with mordant matter-of-factness. Working within the venerable tradition of socially conscious fiction, she brings to it a feminist understanding of the impact such things as class and money have on personal interactions without ever losing sight of the crucial role played by individuals' responses to those things."
—Wendy Smith, *Chicago Sun-Times*

The Colonel Pyat Quartet

Michael Moorcock
with introductions by Alan Wall

Byzantium Endures
ISBN: 978-1-60486-491-5
$22.00   400 pages

The Laughter of Carthage
ISBN: 978-1-60486-492-2
$22.00   448 pages

Jerusalem Commands
ISBN: 978-1-60486-493-9
$22.00   448 pages

The Vengeance of Rome
ISBN: 978-1-60486-494-6
$23.00   500 pages

Moorcock's Pyat Quartet has been described as
an authentic masterpiece of the 20th and 21st
centuries. It's the story of Maxim Arturovitch
Pyatnitski, a cocaine addict, sexual adventurer,
and obsessive anti-Semite whose epic journey
from Leningrad to London connects him with
scoundrels and heroes from Trotsky to Makhno,
and whose career echoes that of the 20th
century's descent into Fascism and total war.

It is Michael Moorcock's extraordinary
achievement to convert the life of Maxim
Pyatnitski into epic and often hilariously comic
adventure. Sustained by his dreams and profligate
inventions, his determination to turn his back on
the realities of his own origins, Pyat runs from
crisis to crisis, every ruse a further link in a vast
chain of deceit, suppression, betrayal. Yet, in
his deranged self-deception, his monumentally
distorted vision, this thoroughly unreliable
narrator becomes a lens for focusing, through the
dimensions of wild farce and chilling terror, on an
uneasy brand of truth.